a MONSOON *of* MUSIC

MITRA PHUKAN is an Assamese vocalist of the Hindustani cla
music tradition, a writer, music critic and columnist. She is the a
of several children's books, and her first novel *The Collector's*
(Zubaan–Penguin 2005) was critically acclaimed. Her works, incl
her short stories, have been translated into several languages.

a MONSOON *of* MUSIC

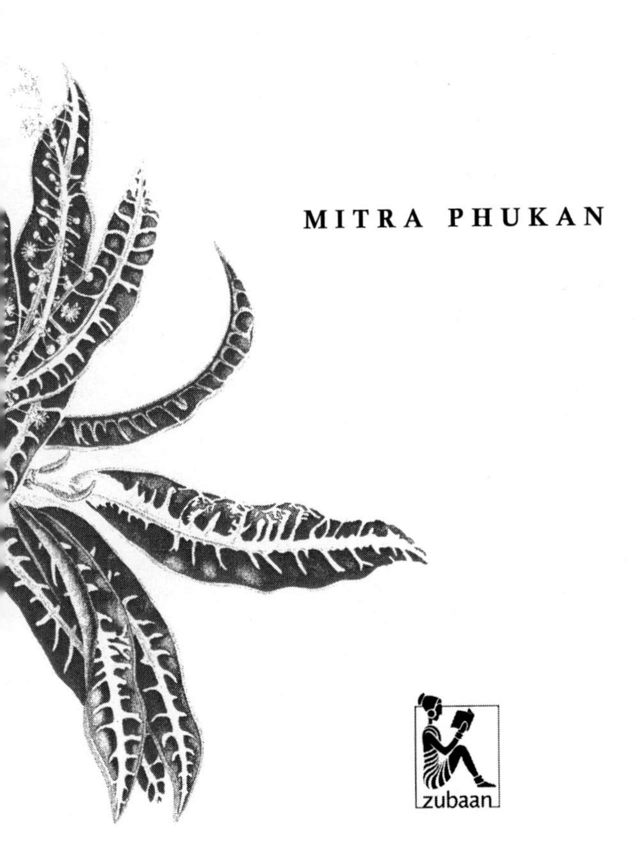

MITRA PHUKAN

zubaan

ZUBAAN
128 B Shahpur Jat, 1st floor
NEW DELHI 110 049
EMAIL: contact@zubaanbooks.com
WEBSITE: www.zubaanbooks.com

First published by Penguin Books India and Zubaan 2011
This edition published by Zubaan Publishers Pvt. Ltd 2018

10 9 8 7 6 5 4 3 2 1

ISBN 978 93 85932 44 1

Zubaan is an independent feminist publishing house based in New Delhi with a strong academic and general list. It was set up as an imprint of India's first feminist publishing house, Kali for Women, and carries forward Kali's tradition of publishing world quality books to high editorial and production standards. *Zubaan* means tongue, voice, language, speech in Hindustani. Zubaan publishes in the areas of the humanities, social sciences, as well as in fiction, general non-fiction, and books for children and young adults under its Young Zubaan imprint.

Typeset in Arno Pro by Jojy Philip, New Delhi 100 015
Printed at PrintShoot, www.printshoot.com

For Luku, wherever you are,
in memory of three wonderful decades ...

Acknowledgements

My Gurus, who have taught me to appreciate the luminous beauty of Hindustani shastriya sangeet.

The very supportive readers of my column, who have been urging me to write "a novel about music".

Dr Rekha Khaund Borkotoky to whom I have always turned for advice whenever one of my characters develops a medical condition that needs explaining.

Preeti Gill, my sensitive and supportive editor who is now such a very good friend.

Mitali Dey, amazing musician and wonderful human being, who so readily agreed to let us use her photograph for the cover.

Prabhakar Dey, photographer, who shot Mitali's pictures with such care, keeping in mind exactly what we needed.

1

I'll be late, thought Nomita in her usual pre-show panic. They'll keep announcing our item, and the audience will sit there expecting the curtains to open. But of course they won't, because here I am, stuck in traffic while the others are sitting with their taanpuras and surmandals, waiting to begin the Shiva Stotra ...

Her thoughts raced ahead, as they always did, to worst-case scenarios. The organisers would try to calm the increasingly restive audience by assuring them that the show would begin in just a few minutes. They would then rush backstage to yell angrily at the other singers. "Come on now, stop waiting for that irresponsible person who's not yet arrived, just go ahead and sing. What does it matter anyway if one person is missing, there are still six of you around aren't there, to fill the gap?" The Chief Guest, probably a Minister or an MLA, would look pointedly at his watch, and tell them about his other impending meetings. He wasn't used to waiting, it was usually others who waited for him ... no, surely he wouldn't say that! But he would be very annoyed.

But of course, and as always, Nomita was well in time. Much ahead of time, in fact. The Mangalacharan, the auspicious song that was supposed to begin the evening's concert, was due to start at six sharp. At six sharp, however, the maroon velvet curtains remained closed, their dirty yellow fringes forlornly showing their bald patches to whoever cared to look. The men in charge of the sound system were still fiddling about, going up to the stage at intervals, looking very self-important saying "One-two-three-*check,* one-two-three-*check,*" in tones that sounded almost professional.

She looked into the auditorium on her way to the greenroom. Just a scattering of people. There was no sign of the Chief Guest, nor of the other important personages who would occupy the front seats and invest them with dignity and grandeur. Everybody in the town of Tamulbari, except Nomita Sharma, knew that functions never began on time here.

Only Panchali and Rupa were present in the first floor greenroom. They were standing in front of the open window, leaning out to look at something or somebody below. Two men were ambling in and out of the greenroom at intervals, talking of a third who apparently was not taking his duties seriously. From the cloth rosettes pinned to their chests, and the gamosas slung around their necks, it was obvious that they were part of the Organising Committee. They ignored Nomita as she appeared at the door, taanpura in hand.

"Here I am, where's everybody?" she asked, taking off her sandals and walking to a corner of the white-sheeted gaddi. She listened critically to her voice as she spoke. It sounded all right, at least so far. Sometimes the journey from her home to the venue of a concert would be so full of billowing smoke from passing trucks and buses that her throat would begin to itch, and her voice would start acting up. A kind of hoarseness would edge her normal soprano, and hitting the high notes, if she was not careful, would sound strained. This hadn't happened yet, thankfully. Since she was the lead singer today, large parts of the Stotra were to be sung by her. She put down her taanpura carefully, making sure that its delicate resonator, created from the hollowed shell of a single fragile gourd, was safe.

Panchali and Rupa turned from the window. "It's early," Panchali pointed out. "Hardly six o'clock. We came so much before time only because we got a lift. The others will be coming soon, I suppose."

Nomita nodded. She remembered that it was a status symbol among musicians in Tamulbari to arrive late for performances. It was an attitude that they carefully cultivated. To come ahead of time, or even on time, would imply that they were nervous beginners, with no experience. To get around this, event organisers had evolved their own strategy of telling performers that the show would begin a good half hour before its actual scheduled time.

Well, never mind. She needed some time to catch her breath, anyway. Calm herself, get into the mood of the Raag on which the Stotra was based. Yes, group performances could be tricky. Especially when the group consisted of people like Rupa and Panchali.

She pushed away the uncharitable thought determinedly. Guruma had said that these two were to be included in today's Mangalacharan performance and it was unthinkable that Nomita should argue with her teacher. If Guruma had decided to include two of her lesser students in the group, well, she knew best. In any case, they were fillers – their duty was to steep the spaces with a background drone of melody.

"Shall we tune the instruments, then?" she asked brightly. "You've brought the other taanpura from Guruma's place, haven't you? And the harmonium? Ok, let's begin."

Somewhat reluctantly, the two of them came away from the window. Nomita wondered what it was that had attracted their attention there. Probably a man, going by what she knew of these two. So what if they were married? In the art circles of Tamulbari these days, marriage vows were hardly ever regarded as barriers to conducting romantic liaisons of varying degrees of intimacy.

Nomita was thankful that today the mattresses on the ground were covered with clean white sheets. Sometimes, in some greenrooms, there would be nothing at all to sit on, neither chair nor floor covering. Today the greenroom had been swept, and the toilet cleaned. Otherwise the strong stench of urine would be powerful enough to fell even a muscular pakhawaj player! One of the hazards of being a musician, she thought wryly, was that one was expected to accept all this and to overlook the flaking paint, the walls splattered with betel-nut spittle, the filthy windows almost opaque with dirt, and the fan heavily encrusted with the grime of decades that creaked ponderously in slow arcs.

She had noticed that this time, the organisers had tried to camouflage the seediness of the stage with a brave show of bright flowers. But of course they could do nothing to repair the ravages of time that had left this Government-owned auditorium in such bad shape. The black cloth wings had holes, the wooden floorboards had nails protruding at one or two places, and a number of chairs in the auditorium had broken seats. Besides, the heat on the stage would be horrific, for there would be no fans, leave alone air conditioners.

Nomita sat down and pulled the harmonium to her. The other taanpura and the harmonium were from the music institution that Guruma and her husband ran, the "Jhankaar Music Academy." A name that was as sonorous, resonant, melodious as the instrument.

"Please, will you play the note on the harmonium while I tune the taanpuras?" she asked.

The two women sat down. Panchali pressed down the fifth black key for the tonic of B flat, the pitch at which they were going to sing. She began to pump the instrument sulkily.

Oops, I've insulted her, thought Nomita as she began to tune the strings of the taanpura to the note on the harmonium. There were all kinds of nuances, all kinds of hierarchies that loomed behind even the minutest of actions at this time, backstage. To tune the taanpura before a performance was supposed to be the prerogative of the senior most person in the group, the implication being that this person had a more sensitive ear for microtonal nuances, and was, therefore, better suited to tune the instrument to the perfect pitch. By extension, the taanpura tuner was supposed to be the better performer and junior artistes were expected to jump to the lesser task of pumping the harmonium. It was even better if the harmonium player could muster up a sycophantic air at this critical time. A few "wah"s judiciously placed, the head nodded flatteringly from time to time, a look of reverence when the tuning was finally over: all this was routine. It was good for the taanpura tuner's ego, and could perhaps even lead to a better-tuned taanpura!

Neither Panchali nor Rupa, however, seemed inclined to flatter her on her tuning abilities at that point of time. Of course they were probably older than her, but her musical seniority at Jhankaar was unquestioned. Still, she glanced with a placating smile at the two women, and said, "Both of you are wearing lovely mekhela sadors"

It was the right thing to say. The two of them were instantly mollified. “Oh, this old thing?” said Rupa, patting her ample chest smugly.

It had been agreed yesterday, after the rehearsals that the women should wear white mekhela sadors, in keeping with the sanctity of the invocatory Mangalacharan. Panchali and Rupa were indeed in white, but the silk was so heavily encrusted with multicoloured woven flowers and zari patterns that the background colour was barely visible. Their hair was coiffed in a manner more suited to a wedding reception than a fifteen-minute stage performance. Heavy bangles jingled on their hands, chandelier earrings cascaded down almost to their shoulders. All this finery made the two look even plumper than they already were. Wide swathes of sindoor burned brightly on their heads. They looked hot and sweaty, with perspiration streaks in imminent danger of appearing on their heavily made-up faces. Nomita looked wonderingly at the ornate rings on their fingers, the long chains around their necks, and smiled again in what she hoped was a complimentary manner.

“I came out of the house in such a hurry, I hardly had any time to dress up,” added Panchali.

“Of course,” agreed Nomita. She bent down to the taanpura, and, clearing her mind of all other thoughts, concentrated on the work at hand.

Tuning the four strings of a taanpura was fine, finicky work, especially in this hot and humid weather. By the time she was satisfied, the greenroom had filled up. The other vocalists had arrived, as had the accompanists.

“Shall we have a rehearsal then?” she asked.

But two of the organisers bustled in, their ennui of some time ago replaced now with an air of fussy importance. “All right, he’s come, the Chief Guest, it’s time for your item now, get ready, go, go up to the stage.”

They had decided on the order of seating last evening. Nomita, as lead singer, in the middle, the two pairs of tablas at the far right, the harmonium behind them, the violin to the far left. In between the tablas and herself would be seated Geeti and Sujata, while Shrabana and Indrani would be between her and the violin. Panchali and Rupa were to sit behind the others, because their parts were small, and they were comparatively new.

But in the seconds before the curtains opened, even as the mikes were being adjusted Nomita saw that Panchali and Rupa had elbowed their way to the front row, edging aside Indrani and Sujata, who were left peering ineffectually over the formers' shoulders. Worse, Panchali and Rupa were directing the microphones to be placed in front of them. Subrato, Dibyajyoti and Chinmoy, the tabla players and violinist, were looking at her helplessly. The organisers were already signalling to her from the wings, indicating that if she was ready, the curtains would open. The presenter had already made his announcement. He, too, was looking at her expectantly, so that he could say his final words before their piece began.

Hurriedly she had the position of the microphones changed. It was too late to shift Rupa and Panchali back to the second row, but she made space beside herself for Indrani and Sujata. Finally, she rechecked the tuning of the taanpuras. Thank God, in all this jostling the wooden pegs that held the strings in place hadn't slipped.

"Right, we're ready," she said, nodding to the by now almost hysterical organisers at the wings.

The curtains began to slide open. The lights on stage brightened, those in the auditorium dimmed. Nomita glanced up. Dusty and cobwebby, the chandelier-like fixture above them was heavy and ornate. Its many bulbs emitted only a feeble light, dimmed as they were by dirt. Nomita strummed her taanpura, Indrani played the other. Chinmoy began to play the Shadaj on the violin.

Everything sounded soothing, sacred. Nomita took a deep breath, and hummed the tonic softly, her face away from the microphone, so that her voice would not reach the auditorium below. In a solo performance, it was easier to gather her concentration to a point, and begin her recital. But a group performance was different. The heat was already creating runnels of sweat on her scalp. She could sense Panchali and Rupa jostling as they attempted to regain their lost positions near the mikes, and was aware of their simpers directed towards the auditorium. With all this going on, it was much more difficult to shut out everything else from her mind and begin the song itself.

The announcer, sitting beyond the wings at a console, nodded.

"So, here we are, ladies and gentlemen. An invocation song, a sacred Shiva Stotra being performed by Nomita Sharma and her group from the Jhankaar Music Academy. This song, invoking the blessings of the Lord..."

The drone of the taanpuras was a soothing background to his announcement. Nomita glanced at the auditorium. It was in darkness, but she could see the people in the front rows in the light reflected from the stage. The Chief Guest was a large man in white kurta-dhuti who was deep in conversation with the man beside him, possibly the President of the organisation that was arranging this show. The presence of security men behind and beside him proclaimed him to be some kind of politician. Nomita had no curiosity to know who he was. It was mandatory in Tamulbari to have an "important personage" in attendance whenever a function of this kind was organised and stage artistes were fated to wait endlessly for these people.

"So ladies and gentlemen, we present before you the well-known artiste Nomita Sharma and her group, with an invocation song."

In unison, the Jhankaar troupe folded their hands in a namaskar to the audience. This, too, had been rehearsed several times last evening, so that the action would by synchronous. From the corner of her eyes, she could see Rupa and Panchali hold on to the namaskar several seconds longer than necessary, so that the audiences' eyes would linger on them. No doubt, thought Nomita with irritation, they would have bright smiles pasted on their darkly lipsticked mouths.

Without any smile on her own, Nomita began the alaap. The shloka was in Raag Bhupali. Starting on Sa, she began to outline its deceptively easy sweep. Most of her mind was concentrated on the song, but she also listened carefully to the feedback from the amplifiers placed on the sides of the stage. Was her voice overloud? No, it was probably all right, though it would need to blend in with the others when they began their chorus. Nothing sounded as bad as a single voice ringing out stridently in a group performance, drowning the others to a feeble background murmur. The violin was fine, the taanpuras beautifully tuned. Prashant on the harmonium behind her was not heard, but that was all right. His role today was to give support to the singers, so that they could synchronize the beginnings and ends of their lines. She would have to see that the percussion, when the tablas joined in, was not too loud, there were two tabla players after all...

The audience seemed quiet, focussed on the first few moments of the recital. Even the Chief Guest was looking towards them. Only the securitymen were glancing with quick, darting professional looks all around the auditorium, and at its doors. In spite of them, all was peaceful, all was serene. The atmosphere was just what any Mangalacharan singer could have wished for.

Suddenly, a huge crash, sounding like a cross between a gunshot and a car accident, shattered the calm.

The screams came immediately afterwards, with no intervening moment of silence, stunned or otherwise. Nomita was not one of those who screamed, but her song was stilled on her lips as shouts and shrieks erupted all around her. The auditorium was in pandemonium. Panchali and Rupa were screaming hysterically, even Indrani and Sujata were moaning with gusto. Nomita's mind, dazed and bewildered, registered that the security men were now everywhere. Two had formed a cordon around the portly Chief Guest, several more had stormed up to the stage, and were standing there, guns at the ready, watchful and alert, but not worried.

They had already grasped what the rest of them were still trying to. The chandelier above the stage had given up the decades-long battle with gravity at last, and had separated from its moorings. It had crashed down to the stage in a torrent of plaster and dirt.

It had missed braining Nomita by just a few inches.

2

The senior students of Jhankaar Music Academy were waiting for Guruma. It was almost five o'clock. The sunlight was a mellow gold, its sharp noonday heat now blunted by the breeze that came wafting in from the Red River that edged the town. The cream-coloured curtains fluttered as the fresh draft drifted in through the windows, bringing more coolness to the space than the ceiling fan whirring over their heads did.

The long room, dim in spite of the windows on the walls, was lined with instruments. It was undoubtedly the most important area in the home of the "First Musician Couple of the State", Vidushi Sandhya Senapati and Pandit Tridib Barua of Tamulbari. On the far wall were the taanpuras, more than half a dozen of them, covered in cloth drapes as they leaned against the wooden stands. Of different sizes, their gourd resonators varied from large to tiny, depending on whether they were meant for male voices, or female ones. Ranged along a quarter of one of the longer walls were the tablas, covered with bright cloth discs, resting on maroon rings which were braided through with gold strings. Two harmoniums, one a scale-changer varnished to a warm gloss, the other an ordinary but still fine-looking instrument, stood beside them. Two surmandals, the small harp-like instruments that were played by Sandhya Senapati and Tridib Barua while singing, lay in their cases, their dozens of strings protected from the damaging and corrosive damp river air with wraps of thick cotton and velvet.

"What I want to know," demanded Pranab, his usually low-pitched voice edged with a sharp note of excitement, "is what you did after that. I mean, did you just sit there shrieking hysterically, did you pack up your instruments and go, or…?"

"Haven't you read today's papers? The local ones are full of our 'brave and unruffled calm in the face of such a grave mishap.'" Nomita could laugh now, but she still felt a tremor go through her at the thought of what could have been. "We waited for the security men to move off, and the organisers to get the rubble cleared, at least some of it. They closed the curtains, and actually had the stage swept. Half an hour later, we were back on stage, having taken the deep breaths that Guruma keeps prescribing to calm panic attacks. They work, you know. If anything, our Mangalacharan was better than it ever was." She struck a dramatic pose, and added, "The show must go on, they said, and it did!"

The plain, off-white walls of the room were brightened by numerous pictures of well known musicians. A bright print of Pandit Ravi Shankar, Ustad Ali Akbar Khan and Alla Rakha performing in their heydays lit up one wall with the sheer vitality that seemed to spill out from the body language of the performers. There were others, too, of revered musicians. Ustad Bade Ghulam Ali Khan's picture highlighted his impressive moustache and muscular physique, giving him the appearance of a bodybuilder who had strayed into this music room by mistake. Barkat Ali Khan was there too, as was Abdul Karim Khan Saheb, Bhimsen Joshi, Jasraj, L.K. Pandit, Kishori Amonkar, Kesarbai Kerkar, Chhannulal Mishra, Mogubai Kurdikar, Vilayat Khan Saheb, Begum Akhtar, and indeed many others.

Pride of place was given to two pictures. One was of Sandhya Senapati's own Guru, the famed musician from Kolkata, Pandit Chiranjeev Mukherjee. A garland of dried blossoms framed his round, good-humoured face. Next to him was another framed portrait, this one of Tridib Barua's teacher, Ustad Nooruddin Khan from Lucknow. This, too, was encircled with an identical garland of dried blossoms. The Ustad's face looked fierce like a pugilist's. His nose was so small that it looked as though it had been broken in some fight, but he had actually been born with it. In any case, appearances were deceptive, for the man had been gentle, with his whole being concentrated on music, unlike the Pandit who was known to have had a rather colourful life, dotted liberally with wine and women in addition to the song that had earned him his living.

The only area in which the Ustad had allowed ill-will and unseemly competitiveness to enter his otherwise calm and music-centred mind, was in his relationship with Pandit Chiranjeev Mukherjee. Though belonging to different Gharanas, and therefore proponents of different musical styles, the two had been at loggerheads with each other throughout their adult lives. This fact was widely known in musical circles, and organisers of Sangeet Sanmelans and All Night Music Conferences had been careful never to slot their programmes together. The Ustad's voice, normally so gentle in conversation, would acquire harsh overtones whenever the subject of Chiranjeev Mukherjee came up. Indeed, he himself brought it up in front of anybody who cared to listen, including his students, as often as he could. He was like a dog with an itchy patch that he couldn't help scratching.

For some reason, till his dying day, the Ustad laboured under the delusion that Chiranjeev Mukherjee, his students, and his many hangers-on, were hell-bent on denying him his rightful place in the musical firmament. He attributed the Pandit's popularity all over the country, and his success during his frequent shows abroad, not to his musical ability, but to his acumen in pulling strings and his skill in hobnobbing successfully with people who "mattered". After music lessons were over, he would often launch into tales of the latest injury done to him by Chiranjeev Mukherjee and his cohorts. If, for some reason, his radio and TV programmes showed a drop he blamed the Pandit. If he was not invited to a particular music conference, he saw in that his rival's hand. If a particular cassette company chose Mukherjee to sing several Raags for its Classical Music series, he attributed the choice to his machinations. He was even known to have averred, on occasion, that Mukherjee's large cassette and CD sales – indubitably larger than his own – were because he ordered his students to buy as many copies as possible! In any case, he fulminated, Bengalis were known to hang together, and any Bangla fellow who came to Kolkata from anywhere across the world considered it his patriotic duty to buy up all the CDs of the Bengali artistes of the day. How could he, Nooruddin, compete against such chicanery?

Mukherjee's name was a bigger draw than Ustad Nooruddin's at concerts, but this too, the Ustad said, was due to the fact that Mukherjee, with his deep pockets, bought up most of the tickets at the venues well in advance. According to him, Mukherjee would seed the art pages of daily papers and other journals with stories, planted through journalists who had been paid off by him. These stories would comment in awestruck tones about how it was impossible, even a month in advance of the concert, to get any seats for Pandit Chiranjeev Mukherjee's recital.

As for the critics, the Ustad sneered at the very mention of their names, for didn't everybody know that critics were notorious for being up for sale to the highest bidder? Mukherjee always treated them to a lavish dinner at a five star hotel after every show of his, a dinner where wine flowed freely. Touba touba, he would continue, touching the tips of his ears devoutly, how could he, a practicing Muslim who said his namaz five times daily, and kept the Ramzan fast every single day, how could he even think of stooping to such tactics? He had never touched liquor in his life. It was obvious, in any case, that the critics had all been bought, for none of them talked of Mukherjee's pronounced Bengali accent which made the lyrics, in spite of being couched in Hindi, or Sanskrit or some North Indian dialect, all sound like variants of Rabindrasangeet.

In all these tirades, he was egged on by his students, who would sit in a semicircle at his feet, and utter exaggerated exclamations of surprise and shock at appropriate moments. To fuel his ire still further, they would add their own stories of how Mukherjee was now hobnobbing with Chief Ministers and even the Prime Minister, in order to get himself nominated for honours such as the Padma Shri or the Padma Bhushan. The Ustad's features would furrow in hate, for he himself could not claim any such Government honour, even though honours from highly respected music organisations had been heaped on him for many years now. He would burst out that Mukherjee was a disgrace to the very name of his Gharana. He dared to call himself a follower of the Patiala Gharana, one who had learned at the feet of Bade Ghulam Ali Khan Saheb himself. Patiala, hah! His voice had none of the throwing ability, or the capability of negotiating sapat taans at lightning speed, which were the hallmark of that Gharana. As for learning at the feet of the Khan Saheb, well, he, Nooruddin, knew for a fact that he had only done so metaphorically, through recorded songs, rather than in real life. He would lower his voice, touch his ears, and aver that *his* Guru, his father, the great Shamsuddin himself, had said that Khan Saheb had refused to take Mukherjee as a shishya, because of the feebleness of his voice. Of course he pretended that the thumri *Aaye Na Baalam* had been taught to him by Khan Saheb himself. But for those in the know, it was apparent that he had learned it, almost by rote, from the recording, and had merely added a few embellishments of his own here and there, to disguise the fact.

All these fulminations were dutifully carried back to Pandit Chiranjeev Mukherjee by the numerous chamchas and hangers-on who frequented the camps of both the maestros. But Chiranjeev Mukherjee, as he listened to them, did not feel any ire. At least he did not show any, secure as he was in the knowledge that his royalty cheques were coming in on a regular basis.

Indeed, it was strange that the portraits of the two Gurus now hung on the same wall, in such close proximity to each other. As Chiranjeev Mukherjee's star had waxed, the Ustad, otherwise so gentle, had grown more and more irritable and crotchety, his original good-humoured nature giving way under the weight of his irrational jealousy. He could not reconcile himself to the fact that he, scion of a family of traditional musicians whose roots could be traced back fourteen generations to the time they had migrated from Afghanistan, was now less well known than that upstart Bangali Babu whose father had been a mere weaver, not inclined to music at all. What rankled even more was that the entire world... well, those who listened to Khayal in its pristine form... knew that his own style was pure, untainted by the mixture of gharanas that Mukherjee passed off as his version of the Patiala style. He, Ustad Nooruddin Khan had always been true to the musical lineage of which he was the proud torchbearer. The bandishes that he sang, the compositions in his repertoire, the way he presented the Raags themselves, were all part of his glorious heritage.

Till his dying day, the Ustad never realized that tastes in music change, as in all other things, even in tradition-laden Hindustani classical music. And in this age when the influence of the media – the radio, gramophone records, inexpensive cassettes, TV – was so ubiquitous, the changes came rapidly. The Ustad never suspected that the era of the Nawabs and Rajas was over, and democratisation had set in, firmly and inevitably, in Classical music as in all else. Clinging to the pride of his lineage, he failed to realize that an artiste was judged by his ability to move the crowd with his performance, not by how many of his forefathers had been singers or musicians themselves.

Chiranjeev Mukherjee, man of the people that he was, knew perfectly well how to tailor his performances to the crowd. The Khayals he sang at small baithaks with an audience of aficionados would be memorable. But if he was performing in a hall or a pandal housing thousands, he would give a token nod merely to the vilambit, and plunge straight into the taans and swift sargams that were his trademark. In any case, he would not dwell on the Khayal at any length at these places. Twenty to thirty minutes– that was the maximum he allowed himself on this cerebral form at these huge popular Sanmelans, full of people whose acquaintance with it was slight. He would then dive into thumris and dadras, taking care that the tempos he chose for them were at least swift, if not plain rollicking. He sang bhajans too, setting aside his taanpura and taking the harmonium from the accompanist who had been playing it all this while. He would accompany himself on that instrument originally borrowed from the West with such aplomb and fluency that the bhajans sounded as though they were – sacrilegious to mention this – song from films. He was not averse to singing in the vernacular as well at these concerts, in his native Bangla. These were songs which were based on Raags and were therefore called

Raagprodhans, but which were many times more populist than the much more austere style of the Khayal. He also sprinkled these recitals under the huge pandals with ghazals, to the enthusiastic "wah wahs" of those who fancied themselves to be connoisseurs. The crowd, especially the younger lot, and those who attended these concerts for their snob value, loved it. His record and cassette sales soared, and he was invited everywhere, while the Ustad, wrapped in his stubborn pride in the past, sulked and ranted, unable to change his style, or even comprehend that there might be a reason to do so.

Playing to the gallery had paid other dividends for the Pandit as well. Though physically he resembled the rasgollas of which he was inordinately fond, his star status at these numerous shows ensured a steady stream of female fans. They were there, among the hordes of autograph-seekers who thronged backstage after every concert. Although not-quite so-young or nubile, but beautifully dressed and bejewelled, among the cognoscenti who attended his baithaks, all toadying up to him, savouring his every glance as he sang his songs of love. They were women who left their legally wedded spouses and followed him, secretly, to his room at night, as though his voice was Krishna's flute, and they were but the gopis whom he had ensnared with his music.

But Chiranjeev Mukherjee's relationship with Sandhya Senapati had been different from the start. In this quiet, slim girl, with her long black hair, ivory skin and huge, tranquil eyes, he had seen, from the very beginning, a spark which spoke to the urge for musical immortality in him. From the moment he auditioned her he knew that this girl was different. With this girl, he would not have to worry about who would carry on his musical style, who would be his musical heir. He had been well into middle age by then, his body full of hardened arteries and gouty digits, the inevitable result of his fondness for good living. Only his voice was as supple as it had been in his youth. His own two sons had turned their backs to music, and had reverted to the genetic heritage of their grandfather. Though not actually weavers, they were now firmly ensconced in the textile trade, one ran a successful garment business and the other was a sought-after dress designer.

Of course he had always had students, multitudes of them, ever since he had got his B High grade from All India Radio. At a very young age, a mere forty or so, he had climbed the ladder of gradations that All India Radio had evolved. From B High he had gone on to A, then, finally, to A Top and the Super Grade, itself, so that he could officially prefix his name with the respectful honorific, "Pandit", or Maestro. If he had been a Muslim, he would have been called "Ustad", by which appellation his rival Nooruddin was known. Kolkata was at that time Kolkata, but in spite of the anglicised spelling, it was the place where Hindustani or North Indian classical music flourished. People thronged to the all-night music conferences where stalwarts of the various Gharanas would present their items, often prolonging their scheduled time of performance to accommodate the encores of their audience. Beginning with the evening Raags, artiste after artiste, with their tabaliyas, taanpura players, and other accompanists, would unfold melodies suited to the time cycle in which they were performing. Puriya, Marwa, Behag, Malkauns, Chandrakauns, Darbari Kanhra, the melodies would become, as the night deepened, progressively more serious and grave, till the faint light in the eastern sky would be ushered in with Lalit, then perhaps Todi, as the rays of the sun grew progressively brighter. And finally, when it was time for the Conference to come to an end, on the last slot of the last day, the final artiste would sing or play Raag Bhairavi, that melody that could be moulded to contain all twelve notes of the octave, tones as well as semi-tones. After Bhairavi, etiquette forbade any more music for that day, at that venue, even if the audience was thirsty for more melodies. And the listeners, who had sat throughout the hours of the night, wrapped up in scarves and coats and shawls against the winter chill, would go home, humming the Raags they had heard sung or played on sitar, sarod, esraj, dilruba, sarangi, and many other instruments, their heads whirling with the tehais of the tabaliyas who had accompanied them.

And there were the baithaks, the small, intimate soirées, held in the homes of those connoisseurs who could afford the expenses involved. These too would stretch into the wee hours of the morning. Here, the artistes would put in even more effort than they would during the Conferences. For their hosts were always men of discernment as well as money, who would immediately notice if a note was not at the correct shruti, the exact semi-tone. The hosts and their guests would look askance if the taal cycles of the tabaliya and the sitarist did not coincide by even a fraction of a second. Painstakingly-built musical reputations, nurtured over a lifetime of rigorous riyaz and sadhana, could be shattered in one evening, if this happened.

In his heyday Pandit Chiranjeev Mukherjee was the darling of the Kolkata crowd, the man who was often given the honoured slot of the last artiste of the last night of the Music Conferences, the person who, with his mellifluous voice, would usher in the dawn with a Bhairavi thumri, or a Bhajan of a superbly meditative quality. He made it a point to be available in Kolkata during the months of November to March, so as to be able to fit in the city's Conferences into his schedule. Often, he would refuse programmes in other places, even places known for their classical music conferences, such as Mumbai, Pune, Delhi, or Gwalior, in order to sing at a Kolkata Conference, sometimes at lesser remuneration. For the Kolkata Conferences of the time were prestigious in a way that many others were not. True, Conferences such as the Tansen Sanmelan in Gwalior or Mumbai's Haridas Sanmelan were legendary, but then so was the Dover Lane Music Conference, the West Bengal Music Conference, or the Borsha Utshob. And Kolkata crowds, it was well known, could make or break artistes. Their knowledge of the form was immense, their musicality inherent. Big names did not awe the Kolkata crowd: if the man's performance that evening was not up to the mark, he was made aware of it in no uncertain terms. And conversely, they were indulgent of newcomers, condoning their initial nervousness and encouraging them with laudatory "*Arrey Bhai, jawab nahin*!" and "*Ki Shundor, Aah*..."

Pandit Chiranjeev Mukherjee strode this world like a colossus for many years. His name would be announced repeatedly before he appeared on the dais, confident that he could get away with keeping his audience waiting, secure in the knowledge that the magic he could weave with his voice would have them eating out of his hands in a few minutes. Senior students would enter the white-sheeted stage, and climb the dais with their large, beautifully decorated taanpuras. After them would arrive the accompanists – the sarengi player, the harmonium player, and finally the tabaliya. The Pandit's accompanists were stars in their own right. They were always men, for no woman, in those days, played either harmonium or sarengi or tabla professionally. Their entry to the stage would be announced with a flourish, and marked by enthusiastic applause from the audience. With deep namaskars, they would take their seats on the white-sheeted dais, balancing themselves and their instruments against the deep bolsters, the takiyas that were placed there for their comfort. They would leave a place for the Pandit in the centre, but he himself would not show up on stage till the final tuning of the taanpuras, the tablas, and the sarengi was complete. The audience would not grow restive even at this, even though most of them knew that the Pandit was probably taking a last swig or two from a hip flask tucked away in the bag carried by a trusted student.

And finally, he would appear. Surmandal in hand, attired in a deep bordered white dhoti and kurta whose diamond and gold buttons twinkled in the stage lights, he would climb onto the stage, his short stature, rotund body and ungainly gait forgotten in the halo of stardom that surrounded him. The applause would swell to a crescendo as he came forward and folded his hands together in a deep and seemingly humble namaskar to all the members of the audience, and especially to those patrons and influential people who sat in the first rows. A maroon or olive green pashmina shawl would be draped around his shoulders, its rich colours picking out the hues of the deep borders of his Bengali-style pleated dhoti. Finally, he would seat himself in the exact centre of the stage, strum the surmandal in his hand, and begin the task of testing the microphones, each one of them. There would be three placed before him, two before the tabaliya, and one each before the others. He would make sure that the base and treble of each was pitched just so, taking a few practice runs of alaaps and taans in taar and mandra saptaks.

The expectation levels of the people in the pandal would by this time be at fever pitch, yet they would not show any impatience at all while Chiranjeev Mukherjee went through these tests, asking for the volume of the tabla to be raised a bit, for the drone of the second taanpura be lowered… Finally with a nod and a dismissive "*Hobey, thik achhey,*" to the scurrying men in charge of the sound system, he would indicate that he was ready. Of course all this was nothing but showmanship, nothing but a way of getting the audiences ready for his music, but few in the auditorium realized it as they allowed their responses to him to be manipulated in this manner.

Students flocked to him as much for his star appeal as for his genuine and wonderful musicianship. Those who came to him merely for his "name" certainly vastly outnumbered the genuine students. For there was a kind of glamour that rubbed off on aspiring musicians who mentioned that they were pupils of the great Pandit Chiranjeev Mukherjee.

But in spite of all this, the man was an excellent musician. Though he was careful to treat all his students alike, he cherished the handful of genuine students with the talent, dedication, and willingness to go the long haul in the pursuit of their music. As he approached late middle age, he became increasingly troubled by the consciousness that this knowledge that he had garnered painfully over the decades, must indeed be passed on to another. His music could not be passed on through the written word, or musical symbols. It had to be handed down from teacher to student through a one on one interaction. In the guru-shishya parampara or tradition of teaching, the ultimate accolade that a musician could get, in the evening of his life was to have students who were acknowledged by connoisseurs to be the true torch-bearers of the tradition. These students were the parchment on which a true Guru could stamp the imprint of his musicianship, the blank pages that awaited the stylus of the Guru's knowledge.

Pandit Chiranjeev Mukherjee had perhaps five or six of them. They were progressing well under his tutelage, and had already begun to make a name for themselves in the classical music firmament. But he feared that most of them were only using his training as a base from which to fly off to modern music. With their flexible voices that ranged over the entire span of three octaves, a feat that had been achieved only through the training he had imparted to them, they were now being snapped up by the film world. Two were well known in Bangla films, their classically-trained voices adding a depth and musicality to even the most mundane of melodies, making them a music-director's delight. Two others were trying their luck in the world of Mumbai filmdom, and, given the beauty of their timbred and nuanced voices, Pandit Chiranjeev Mukherjee was quite certain that they would soon be able to work there. Where, then, was the student who would carry his torch– carry his own personal gharana, his style, forward?

He was in this despairing frame of mind when Sandhya Senapati came to him. Or rather, was brought to him, by her father, from some place whose name he had never heard of, way up in the North-East of the country, a town called, it seemed, Tamulbari.

Sandhya Senapati was that anachronism in the generally narcissistic and intensely competitive world of Hindustani Classical Music, a person who did not care in the least about Image. Or about material success. True, like all performing artistes, even back then when she had been a student of Chiranjeev Mukherjee's sunset years, she needed an audience. An audience was after all the sine qua non for performing artistes, the mirror that reflected their art, and expertise. But she was not willing to compromise her years of hard-won knowledge and expertise just to suit the tastes of her audience. And Chiranjeev Mukherjee, who, in spite of the musical gimmickry that he indulged in to placate a restive crowd, and win them over to his side, was at the core of his being, a person who was thoroughly conversant with the classicism of Hindustani Shastriya Sangeet.

The emotion he felt when he agreed to take on Sandhya Senapati as a student was one of huge relief. Here, at last, was the One, the voice, the vessel that would carry the riches of his hard-won knowledge into the future.

It would have been better if she had belonged to Kolkata. He could have groomed her even more extensively, he thought, even as he marvelled at the way she reproduced with seeming ease the meends, the glides and glissandos for which he was famed. They were recognizably his own style, yet she had imbued them with a freshness that was her own, a new dimension that came with her voice which was, even in those early days when she came to learn from him, richly timbered. Yes, she would reign like a queen if she made Kolkata her address. He therefore offered her a home, telling her that she could stay with his other girl students in the flat he had bought across the road. He would pay for her food, her lodgings, even her college education a good Kolkata college. For she was only sixteen at the time, fresh out of school, from that place she called home, Tamulbari. Tamulbari! He was careful not to show her his contempt for the small town where she came from, and its no doubt betel-nut-chewing populace.

An artiste needed a nurturing environment, and surely Kolkata could provide it. He was tempted to tell her to give up academics but refrained, for he knew that these days it was necessary for musicians to be educated, at least graduate. But yes, he had offered to pay for her academic studies out of his own pocket, if she would stay with his other students in close proximity to him. With her almost perfect aural memory, her ability to understand and reproduce every small nuance of his style and his treatment of Raags, she would be able to learn much more. And how much more he himself would be able to teach her if she remained with him through all the days of the year, through lessons, rehearsals and performances.

Her father, a schoolteacher, had sold his ancestral land in order to be able to bring his daughter to Ustad Chiranjeev Mukherjee for lessons. He was not a little relieved to turn over his daughter to this man of formidable musical reputation. Luckily, he lived too far away to have heard anything about the man's womanizing and drinking, otherwise he might have changed his mind. Sandhya Senapati had learned the basics of music at Tamulbari from a local teacher, but had far outstripped her Guru in a matter of a few years. Already, at sixteen, she was well known in the music circles of the region that she came from.

Chiranjeev Mukherjee's secret contempt for the place remained a fixed constant in his mind. Tamulbari, near Kaziranga that place that was famous for rhinos and floods. Who in that Godforsaken place would listen to the music that she created?

In his efforts to get her to leave the place, Pandit Chiranjeev was only partially successful. Her father was willing enough for her to stay with her Guru in Kolkata. He was a forward-looking man, not a musician himself, but quite aware of his daughter's stupendous talent. He felt the weight of his responsibility and wanted to make sure that her talent was nurtured as best as possible. For her to stay in Kolkata for most of the year would solve many problems, not least of which were financial.

But it was she who had refused to uproot herself completely and make Kolkata her home. True, she did stay with her Guru for a large part of the year in the flat across the road where his girl students were housed. She was given a room of her own, so that she could do her riyaz undisturbed. She was enrolled in a college where she pursued an academically-lightweight course leading, eventually, to a BA degree.

Chiranjeev Mukherjee would have liked her to forget her home town completely, but Sandhya, delicate-looking though she was, insisted on going back there every time there was a holiday lasting more than five days. In the Kolkata of that time, bandhs and hartals closed everything down quite frequently. Besides, there were those endless holidays in summer when she went home for months at a time, and during Durga Puja, when she sang, it seemed, at some temple opposite her home back in Tamulbari. She was conscientious in maintaining her riyaz but he constantly had a sense of time rushing by. He could have taught her so much more, she could have progressed so much faster if she had remained near him throughout the year.

Why? Who knew? She had some notion of rootedness, some feeling that she should not lose touch with the land of her ancestors. For her, he had made an exception to his rule against using modern aids such as tape recorders and cassettes for teaching. For her, he himself would order that the cassette player be switched on, right at the beginning of lessons, so that every note, every phrase, every ornament was recorded. Of course if Sandhya had stayed in Kolkata these technological aids would not have been necessary, for her aural memory was prodigious. But he wanted to take no chances. She was often away for weeks at a time, sometimes even for a span of two or three months. What if she forgot, or ignored, some vital points in his lessons, some murki or sapat taan that had to be performed just so in a particular Raag, in order to get the full bouquet of its flavour?

Yet, even though she was frequently absent from Kolkata, the music circles soon sat up and took notice of Sandhya Senapati. Within just a few years of tutelage under Pandit Chiranjeev Mukherjee, she was a graded Classical and semi-Classical artiste of All India Radio. Though she was often away in that godforsaken hole of hers during the winter music season, her Guru saw to it that a few programmes in judiciously chosen Conferences were booked in her name when she did come down. At first, she was naturally given the early slots meant for beginners. Quite swiftly, however, she rose to the middle ranks, so that she was soon performing melodies such as Raageshri in the eleven PM slots, when the crowds had settled down, and they looked forward to good music. It was to her credit that she could always satisfy them, with the variety of her repertoire, her sweet voice that ranged freely across three octaves, her tonal richness, the purity of her aesthetics, and, yes, her serene beauty. Always simply dressed in white or pastel colours, her plaited hair a long black snake, her calm and decorous bearing had the papers calling her Saraswati and Binapani, even at that early age.

Pandit Chiranjeev, he of the numerous illicit liaisons and quick, one-night stands was not above breaking a taboo when it came to having a relationship with a girl student. But as far as Sandhya was concerned, Pandit Chiranjeev Mukherjee never felt anything that he should not. Her ivory skin and tranquil eyes appealed to him aesthetically, but he noted them with approval, only as wonderful aids to having a pleasing stage presence. He sometimes looked at her body under its salwar kameez or sari, but only in the context of wishing it was a little taller, and heavier, so that there was some flesh on her bones. He was only thinking of Sandhya's musical stamina when he told her to eat more of the traditional foods meant for musicians, especially vocalists, such as ghee, almonds, pistachios, along with aromatic biryanis, potato-stuffed parathas and of course chicken and mutton swimming in curries thick with cashews and raisins. He told her she could even gorge on ice cream if she wished, or pickles if they helped to whet her appetite for more food during lunch and dinner. Traditionally, vocalists avoided these two things, for they irritated the sensitive linings of the throat, and caused coughs and soreness that could be disastrous if one had a concert coming up. But as Pandit Chiranjeev Mukherjee told his students with pride, the vocal exercises he had evolved, ensured that they could eat whatever they wished, drink ice cold water during a concert if they wanted to. He practically guaranteed that if they faithfully carried out these vocal exercises, they would never be bothered by the irritants that could mar the concerts of the most well prepared vocalist. And it was certainly true that none of his students needed to go around with their throats wrapped in warm mufflers and scarves as many other vocalists did even in summer.

But Sandhya Senapati never put on weight. She was a light eater, and did not like either oily food or ice cream. And in spite of her thinness, her stamina during a recital remained quite robust, unlike those of some of his plumper students, whose voices would lose volume as well as flexibility after a couple of hours on stage.

Over the years, Sandhya progressed rapidly under Pandit Chiranjeev Mukherjee's tutelage. Her voice, already sweet and timbered, acquired a range and versatility that became her trademark. She could climb right upto the Sa of the ati-taar saptak, and plunge, within moments, to the shadaj of the mandra saptak, with such effortlessness that even the most jaded listener was forced to sit up and take notice. Her taans acquired speed and variety, her bistaars in the slow portion were spiritual as well as sensuous. Most of all, her mind, under her Guru's guidance, learned how to home in straight into the essence of a Raag, and produce the exact sequence of notes that would accentuate its soul, its spirit, in such a way that listeners would be moved to joy, or tears, according to the emotion that she wished to evoke. Remarkably, for one so young, she understood the character, the essence that was at the core of each Raag. She realized, right from the beginning, that mastery over techniques was just a means towards an end, just a method and a process by which the soul of the melody could be glimpsed.

Her father, the schoolmaster, began to talk of getting her married. Pandit Chiranjeev Mukherjee, with his long experience of students, well knew the hazards that this implied. Marriage was something that almost invariably, cut short even the very promising musical career in a woman, and even though the old disapproval of conservative families about the daughter-in-law of the house singing, playing, or dancing on a public stage had by then almost vanished, the very fact that music was not a nine-to-five job made it a very difficult career option for women. They had to wake up early, and do their morning riyaz, without fail every day and not too many husbands would take kindly to getting their own breakfasts or doing household chores while the wife sat singing scales and Raags. Add to that the fact that musical functions took place in the evenings, and went on till quite late at night and that musicians often had to travel to outstation venues it would be a difficult proposition at best. And once the babies came, the riyaz and concert schedules would inevitably take a back seat, at least for a few years. After staying awake the whole night with a squalling infant, which woman, however talented and dedicated, would have the energy to sit down for her riyaz at dawn? Gradually, concert appearances would start dwindling, and her proficiency would fall from the peaks it had scaled previously. Yes, marriage was a dicey business for a woman musician.

Pandit Chiranjeev Mukherjee hinted to Sandhya's father that his daughter should remain a spinster, a votary at the feet of Saraswati. Her enormous talent would only be wasted in matrimony. But his hints fell on deaf ears. Sandhya's father came from a milieu where matrimony was the goal of all women. He would be failing miserably in his duties as a father if he could not get his daughter married. Of course he would see to it that she would remain in an environment where her music could be nurtured, and would flourish.

Chiranjeev became desperate not to lose his prize pupil to some insensitive man who would insist on putting his own comforts and needs before Sandhya's dedication to music. He began to toy with the idea of bringing her to his own home, as a daughter-in-law for one of his sons. Both were by then well settled in their chosen professions, and were earning, from what he could make out, very well. He had never really been close to his sons, his routine of riyaz, teaching, and concert performances not having given him much time for it. Luckily, his wife, Noyona Devi, was a competent and practical woman, totally unmusical and with not a single artistic bone in her angular body. It was she who had run the household smoothly, in spite of the erratic schedules of the master of the house, she who saw to it that her sons got the best education available in the city. She turned a blind eye to her husband's peccadilloes, considering them to be part of the hazards of the profession. In any case, she held the purse strings firmly in her hand, the two apartments were in her name, and all the family's monetary investments had her name on the title deeds.

Noyona Devi's relationship with the pale, beautiful student from Tamulbari was maternal. Indeed, she was maternal to all the students who came to their home, and especially to those who stayed in the flat. She made sure that they got their meals on time, that they were not disturbed, that they devoted enough time to their riyaz while in her care. And Noyona Devi, mother of two sons but no daughters, was particularly affectionate and caring towards her husband's favourite student. She tried to coax her to have more almonds in the morning, more milk, so that she would put on some weight. Body weight was something that was traditionally thought desirable in musicians. The portlier they were, the heavier, the more stamina they were perceived to have. Nobody correlated the early coronaries and fatalities that musicians of those days suffered, with the traditional diet high in fats and carbohydrates that they followed. But Sandhya Senapati would not, could not eat more than mere morsels of what Noyona Devi tried to feed her. She remained as undesirably slim, in her Guru's eyes and his wife's, as when she had first come to them.

Chiranjeev Mukherjee broached the subject of marrying his favourite student to one of his sons to Noyona Devi one evening. Though surprised initially – she had never thought of the rather dreamy girl as good daughter-in-law material – she agreed to find out what her two sons thought of the idea. But before she had a chance to do so, the older one brought home a laughing, pretty girl one evening for dinner. Later, after he returned from dropping her home, he confided to his mother that he meant to marry her. Of course there was no question of opposition, especially since the girl herself was already finding her feet in the Civil Services.

And then Sandhya's father went and did something that shocked Chiranjeev Mukherjee so much that he actually suffered a coronary a few days after he came to know of it. The ex-schoolteacher Senapati went and fixed his daughter's marriage with a student of his arch rival, Ustad Nooruddin Khan of Lucknow.

What could the man have been thinking of?

Actually, Sandhya's father was extremely pleased with the alliance. He felt he had pulled off something of a coup when the marriage negotiations finally reached a triumphant conclusion. Not only was the "boy" a well known vocalist himself, he was also from a very good family, the son of an engineer, no less. What more could a school teacher like him aspire to? Of course it was Sandhya herself who had actually swung the negotiations in her favour, Sandhya with her ivory skin and snake of black hair, her large tranquil eyes that were so much like her mother's, her quiet nature and tidy looks, and of course her growing fame as a musician.

Sandhya had never told her father what she required in a husband. It was not the done thing in a household such as theirs to demand this kind of bridegroom or that. It was assumed that the parents knew best. In any case, what did a girl, even a girl as beautiful and talented as Sandhya really need? A husband who would be a good provider, somebody who would see that her interests were not stifled, somebody whose mother was hopefully not a harridan. Senapati the schoolteacher preened in secret when the marriage was finalized.

Tridib Barua, a good eight years older than Sandhya, was so devastatingly handsome that many people thought he was a model or an actor rather than a classical musician. Though he spent the lean season in his home state, he was very frequently with his Guru in Lucknow, or on concert tours across the length and breadth of the country, and abroad.

Tridib Barua's parents too were looking for a suitable girl. Somebody who would understand the nature of their son's work, somebody who would support him, somebody who would be a helpmate and a muse both. They were delighted when Sandhya's father approached them with the proposal. They had of course already seen and heard the girl at concerts. There was nothing that they could dislike about either Sandhya or the family, and since dowry did not figure at all in their community, the negotiations were quickly concluded.

The only problem was in persuading their son to get married. He had resisted all offers of marriage so far, waving them away good-naturedly when his mother had broached the topic to him. "How can I live my life with an engineer, Ma? I don't think I'll be happy with a girl who most likely thinks in figures and numbers, instead of in sur and taal." Or "Did you notice the girl's voice, Ma? No? Well, I won't be able to marry anyone with a less than perfect voice. Imagine waking up to something like a crow's cawing every morning ... !" His parents chided him for being over-fastidious, for being so choosy. But he remained adamant. They even asked him if he was behaving like this because he already had a sweetheart tucked away somewhere. Was it, they asked with trepidation in their hearts, for after all their son's Guru was a Muslim, of another religion, while they themselves were practicing Hindus, was it that girl, Shanaz, the Ustad's daughter? If it was, they would accept her as a daughter-in-law, after all she was a nice girl, though not very educated. Besides, true to the traditions of his Gharana, Ustad Nooruddin had not taught his daughter anything about music at all, not even the basics, for after all she was but a girl who would be married into another family. If he had taught her, she would end up taking with her the hard-won knowledge of her Gharana, and enriching that of her husband's.

But no, it seemed that neither Shanaz, nor any other girl, was part of their son's life. All he would tell them was, "Where's the hurry? Let me build my career, you see how much time I need to devote to it just now. You, of all people, should know just how critical it is at this point of time to travel to distant venues, so that music lovers can hear me first hand, and know my music. In a few years, eight, ten at the most, I won't have the stamina to travel so much. I won't have the energy to stay up all night, performing for hours at major conferences, and then going straight off to the airport at dawn, without a wink of sleep, in time to catch a plane to another concert venue for a performance that same evening. If this was forty, fifty years ago, you could have married me off to somebody who would be content to sit at home and take care of the house, and the children. But which modern girl will like a man who's hardly at home?"

He had said all this gently but firmly to his mother over and over again. But now here suddenly was this girl. Sandhya Senapati.

It would be a match made in heaven.

Tridib had already met and spoken to Sandhya at several concerts, in Kolkata as well as in other places.

It could not be that he had anything against her looks, or her behaviour. Could it be...? These musicians were a strange lot, and Tridib had spent so much time at his guru's house in Lucknow that it would be no surprise if he began to think like him in some ways. Could it be that he was so influenced by his Guru's well-known dislike of Sandhya Senapati's guru that he could not see beyond it to the kind of person that Sandhya actually was? Or could it be that he held on to some purist notion of gharanas, that it would not be proper to mingle the purity of his guru's gharana and his own with the eclectic style of Sandhya's singing, and her guru's?

But no, it seemed that that was not the problem either. At least he did not admit it. But Tridib remained impervious, to his mother's cajoling and his father's unspoken but nevertheless eloquent entreaties, till his parents began to lose patience. His mother began to cast about for another way to make her son fall in line, and get married.

Eventually, she took recourse in the time-honoured trick of falling sick. Like so many parents of recalcitrant children down the centuries, she clapped a hand to her chest, and had a heart attack. She was rushed to hospital after she slumped down in her chair while having breakfast. No, she didn't fake it. The ECG monitors and all the other machines that were brought to bear on her confirmed that she had, indeed, had a real, if not very major, heart attack.

Her son cancelled all his engagements for a month, and rushed back from London, where he was taking part in a workshop on Raag as an Expression of Emotion, to be with his mother. Never one to miss the chance to make the most of an opportunity when it presented itself she began to work quite shamelessly on her son's sentiments. She knew fully well that what she was doing was nothing short of emotional blackmail, but she cared not a whistle about being labelled manipulative, or even scheming. It was high time her son assumed the duties and responsibilities of a householder.

She began to work on her son. She had a whole month to do it in. She began in hospital, continued when she returned home, and finished, triumphantly, when, three weeks into Tridib's stay, he agreed to marry Sandhya Senapati.

Things moved swiftly after that. Tridib's mother got up briskly from her sickbed, and in a voice that was suddenly no longer weak or infirm, began to arrange things. Senapati the schoolteacher was summoned, dates were discussed. Sandhya's father wanted her to at least "see" the "boy" before she agreed, formally, to get married. But Sandhya herself said that from her side, it was not necessary. The reason she gave was that Tridib's mother was still recovering from a heart attack, and it would be insensitive to place this added stress on her. There was also Tridib's hectic schedule. She had met him several times, and had found him pleasant, and not in the least bit arrogant, unlike many other musicians she knew. True, he had never shown much interest in her, but then that was perhaps to be expected. After all, he was a musician who was senior to her on the circuit, and it was enough that there was no gossip about him at all. She had noticed that he never looked at women lecherously, and she appreciated the fact that he never showed any unseemly interest in her. She herself was always careful to remain within the boundaries of what was conceived as "correct" behaviour.

What she wanted now were not signs of romantic inclinations in the man who was to wed her, but an assurance that his family would not stand in the way of her pursuing her own musical career. In this, she had been more or less given a guarantee by her father, who had conveyed Tridib's mother's words to her.

And so it came to pass that both Pandit Chiranjeev Mukherjee and Ustad Nooruddin Khan shared the same place of honour on the wall of the music room in the home of their students. Both pictures had garlands around them now, for they had departed from this world within a few months of each other. Perhaps it was a coincidence that their deaths had been timed thus, perhaps not. The fact was that they had both left this earthly abode within a little over a year of their favourite students getting married to each other.

Nomita, laughing, had just finished telling the other students about her experience with the crashing chandelier, when the curtains at the end of the room parted. Guruma, Vidushi Sandhya Senapati – she had kept her maiden name for professional purposes even after marriage – entered the room.

3

Usually, Nomita took her lessons from Sandhya Senapati alone. She was an "advanced" student, and, people said, her teacher's best. But sometimes, perhaps when a Vedic Chant or a Saraswati Vandana was under preparation for a show somewhere, Sandhya Senapati asked her to be present in her group classes. Nomita's was always the leading role in these group affairs.

As soon as Guruma entered, the students got up and, bending low, touched her feet. It was a time-honoured ritual, this mark of respect for their teacher, and by implication, to Saraswati herself, the Veena-playing goddess of learning and music. But as she waited for her turn to go up and pay obeisance to her teacher, Nomita felt uneasy. As the other students jostled each other to get to their teacher's feet, it seemed to her that even here there was a sense of competition: who would bend down lowest, whose would be the greatest show of respect, who would take the most time to actually finish the ritual? It was as though they believed that the knowledge that they had come to seek at their teacher's feet would, in some way, be transferred to them, in direct proportion to the elaborateness of their ritual greetings to their Guru.

Quickly, Nomita pushed down the disloyal thought. Sandhya Senapati's face looked as serene and calm as ever, and whatever the motivations of her students she certainly took this daily ceremony, with due seriousness. She placed her hands, palm down, on the head of each student as he or she paid her obeisance, and said brief words of blessing to each. Nomita, watching, reflected that in all these years that she had been Sandhya Senapati's student, she had never seen her impatient while this was going on. It would be repeated again at the end of the lesson, and Sandhya Senapati would remain as calm and unhurried as always.

Time had touched Sandhya Senapati lightly. She was probably over forty, reflected Nomita, perhaps forty-two? Forty-three? Certainly she was as slim and graceful now as she was in the photographs in her albums, taken at musical events when she was in her twenties. With her ivory colouring, cream coloured clothes and tranquil demeanour, she seemed to light up the shadows of the music room at Jhankaar now.

Finally, when it was her turn at last, Nomita went up and placed her hands on her Guru's feet. She felt the light touch of Sandhya Senapati's palms in blessing on her head.

"It was terrible, that lamp crashing down like that," she said as Nomita stood up again. Her voice, was as soft as usual, but her words conveyed the same anger as her eyes. Normally calm and unruffled, they had at this moment an uncharacteristic spark of displeasure. "I mean – a few inches this way or that, terrible, na? ...."

Some of Tamulbari's papers had carried the news item about the crashing chandelier, along with a description of the function itself. A couple of them had carried pictures too, of the singers of the Jhankaar Music Academy carrying on dauntlessly, after the debris had been cleared, and presenting, as the papers said, the Mangalacharan in "as tuneful a manner as they always did." Nomita's face in these pictures was practically hidden by the microphones before her. This was normal. As a vocalist, she was more or less resigned to having her pictures showing her face either distorted, with her mouth wide open in a taan or bistaar, or hidden behind the microphones. Panchali and Rupa, she had noted with irritation that morning as she had glanced through the papers, had looked rather good in the pictures.

Sandhya Senapati had telephoned Nomita that morning to express her concern and, Nomita had brushed off her concern saying, "Well, thank goodness it didn't. I hope they fix it up properly this time."

Sandhya Senapati continued, "You did well to continue after the cleanup. The whole thing must have shaken you, it must have been difficult to settle down again and sing. But you did well."

Unlike many other teachers, Sandhya Senapati was not chary with praise where it was due, though she was quite conscientious too, about pointing out flaws. Nomita was gratified, but she said nothing, only smiled.

Sandhya Senapati moved towards the centre of the room. A large mat of split bamboo was scattered with cushions. Her walk, like the rest of her demeanour, was unhurried, her steps small and graceful. She sat down cross-legged on the floor in a fluid motion, and waited while her students arranged themselves before her. Straight-backed as always, already her eyes were closed, already she was thinking of the lesson ahead, the music before her, the knowledge that needed to be transferred to the boys and girls who were now seated in a semi-circle around her. Taanpuras were fine-tuned till they came to rest at the exact shruti. Throats were cleared. The lesson began …

They were preparing, for the inauguration of a new branch of a bank in the town. In Tamulbari, it was considered auspicious to start any venture with a recitation or, better still, a musical rendition of a Sanskrit sloka. The hoariness of the words was assumed to have some kind of talismanic effect which would ward off bad spirits and the evil eye.

It was a piece that all of them knew, yet a great deal of co-ordination was needed to get the diverse voices of the group to sing in a cohesive manner. It was an ancient hymn.

Yajja Grato Doorang Mudaiti Dwaivang …

Nomita, moved as usual by the beauty of the words of the hymns that they often sang, paused as Guruma corrected a couple of wrong notes that had crept into the song. Her ear was unerring: a minor slip on the part of a single singer in a group of six, eight, even twelve, never went undetected, or uncorrected. Nomita looked around her, at the singers, taking note of the way their bodies, too, responded to the music that came from their minds, and voices. It was a diversion, these mental notes she collected of the gestures that musicians made while practicing, or performing on stage. Depending on their own personalities, their hands and bodies and necks and faces moved as though they were performing in step to the music.

Nomita had noticed that as musicians evolved, so did their hand and arm gestures. Though no formal lessons on hand-gestures and body language were ever given, the mudras of the guru were always echoed by the student. The twitch of the eyebrow found a faithful shadow in the mirrored tic of the student. There was a whole body of knowledge enclosed in these twirls and wiggles, which students faithfully emulated, though no word ever passed from guru to shishya about this.

In the beginning, Nomita had seen, students were always self-conscious in their hand gestures. Their elbows would remain stiffly by their sides as their fingers moved in inhibited little circles. But as their voices soared, their arms, too, were freed. Before long, they reached the point when voice and hand moved in synchronization, each one drawing the picture of the Raag in different but complementary ways. The more media-savvy among the students used their arms and hands to dramatic effect, almost as though they were dancers, like Sufi saints and not just singers. They used these over-the-top gestures even when singing a simple bhajan, though this show of devotion was not strictly necessary, and was sometimes so incongruous as to be ridiculous. The mismatch between the singer's musical ability and the theatricality of her gestures were often the source of secret merriment to Nomita, secret because there were very few people she knew with whom she could share her observations. Rahul was the only person she could talk to about this.

She noticed now that as usual, Panchali and Rupa were adding punch to their singing by closing their eyes and swaying soulfully. Pranab had a tendency to wave his palm in the air when he approached the sam, the first and strongest note of the taal cycle. Sometimes his palm seemed to wave of its own accord even when, as often happened, Pranab pounced on the wrong beat, mistaking a subsidiary one for the dominant sam. Sujata's hand made small, constrained arcs, as though she was a timid sparrow trying to break free of restraints. Her gaze travelled to Guruma, who, with her eyes closed, was singing the hymn now. Her hands moved in beautiful swoops and swirls along with the melody, they were almost a dancer's mudras in their beauty and expressiveness. Somebody should make a film on her hand gestures alone, thought Nomita as she watched and listened to the melody and the mudra become one.

Towards the end of the lesson, Tridib Barua entered the music room. Or rather, that was when Nomita, along with the other students actually noticed him. When he was in town and free from his own commitments, Tridib Barua sometimes sat in on their lessons with Guruma. Guruji, they called him, and accorded him the same reverence they would have if he had been their teacher, and not their teacher's husband.

In a way, he was, for he sometimes gave a suggestion here, or a tweak to a composition there, which would enhance and illuminate the entire piece of music. But unlike many husbands of musicians who were also musicians themselves, Tridib Barua never gave an opinion on his wife's students unless he was asked, nor did he give suggestions unless specifically requested to do so. This, Nomita knew, was highly unusual. It was more or less taken for granted, that when a husband and wife were both professional exponents of Hindustani Shastriya Sangeet, it would be the male who would be higher in the pecking order. It would be his word that would be final, it would be his judgement that would be deferred to, in all matters pertaining to music. In the strict hierarchy that prevailed in the world of music, the wife would automatically defer to the husband. Sometimes, indeed, the husband never mind if his music was much worse than his wife's, would actually declare himself to be his wife's Guru, and therefore all her students would also become, by default, his students, twice over. And of course the students themselves were usually too gratified by this show of condescension on the part of their Guruma's Guru to feel, even in the slightest, that this was not interest, but interference: a show of ego, and quite uncalled-for.

Nomita, covertly watching Tridib Barua as he sat quietly in the shadows at the back of the room, had long realized that the relationship between Sandhya Senapati and Tridib Barua was highly unusual. It was almost unheard of for two musicians, both vocalists in the same tradition, though with different styles and from different

Gharanas, to live under the same roof, without any perceptible ego hassles. She had seen it happen, or heard about it, all too often. After marriage, the woman's star would wane. The time that she should have spent practicing would be allotted, instead, to domestic duties. Or if, by excellent time management, she did find herself actually continuing with the demanding hours of riyaz required to remain and rise above a certain level, she would find that it would not be possible, after a time, to go out of town to perform at all the important functions to which she was invited. There would always be more pressing demands on her time. And since her husband was always out of town, or even out of the country for long periods, the smooth running of the house, and management of the children, would always fall on her. Of course there were exceptions, and this was certainly clear in the case of Tridib Barua. He himself had now become a much sought after concert artiste, spending weeks, even months at a time on tours around the country, and the world. His cassettes and CDs were greatly in demand. Much sought after by the best recording companies of the country, at least two CDs of his music appeared each year, and to add to that his concerts were recorded too. Nomita was aware that each CD went into several editions.

The unusual thing was that Sandhya Senapati's career too was curving upwards in a line parallel to Tridib Barua's. She too was much sought after in venues all around the country, and was often abroad. It was of course rare that organizers booked them for the same concert. After all, there was a format that had to be followed in these classical concerts, especially the shorter ones that lasted for four or five hours at the most. A group song, perhaps a Mangalacharan, or maybe a devotional bhajan, to open the show. A vocal performance, either by a male or female artiste. Dhrupad or Khayal to begin with, then, perhaps, a dhamar, thumri, or dadra. This would be followed by a dance recital, perhaps a vibrant Kathak, a meditative Bharata Natyam or a peaceful Sattriya from the ancient monasteries of the valley of the Red River. And then, to wind up, an instrumental piece, perhaps a sitar or sarod, or maybe a santoor or flute. If the vocalist was much more senior than the instrumentalist, their order of appearance would be reversed, but it usually followed the pattern. There was usually no place in these programmes for two separate vocalists, even if they were husband and wife. And the two rarely sang jugalbandis, the classical duets together, no doubt because of the difference in the pitches in their voices, and also because of the different styles that they sang in. Mostly, therefore, the two performed at different venues. Nomita wondered now, as she had wondered several times in the past, whether the couple had consciously decided not to have children. After all, there would have been demands then that would certainly have interfered with their careers, most likely Sandhya Senapati's. Quickly, she pushed away the thought. Sacrilege to think of such things in connection with one's Guru!

It was therefore quite in keeping that Tridib Barua had entered the music room so unobtrusively, without making a production of it. No students or even a ubiquitous toady fore and aft to herald his approach. No self-important "Carry on, carry on, I am here to listen only, don't mind me…" that sometimes managed to be so much more disruptive than a routine entry.

Now, as Tridib Barua sat quietly with his eyes closed in concentration in the shadows, Nomita observed him covertly. He was still amazingly handsome. Indeed, the two of them, Guruma and Guruji, were both very good looking. But when it came to physical attractiveness, the beauty of perfect proportions Tridib Barua won out. Much of Sandhya Senapati's beauty came from within, from the tranquillity that was so much a part of her persona, a tranquillity embodied in her name, Sandhya, Dusk, Godhuli, the magical time when the cattle came lowing home, tinkling bells around their necks, the sound of which merged with those of the temples as evening prayers and aaratis were offered. This was a time encapsulated in the serenity of her eyes and in the raags sung at that time, Marwa, Puriya, Puriya Kalyan…

On the other hand, the sheer perfection of Tridib Barua's looks overshadowed his individuality, even personality. Nomita knew him to be a very artistic, creative, sensitive man, courteous and helpful. But none of this was apparent by just looking at him. Everything from his still-thick, but now beautifully greying hair, to his face with its Grecian features, perfectly proportioned torso, limbs, and unblemished feet, spoke of a classical beauty that would have delighted painters looking for a model to portray an older David. Older, but still at the peak of physical perfection. Life, and its many experiences, had left little imprint, on Tridib Barua's face. To reach the place where he was now, professionally, must have taken him a great deal of effort and work, physically as well as mentally. Yet none of the hardship that this had entailed had left any imprint on his face. The strains of travelling, the stresses of performing, making sure that one always took one's audience along on the journey through melodies, the late nights and irregular timings, had left almost no mark on his face or frame. Indeed, it was on Sandhya Senapati's face instead, that the under eye shadow and small forehead creases were beginning to be visible, if one looked carefully. Nothing disfiguring, far from it. Indeed, if anything, they added to the interest generated by her face and demeanour. But when husband and wife were together, the gaze, whether a man's or a woman's, would inevitably be riveted on Tridib Barua, at least at first. It was the sheer perfection of his face and body that drew the eye as irresistibly as did some mesmeric mountain scene, for instance, or a beautifully laid-out garden.

Tridib Barua's quiet "Wah," after they finished, the universal expression of appreciation in these parts, was expected. So was his wife's questioning look at him. "What do you think? How can it be improved?"

Unless he was asked his opinion on a piece of music, or about a musician, Tridib Barua would never comment. But when his advice was sought, he gave of it unstintingly, and thoughtfully. "The voices should come at the exact moment of starting. To make an impact, you know. A few voices stand out more than the others, that should be remedied by a proper placing of the mikes. Be careful about those high notes, a few of them sounded a little off to me. Nothing really discordant, just a bit… Otherwise it's sounding just fine."

Guruma nodded, and turned back to the students. "We'll work on that next time. Meanwhile, make sure your individual parts are perfect. It's the parts that make up the whole, even though our aim is to make the whole greater than the sum of its parts… Yes, we'll meet again tomorrow, this time."

Once more, the ritual of touching Guruma's feet. This time, the whole exercise was doubled, for it was unthinkable that they could depart without showing Guruji the same respect.

Finally they filed out of the house. The various rivalries within the group, held back for more than two hours by Guruma's calming and inhibiting influence, came rushing out to the forefront again.

"Those off-key high notes…yes, I heard them very clearly, too, over my own singing. Thank goodness it's not me…how embarrassing if it was, but only last week Guruma had praised my voice in the high notes…" Pointed looks were exchanged, offence was given, offence taken.

Ignoring all these rapier thrusts, Nomita stood outside the gate, peering into the deepening dusk, waiting, like the others, for a rickshaw or auto. It was pointless paying too much attention to this lot. She knew that once her back was turned, there would be unanimity among them in tearing her voice, or her manners to shreds.

"Will you be coming to the concert then, Nomita?" asked Sujata, one of the nicer persons in the group. "It's only about a fortnight away now, you know."

"Of course!"

"The Concert" in this group of people could only refer to thing. This was the sitar recital that was being viewed, and projected, not just as a musical programme, but as an Event. Already, the papers were full of advertisements about the "Show," already there were "Previews" in the culture sections of various journals of the town about the maestro for whom all Tamulbari was waiting with bated breath. Kaushik Kashyap's first visit to this town was being tom-tommed as a social event as much as a musical one.

Nomita hesitated, wondering whether she should add more. Should she tell this group of music students about…no, better not…

But her thoughts were cut off by the many voices around her, for whom the reference to Kaushik Kashyap's concert had served as a signal to change the subject. Like a group of chattering birds, they commented excitedly,

"The tickets are almost sold out, you know! Just very few are left, that too in the thousand-rupee-per-seat bracket. Lucky we got ours in the two hundred rupee ones last week."

"Of course Kaushikji will donate it all to charity. He's not going to take any of the proceeds for himself. The organizers told me so themselves. He's coming here for free, not taking any money at all for the show. Only the travel expenses, and those of his accompanists, will have to be reimbursed. An amount equal to his normal fee will be given to some charitable institution."

"This is the first time he's coming here, of course. The first time he's coming to any town of the size of Tamulbari, I believe. Of course he's mostly abroad these days, except during the winters. He's so much in demand at that time at the Music Conferences and Sanmelans that he sometimes has no sleep for several nights at a stretch!"

"He's taking time off from his work as Visiting Faculty Member in a university in California, just to come here, it seems. Now that's something, isn't it? It shows something about the importance of our town on the musical map..."

Each voice cut off the other, clamouring in un-musical tones to be heard above the rest. This desire to be perceived to be "In the Know" about such an important event was routine. Much of what they said on these occasions was a result of creativity, arising out of competitiveness. If one didn't have a piece of authentic "news" to show off one's being "In the Know", it was all right to invent something. Today, however, thought Nomita distractedly, what they were saying about Kaushik Kashyap was all true, more or less.

"He's on the National Programme on the radio tonight," said Sujata. "Must remember to change the batteries in our transistor."

"This is the second time in less than two years that Kaushikji's been featured on the National Programme," said another voice, confident in the knowledge of knowing more than the others. "That's really unusual, it's practically unheard of, you know. That's the kind of stature he enjoys…" as though he himself was personally responsible for Kaushik Kashyap's immense popularity all over the world.

A motor bike, its rider helmeted beyond recognition, roared to a stop in front of her. Even before he took off his headgear, even though she hadn't seen him for quite a while now, Nomita knew from the way the rider sat on the seat that this was Rahul.

"Want a lift?" he asked, ignoring the pack of singers around Nomita.

Quickly, she climbed up behind him. Forgetting to say or even wave a farewell to the others, Nomita was soon whizzing down the lane at a speed that would have seemed impossible, given the density of traffic at this peak evening hour.

"When did you arrive?" she yelled into the general direction of Rahul's ear.

"This afternoon!" he yelled back, his words whipped away by the roar of a passing truck. "Wait, we'll talk…"

A few minutes later, in the cooled space of a restaurant, with the helmet sitting on the table between them like a polished black skull, it was much easier to talk.

"So, how are the Gurus?" Rahul's tone was flippant. Nomita was used to the way her fellow students, and those others whom she met in the world of classical music, dipped their voices to reverential levels whenever her Guruma was mentioned. She found herself reacting, as always, with something like surprise. Yet why should she be surprised, she thought, as she murmured the expected responses, "Oh they are fine, busy as ever," and sipped the tea placed before her. After all Rahul was from a very different world, a world where music was treated as entertainment, or a "Time Pass" affair. Whereas in the world of classical music that she was familiar with, music was a spiritual quest, a means to merging with the Godhead, at its best. And Gurus, keepers of the flame, responsible for passing on the knowledge to the next generation, were revered just this side of divinity.

"So, your flight was on time?" she added.

"Yes, bang on, can you imagine, I hopped on the plane at Bangalore at six in the morning, at eleven I was peering down from the window at the betel nut trees around Guwahati airport, and by three I was here in Tamulbari. The trees look rather pretty from the air, don't they? Especially when you contrast the green of their leaves with the blue of the skies, and the river..."

Nomita quirked an eyebrow at him. It wasn't like him to wax eloquent about nature. He grinned somewhat self-consciously, and said, defensively, "Well, I've been homesick, a bit. Haven't been here for more than a year now. But," he looked around the place, gradually filling up with the young crowd of Tamulbari, "home is changing, too. This place wasn't here when I was last in town... and now look at it. An established eatery, as they say..."

"Isn't that just typical of you, all of you who go off and expect your hometowns to remain the same, frozen in time, and the rest of us waiting in endless expectation of your return...!" It was so easy to slip into the banter that was habitual between the two of them. Nomita realized, suddenly, that she had missed this easy camaraderie very much. Engrossed in her music, busy with her job, she had hardly realized it, till now. There were very few people, hardly anybody, in fact, with whom she could talk in this way.

Rahul laughed. It was the same laugh she remembered, carefree and cheerful, the same laugh she had grown up with. As far back as she remembered, Rahul Borkotoky, and his family, had been a part of her life, and that of her family's. His father and hers were both doctors, colleagues in the hospital. Their mothers, too, got on very well, though Rahul's mother worked in a bank, and hers was a Science teacher in the same school as she, Nomita herself worked in now. She and Rahul were friends, back from when they had been in nursery school together, howling for their mothers to take them home. Their families met up in each others' homes at least once a month, often more. Over the years, they had gone on holidays together, had shared their problems, laughed together, supported each other through the good times and the not-so-good. When Rahul's father had gone abroad for six months, it had been possible for his mother to take leave from her work and accompany him there only because they had been assured that Rahul would be well looked after in their absence by Nomita's family. Rahul's father, a pediatrician, had been a constant figure in her life through mumps, measles and chicken pox, but also at the get-togethers that happened at frequent intervals. Even after Rahul, an only child like Nomita herself, had gone away to study engineering in a college across the length of the country, and had then begun to work there, Nomita still went to visit his parents, sometimes along with hers, sometimes on her own. To her, they were "family", just as her parents were to Rahul.

And Rahul himself? Nomita studied him as she listened to his account of his journey this morning back to his hometown. He was the same age as her, but he looked, she thought, so much more carefree. But why should that be so? True, she was a student of a difficult, serious and highly philosophical discipline but that did not mean that she needed to become sombre at this age.

She gave herself a mental shake, and soon found herself laughing at his stories. It was true, she thought, that she had much more fun in his company than she did with others. Besides, she could talk to him freely, in spite of the fact that they did not meet nearly as frequently as they had earlier. Still, there was always email. And telephone, and sms. It was so easy to keep in touch these days, even if one was in the South, and the other thousands of kilometres away, in the North-Eastern part of the country. She was quite up-to-date in the events of his life, as he was in hers.

She was glad he hadn't mentioned the Other Matter. But he was like that. He wouldn't talk about it unless she brought it up herself. "So how are preparations for the trip?" she asked now. The software firm that he worked in was sending him to the US on a project for three months.

"Well, I'm leaving right after I get back from here... in fact they were cribbing about me taking time off to come here now, just before the trip. Thank goodness I could make it... I always think it's really amazing," he frowned at his empty tea cup, "considering the fact that Tamulbari is smack in the middle of tea gardens, that the tea in most of these places is so awful. Shall we leave? You're done? You can give me a second cup in your house, I can meet Moha and Mahi, too. How are they?"

It was easy falling into the same pattern with Rahul once more. Talking to him, she realized how engrossed she had been in her own world of music. It seemed he was more in touch with what was happening in Tamulbari, about their old school friends, than she was.

"So Priya and Sudesh have hitched up, at last... I was glad to hear about that."

"They have? When?"

Rahul laughed, and got up, ready to leave. "You're really out of touch. Well. So what are you doing tomorrow? Drop in for lunch, it's Sunday, the old school's closed. You'll meet some of the gang there."

For a while, she felt buoyant and light. Rahul had that effect on her. At dinner that night, her mother asked her,

"Strange that Rahul hasn't called yet. He was supposed to have come in today, wasn't he?"

"Oh sorry Ma, he did come, you were out. He wanted to meet you... you weren't home at that time."

Her mother nodded, her mind preoccupied with something else. The Other Matter, Nomita realized.

"Tirna rang up again today. She wants to know how you feel about the whole thing. Of course her son is coming to Tamulbari, that's fixed, the concert dates and hotel bookings are all ready, no question of backing out from those. But what she wants to know is: will it be all right with you if he comes to our house? You know, kind of..." her voice trailed off.

"But Ma, won't Kaushik Kashyap be too busy to come to this... this humble abode?" She exaggerated the irony in her voice, but her mother didn't react. "I mean, I know you and Tirna Ghosh have become great friends. But he's a star, and I'm sure his schedule will have been packed to bursting by the organizers of the concert. Interviews, press conferences, radio recordings, the works. Just because his mother and you are friends, why should he...?" She trailed off, knowing what her mother's reply would be.

"Nomita!" Her mother's voice was exasperated. "You know if he comes here it won't be to see me, just because I'm his mother's friend.

It will be to see you. Yes, 'see' you. With all that it implies. His mother's choice of bride is fine by him, he says, but Tirna wants him to 'see' you at least, before anything is finalized. And to do her justice, she wants you to 'see' him, too. And so do we. I mean, you know all this. If you don't like him, or even if you don't want to 'see' him, you just have to say so, nobody's forcing you into anything."

Her father, at the other end of the table, cleared his throat and said kindly, "Of course she knows that. But he *is* after all a good match, especially for someone who's taken to music as seriously as you have."

"I'll ... let you know, give me some time." She hesitated, then said, "I know, I mean I suppose I should feel grateful that the great Kaushik Kashyap is taking an interest in me, is actually coming to this tiny town so far away from his usual tours, just to 'see' me. But 'seeing'... well that is a step in itself, isn't it? Let me think ..."

"Of course!" The talk turned to other matters, about school and the heat and inevitably again, the chandelier dropping on stage.

"Be careful where you sit on stage from now on," her mother fussed. "I mean, not just the placement of the mikes and things, that of course is routine for you. But always look up at the lights, make sure that you're not directly below them ..."

She didn't tell her parents that Kaushik Kashyap would be on air that night. As she went to her room, she said, "The National Programme is about to come on. Ma, if there's a call for me, tell them I'm busy, I'll call back." She knew her parents, supportive as they were of her own deep interest in music, were unlikely to listen to programmes of classical music themselves. They would rather read, watch TV, or catch up on the day's happenings. And if she told them about the programme, they would feel obliged to listen, to humour her, perhaps. Certainly they would feel that because of the impending "viewing" of their daughter by the sitarist, they should at least be able to talk knowledgeably about his music when he did arrive.

As usual the brief introduction at the start of the country's premier classical music programme on air, the National Programme on All India Radio gave a brief bionote of the artiste. Where he was born, what year. Nomita rapidly did some calculations in her head: Kolkata, some thirty-five or thirty-six years ago. That made him how much, nine or ten years older than her. Certainly he had achieved a huge amount in this time. He was surely greatly talented to have achieved such recognition, from connoisseurs as well as lay people around the world. She listened carefully to the names of his Gurus, his musical genealogy, his pedigree. They were all highly respected sitar players from Kolkata. But his present Guru lived most of the year in America, in spite of his advancing age. Nomita, familiar with the name of Kaushik Kashyap's guru, also knew that he had established a centre for Indian Culture there, and now lived there with his far younger American wife and two toddlers.

The announcer ran through a brief list of honours that Kaushik Kashyap had received so far. They included some of the most prestigious ones from around the country, including the "Kal Ke Kalakar", of Sur Singar Sanstha of Mumbai, "Tomorrow's Artistes" of the Bhopal Music Society, the "NewsMakers Award for Young Achievers" from a popular music channel, the "Samman Award" from Shruti, a greatly respected musical organization in Kolkata, and much else besides. A Padmashri already, a Government honour even though he was only in his thirties. Highly unusual, that. Already, he had been nominated for a Grammy for his fusion music with a renowned flutist from Sweden. The announcer ended by naming the raag that Kaushik Kashyap would be playing. None of the Yamans or Puriyas that were routine raags for performers to begin the National Programme with. He started with Sohni, a raag uncommon as a main item not because it was rarely heard, but because it was believed to have a limited canvas for an opening item. Musicians preferred to play it as a shorter second item. It was also unconventional to start at ten at night with this raag, which was traditionally played later, at about two or three in the morning, before the dawn raags.

Kaushik Kashyap, his trademark sweetness evident from the very first note that he struck on his instrument, played this raag for a full forty minutes. Incredible, thought Nomita, riveted to the river of sound pouring from the radio. The man's musical imagination was amazing. The note combinations, the mood he evoked, all spoke of his huge talent and of course also his unflinching dedication.

Listening to the melodies now, Nomita knew that here was a musician for whom the hours, minutes of each day would have just the one focus: his music. It was astonishing, thought Nomita. Not only was the technique perfect, his innovations too were amazing. Sticking rigorously to the framework of the raag, he infused it with an astounding freshness. He brought in hints, elements of a kind of music that was very different from anything heard under the category of Indian music. Hints of harmony, a Western concept, swam in and swam out of the river of music without in the least disturbing the elements of the raag itself, merely enhancing it. He stuck scrupulously to the accepted and traditional patterns of taans and tukras, the time-honoured ornamentations with which the exposition was embellished. But each taan, each tukra, was combined with another, each pattern of notes was given that slight tweak in such a way that everything sounded new, as though this particular raag had never been heard by connoisseurs of music ever before.

Next was a dhun, a lighter piece, where the musician had the liberty of bringing in elements of other Raags if he wished, a piece that could be less "classical" and more emotive. Kaushik Kashyap chose a self-composed piece based on a river melody. River melodies from Bengal had been brought into the repertoire of light classical music by other sitar players, she knew. They had given it a base of a raag, and the respectability of a concert platform. But once more, Kaushik Kashyap's exposition was startlingly new, romantic yet grounded in classicism. His sitar sang in ways that she had never heard before.

It was easy, at the end of the programme, to understand the man's position in the world of music today, not just Indian classical, but increasingly, world music. There was a breadth to his music, a wide vision, an inclusiveness, that was not often found in Indian classical musicians. Without sacrificing any of the meditative spirituality that formed the bedrock of this genre of music, Kaushik Kashyap had also managed to include an awareness of different worlds, different systems, different cultures even while being very faithful to the tradition in which he had been groomed.

A man who possessed this kind of vision, and more importantly, even managed to convey it through a music that was pure and sweet and attractive even to the rankest beginner or a layperson, this kind of man must surely, thought Nomita, have a world view different from the routine. His music spoke of a personality that was perceptive and empathetic to the needs and aspirations of others. A person like this would surely be indulgent towards the weaknesses and flaws of others. Surely he would be easy to get along with for wasn't it well known that the better the artiste, the more genuinely humble he was.

4

Nomita's classes at the Tamulbari Public School were usually in the afternoon, since the morning hours were given over for subjects perceived to be demanding, such as Mathematics and Science, which were supposed to tax the brain much more than such "soft" subjects as Art and Music. Her classes were scheduled for the time when students were sleepy, or restive

Still, even though she rarely left for work before twelve in the afternoon, her mornings were always busy. She got up before her parents did, though they themselves were no late risers. Her morning riyaz usually stretched to three hours, sometimes more, if she was due to perform solo somewhere. At the end of that time, she felt so drained, physically as well as mentally, that she needed to sit down for a while in solitude to recover. But Sandhya Senapati had told her that she should rest her voice one day a week. They were no longer living in an age when it was assumed that practice, practice and more practice was all that was needed to make perfect. Ancient techniques were now tempered with scientific knowledge. Of course there were still some gurus, mostly of the older generation, who prescribed the old ways to their students, not realizing that it was this demanding regime of riyaz for five, six hours at a stretch that was to blame for the chronic laryngitis that their students began to suffer from. But the new gurus now knew that the throat was a delicate part of the human body, and needed time to rest and recuperate.

Sunday, therefore, was her day of rest. It always took her a while, an hour at least, to get adjusted to the pace of this day without her riyaz. Usually she woke up late, for quite often this was also the day after a programme, from which she had returned late, either a programme where she herself had performed, or where she had gone to listen to somebody else's music. Her mind, on waking, would be full of the melodies that she had heard the previous evening.

Just as, this morning, it was filled with thoughts of Kaushik Kashyap, his music and, his mother's proposal of marriage. He himself seemed to be the good son who would go by whatever his mother suggested, a perfect Indian boy who would only marry according to his mother's wishes.

So did this mean that Kaushik was a devoted son, and would likely make an equally devoted husband? Or would he remain only a devoted son, while neglecting the wife chosen for him by his mother? Or, worst of all, did it merely mean that he was indifferent to the whole question of matrimony, and was agreeing to "see" her and "be seen" only because his mother was nagging him to get married soon? Had he agreed to his mother's choice of bride for him because he needed this matrimony thing out of the way, so that he could concentrate on his career?

But his music still reverberated through her mind as she walked out to the dining room for her breakfast. A man who made music such as this surely had more depth in him than most. Certainly the cascades of melody that he had created spoke of a sensitivity that would undoubtedly carry over to other areas of his life, and relationships, as well.

Over the pheni pitha and potato curry that usually made up their Sunday breakfast, Nomita brought up the topic that had been discussed the previous evening. Wrapping the fried and flavoured rice flour disc around a potato cube, she said, "About this 'seeing' thing..."

Her parents looked questioningly at her.

"Tell his mother that okay, it's fine by me if he comes to our house." Quickly, she added, "I hope I won't have to be dolled up or something for him. I mean, we can keep it casual, can't we?"

In her usual brisk and commonsensical voice, her mother said, "Don't be ridiculous. Those things happen only in Hindi movies, I would imagine, or those serials on TV that everyone talks about. Well that's a decision taken at least. Don't think of it as an irretrievable step in one direction. You can always back out... so can he."

"Of course *he* can. He's a man, isn't he? And already such a huge star. Maybe he expects me to feel grateful about all this..."

"Nomi!" Her father's voice was concerned. "If you don't want to go ahead, you just have to say so. Any decision you take is fine. We're not pressurising you or anything, surely you know that."

The music in her head grew louder. She smiled and said softly, "No, I know there's no pressure. It's my decision. See? I'll be responsible for all the consequences." Brightening up at an idea, she turned to her mother, and said, "Actually, why don't you *order* me to see him, then if he agrees, get married to him? Things would be so much easier for me! I can just remain sitting there like a mannequin or something, while you people decide everything for me. *I* wouldn't have to take all these decisions. Lovely! If things work out, fine, if they don't, I can always blame you, and make you feel guilty for the rest of your life! All this empowerment is terrible."

Shikha Sharma rolled her eyes, but smiled. "All right then, I'll call Tirna today and tell her. All this fuss... when my parents arranged my marriage with your father..."

"I know, I know. You made it clear to them that the final say would be yours. And it was. But don't you see, Ma? He's so much above me, professionally, so much better... it's almost as if..."

Nomita stopped. How could she put her ambivalence about the whole thing into words? She knew many women would jump at this interest shown in her by Kaushik Kashyap's family. The artiste, like most successful ones today, was rich, by any standard. Besides, his family and parents were like hers. Indeed, Tirna Ghosh, a teacher like her mother, had become friends with Shikha Sharma at a refresher course for teachers. It wasn't as though Kaushik came from a family of traditional musicians, where the women were always relegated to the background.

As for her parents, they felt that this was something that Nomita herself should be delighted about. They knew that she had no romantic interest in her life. Marriage to a person like Kaushik

Kashyap – Kaushik Ghosh actually, but he had adopted the name Kaushik Kashyap for the stage – would be just right for her. His home would be a place where her own talent would flourish. Indeed, they themselves were a bit at sea about how to go about nurturing this talent in their only offspring. They were lucky indeed that Sandhya Senapati had taken Nomita under her wing at a young age, and was grooming her talent with so much care. But certainly a move to Kolkata, with its vibrant musical scene, could only be good for Nomita's career. In any case, Tirna and her husband were wonderful people, and though Nomita's parents hadn't yet met Kaushik, any son of such parents would surely be fine for their daughter.

Shikha Sharma, looking at her daughter's face, sensed the turmoil in her mind. She had an idea of what was worrying the girl, but then she herself had given the go ahead just now. Well, she would pursue the matter later. Changing the subject, she asked, "Rahul rang up a little while ago, while you were still asleep. You're to call him, he said, as soon as you're up."

"They're having a party," remembered Nomita, "lunch with the old gang. Strange how it's Rahul who's in touch with them. I live here, but hardly meet them! Anyway, it'll be good to see them. I hope the thing hasn't been cancelled..."

But it hadn't. In fact, she thought, as she replaced the receiver after ringing up Rahul to find out why he had called, it was extremely unlikely that any party of Rahul Borkotoky's should be cancelled.

"Come early!" he had commanded on the line. There had been music playing in the background already, music very different from the melodies of yesterday, melodies that were still running incessantly through her head now. "No, one o'clock won't do, what are you *thinking* of Nomi? It's almost ten now, get ready quick, I'll fetch you just now. No? All right, but come by eleven latest. "

But it was almost noon by the time Nomita walked up the familiar path to Rahul's home. Sounds of talk and laughter came down to her as she rang the bell and waited for someone to open the door. Vibrant voices, quick sentences, energetic and forceful, quite unlike the measured tones she was used to at the Jhankaar Music Academy.

There was energy in the music coming down from the windows above, music that she was not familiar with. The rhythm was simple, nothing like the seven or fifteen beats that she routinely heard on the tablas, but a two-two beat in a foot-tapping tempo.

Nobody seemed to have heard the bell. She stood back and looked up at the windows of Rahul's room upstairs. The curtains were billowing out, dancing to the rhythm of the music inside. It was unlikely that they could hear the bell over the sounds of music, talk and laughter.

She rang the bell again, and waited. Nothing happened. She pushed at the front door, but it was, as expected, locked. Where was Shakuntala, their help, then? And weren't Rahul's parents at home? Maybe they'd fled, who knew?

She walked around to the back, and found the kitchen door ajar. Shankuntala was washing dishes, and what with the sound of running water and the reverberations from the booming music, it was no surprise that she hadn't heard the chimes of the doorbell.

"Go straight up!" she yelled, waving a soapy hand cheerfully when she saw Nomita.

Upstairs, standing at the doorway to Rahul's room, Nomita stood unobserved for a few moments. The room was bright with light, music and laughter. Two girls were sitting on a floor cushion, their backs leaning against each other, tapping out the rhythm with their feet. Their necks were angled sharply away from their bodies, their faces almost hanging over each other's shoulders. Long, jeans-clad legs ending in bright green and deep purple toenails were propped up on low cushions in opposite directions. A boy lounged on Rahul's bed, head on palm, elbow on a pillow. His legs, also in jeans, bent at the knee, were at right angles to each other. He was adding his voice to the music that filled the room. Rahul, dressed in his usual jeans and T shirt, bright magenta today, was dancing in quite an abandoned manner with another girl, whose long, black, crinkly hair whirled around at every turn, making her look like a dervish at some Sufi gathering. She too was in the compulsory jeans, slung so low that it seemed they would fall off her slim hips any moment. Yet another pair of jeans was stationed at the window. Probably this was a boy, but she couldn't be too sure, for at that moment for some reason, the upper half of the body was leaning out of the window.

She realized that she hadn't dressed like them for a long time. Her own salwar kameez, pretty and demure with its pastel floral design, suddenly seemed dowdy in comparison. The Ts of the other girls clung to their bodies, accentuating their slim waists and rounded breasts. Her own clothes felt like a tent.

Rahul, spotting her in the middle of an energetic whirl, yelled over the music, "Nomi, what are you doing standing there? Come and dance..."

But Nomi went to the floor to sit next to the two reclining girls, who were now looking towards her with welcoming smiles on their faces. They were, she realized, batch mates from school, Ranjita and Jimli. She hadn't seen them for a long while. How different they looked now! Not just their looks. Even their clothes, and indeed their postures, spoke of a life very different from hers. Force of habit made her sit cross-legged on the floor, straight-backed, as though she had a taanpura in her hands, and was about to perform somewhere in front of hundreds of people who were looking critically at her. Suddenly self-conscious, she relaxed her posture.

Impossible to talk right now. The air of the room seemed to vibrate in time to the rhythm. It was invigorating. The undecipherable lyrics had an energy of their own, the male voices singing in perfect tune, but in a pitch that would have had her Gurus putting their palms over their ears in pain and horror. Nomita found herself smiling back at Ranjita and Jimli. Suddenly, she felt lighter, freed of the burden of decisions. She was, she decided, beginning to enjoy herself here.

The third girl, laughing at nothing in particular, came dancing up to them. With expressive gestures of her hands, she indicated that she was too hot to dance any more. She flopped down next to Nomita, sending a wave of some cool, citrusy perfume in her direction.

The beat, simple though it was, was full of life. Nomita's feet continued to tap out the tempo as they rested on the floor, but she forced herself stop analyzing the music. This was not *her* music, it was not required of her to be constantly on learning or critiquing mode. She realized that her body was swaying, more or less of its own accord, to the beat. The air of the room was electric with sound waves that vibrated all around her. Nomita found herself smiling warmly back at the girl, and waving her hands around in response to indicate that she felt hot too.

Rahul, suddenly left partnerless, came dancing up to her. Ignoring the shakes of her head and her laughing protestations he pulled Nomi up to the middle of the floor, where he continued his twirls and whirls in time to the music. Nomi felt the beat take over her body. The tempo climbed up through her toes, past her ankles and knees, to her shoulders, neck, and then her wrists and fingertips, so that, before she knew it, she too was moving to the rhythm. She was enjoying herself too much to wonder at the spontaneity with which her body responded to the music.

The other boy joined them on the floor, whirling his lithe body around as he balanced on the toes of his left foot. Ranjita joined him, swaying, arcing and bending her body at impossible angles. Nomi realized she was smiling, it was stimulating being here. The melodies of last night fled from her mind and she didn't even notice.

Introductions were made later, when the music was turned down. The third girl was Sheila, working with a mobile phone company in Tamulbari itself, and the boy, Reza, was in tea. Sheila and Reza, she gathered later, were married, though there was nothing of the married couple, or what Nomi thought was "married couple" behaviour about them. The figure by the window, now standing beside them, was Shyam, who owned a rather trendy new restaurant in town.

Ranjita's voice was low and pleasantly throaty when she spoke. "Saw you on TV the other day," she said. "Wonderful programme! I was so proud of you! I keep telling my colleagues at the bank that the famous Nomita Sharma is my classmate. But we haven't actually met for a long time, right?"

Nomita felt faintly ashamed. Here was her old friend, quite up to date on her doings and career, and she, Nomita, had practically forgotten her. In order to cover up her ignorance she asked, enviously,

"How have you managed to remain so slim?" Her own figure was curvy and well rounded verging on plumpness if one was being uncharitable. All those hours of sitting with a taanpura were never conducive to a slim figure. Most of the singers she knew had "Khajuraho figures", as somebody had once pointed out. Instrumentalists, especially those who played on large instruments like the sarod and sitar, tended to be slimmer, because of the sheer physical energy they needed. Their shoulders were often well developed but the pencil slimness of these girls was alien to the classical music world. Even Sandhya Senapati was nowhere near this slim.

Ranjita laughed. "Gym, what else? Sitting on my ass the whole day at the bank would make me look like a pumpkin in no time at all if it wasn't for the gym in the office basement! Jimli," she turned to the other girl "now, she's the person to learn from. She's into yoga, you know, and she can do all kinds of postures. I wouldn't be surprised if she can stand on her head for hours by now..."

Jimli laughed. "Don't exaggerate, Ranjita." She turned to Nomita and said warmly, "You look wonderful, too. No, I mean it. You have such a glow to your face. I've noticed most musicians do. It must be something to do with your breathing exercises, they are also yogic, aren't they?"

They plunged into a discussion of breathing techniques and exercises that classical vocalists were taught, and also about pranayama, and health tips that gym instructors gave. Sheila practiced meditation, listening to Buddhist chants as she did so, and Reza, in spite of being a devout Muslim, loved to unwind to their soothing tones at the end of a working day. It was all related.

The talk turned to her profession again.

"You're quite famous here, you know, Nomita," said Jimli. "The only one in our group..."

"That hardly means anything," said Nomita, embarrassed again. "I have a long way to go..." It wasn't false modesty that made her say this.

Rahul suddenly got up and vanished downstairs. He reappeared in a little while with a tray of food, with Shankuntala following him with another. Beer and snacks were already laid out at a table near the door.

"Lunch," he announced unnecessarily.

It was decided that the party should move outdoors after lunch. Nomita couldn't help thinking of the heat but it seemed that the last thing on anyone's mind was the temperature.

"A boat ride!" decided Rahul. "It'll be wonderful to be on the river again!"

Half an hour later, they were clambering on to a frail canoe-like craft on the ghaat of the Red River. It was hewn from a single log of some wood that was now blackened by the elements. The ferries that routinely plied from shore to shore, as well as the floating restaurants that took a sedate hourly turn up and downriver, had been summarily rejected by most of the party, mainly the girls, as being too dull. And also too crowded. Not that the narrow, delicate looking canoe was not crowded, once the seven of them had clambered onto it. The two boatmen advised them on the best seating arrangement to balance the little boat that rocked alarmingly as they clambered in.

Ranjita, Jimli and Sheila climbed on nimbly, scorning the offer of helping hands from the boatmen who stood with their feet akimbo on the craft, balancing it expertly as it settled lower into the water as people climbed on. The three slim women strode in with long, even steps, creating hardly a stir in the boat as they settled down in their allotted seats. The boatmen directed them to the wooden bar that straddled the middle, Reza and Shyam to the prow. Nomita, plumper than the other women, would sit with Rahul on the last seat. Clumsy in her open sandals and floating chunni, Nomita gratefully accepted the support of the boatmen's rough hands. The boat protested with embarrassing sways as she moved towards where they led her. With Rahul settled beside her, the sails were trimmed on the little craft, and they were off.

The crowd at the ghaat was soon left behind. The silence when the vessel moved midstream was broken only by the creak of the rudder being moved. The people on the boat too had unconsciously lowered their voices, and now spoke in murmurs.

"Beautiful, as always!" Rahul breathed in deeply of the air, fresh and clean. The heat of the city was nowhere in evidence here, even though the late afternoon sun shone down on their bare heads. The breeze whipped their clothes, cooling them. Above, a few birds wheeled about, their cries deepening, rather than breaking the silence around. "This ride, this river – these are the things I really miss when I'm away. Lucky you, to be able to come down here whenever you want..."

Nomita recollected that the last time she had been on the river was more than a year ago. And Rahul had been her companion even then. The intervening months had been busy so that she had not had the time... No, she decided, that was not strictly true. She could certainly have made the time. The truth was that none of the people she met were interested in this. The musicians that she moved around with were indoor types and their world revolved around auditoriums and stages and recording studios. Even though they routinely sang of nature, and the beauty of flowers and birds figured very often in their lyrics, theirs was not an appreciation that was gained first hand.

Rahul was busy, taking pictures of his surroundings. The blue hills ahead, the gossamer shimmer of the steel girders of the bridge spanning the river, and the city of Tamulbari which, screened by trees, looked, rather pretty behind them.

"I'll put this in the computer, and mail it to my friends back in Bangalore. They think I'm joking when I tell them about our river, its huge size, its beauty... anyway I want to take these pictures with me when I'm in the US." He turned to her, and added, "I did tell you that I'm leaving for the US shortly, didn't I?"

Nomita replied, "Well, only very casually. For a few months, three, you said."

"No, that's old news. I heard from them last night. The latest is that they want me there for two years. At least."

But why should she be surprised, thought Nomita distractedly as she half listened to Rahul telling her about his firm sending him to their headquarters in California. After all, he was a software engineer, and he had made trips to San Jose in the past, too. But never for more than four, five weeks at a time, a couple of months at the most. Two years...

"When will you be going?"

"Quite soon, though the exact date hasn't been fixed yet. I'll be leaving for San Jose from Bangalore so this is a kind of farewell home visit, I ..."

"Two years. Well, it's not as though you come in from Bangalore every week, or every month. you come barely once a year, isn't it?"

"Yes, but there is always the feeling that one can fly in from there and reach Tamulbari the same day. Actually, within a few hours. But America... one can't think of dashing in and out. Two years. I don't think I can make a visit in between either. I..."

The three women sitting before them pointed excitedly to a spot to their right. Ripples circled out from the place. "There! We saw a river dolphin! Right there!"

All of them craned their necks, trying to catch a glimpse of the animal when it surfaced again. Sure enough five minutes later, and then again at intervals, the dolphin arched darkly over the water, receding each time into the distance as it made its way downstream.

The topic of Rahul's departure did not come up again. Nomita got the feeling though, that there was something more he wanted to say. She too had wanted to talk some more about it. She was aware of some vague feeling of unease, or was it dissatisfaction? But why should she feel uneasy?

The rest of the boat ride was uneventful. The noise of the ghaat as the canoe glided up to the landing dock hit them solidly. Their voices rose in volume again as they tried to make themselves heard over the din.

Farewells were said, plans made to catch up with each other again while Rahul was here. Nomita was included in them, but it was she who remembered, "Sorry, I can't make it anywhere next Saturday. I have a show."

"That's in the evening, surely? Can't you come with us in the daytime? We'll be back well before dusk..."

Nomita smiled at Sheila. Obviously she did not know a classical vocalist's routine on the day of a show. Riyaz in the morning preferably with the accompanists. Rest in the afternoon, the careful nurturing of one's voice throughout the day, not talking too much in case the vocal chords tired. Meditating on the raag that would be performed. Listening, if possible, to recordings of performances of that raag by the top masters, so that one would be steeped in that particular melody. But she did not explain any of this to Sheila, and only said, "Sorry, I would have loved to come, of course, but there's always a lot to be done before a show. But we'll meet..."

They piled into the two cars. Getting off at home she watched Rahul chat in a carefree way to Ranjita and Jimli as he drove away.

5

Today, the raag being taught at the general classes at Jhankaar was Madhuwanti, the late afternoon – early evening melody. The bandish in the sixteen beat medium tempo was a traditional one, and Nomita sang it along with the others.

Ghunghat Mat Kholo Shyam,
Mat Chhuwo Naram Kalai…
Do not part my veil, Shyam,
Don't touch my wrist, it's delicate…

Was it her imagination, the conditioning of her mind only, or was there really something in the melody that brought in the atmosphere of a declining day? True, Madhuwanti, by a coincidence, was being taught today at the specific time that was prescribed for its performance. But even if it had been taught late at night, the melody would have brought to Nomita's mind this particular kind of sunlight, the slant of the rays as they lost the fiery heat of midday and sloped down to a gentler temperature. She looked at the curtains that swayed in the breeze along the walls, the golden light filtered and tempered by the waning day. Whenever I sing this, she thought, wherever I am, in a closed auditorium or a city flat, I will remember this light, this subtle radiance that is so different from the morning light. To her, the sunlight of Madhuwanti was a melody that captured a fleeting moment, the exact time when late afternoon blended into dusk. It was not grey like the latter, it did not evoke the spirit of "Go Dhuli", the dust raised by the hooves of the lowing cattle as they came back home for the night. Nor did it bring to mind the brighter yellow, sometimes bordering on harshness, of an earlier afternoon hour. The evanescence of this moment was magically captured by Guruma's musical imagination today as she wove her way through the nuances of Madhuwanti. The fleetingness of that particular light was expressed with exactitude by Sandhya Senapati's voice, by the nuances she brought into it, by the shadows and brightnesses that moved through the aural landscape that she created so effortlessly. And on the extended windows at one side of that long music room, the curtains that fluttered in the gentle breeze let in the light that matched, unerringly, the light that was evoked by Madhuwanti.

The rest of them, trying to repeat what they heard, sounded, at this point, like clumsy oafs clod-hopping through the delicate landscape, ruining its gossamer fabric. Of course this was the first time they were attempting the Raag under Sandhya Senapati's guidance. With practice, they would sound better, but it would take months, years, before they began to sound like Guruma herself. It wasn't just the accuracy of her manner of touching the relevant notes, the specific semitones, and shrutis that made up the Raag. It wasn't even the way she glided and slid from one note to the other, so smoothly that it was impossible to pinpoint when one ended and the other began. It was the timbre of her voice, the soft yet resonant tonal quality that imbued the whole melody with an evocativeness that was like the best poetry, which were things that could only come to a singer, if at all, through constant practice. This was sadhana, that prayer-like quality, meditativeness, which imbued the physical act of giving voice to a particular lyric with an uplifting spirituality which came to only a few practitioners of vocal music.

Nomita, playing the taanpura, was sitting to the side of the little group. She was able to take in their expressions, and listen to their individual voices from this point. Rupa and Panchali, she noticed, were as boldly dressed as ever. Though Shrabana and Sujata were at least attempting to get the softness of the melody into their voices, Rupa and Panchali were singing with gusto.

Guruma, listening to the students as they repeated the stanzas after her, raised her right hand.

"The mood is delicate, like the Nayika's wrist. It's symbolic...your voice must convey that lightness. Kalai...wrist. The word has long vowels, diphthongs...but you must resist the temptation to put in a lot of flourishes in that word. Kalaai...it should be insubstantial. If you put in strong embellishments, both will break...the wrist and the delicacy of the melody."

Nomita looked covertly at Rupa and Panchali. But they did not seem to realize that Guruma had meant these words for them. She had been tactful thought Nomita. She must remember to be as tactful with her own students, though of course neither the children at the Tamulbari Music School, or those at Shishu Kalyan were as sensitive to criticism, as these two were apt to be.

"You must keep in mind," said Guruma, her voice like a piece of music even though she was only taking a routine lesson at the Jhankaar Music Academy, "that vocal music has a very important component. Words. Lyrics. Unlike instrumental music, vocal music needs to constantly keep in mind the fact that melody is only a part of the whole. An important part no doubt but still, a part. The lyrics, the poetry, that's the other part. The melody adds to the poetry in a way that just reading or even listening to it being recited would never do. In fact vocal music is a genre that takes the best of the two, that is music and poetry, and combines them. Vocal music is more than just the sum of these two genres, it is an entity in itself. Since it fuses the richness of these two forms, it becomes a category on its own. It has the suggestiveness of poetry and the emotive content of melody, honed to perfection down the ages..."

She paused. The sounds of the two taanpuras and the electronic box that perfectly emulated the sound of the original, added to the calming atmosphere.

"Actually, it's only now that the words, the lyrics have become so very important. Till about thirty, forty years ago, the poetry was not as important as the melody. You must have heard those old recordings of the mid-twentieth century maestros? These were the musicians who learned at the feet of their Gurus in the early part of the last century. They sang the traditional bandishes, the compositions that were handed down to them from generation to generation as gifts from their Gurus. Sometimes, the Guru composed a lyric of his own. But the images, the poetic conventions, were always conservative. You know what I mean?" She hummed for a few moments, then sang the famous lines,

Kya Karu Sajani,
Aaye Na Baalam.
Rowat Rowat Kal Naahin Aaye
Nisdin Mohe, Birha Sataye
Yaad Awat Jab Unki Batiya...
Aaye Na Baalam.

"Yes, it's Bade Ghulam Ali Khan's famous thumri. The sentiments are totally feminine, because the thumri is meant to portray the woman's point of view in the conventions of love. There were few women singers who performed in public in those days. And in any case neither audience nor performers thought anything of the fact that these sentiments were being sung by a heavyset mustachioed man. Well, such was the magic of his voice, I suppose."

She paused again.

"Suspension of disbelief?" wondered Nomita.

"Something like that, yes, I suppose you could say that. The sheer mellifluousness of his voice and the emotions he put into his music makes us forget the gender of the singer, his physical presence. Just like Kellucharan Mahapatra for instance. I had the good fortune of watching him dance many times, and it was always enchanting. Even when he was old and frail with a sick body, it was always amazing. With the slightest of gestures, he would make hundreds, thousands of people at a time believe that he had been transformed into a young girl, a Nayika, at her toilette. The magic of Odissi changed the ageing, balding man into a beautiful woman before the eyes of the audience. It's the same with music, especially vocal music. Every great musician transcends her gender, his or her very identity in fact, to give voice to the thoughts, the emotions that are encapsulated in the melody. The singer – all of you – should aspire to become a vehicle, a vessel, for the ideas and emotions portrayed."

Once more, the drone of the taanpuras filled the room. Nomita had been listening raptly, but now she was distracted by rustlings. Panchali and Rupa were becoming restless.

"What I was saying...yes..." continued Guruma, ignoring the two at the back "was that the lyrics, the compositions, always had the conventional images. The pining Nayika, sometimes a joyous one, but then even that joy was dependent on the arrival or the presence of a male Beloved. In fact, the words of the lyrics are sometimes quite indistinguishable in the old recordings. That was the style. It was the melody, not the words, which were of prime importance. These days, of course, we realize that the words enhance the melody. The enunciation should be clear, the words should be intelligible. Most of the old bandishes, the lyrics, are beautiful, in fact that's why they've survived the test of time, and come down to us, through this oral tradition. After all, it was only after people like Bhatkhandeji and others began to document them that they have been put into notational form."

Once, more, she hummed, and then sang a fragment of a bandish. Nomita recognized the Raag Malkauns immediately.

Mukh Mor Mor Muskaat Jaat...

"Forget, for a moment, the predictability of the imagery...a beautiful woman has adorned herself and is on her way to meet her beloved. But just look at the melding of the melody with the poetry, look at the use of the words, the alliteration, the beauty of the poetry itself...

"But of course things have changed today," she continued. "The twenty first century woman probably will not identify with this Nayika. She will not conform to the image that comes to our minds through this lyric. Shringar, beautifying oneself, adorning oneself with jewellery and fine clothes before meeting the beloved, was a recognized poetic convention. Today of course we don't identify with that convention, though we can still appreciate it. And in any case the contemporary woman hardly has the kind of lifestyle described, in those lyrics. Twenty-first century women travel out of their homes, they no longer sit pining, gazing at the monsoon clouds which envelop the skies, waiting for their men to return. A lot of these lyrics are rooted in the lives of the women of the merchant class. The merchants would travel sometimes for months at a time, leaving their wives behind. But modern sensibility has made that a little redundant, isn't it? In fact I myself know a woman today who travels the world, looking after her business. Unthinkable even a hundred years ago."

The class smiled. Rupa and Panchali tittered, in the fashion of chamchas. Or perhaps it was just the mention of romance that made them simper. Guruma however did not notice.

"But even though the sentiments might seem a little outdated, you must remember that the lyrics that have come down to us, the traditional ones, are beautiful, in their own right. They give us the essence of the raag. They give note combinations that are absolutely stunning. They inspire us to create our own combinations, through our own creativity... But today, just because those conventions described in these lyrics are no more, we all have to try that much harder. We have to infuse our voices with the moods that the raag, the melody evokes. We have to convince our audiences of the picture that we try to call to mind. Not just the literal picture, but the totality, the evocation of a mood, an emotion, a rang, a colour. A Raag, and the mood it evokes, 'colours' the mind, in the way poetry does, but also in the way music does..."

After lessons, as they trooped out of the music room in a group after Guruma, they met a man who had obviously been waiting there for a while.

"Ah, Haren Babu, when did you come...?" asked Guruma in Bangla. She sounded surprised.

"Not long at all... I was just..."

It was obvious that he was being polite, that he had probably been sitting on one of the cane chairs in the verandah for a while, waiting for Guruma to finish her class and come out so that he could meet her. It was of course courteous of him not to barge in, and disturb the class in progress, but Guruma nevertheless said, "You should have come in... I didn't know you were outside..."

"Of course, Didi. In any case I didn't want to disturb you while you were teaching." The man was very well-mannered.

Guruma said to the students waiting behind her, "This is Shri Haren Das from Kolkata. He's an impresario, a very good promoter of music and dance, a great organizer of functions. Quite a few of the top functions are organized by him in Kolkata these days. Haren Babu, these are my students..." She made the introductions, briefly, and asked, "When did you come from Kolkata?"

"Just this morning. Actually I'm on my way to Imphal. They are having a festival of Manipuri dance, and they've invited me. I'm hoping to discover some new dancers there... I believe they have some fantastic new artistes... I had a few hours before my connecting flight, so I thought I would look in on you."

"That's really nice of you, Haren Babu, but I wish you had called. I would have kept myself free. You're staying for lunch of course?"

"No formality Didi, just a cup of your Assam tea will be fine," said the man, smiling. He was thin and short with teeth that protruded alarmingly at an almost ninety degree angle from his mouth, but he spoke pleasantly. The angle of his teeth gave the impression that he was permanently smiling.

"Actually, Didi, I'm in a bit of a hurry," he added. "But since I was due to be here in any case, I thought I would speak about it to you personally."

"About what?" Guruma asked.

"Well, this Borsha Utshob that we're having this year. I am as you know part of the organizing committee. We wanted you in it this year..."

"Gladly," replied Guruma instantly. "You know I never refuse anything in Kolkata, as long as it doesn't clash with some other programme. But let me get my programme book, why don't you come in?"

"This is a wonderful place, Didi, so much greenery it's beautiful. We don't get to see much of this in Kolkata after all."

"One minute then. I'll ask for the tea to be brought out as well..."

Guruma walked into the other part of the house, the portion

that was their living quarters. She was barely out of sight before the other students clustered quickly around Haren Das and whipped out their CVs and brochures and pressed them with soulful and sober expressions into the hands of the man. Nomita watched quietly, trying not to show her amusement.

"How nice that you are here," said Pranab, his voice squeaky with excitement. "I am so pleased to meet you." The glossy folder that he had taken out as though by magic from his jhola looked impressive in his hand. He pressed it urgently into Haren Das's palms, saying, "This is my brochure, I am one of Guruma's most busy students, she will tell you about me ... I mean I would be delighted to perform at any event you may organize ... just a brief write-up about my achievements."

But he was quickly jostled out by the elbows of Panchali and Rupa. Both had large pamphlets in their hands. Nomita noticed that they opened out, accordion like, into a tail that was surely not as lengthy as Panchali's and Rupa's musical careers warranted.

She stepped away from the jostling group before Guruma came back again. Haren Das was unfazed. Smiling still (or was it because of those teeth?) he put them all into an outside pocket of the overnighter he was carrying, and said in a voice meant to instill confidence, "Thank you. I will certainly keep them, and consult them when necessary... thank you ..."

But Guruma had emerged from the other side of the house, a notebook in her hand. It was the diary where she recorded her engagements. Murmuring their farewells, the group of students melted away, barely able to conceal the satisfied expressions on their faces. It was obvious that the act of passing on their brochures had made them confident of bagging a programme quite soon, at a concert in Kolkata.

Kaushik Kashyap's visit was shaping up to be a landmark event in Tamulbari. This was surprising, for Hindustani Classical Music was not that popular in the place. It was perceived to be an elite activity, and only occasionally, a recreational one.

Paradoxically, though, Hindustani Classical Music was still an aspirational genre. Those who sought to project a "cultured" image, along with those who actually loved the music, taught their children the genre, and even sent them to different places around the country to learn. Mostly, it was the daughters who took the path of performers, for economically, it was a chancy business. Sons, with homes to run, hardly ever went on, these days, to become professional Hindustani Classical musicians in Tamulbari.

It was this aspirational aspect that made people buy tickets for classical music concerts. Being knowledgeable in the High Arts still carried an aura in Tamulbari, especially among the middle aged. Indeed, Classical Music had always been exclusive, always classist whether it was performed in temples or the courts of kings, in small private baithaks or concerts where entry was limited.

Kaushik Kashyap's star value was being proved over and over again in this small city at the edge of the country. People thronged to buy tickets for his show. Even Friends Club, the charitable association of the city that was organizing this as a fund raising event for their benevolent causes, was surprised at the response. Not since Ajoy Chakravarty, the vocalist from Kolkata, had performed in the city several years ago, were the ticket sales this high. Indeed, sales rivalled those of the concerts, quite some time ago, of famed flutist Hariprasad Chaurasia, and santoor player Shiv Kumar Sharma.

This, of course was understandable. For Kaushik Kashyap had, in recent years, pulled in people from many different sections of society to his concerts. Teenagers and young people were drawn by his youth-friendly persona, his aura of stardom. He was definitely hip. Right from the long, curly locks that made him look like the tabla player Zakir Hussain, to his designer clothes and mojris, Kaushik Kashyap was perfectly in tune with what the younger generation required in a Classical performer. Knowingly or unknowingly, whether by accident or design, he now occupied a special place in the pantheon of stars of the country. Globe-trotting was a phrase that was routinely used when referring to successful classical musicians, but with Kaushik Kashyap, the words acquired a new dimension. He was quite at home in California, where he spent several months of the year as Visiting Faculty Member at his Guru's institution.

Besides, Kaushik Kashyap's appointment book was always full, months ahead, for concerts at prestigious venues worldwide. His distinctive kurta-clad person was also at home in all the major airports of the world. Along with an accompanist from his roster of tabla players he crisscrossed the globe. Jet lag seemed not to bother him at all, as often, after a red-eye transatlantic flight, he would sit down to practice in his hotel room, and then move on to the concert venue without his head having touched a pillow at all in the country where he found himself. He had cultivated the habit of sleeping soundly while travelling, a skill he had perhaps wilfully acquired as being essential to the star musician of today, living, working and performing at a time when time zones needed to be frequently crossed. His travelling habits were a far cry from those of his Guru's Guru, a person who had preferred the ashram-like surroundings of his home, teaching his few live-in students under the shade of the fruit trees of his garden. He had travelled reluctantly, that too on stately bullock carts with stops at villages by the wayside, and had graced only some of the concerts to which he was invited.

In contrast, even Kaushik Kashyap's instruments – the beautifully handmade sitars whose crafting by the best instrument maker in Kolkata he personally supervised – were geared to travelling. His sitars flew from one continent to another in wheeled fiberglass boxes that were not only strong, but also light enough to ensure that the large instruments were easily transported from venue to venue. Their padded interiors also protected them from the extremes of heat and cold while travelling.

Besides, Kaushik Kashyap was in touch with several experienced metallurgists, both in India and abroad, in places as diverse as Jamshedpur and Italy. He was always searching for newer alloys for his strings, so that the ones that had traditionally been used on his instrument, made of steel and copper and gut, could be improved upon. He was on a quest for the ideal material that would both sound perfect, and be flexible enough to never break in mid-concert. He took pains to explain to audiences around the world that the bridge and decorations on his instrument were environment-friendly. He never used the traditional ivory, nor its replacement, plain white plastic, which was serviceable, but, to his eyes, ugly. Instead, he used deer antlers, picked up from forests after the animals had shed them naturally.

But in spite of these peripheral interests and activities, not even the harshest, most conservative critic back home, in a traditional Conference or Sabha in India, could find fault with his music. True, he tailored his programmes when he was abroad, cutting short the slow alaap, and increasing the length of the fast-paced portions, going through all kinds of gimmicky gestures such as flourishing his hands in the air when he arrived at the sam during a speedy portion. He also used his eye-catching hairstyle to marvellous effect at these shows, and also at those in India where he knew that the bulk of the audience would be people whose knowledge of classical music was not that of connoisseurs. At the beginning of the concert, his locks would lie neatly on his head, the curly black spirals resting quiescently on his shoulders. But as the tempo increased, the locks would fall forward, and he would have to brush them back with an impatient right hand. A single large diamond flashed and glittered prominently on a finger. As both tabla and sitar reached their melodic and rhythmic crescendo, his hair, whirling around his head in a dark halo, would acquire a life of its own, and he would resemble a Medusa, or a Sufi saint, as his head dipped and rose, rose and dipped. Indeed, his hair at these venues was as much a part of his playing persona as were his hands, long-fingered and sensitive-looking, as inevitably, almost all sitarists' and tabaliyas' were.

But in the solemn, sober Sabhas of Chennai, or the Conferences of Kolkata or Gwalior or Pune, his hair, in spite of the brisk tempo of the latter parts of his concerts, remained much neater. The slow paced alaaps would invariably be longer, deeper, more profound at these venues. In the concerts that were held in the Southern parts of the country, particularly in Chennai, and also in Kolkata his native town, his music, his mannerisms, his very persona, would be different from when he performed in the North. As he sat down on the dais in these other places, with the front rows filled with traditionally dressed vidwans, learned connoisseurs and extremely knowledgeable rasikas, their foreheads invariably marked with the sacred vibhuti ash, his clothes would be pristine white, kurta and dhoti. His hair would be neatly combed back. Even his sound checks, those requisite drills involving trial plays from all the instruments on the dais, balancing and checking them, would be brief, efficient affairs, unlike in other venues, where they would stretch on for quite a while, till the auditorium had quietened down and he was sure that he had their complete attention.

And the critics and vidwans, the connoisseurs and experts, would not be disappointed. Kaushik Kashyap's recitals at these venues would invariably consist of ancient raags, and those ideas that had found honourable mention in centuries-old treatises on raag music, such as Bharata's *Natyashastra*, Matang's *Brihaddesi*, the *Sangeet Ratnakar* of Sharangadev. And the critics and vidwans could not help but be impressed by Kaushik Kashyap's performances. Sitting in the front rows, with the weight of their learning obvious from the stoop of their shoulders on which elaborate angavastrams rested, they presented an intimidating sight to the most seasoned musician, as they kept impeccable time to the beat with their right hands. A small nod of approval from them was equal to a hall full of thunderous applause at other venues. And yet, in spite of the fact that they knew Kaushik Kashyap's other facets, his penchant for showmanship, they could not help but be impressed by the man's deep knowledge of the nuances of whatever raag he chose to play, Malkauns or Marwa, Behag or Puriya. Indeed, his physical presence seemed to become immaterial at these concerts, as he became a conduit for the cascades of music that flowed out of his fingertips. No wonder even papers like *The Hindu* bestowed unstinting praise on him.

And yet it was this same person who was not averse to appearing in ads in the electronic and print media. He endorsed products that ranged from textiles and airlines to shampoos and conditioners. Kaushik Kashyap, it was well known, minted money from these. Besides, one of his fusion albums with noted rock groups from Europe and America had brought him a Grammy nomination not very long ago, and sales of the CD had been phenomenal, worldwide.

The ease with which Kaushik Kashyap straddled two worlds within the sphere of classical music was a new phenomenon. He was one among a handful who realized the need to strike a fine balance between the vast and majestic treasure that was his musical heritage, and the need to package it in such a way that newer audiences would still find something to savour in the classical music of this country.

Of course Kaushik Kashyap, unlike many of the great musicians of the past, was an educated person, even, one could say, a highly educated one. In previous generations, the classical musician was respected, even revered, for his music. Several of the legendary names in music were, by today's measurements, functionally illiterate. But knowledge of the alphabets was not really needed at the time if they were excellent as musicians. The art, after all, was passed down from guru to shishya, teacher to student through years of rigorous training. It was not necessary, if one had a good aural memory and an excellent musical sense, to refer to books at all. Their general knowledge was poor, even though they were lauded as Ustads and pandits in their own fields.

The story commonly told for a while in the early fifties of the last century about a revered Ustad was not apocryphal. He had arrived for a recording in the studios of All India Radio, when the Station Director politely informed him that his recording had had to be rescheduled at the last moment. Inconvenience was greatly regretted, but the Station Director had had to do this, as the place was needed for a broadcast from Pandit Jawaharlal Nehru who would be arriving at the studios soon. The maestro, a spry and genial man, was not in the least offended, for he was quite free of any ego hassles. But he was curious. "Arre, don't worry, I understand, you must have your own compulsions," he said affably as he had repacked his surbahar into its case preparatory to leaving. "But tell me, who is this Pandit Nehru? What gharana does he belong to? What instrument does he play, or is he a vocalist?"

Kaushik Kashyap, though a musician of the highest calibre,

was in other ways not in the least bit similar to that simple Ustad. His degree was not in music, as was often the case with today's musicians, but in the unrelated subject of Physics, in which he had majored from Calcutta University with a First Class. His mother, Tirna Ghosh was after all a teacher, with a teacher's respect for book learning. And though his parents had been careful not to discourage their only child from entering a field in which, he was highly talented, they insisted on his having a "proper" degree. By which they meant a degree in the Sciences, or Liberal Arts, or some professional course such as engineering. And Kaushik Kashyap had certainly done them proud even in the academic field, with his grades throughout school and college, even though he had barely made the requirement for attendance records during his last year at college. By then, he was already busy with concerts. He had won prestigious competitions such as the All India Radio Competition for Young Classical Musicians. Indeed, he was a regular performer on the exalted National Programme of Classical Music of AIR, that benchmark of a fine artiste, from a young age. Now of course he was A Top, at the very apex of the pyramid of classical musicians of the country, a spot which few occupied.

He was quite adept, also, at remaining in the public eye without seeming to try very hard. He would juggle his dates and go to quite great lengths in order to appear on TV, not only on the music programmes, but also music competitions and quizzes. These were sometimes inane events, but they always had a huge viewership. He was always accorded the most deferential treatment by the hosts, and in any case it was an easy enough job, a few hours every week, while the recording of the show was in progress.

Perhaps it was envy then, jealousy pure and simple, that made many other musicians adopt a supercilious air when they spoke about him. Nomita heard several such comments made around her by musicians as the countdown to Tamulbari's big Classical Music Nite began. (It was always, for some reason, Nite on the banners advertising the event that sprang up all around town, never Night.) True, except for Sandhya Senapati and Tridib Barua, there were really no other top notch Hindustani classical performers in Tamulbari. But there were quite a few who were learning from other teachers around the country, going sometimes to great lengths to get their lessons. The envy of the guru was transferred to the student, who waged battle on the guru behalf of whenever the topic of Kaushik Kashyap cropped up during the run-up to the concert.

Nomita watched and listened to all these thrusts, sideswipes and deflections at the various musical events she attended in Tamulbari in the interim. At first she was amused. But gradually, even listening to these loaded statements began to irritate and exhaust her. Not least, she was honest enough to admit, because Kaushik Kashyap was coming to town to "see" her.

Sometimes, as she sat listening to the endless conversations about Kaushik Kashyap this and Kaushik Kashyap that around her, Nomita couldn't help wondering why Tirna Ghosh wanted to have her as a daughter-in-law. True, her meeting with Shikha Sharma at that teacher's conference had, over time, deepened into a friendship that scorned the distance between Kolkata and Tamulbari. They had met at other venues, at other conferences, and also when Shikha had accepted Tirna's invitation to spend the Pujo holidays with her in Kolkata one year. In return, Shikha had extended her own invitation to her friend to visit them during Bihu, the Spring Festival when the entire valley of the Red River sang and danced to the ancient rhythms of that folk celebration. Tirna had not been able to make it for that particular Bihu, instead, she had come another time, when an Educational Conference had taken place in their town.

Nomita had often spoken to Tirna Ghosh on the phone after that time when she had come to their house. It was usually when she rang her mother, and Nomita, had happened to lift the receiver. She was always pleasant, and interested in Nomita's doings, how her music was progressing, what raag she was learning, where she had performed lately. "Performances are such an important part of learning. After all music is a performing art, and our kind of classical music, which relies not on anything that is written down, but on spontaneity during actual performances, depends to a great degree on being at home on the stage. Being self-conscious, or a victim of stage fright just won't do! Which is why actual performances are so important. But your Guruma has told you all this, I am sure. How is she? Please give her my regards...."

Nomita liked this about Tirna Ghosh, that she always spoke with respect and regard for Sandhya Senapati. Indeed, she liked many things about this person she had met just once, this voice on the phone, a rich contralto edged with kindliness and laughter. Nomita tended to judge people by their speaking voices, the warmth, tone and timbre. Not by the sense of it, but the sound.

Still, she wondered why she had chosen Nomita. Surely there were lots of girls in Kolkata, even lots of musical girls, whose parents would love to give their daughters to Kaushik Kashyap in marriage.

Kaushik, Kaushik Kashyap. And that was another thing. What, wondered Nomita, had his parents felt when he had changed his name, from Ghosh to the punchier Kashyap? What kind of a person would change the name that was his by birthright, and take up a stage name? Her own name was tame but she would certainly not want to change it. Though if she did marry him, she would become Nomita Kashyap. Or would she be Nomita Ghosh? No, maybe she would retain her name. Nomita Sharma was good enough, she quite liked it. There was no question of changing her name even by marriage. Perhaps, like thumri queens Girija Devi and Savita Devi and so many others, she would quietly eschew all these complications of patriarchal family setups, and become Nomita Devi instead. And then, if she was good enough at her music, the name would fit the persona, instead of the other way round.

But no, not Nomita Kashyap. Certainly not.

But then, she thought, coming out of her reverie with a start, she was putting the cart before the horse. Or indeed, the jhala before the aalap, the drut before the vilambit. With a non-committal smile, she listened to the swirl of conversation around her.

A concert featuring well-known classical vocalist Rajeshwari Mishra of the Benaras Gharana has just finished, and Nomita was waiting outside the auditorium. Rahul had come with her to the concert, and had gone off to fetch his bike. She had been somewhat surprised when he had shown an interest that morning in coming along with her to the performance. When she had declined his invitation for a movie that evening, he had said, "Rajeshwari Mishra? Ah, she's from UP, isn't she? Benaras? She has a lovely voice, so unusual. One doesn't hear voices like that any more. Every female voice these days is the same, as though they are all clones of some template somewhere. Everything is sweet and silvery. Must be the exercises that are taught to vocalists these days. Now her voice, Rajeshwari Mishra's. I like it, it has that unashamed nasal twang. And it gets accentuated when she puts passion into her music, which is almost always, isn't it?"

Rahul had always been well informed about music, and his perceptions and judgements about musicians had always been down-to-earth, based on what he heard. Whereas she tended to be swayed by such factors as the name of the artiste's guru, and even his gradation, which always coloured her judgement of the actual music.

The conversation that swirled around her now was not about the artiste that they had just heard but of the upcoming concert.

"Of course I've bought tickets for the Kaushik Kashyap function." This from Jiten Dutta, a flutist whose guru lived in distant Mumbai. He went once a year to that city and stayed with the teacher for a month. By virtue of these yearly trips to the metro, he had set himself up back in Tamulbari as a kind of authority on music and musicians. Right now, there was a note of irritation in his voice. "They're very pricey, but what to do? Since he's in Tamulbari, one must go I suppose. When I was in Mumbai last month, I listened to his concert along with Guruji, I must say I was disappointed."

None of the people around him asked why, but Jiten Dutta continued, "I mean the man knows how to draw crowds, no doubt about it. But it's not with his music, is it?"

The musicians around him murmured agreement. "That's right, it certainly isn't," said Reena Goswami, a sitar student of a Guru in Kolkata who was much less famous than Kaushik Kashyap. "His expositions of the raags he plays are scandalous. I mean, he uses all kinds of extra notes, notes that aren't allowed. I believe when he played at the Dover Lane Conference last year, he put in a shuddha nishad into his Malkauns! Can you imagine! Yes, that made it Chandrakauns, true, but he had specifically announced that he would be playing Malkauns. Sometimes he puts in a pancham into that raag too, I believe, and we all know that that's specifically forbidden, don't we?"

The others nodded, their faces aglow with a kind of viciousness that was not an uncommon sight when Hindustani Classical musicians discussed each other.

"Kaushik Kashyap's strong point is his PRO, of course." This was from Chandra Patowary, a vocalist who also accompanied other musicians on the harmonium. "He takes care to be in the good books of those who matter. He does a lot of politics, you know." Chandra made it sound as though he knew many things first hand.

This seemed to rouse the competitive spirit in the others. How could they let it seem that they, musicians all, did not have inside information about the nature and habits of someone as well known as Kaushik Kashyap? Nomita listened as all around her people discussed him with an air of authority. He had made friends with powerful politicians as well as rich businessmen. The former dropped a word to organizers when artistes for big shows were selected, thus ensuring that he was chosen, for obviously, organizers liked to keep politicians in power happy.

As for business people, it seemed that here the plot was even more complex. According to the gossipy musicians, three or four of the richest business houses in the country had committed themselves to sponsoring all Kaushik Kashyap's shows in India. This way, the organizers themselves never had to pay the man a single paisa. The budget allotted to him could be divided up among themselves. The fact that they could make money off him made Kaushik Kashyap immensely popular with organizers. What did the business people who sponsored him get in return? Well, he appeared in their ads, free of cost, didn't he? As for the media, don't ask. He held frequent press conferences in Kolkata and Mumbai where each journalist was given a bag of goodies, not your common IMFL foreign liquor but Scotch, and things such as free stays for the entire family at pricey resorts....

On the other hand, Tambulbari also had a group of musicians who belonged firmly to the other camp. They were the ones who spoke now of Kaushik Kashyap with exaggerated deference. What they said about him was common knowledge in the world of music in any case. Yet the way they said it, with much significant pursing of lips and lowering of voices, was meant to give the impression that they had heard all this from the Great Man himself, that, indeed, they knew many more things about Kaushikji, which only discretion prevented them from divulging.

Listening to these chattering musicians around her was amusing no doubt, but Nomita was relieved when Rahul came roaring up on his bike, and she could leave after waving polite goodbyes to them.

6

Within the precincts of the Jhankaar Music Academy, however, talk about Kaushik Kashyap's impending visit was quieter. Neither Tridib Barua nor Sandhya Senapati found it necessary to be drawn into the hysteria that was being built up in and around Tamulbari.

When Rupa asked if she would be going to the concert, Sandhya Senapati replied, disappointingly, "Of course! We have been invited by the Friends Club and even if they hadn't done that, we would certainly have gone. After all Kaushik Kashyap is an amazing musician, isn't he? There is much we can learn from him. I hope all of you are going? His Raagdaari, his theoretical knowledge of the raags is amazing, and the way he translates it into practice is absolutely miraculous. His technique is perfect too, but it is always a slave to the Emotion, the Rasa, the spirit of the raag. Which is exactly as it should be. One never gets the feeling that he is indulging in mere gimmickry for the sake of showing off his taiyyari, his prowess over the technical aspects of playing the sitar. There's always the temptation to do that, especially when one has spent such long hours mastering the physical difficulties of playing this instrument. After all, one's voice is part of one's body, it is comparatively easier to get it to do what one wants. But to produce such amazing melody from a few strings stretched over a length of wood - now that requires intense, rigorous riyaz, for years on end. His fingers must have bled till the callouses set in, and now the tips must be numb. And yet such sensitive music flows from them! It is a tapasya he has undertaken, an amazing thing."

This answer seemed to leave Rupa and a few other students who had been eagerly waiting for her reply vaguely dissatisfied.

On the weekend before Kaushik Kashyap's scheduled performance, Nomita accompanied Sandhya Senapati to an out-of-town concert. This was not unusual. After all she was Sandhya Senapati's senior-most student, and though her Guruma was at the peak of her powers as a vocalist, she liked to have Nomita's voice accompany her recitals on occasion. In any case, this was the time-honoured way of getting a student used to stage performances. In the beginning, the student would be allowed to play only the second taanpura, sitting at the furthest end of the dais. Gradually, he would graduate towards the centre, behind the Guru, and play the all-important first accompanying taanpura. In past centuries of course it was always boys and males who were accepted as students, never girls, even if they were daughters or nieces. After the student was closer to the teacher on stage, sometimes the Guru would remember the young person sitting beside him, and would occasionally ask him to sing the bandish, the actual lyric, along with him. When the Guru judged the shishya to be sufficiently advanced, he would be made to sit beside him, playing if not a taanpura, then a surmandal, and actually singing some portions of the Raag extempore, along with the teacher. In the meantime, the student would be giving solo performances of his own. This was the way a shishya was groomed for the stage.

For Nomita, it was always a nerve-wracking experience to accompany Sandhya Senapati. On these occasions, she got stage fright, and sang timidly, though when she was on her own, she never, or hardly ever, got an attack of nerves on the dais. After all, accompanying one's Guru was a daunting task. For one, Sandhya Senapati was so much better than she was. True, when she nodded to Nomita to continue the melodic phrase she had just begun, the tune always came out steady and pure. But Sandhya's voice, honed by decades of constant riyaz, was much mellower, than hers was. To Nomita's ears, her voice, in comparison, sounded like a novice's when she accompanied Guruma. Besides, there was the tension of trying to anticipate exactly what Guruma would be singing at a particular point of time, what melodic idea she would be developing, and being ready to continue with that idea the instant she was asked to do so.

But of course it was also a great honour to sing alongside one's Guru, and Nomita was always, therefore, prey to mixed feelings whenever Sandhya Senapati asked her to accompany her on stage.

This time, the venue was a town a hundred kilometres or so away from Tamulbari. The leading Culture Club of the town, Krishnanagar, was holding a classical evening (not, Nomita was relieved to note, a Nite). Nomita was glad to have an excuse to get away from Tamulbari, and the constant talk of Kaushik Kashyap, which now seemed to be the city's sole topic of conversation. Even at home, Shikha Sharma was getting into an uncharacteristic flap about how she would arrange things for the "Seeing Ceremony," as Nomita called it, what food she would offer the guests, who else she would invite, or indeed, would it be proper to invite anybody else at all...

The organizers, as usual, had made arrangements for two vehicles to pick up Sandhya Senapati and her accompanists. Subroto, Chinmoy and Prashant, along with their instruments, had gone on ahead in a Qualis. The two taanpuras, too, had been carefully packed into that vehicle.

Unlike folk or modern musicians, classical musicians did not carry their own sound equipment. This was a relief, as well as a worry. A relief because it freed them from arranging for bulky sound systems to take along with them wherever they went. But also a worry, because they were now dependent on the sound systems that the organizers provided them with. Of course everyone had progressed beyond the tinny sounds that had issued out from the horn-like amplifiers of some decades ago. But there was still the danger of the dreaded squeals and moans coming out of the system, effectively blocking the musicians' voices and ruining the concentration of the audiences. Such sounds understandably provoked hilarity among the listeners. Once that happened, it was practically impossible to get them back on track again, no matter how good the performer. No wonder artistes such as Palghat T.S. Mani Iyer, the famed mridangam player, had resisted performing in front of microphones till the last.

Their own styles depended greatly on amplification, of course. In fact, the names of microphone technicians, "Sound by...." were beginning to find their way into the programme sheets of most performances. No longer were they known as humble "mike men". Their indispensability to the overall success of the programme was underscored by the fact that they were now known as "Sound Engineers," just as the people who created the lighting for dancers and theatre people were now known as "Light Designers." Gradually, technical people were becoming as important as the accompanying tabla or mridangam or sarengi or ghatam player. Hiring good sound systems, along with their accompanying "engineers" formed a large percentage of the total costs of any concert. Soon, reflected Nomita, even Hindustani classical musicians would need trucks, airplanes, like the travelling rock bands that Rahul kept talking about, to transport their sound requirements from place to place.

Nomita remembered the sound of Kaushik Kashyap's sitar. He must have had an inbuilt amplifier near its resonator. This had no doubt added to the mellowness of his total sound. Probably, she realized now, it also allowed him to take his superfast taans at such lightning speed. When volume was provided by technology, the artiste could develop the technical side, the speed of his musicianship.

Perhaps, she thought now, pleased at the idea, their marriage would have stimulating discussions on these lines. What technology did to even traditional music, the way it changed things, though the spirit of the music remained unchanged. She remembered reading about veena player Ravi Kiran's slide. His variety of veena, the gottuvadyam, had to be played with a slide which, previously, had been made of ivory. With constant use, the slide became a smooth, polished piece that glided over the strings. But now that ivory was banned, instrumentalists had to look for other material. Bone, the antlers of deer – many substances were tried. But finally, it was Teflon that was found to give the best effect.

Yes, Kaushik Kashyap was such a well-travelled man, and she only a small town girl. There was that rather large age difference between them, too. He had experience of the world, an attractive quality in any man. There would be much she could learn from him. Not just about music, but about many other fascinating little things, in the same way that proximity to Guruma had enriched her.

Nomita, sitting beside Sandhya Senapati in the back seat of the second vehicle, a flame red Indica, felt none of the restraint that was usual between a student, even a senior student, and a Guru of the stature of Sandhya Senapati. Perhaps it was because they were both women. Women teachers of classical music were still, even in this twenty-first century, rarer than male teachers. The topmost echelons of Hindustani Shastriya Sangeet were populated with many more males than women, unlike Carnatic Classical music, where the gender balance was not nearly so skewed.

But she was glad that Sandhya Senapati was her Guruma, not just because of her knowledge of music, her empathetic nature and her teaching skills, but also because of her gender. Practically, it was a big help. Living in a small town it would not have been possible for her, a woman in her mid-twenties, to accompany her teacher on an overnight trip out of town if the Guru had been a man. Even the Guru-shishya relationship was not strong enough to withstand the gossip and innuendo that would inevitably follow if such a thing happened. Now, of course, Guruma was a chaperone as well as a teacher. In fact, over the years, Nomita had begun to think of her as a friend too, a mentor certainly, but also a person with whom she could talk freely. There was no need to be unduly circumspect with her, as she often was when Nomita found herself in the company of other musicians in Tamulbari.

At this moment, Guruma was looking out through the tinted glass at the view streaming past the window. It was hot weather, but from inside the air-conditioned car, it looked cool and pleasant outside too. The light fell on her ivory face, highlighting her calm features. As usual, her lips held a hint of a smile. She was humming a melody softly to herself. Nomita recognized the thumri, "Aaye Na Baalam". It was one of Guruma's favourites. "What can I do, my friend, my Beloved has not come." Such a romantic song! It was difficult to believe, however, that Guruma could be missing Tridib Barua. In Nomita's mind, their relationship as husband and wife always took second place to their more apparent relationship as two top notch musicians sharing the same living space in creative harmony.

Sandhya Senapati turned and smiled at Nomita. She was not embarrassed to find her student staring at her, nor was Nomita disconcerted to be discovered doing so. She smiled back warmly, and asked, "Will you be singing that thumri today, then? I'm not very good at it..."

"We'll see. Don't worry, even if I sing it, I won't ask you to support me. Actually, this thumri is a favourite of a very good friend of mine. He'll be there, he sent word."

Nomita looked questioningly at her Guru. "You'll meet him," responded Sandhya Senapati.

Nomita nodded. A flash of river as they crossed a bridge caught her eye beyond Sandhya Senapati's shoulder, through the tinted window. How pretty it was! She wished she could get the car to stop, and walk down the bank to the river. She wanted the sun on her face, the wind in her hair. If she had been travelling with Rahul, instead of Guruma, undoubtedly by now they would be splashing the clear waters of the river at each others' faces, shouting with delight. She felt as though she was chafing at some bond. Everything she did as a musician was indoors, away from the very nature that they praised in their songs. But then this was her choice. She had chosen classical music, not folk, or even Sattriya. These other genres had sprouted from the soil, and were performed under the open sky. Whereas hers was a genre that needed the artifice of the proscenium stage, the technology of the microphone, and the attention of an audience that was well versed in the style. It was part of the deal, she supposed. She glanced at Sandhya Senapati, wondering if she ever felt the same way.

Once more, she wondered why this man, this star, had agreed to "see" her. And come to think of it, it was also strange that he hadn't yet chosen a partner for himself. Surely he had met enough nice young women by now to make a choice? Perhaps he hadn't had the time? Perhaps he was single minded in his devotion to his music, and was now agreeing to "see" her just to humour his mother?

Where, then, did this place her?

Of course it was routine, almost a given, for most male classical musicians to neglect their homes and families in the pursuit of their art. Especially the older Ustaads and Pandits. There were stories galore about that aspect of musicians. There was, for instance, that renowned violinist, a gifted musician and a path breaker, too, who was widely credited with popularizing this western musical instrument in such a way that when he played, it was as though the violin had always been an instrument through which Raags and not symphonies or concertos had flowed. Honours had been heaped on him, money, too, and students from all over the world had flocked to his doorstep in order to learn the intricacies of this instrument that was now known on the subcontinent as the Behala, instead of the violin or the fiddle. And yet he had not found the time to teach any of his three daughters anything about the instrument, the music, or indeed much else. He had been conspicuous by his absence at their birth. His wife, a long suffering woman, had in fact given birth to the older one in the drawing room of their two roomed house in Kanpur, for the musician himself had gone off to a concert the previous night, and had become so engrossed in the music that he had simply forgotten that he was supposed to take her to the hospital on that day. It was only due to the kindness of the elderly landlady that both mother and daughter had survived at all. And at the end of his life, when arthritis had dulled the sensitivity of his fingers and the speed of his bowing arm, the money had simply run out, nobody knew how or where. Once a giant of a man who had swayed thousands at a time to tears or smiles with the magic of his music, he was now dependent for survival on the same daughters and wife whom he had neglected so badly before.

Her mind, which had so far circled the essence of a problem that sometimes worried her, finally came face to face with the core issue. In those families where the breadwinner was a male classical vocalist, it was more or less a given that the wife played a domestic role. And even if the woman in question had musical talent, it would wilt and wither under the sheer weight of these domestic responsibilities.

Perhaps she was worrying unnecessarily, she thought, settling back in the seat of the speeding car and closing her eyes. Maybe she should just go with the flow, get married to a jet-setting star, and enjoy the happy moments when they came. Maybe he would create raags and name them after her. Now that would be nice. "I dedicate this Raag to my wife, ... no, my *lovely* wife ... no, maybe even my *beautiful* wife, Nomita," he would announce in shows around the globe, "and I have named it after her. Raag Nomiteshwari." Oops, that sounded silly. She tried not to giggle. She must remember to share this with Rahul when she spoke with him on her return. No, not Nomiteshwari. Perhaps Raag Nomita Dhwani. She stifled a laugh, looking across to see if Guruma had noticed. But Sandhya Senapati seemed to be dozing now.

Then, there was the question of her teaching music. Nomita enjoyed her classes hugely. The children shone during the music concert, and the weeks of preparation leading up to this annual event were as fun filled as they were satisfying, as much hard work as inspiration. Indeed, since her coming to the Tamulbari Public School as a teacher, the institution's annual concerts were becoming quite famous around town.

There was also the teaching that she did at the Shishu Kalyan for children who were differently abled. It was challenging and satisfying in a way that being a concert performer, even a top notch concert performer, could never be. She was sure of that.

If she became Kaushik Kashyap's wife, would she be able to continue with these activities? Even if her musical career and performances on stage and radio continued, it was unlikely that Kaushik Kashyap would encourage her in her role as music teacher in a school.

But perhaps she was doing him an injustice. Perhaps after all he was just a nice, normal guy, ready to marry, in true Indian fashion, a girl his mother chose for him.

7

As expected, a small reception committee was waiting for them in front of the hotel in Krishnanagar. The other vehicle had already thundered down the highway and reached the place much ahead of them. Three or four men, all middle-aged, bordering on elderly, ran around opening the doors of their Indica, introducing themselves, sounding effusive and officious all at the same time. They were the office bearers of the Krishnanagar Culture Club, their hosts for the evening. With some ceremony, they were shown up to their rooms on the second floor of the three storey hotel. Subroto, Chinmoy and Prashant, it appeared, had already settled in, and were now deep in a post-lunch siesta.

Nomita's room, adjacent to Sandhya Senapati's was surprisingly large for a town of Krishnanagar's smallish size. She remembered that they were in tea country. No doubt there were visitors from distant places, buyers or planters or executives, who stopped here on the way to and from their gardens. They would demand some comfort when they halted for the night.

"Get some rest," advised Sandhya Senapati after they had finished the light lunch that was sent up to them in her room. "The function is likely to go on rather late, that's normal in these smaller towns. You'll find the audience very appreciative, if my guess is right. They're much less apathetic than big city ones tend to be."

The white noise of the fan in her room drowned out most sounds from outside. In spite of the heat, Nomita resisted putting on the AC. She knew that in the next room Sandhya Senapati too would refuse to be tempted by the AC. With a performance due in a few hours' time, changes in temperature, especially while asleep, were notorious for making the voice hoarse and sluggish, unable to negotiate a taan or the higher notes of the taar saptak. Indeed, the more elderly performers sometimes refused to even use a fan before a performance, no matter how sweltering the weather, saying it affected their voices.

It was almost four o'clock by the time Nomita awoke, rested. She wondered if Guruma was awake. She probably was, she decided. The function was due to start at six thirty, she knew, so it was time, now, for them to begin their warm-up rehearsals. Freshening up a bit, she walked up to Guruma's room next door, and knocked.

There were voices coming from inside. Guruma's voice, and a man's. She knocked again, louder this time. Guruma asked her to enter. Nomita opened the door and walked in.

"Ah Nomita, hope you managed to rest a bit? Good. Let's have our tea..." Guruma smiled and turned to the man, "This is Nomita, my student. And Nomita," she turned back to her, "this is my friend, the person I was telling you about. Deepak. Deepak Rathod."

Nomita, hands folded in a namaste, looked at the man. He was tall and strongly built, with a thick mane of dark hair that was sprinkled with white.

"Ah yes, Sandhya has been telling me about you," he said. Deepak Rathod's voice, Nomita noticed, was pleasantly low pitched. "Wonderful that I will get to hear you today."

"Only as a vocal accompanist," protested Nomita, embarrassed. "Guruma is the performer, of course."

Sandhya Senapati, watching the discomfiture of her student, came smilingly to her rescue. "Deepak has tea gardens around Krishnanagar, and since he was here, he decided to drop in on our concert when he heard of it."

"You're a tea planter, then?" asked Nomita, settling down on one of the deep easy chairs.

"Only somewhat, I'm afraid," he replied. Seeing Nomita's questioning look, he added, "It's one of the things my firm is into."

"Deepak's company has interests in several things, tea is one of them," explained Guruma. Turning to the man, she asked, "Tyres, and tea, and transport, wasn't it, Deepak? Three 't's. Though of course now you have your other businesses too..."

Deepak Rathod smiled, but changed the subject. "You'll be practicing now, I guess... I won't disturb you. I'll be around."

"You can stay while we rehearse, you know," said Guruma.

But the man was already standing up. "No, somebody is coming to see me. Besides, you'll need to rest your throat a bit. We've been talking for hours, haven't we? I'll see you later, in any case..."

"What a nice man," thought Nomita as she smiled goodbye to him. "A person one can talk to easily. Friendly. " But she didn't voice any of this to Sandhya Senapapti. No matter how close she felt to her Guru at times, there was still a distance between them and Guruma was obviously good friends with this man.

Besides, Guruma was pre-occupied with a tiny object in her hand, from which wires snaked out to end in headphones. Looking up, she said to Nomita, "Have you ever heard this? Or heard about it? It's something called an i-Pod Touch... Deepak brought it over for me, from Singapore I believe. He's filled it up with my songs, from radio recordings and CDs and cassettes. And there's still lots of space for more, it seems! Listen to the sound, it's unbelievable!"

"Ah, an i-Pod!" She had listened to the music on Rahul's, but it had been his kind of music, not this. Guruma's voice, each note and syllable, sounded out with unbelievable clarity through the earplugs. The accompanying instruments, harmonium, tabla, taanpura and sarengi had their own individual identities, yet blended in seamlessly with her voice, not overpowering it, but providing the support so essential for a well-rounded performance.

"Soon, perhaps, these gadgets will replace live performances?" wondered Nomita as she took the headphones off reluctantly. "I mean, these actually enhance the music, don't they?" She saw Guruma smiling, and realized what the connotation of her words was. "No, I don't mean that they make you sound better than what you are, I mean..."

"I know exactly what you mean," said Guruma, laughing, "and I agree with you totally. The sound quality, the balancing of instruments, the quality of voice production...of course the music is enhanced. Unbelievably enhanced. But then live performances will always have their value, won't they? The energy of a stage performance, the interaction between audience and performer that boosts the presentation level...these are absolutely essential for good performances. At the centre is the live performance. Audio and video recordings, no matter how perfect in sound quality, are only subsidiary." She took back the little gadget, and added smilingly, "Even the mistakes are magnified in this, I would imagine!"

The three accompanists, looking fresh and rested after their long nap, joined them, instruments in hand. Soon, all of them were on the mats spread on the floor, going through the paces of the Raag that would be sung, and the thumri afterwards.

"No, Nomita, don't stay quite so long on the Komal Rishabh, it's Puriya Kalyan, remember, it doesn't call for such a long pause on that note," or "Nomita, don't be so diffident, go ahead and sing for a longer time, you don't have to stop so apologetically each time, as though you were taking up my space or something..." or, gratifyingly, "Wah, Nomita, that was good..." Sandhya Senapati, even as she prepared for the coming performance herself, was mindful, as always, of her student's performance, her hesitations and her strengths. This encouragement, not always forthcoming from other Gurus, reassured Nomita.

Performing in front of small town audiences was, Nomita knew, definitely a different experience from performing in larger places. Krishnanagar was much smaller than even Tamulbari, though it was, unmistakably an urban and not a rural centre. Usually, the halls were crowded, unlike some of the bigger city concerts where the front rows would have the critics and organizers and their families, and very few others. The audience at these places were also, Nomita had found, surprisingly well-informed about raags and also about performers. Perhaps, living in a smaller place, there was time to actually sit and listen to CDs and radio programmes, perhaps there was time to discuss the nuances of a raag with people who knew about them.

But then of course Classical Music was supposed to be enjoyed at leisure. Developed over millennia, nurtured in the durbars of Kings, the courtyards of temples, and the baithaks of aristocrats, it could never be absorbed by listeners in a hurry. It wasn't enough to have it on as a background to your daily chores either. You needed time to savour the way it unfolded, for it was sequential in its logic. A bit from the concluding tehai would make no sense unless one had listened to and understood the preliminary alaap and the jod in the middle. It was a structure that each musician built up painstakingly, building aural edifices of grandeur and bewitching beauty. Each performance, even of the same raag, was a different narrative, even if the basic notes of the melody were the same. There was a strict adherence to the rules of the raag and structure, yet, amazingly, there were also large spaces where the performer was free to project his own individuality, through voice or instrument. And if today the mood, the mizaz of the performer dictated a sober Yaman, perhaps a month later, the very same performer, with the very same accompanists, but under the influence of a different mizaz, would imbue the same Raag Yaman with a delicacy and sparkle that would make it so much less dark that it would sound like a totally different melody. And yet it would be, strictly speaking, the same. Perhaps only small town people had leisure enough to marvel at these ornate structures, to discuss the nuances of the raag and so perhaps the performer needed to be more alert before such an audience.

But this, Nomita knew, was not always the case because so many of the most well-known performers, scorned smaller towns. It was true that not many small town organizers could afford their fees but even when they did manage to do this often the star performer did not really give of his best. And of course small town audiences were usually too polite to tell the performer to his face that he had been mechanical, and repetitive, and uninspired. Besides, the critics from the big newspapers would not be sitting in the front rows to put the performer on guard. There was nothing like a critic from a highly circulated journal sitting in the front row, or TV cameras from national channels recording the programme, to elicit a better performance from the artiste.

There was a routine to this pre-performance time, and also an etiquette. The organizers, especially in these smaller towns, were usually simple people, wanting to be reassured that the arrangements they had made for the artistes were up to the mark, that the hotel was to their liking, the food fine, the stage arrangements at par with those in big cities. One or the other of the accompanying artistes, usually the tabla and harmonium player, would have had a preview of the all-important sound systems, and discussed modifications with the sound people.

Eager hands took out the taanpuras as the vehicle stopped. The reception committee was waiting to welcome them, smiles of genuine warmth on their faces. The auditorium before them was quite large. "We are pleased with our cultural traditions, we've had so many of the best performers here over the last few years," said the Secretary proudly. He was wearing a spotless white dhuti and kurta, with a ribbon rosette on his chest and a gamosa slung around his neck to show his status on the Committee. "Bhupen Hazarika, Zubeen Garg, Parween Sultana, they've all come here in the last couple of years. Even Hari Prasad Chaurasia. And the other kind too, for, you know, our younger people. The Indian Idol finalist, Amit Paul." Thinking perhaps that the enumeration of this list might make the artiste before him feel as though he was being dismissive of her prowess, he added, "And now of course Krishnanagar will have the pleasure of listening to you."

"It will be my pleasure," said Sandhya Senapati courteously.

"Actually, you will be the first to perform here after the renovation," continued the Secretary. They were moving past the auditorium on their way to the greenroom, through a corridor that was fronted by a pretty arch. Nomita glanced inside the hall as she walked past. Despite the fact that this was a small-town auditorium, the seats were well upholstered, the floor marbled. "A benefactor donated a large amount that allowed us to redo the whole thing. You won't believe it looking at this place now, but till last year the place had a mud floor. We just couldn't get the money together till he came forward. And we used to have benches for seats. Of course audiences in our town are really wonderful, but they found sitting on those hard benches a bit of an ordeal, as you can well imagine. You will find the sound system quite good, I think, though I say so myself. He insisted that a sound engineer should check the place for perfect acoustical balance, too."

"That's unusual," commented Sandhya Senapati. "Who is the person?"

"The person who donated the money? Oh, you'll meet him, he's the Advisor of our Committee. A well-known businessman, but not a – don't get me wrong – not a person who thinks only of money. A cultured gentleman. Mr Deepak Rathod. He owns tea gardens here as well as having other businesses around the country. Around the world, actually. "

Nomita happened to be looking at Guruma's face at the moment the Secretary said the name. A flicker of some emotion crossed her face. Surprise? Yes, probably. So Deepak Rathod had not mentioned to her his role in refurbishing this place. As they settled into the white-sheeted gaddis in the greenroom, the man whom Nomita had met briefly a few hours ago rose several notches in her estimation. Not so much for what he had done, but for not talking about it to others.

Tuning was always an elaborate process. It needed concentration, a shutting out of other thoughts, distractions and other sounds as they swirled around the greenroom. It was entering the world of the Nada, that of Sound, the basic component of all music. The drone of a perfectly tuned taanpura was the doorway by which the artiste entered the domain of sur, taal and laya, melody, rhythm and tempo, in which he roamed freely for hours, till the concert came to an end. Many artistes used this time, surrounded by the resonances of the taanpuras, to enter the Zone, to meditate on the Nada Brahma, the Divine Sound, the wellspring of the Universe, from which all Being, all Matter, all Music had sprung. Organizers of the functions usually saw to it that they were not disturbed at this time and they took pains to keep away autograph-seekers and those who wished to meet these performers.

Nomita found herself being drawn into the web of melody. She was only dimly aware of the speeches being made, the introductory song being sung on the other side of the closed door that led to the stage. But before long, the door opened, and the Secretary was before them in a respectful stance, which said, without words, that it was time to go onstage and begin the performance.

A quick visit to the loo. "These are the practicalities of being an artiste, Nomita," Guruma had told her long ago, "always perform on an empty bladder. And on a half empty stomach, so that your breathing is not affected by a heavy weight in your intestines. Besides, remember you won't be able to get up from stage for a toilet visit! It would be embarrassing, na, with a whole hall full of people watching?"

And then they were ready for the performance.

Nomita, following Guruma up to the stage, touched the floor and placed her palm reverently on her forehead, showing the ritual sign of respect for the stage. This space was where they would present the raags that had come down to them from sacred scriptures. No one took their footwear to the stage. To do so would be desecration, a fouling-up of a hallowed area.

From the very first, it was apparent that the sound system would more than live up to the Secretary's high opinion of it. The stage like the auditorium, the greenroom and indeed even the toilets, was beautiful, much better than many of the auditoriums in Tamulbari, in fact. Nomita was pleasantly surprised. Involuntarily, she looked up at the ceiling. No loosely-hung chandelier up there. Guruma saw her look, and smiled. She knew exactly what her student was thinking. She gave her an affectionate pat on her head before they settled down to their places on the white-sheeted mat.

Once the curtains opened, Nomita felt a mild curiosity about the audience. In the auditorium below, the lights had been dimmed. But as always, there was a spillover of brightness from the stage, and the first few rows were clearly visible. Nomita, carefully handling the taanpura, hoped Deepak Rathod was present there. Usually she never thought of particular people in the audience, but rather of the audience as a whole, an entity that had come to listen to her, or to Guruma in this case, at the cost of their time, certainly, and also probably money, and definitely energy. Every artiste owed his or her best effort to the audience before her. It was her duty to make them feel that the two or three hours they had spent inside the hall had been worth it, that it had enriched them in some way.

There were the usual welcome gestures, the giving of bouquets and the garlanding with gamosas. Deepak Rathod was not one of those who came up to offer them floral welcomes. Perhaps he hadn't come after all?

As usual, Guruma began in her quiet voice, after the last tunings of the instruments were over, by speaking a few words. She introduced her accompanying artistes as well as Nomita, spoke about her pleasure in being at Krishnanagar, a place that was so well known for its appreciation of good music. This, of course, was a safe thing to say, for which town did not lay claim to being true connoisseurs of all things cultural? Besides, it was a good way to sweeten up the audience, though Nomita doubted whether Guruma had these intentions when she spoke. She was, as always, sincere in what she said. She mentioned that she would be singing Puriya Kalyan, the serene evening raag, and its bandish, "Aayi Saanjh Ki Bela," celebrating the coming of dusk, describing it, and complementing the melody of the raag itself. She asked for the lights in the auditorium to be switched on, for classical music was supposed to be an interaction between audience and musician to an extent, and how could that take place if the hall, so beautifully redone she had heard, was not seen by the artistes on stage?

The faces became visible. Deepak Rathod was there, looking smilingly up at the stage. Guruma smiled briefly at him, and greeted the others of the Committee who were sitting in the front rows. Nomita and the others, too, made their Namaskaars.

It was time to begin. All other thoughts moved out of her mind as Nomita concentrated on the music, and her part in it. When concerts went well, it was as though she was dipping into some rich mine inside her. Often, she came up with phrases and melodic improvisations that she had never consciously thought about before, and which, she knew, would be difficult to replicate later. Today was one such day. Guruma was at her best, her voice weaving nets of melody that shimmered with the sentiment and mood of the Raag. She brought in the coming of the evening, of Godhuli, when cattle moved in through the dust of dusk, the bells around their necks giving intimation of their return, when homes lit their lamps, when Lakshmi was ritually worshipped, and thanks was given for the successful completion of another working day. All around them sounds of peace were evoked, of calmness, and tranquillity. Nomita, adding her voice at times, was aware that this audience was with them. The hall full of people listened, hushed, as they built up the image, adding the rosy glow of the sinking sun to the picture they were painting, and then adding depth and movement to the canvas, so that, slowly, the orange gold seeped out of the evening, and the luminous grey of dusk appeared to give way, in turn, to the darkness of night.

Earlier, Nomita had been gratified if she could elicit the laudatory "wah" or other such complimentary exclamations from the audience. But she had gradually realised that the true connoisseur was not the one who showered such accolades on the music, or the musician. Indeed, many a time, the "wahwahs" of the audience became a kind of exercise in competitiveness among them, to show off to the others their understanding of this music that had an aspirational aura about it. After each taan or tukra, these people would shout "Kya Baat!" or "Wah!" in ever louder voices.

It was different with this audience though. The mood of the raag was of quietness and serenity. The hall full of people responded by showing their appreciation only through quiet nods. Nothing intrusive, nothing that could shatter the painstakingly-built aural edifice that was now glimmering all around them.

The applause of the audience when they ended was incidental. Those on stage knew they had performed well, to the best of their ability. They knew that it was a recital that would be talked about for a long time in Krishnanagar. They had performed as a team, with each instrument and voice giving support to Sandhya Senapati, enriching the performance, yet never overpowering her voice or ideas. They had, individually, given of their best too, yet they had never, any of them, pushed themselves forward at any time to highlight their own proficiencies. Nomita's vocal support was not just a kind of filling-in of the gaps when her Guruma took a breather during the recital. It was, in its well-thought-out structure and melodic design, an individual presentation, almost, a recital within a recital, a statement that was complete in its own right. Yet every minute during the totality of the recital, she was always the supporting voice, always conscious that her job this evening was to enrich and enhance Guruma's ideas and projections, not bring in her own. And yet that framework, too, was a liberating one for her, allowing her to climb the heights of her own creative skills.

As always when engrossed in a recital, her awareness of individuals in the audience receded to a blur. But they remained vitally important, nevertheless. She, like all the others on stage, remained acutely aware of the impact of every note, every subtle murki, every nuanced kan, on the people in the auditorium.

The true end of music, of art, was to please, in different ways, to differently informed audiences and spectators. And as they finished their first raag, they were aware that they had succeeded in carrying along this audience on the wings of this particular dusk melody. It was with that satisfaction that they moved on to the other, lighter pieces, the thumri in Kafi, and also, then, "Aaye Na Baalam", "for a friend who is here," said Guruma before singing it, the Dadra in Tilak Kamod, and the bhajans on request. Finally, it was with the haunting melody of a Kajri in Bhairavi that Guruma ended her programme.

Though she was sitting behind, and to the side of Sandhya Senapati, Nomita knew what her teacher's expression would be. She saw that ivory face in profile, but knew, from memory, what the audience before them was seeing. Sandhya Senapati was like a traditional sculpture of Saraswati, the same calmness suffused her mind and physical being. Her body language had none of the drama that so many vocalists of her stature often acquired. Her hand gestures were controlled, yet were none the less expressive. Indeed, she barely raised her arm above the height of her elbow, nor did she move it beyond a few inches in front of her body. Yet her fingers faithfully pictured each murki, each little trill, each meend and glissando, each swoop and curve as her voice mined the pool of sound and displayed the music she created from those swaras and srutis in all their splendour. It was as though there were two picturizations in progress, each one perfect in its delineation: one, through her voice using the medium of sound, the other, using her delicate fingers, tracing the intangibility of that sound in the space before her.

Later, through the blur of the congratulatory crowd, and the post-programme dinner, they gradually came down once again to the levels of the routine and the mundane that they normally occupied. They accepted the congratulations of the crowds with smiles and thanks, quietly happy that they had all done their best, yet knowing too, that there was never a set point for perfection in their line of work. Next time, the bar would be placed higher, both by the audiences' expectations, and their own, and they would strive, again, to reach that sweet spot where performer, music, and audience melded into one, and were able to experience the tranquillity and the exhilaration, at one and the same time. Sometimes they would be able to do it, sometimes they would fall back, in failure. It was not, of course, a physical thing only, but a spiritual one. The same notes, produced in the same way by the same artiste sometimes turned the key in the lock, and admitted them and the audience to the experience. And sometimes not. Sometimes they would be able to just have a glimpse of that River that led to the Ocean of Sound, sometimes not even that. And on rare occasions, as today, they would be able to become a part of it. That was what they would strive for, and be thankful for when it actually happened. And a glimpse, however brief, of that Universal Consciousness would imbue them with a deep humility, which would be present in their lives even as they went about their daily routines.

The autograph seekers seemed, at this point, hardly important. They came to all of them, to Guruma of course, but also to Nomita and the instrumentalists, because they had been part of that transcendental experience. Smilingly, they gave their signatures, knowing this was all ephemeral, but if it made them, the autograph seekers, happy, well, then why not? Nomita was glad that their performance had so obviously pleased the audience. Their job, at the end of the day, was to carry them along to an experience that was at once spiritual and sensory, of the moment and eternal, all at the same time. Guruma had achieved it today, and as part of the team, she was happy.

Introductions to the leading lights of the small town were made. Aspiring musicians came up to touch Guruma's feet, to speak to the rest of them with emotions that ranged from awe to envy. With some ceremony, Deepak Rathod was introduced to them.

Sandhya Senapati, smiling in her usual quiet way, said softly, "We've met." Deepak Rathod laughed, and told the other Committee members, "We have known each other, well, for quite some time. Right from her Kolkata days, when she was still a student with Pandit Chiranjeev Mukherjee. The *legendary* Pandit Chiranjeev Mukherjee." He turned to Nomita, and said, making sure that the others in the crowd did not hear what he was telling her, "You should have seen your Guruma at that time. Her Guru was of the opinion that she needed to put on weight, in order to build up her stamina for late night concerts and fast taans. He made his wife give her all kinds of dry fruits, you know, the normal diet of Hindustani classical musicians. Almonds and pistachios and cashews and whatnot. She would pretend to eat them all right, but would salt them away. She was, I think, relieved when I volunteered to eat all she could bring me. I was at Xavier's, studying Commerce, and I was hungry all the time! Poor Panditji never could figure out why, even after all that special food, his favourite student never put on weight!"

After the buffet dinner in their honour back at the hotel, most of the Committee members went away. The two local papers had sent their photographers and reporters, and they had managed to get brief interviews of Vidushi Sandhya Senapati over dinner. Once more, as on so many occasions in the past, Nomita marvelled at Sandhya Senapati's down-to-earth manner. It was so easy, in the face of this kind of adulation, to get carried away, as so many musicians did, to become aloof and distant, to give oneself airs and think of oneself as "higher" than mere mortals. Guruma, and also, Nomita remembered, Tridib Barua, had none of this.

Nomita noticed that Deepak Rathod had still not left. In any case, he had stood out among the small town Committee members, not only because of his obviously more expensive clothes and his height, but because of his personality. Besides, his colouring was dark, that of an outsider, somebody who did not belong to this North-eastern region. Guruma, busy with the last of the autograph seekers, turned around and caught Nomita's eye. Smiling, she signalled that she would be done in a few minutes.

In a short while, the three of them were alone in the dining room. The accompanists had left earlier, probably to "relax" as they put it, over liquor hospitably provided for them by younger members of the Committee. It would be showing the greatest disrespect for an artiste of Guruma's stature if they had the bad manners to drink in front of her.

"Come over to my place," urged Deepak Rathod, including both teacher and student in his invitation. "It's just about half an hour from here, and you have nothing to do now, do you?"

Somewhat to Nomita's surprise, Guruma agreed. "Just give me a moment. Nomita, are you ready? You'll like Deepak's home, besides, we don't have to start early or anything tomorrow..." Perhaps she sensed her student's hesitation, for she urged gently, "It's a lovely place, you know..."

Deepak Rathod smiled. "I don't know about that, but do come, Nomita. Just for a late night cup of tea, from my garden, of course....

Nomita couldn't explain her own sense of slight discomfiture to herself. But she found herself saying, "No, Guruma, you go along. I have a headache, you know I'm always so tense when I'm on stage with you. I'll see you in the morning." She bent forward and touched the older woman's feet ritually, since this would be the last time she would see her tonight.

"If that's what you wish…" said Sandhya Senapati. "See you in the morning, then."

Deepak Rathod smiled and, leaning forward, shook her hand. "Lovely meeting you. We'll catch up later then, maybe in Tamulbari sometime? I'll be passing through in a few days… Good night!"

8

The journey back to Tamulbari the next day was uneventful. As always after a programme, they felt drained, tired, and in need of recharging. On the other hand, the Organizing Committee had been full of energy and vitality as they had assembled once more in the foyer of the hotel to see them off.

Though Nomita herself had not seen it happening, she knew that when farewells were being made, the Secretary had taken Guruma discreetly aside, and passed over a large envelope, which she had put into her bag without comment or indeed overt curiosity. There were artistes who would depute a student or a chamcha to take the envelope and physically count the money before signing the receipt, for indeed short-changing was known to happen. Others had Secretaries who looked after the actual business side of things. Unlike many of the Ustads and Pandits of yesteryears, these new stars were sometimes so worldly-wise that until their Secretaries counted the cash, and checked that the stated amount had been handed over, they would not even step out from the greenrooms onto the stage.

Neither Guruma nor Tridib Barua were like that and she wondered if perhaps Kaushik Kashyap would be like that. Later, Guruma would take portions of the money and put them into individual envelopes, and hand them over to Nomita and the accompanists. Both she and her husband were known to be good paymasters, which was why there was no dearth of accompanists ready to play with them. Nomita, for her part, had long stopped protesting at being given this remuneration from her own Guru. In the beginning, when she had done that, her protests had been overruled. "You've worked hard, they've paid well, and so you deserve this," Guruma would say, placing the envelope in her hand, smilingly. "Your work on stage is worth something, you know, never forget that..."

As the car taking them home to Tamulbari picked up speed, both Sandhya Senapati and Nomita snuggled into the seats, and closed their eyes. They hardly spoke, except on the occasions when Guruma leaned forward to tell the man driving the vehicle, "Drive slowly, I'm not comfortable with speed, you know. There's no hurry, take it easy..."

And indeed, this was a wise precaution. In a profession that entailed so much travel, a lot of it by road, many great artistes had been lost to the world through car accidents that happened as they were travelling to or from programmes. Who hadn't heard of the way the door of Ustad Amir Khan Saheb's vehicle had been flung open as the driver had negotiated a bend at breakneck speed on a Kolkata street made bare of crowds by the advanced hour of the night? The great man, returning from a show, had been thrown out onto the hard pavement, the melody on his lips stilled abruptly as blood had gushed out from the burst skull.

Briefly, Nomita wondered when Guruma had returned last night. But Sandhya Senapati said nothing about the previous night, except to talk, once or twice, about the wonderful reception that the people of Krishnanagar had given them. She did, however, say as they neared Tamulbari, "I'll be glad to take a nap now, once I get home. I'm feeling really tired."

Guruma hardly ever complained of anything, even tiredness. Nomita looked at her, a little surprised as Guruma continued, "I don't know, Nomita, sometimes I feel... I wish... I was a person with a different kind of talent."

To Nomita, this sounded almost like sacrilege, a kind of disloyalty to the gift that one was so fortunate to be born with, and doubly fortunate to be able to nurture. And yet, given the context of the conversation, she thought she saw a glimmering of what Guruma meant.

"Don't get me wrong. I love the music that I've been taught, I love the singing of it. But increasingly, all this travel, all these preparations for shows, the sheer physicality of the performances, these have become… no, not wearying, that's too strong a word. But tiring. Yes, certainly tiring."

Nomita thought of Kaushik Kashyap, for whom travelling from venue to venue across the globe seemed to be an energizing thing, rather than an energy sapping one. But then he was younger. And he was a man. He would not have to contend with the cyclical hormonal fluctuations that all women from ten to maybe fifty-five were subject to: having to take a long haul flight, even though one's body was crying out for some rest after a particularly heavy bout of bleeding for example. As an instrumentalist, he would have his own constraints, but not the ones that Guruma, as a vocalist had to cope with. The careful nurturing of one's sleep and rest cycles, so that the voice was not coarsened by the changes, the constant need to protect the vocal chords. Yes, all this was tiring, physically and mentally.

"I wish I was, you know, maybe somebody who had been given a talent for writing instead. Or maybe a painter. Yes, I think I would love to be able to create canvases with colour, instead of melody."

"But why?"

"I don't know if I can explain this properly, I mean I've never heard any other artiste talk of it. But performing is a physical thing. Just as the body coarsens over time, and loses its purity of line and tone, the voice, too, thickens. Have you heard the early Lata Mangeshkar songs? 'Ja Re Badara Bairi Jaa,' for instance. The silveriness, the flexibility, that too, without any of the technical wizardry that helps today's artistes. And do you hear her songs now? True, she still sings beautifully, but her voice has slowed, and that's apparent in spite of all the technical support she gets now. Maybe there should be a retirement age for musicians, you know, so that they don't become a travesty of their former selves!"

Nomita nodded, remembering the programme she had attended last year, of a singer well past his prime. The musician himself had not realized the changes in his voice that were so apparent to the audience. Maybe his mind still heard the voice of thirty years ago even when he sang today.

"That's the sad part of being a performing artiste, at least for me, Nomita. The mind matures, continues to mature, till well past the age when the body loses its youth. Soon, the time will come when I will not be able to translate the musical ideas I get in my mind to actual sound. A note will slip, the speed will slow...it is inevitable. Whereas if you are a painter, or a writer, your mind need not depend on the youthfulness of the body to continue to create art. Indeed, in these genres, the mind makes the body irrelevant. The art that the mind produces through the greatest painters, or writers, or maybe sculptors, it's not dependent on the artist's body, not to the extent that a performing artist's is."

"You have a good many years of performance before you, Guruma, why are you speaking like this?" Nomita felt a rush of emotion as she spoke. "A good many years. Vocalists go strong right up to seventy, seventy-five, maybe more. Okay, with instrumentalists it's likely to be a little less, playing an instrument is more physically demanding than singing. And with fitness techniques becoming better by the day, who knows? In our lifetimes we will see Gurus of ninety, hundred, performing as though they are at their peak, at forty or fifty..."

Sandhya Senapati smiled, but said nothing. They continued in silence, each busy with their own thoughts.

"Have a good rest now," said Guruma as the car dropped Nomita off first after they reached Tamulbari. "No thank you, I won't get down today...do give my regards to your parents. You'll be coming to class as usual tomorrow? Good, I'll see you then."

It was good to be home, good to be back in her room, good to listen to her parents' chatter and answer their questions about the programme. She watched an inane soap on TV. She had decided, after the party at his house, to learn more about Rahul's music. She put on some channel that belted out vibrant rock melodies. She found herself smiling and tapping her foot and humming along with the lyrics. She realized that the high of the post-function hours had left her, and she had been, without knowing it, feeling down. A kind of restlessness, an entirely alien feeling for her, had robbed her of her calmness.

She wondered where Rahul was, then remembered that he was supposed to have gone with his parents to an outlying town. On an impulse she called him on his cell but he was unreachable. Pity. His refreshing chatter would surely have been a wonderful pick- me-up.

But within a few minutes, her phone rang. Rahul.

"Where are you?" she demanded, suddenly feeling a lifting of her spirits at seeing his name on the screen of her cell. "I've been calling... just a few minutes ago, in fact..."

"No, where are you?" he asked, his voice carefree and light-hearted. "I've been calling you since yesterday... was your phone switched off?"

"You must have called during the function. I had switched it off then... I was at Krishnanagar, remember I told you?"

"You wowed the crowds there, I'm sure."

"Rahul, classical music audiences don't get 'wowed,'" she said, laughing, feeling better already. "They are sober and serious, even to clap loudly is a no-no. And most of them are quite middle-aged anyway. Hardly any young people come to classical concerts. And it was Guruma they came to listen to, not me... I was just the supporting artiste."

"I don't know, when I watch a Hindi movie, it's the extras I look at during the dance sequences. They work so much harder than the main guys, have you noticed? No? You're missing something. The way they fling their arms around, the way they exaggerate every body movement! They're worth every paisa they're paid, I tell you! I..."

"Are you calling me an extra?" Nomita tried to keep the mirth out of her voice. "Is that why you called? Rahul...!"

"See you tomorrow!"

She looked at the cell in her hand, smiling. The lethargy of the past few hours had slipped away. She felt much better, more normal.

She realized, with a heightening of her happiness, that she was scheduled to take a class that evening at the centre for handicapped children nearby. The understanding was that she would go to supplement the work of the regular music teachers there, when it was convenient for them, and she herself was free.

Certainly the atmosphere at Shishu Kalyan was very different from that at Jhankaar Music Academy. This was a place where children with different kinds of disabilities were taught the arts. The classes were held as a supplement to the special education that the children got from their various institutions. Different children had different aptitudes, but they all loved the classes at Shishu Kalyan, whether it was drama, or dance, or music. Especially music.

Nomita taught only very simple songs here, a few stanzas of straightforward lyrics, usually about the Motherland, or Nature. The melodies, too, were nothing like those heard at Jhankaar, being linear, predictable and undemanding. Probably the students there, even people like Panchali and Rupa would be able to pick up the song in its entirety in just about five minutes, if that. But here there was no saying how long it would take her to teach the students of a particular class at Shishu Kalyan the simplest of songs. Whether they were slow learners or spastics, the teaching of the song involved extreme patience and a great deal of repetition on the part of the teacher. Sometimes, it would take two months to teach a class with learning disabilities just the first two lines of a song. Nomita marveled at the way Riniki, the regular music teacher, did it. Her own job here was to give the children voice training, along with teaching them some simple songs.

As usual, the class, with Riniki in charge, was waiting for her. Some of the children made an attempt to get up from their chairs when they saw her, though for the wheelchair bound, there was no question of doing so. Indeed, one or two were literally tied to their wheelchairs to prevent them from falling out. But there was no mistaking the way their faces lit up as Nomita moved to each one in turn, to pat one's hand, or ruffle another's head, and speak a few cheery words before she sat down next to Pankaj at the harmonium on the floor before them. Deba, tablas before him, was waiting, too. They smiled in welcome as she began her lessons.

"Wonderful! Silsila, that was really great. Your voice has improved so much since I last heard you! Rafique, you are really doing well. That Sa you sang was so steady! Seema, yes, good, but let's see if you can do it again? This time, see if you can hold the Pa a little longer? Take a deep breath before starting, nono, not *that* deep, just a little deeper than normal…yes, great, this is how you must practice before you begin the songs that Riniki Baideo teaches you…"

She knew she would have to repeat much of what she was saying the next time she was here, just as today, she had repeated much of what she had said last time. Progress was slow, infinitely so sometimes, yet it was measurable. Today she noticed that Prabha, the child with Attention Deficit Disorder, was listening to her and following her instructions well. In school, Riniki had told her, Prabha was a restless child with a very short attention span. But in the music classes, her attention span was much longer. And indeed, over the last few months, she had begun to sing beautifully.

Before her, the faces of the children glowed with a sense of accomplishment as one of them managed to sing a single simple palta all by herself, without help or prompting from Nomita. Another laughed out loud as he finished holding the Sa of the upper octave for a full ten seconds, as counted off by Nomita with her finger. She knew she would probably have to repeat this again next time, but that did not matter. Today, tomorrow, some day, they would master it, and then their happiness would wash over everyone who was present at the time.

She was also teaching them a very simple Jyoti Sangeet. *Gosey Gosey Pati Dilay, Surorey Sorai…* Every leaf is offering up a melody. She noticed with pleasure that Pallavi, whose memory was even shorter than the others, was actually managing to sing the second line of the song by herself, unaided.

Next to her, Pankaj, playing the melody on the harmonium, looked calm, tranquil. Yet just a few years ago, Pankaj, coming from a disturbed family background, had been prone to violent temper tantrums. As a teenager, he had had destructive fits of rage, fits during which he would seem to lose his reason. A talented santoor player, he also knew how to coax tunes out of the harmonium. His salvation had come when he had begun to work at the Shishu Kalyan part time, as a harmonium accompanist and a teacher. The children had given him much more than he had given them, Pankaj had told Nomita one day, and she had understood.

She discussed this with Rahul when they met the next evening. "Let's go to that new place on the river, that floating restaurant that everybody's talking about," he had said, and they had roared off on his bike together.

The riverfront, in this season of summer heat, was busy with people out to enjoy the cool breeze. Several boats had transformed themselves into restaurants and the Jolporee was the latest and poshest to cash in on this lucrative demand for newer modes of entertainment. The place was comfortably furnished, with cane chairs and pink gingham tablecloths. Long lines of fairy lights and streamers were strung across the deck, giving a festive air to the place. As the ship's bell struck the warning notes, the engine throbbed to life, and they began to move slowly out towards the centre of the river.

They chose their snacks and beverages, and sat back. It was refreshing, thought Nomita, to get away from the town, and feel the clean river breeze streak through her hair. Around her, the sight of people enjoying themselves made her own spirits rise. The sounds of merrymaking were softened by the open air. The gentle wind dispersed the sound and toned down the decibels to less frenetic levels. Even the live band that began to play the latest film music sounded much better than it would have in an enclosed hall. It was complete with a crooner whose sincerity and vivacity were not matched by her unfortunately somewhat off-key voice. But Melody-Queen Anita was certainly popular with the people around them.

"My trip to the US has been postponed, did I tell you?" Rahul asked as the waiter put their orders of momos and ginger tea before them.

"Oh?" She considered, then asked, "Are you disappointed?"

"No, not really." He shrugged, then added, "Anyway, it's only been postponed, maybe for a few months. Not cancelled. And another good thing is that they've given me some more leave now. That's quite a bonus."

"Wonderful!" smiled Nomita.

"Yes, I mean to make full use of this. I'll visit all the people I haven't met up with for years... So, tell me, how was Krishnanagar? "

"Good. It was a good programme. Performing with Guruma is always a..." Nomita searched for the word, "well, it's a pleasure, of course, but so much more than that. It's a learning experience. An intense experience... oh, by the way, I met a rather wonderful man there. Deepak Rathod."

"Deepak Rathod? The business tycoon? Ah yes, he's into tea, too. And tyres, I think... He's bought a tyre company in Singapore, or was it Kuala Lumpur recently, I believe. A very successful business man. His companies are always cited in case studies in *Business Week*. I wouldn't have thought he would be at a music recital in a town like Krishnanagar. What was he doing there?"

Nomita was a little surprised. She wouldn't have expected Rahul to have heard about Deepak Rathod. But then why should she be? He lived in a world which was more similar to Deepak Rathod's than it was to hers.

"Ah, I remember now," Rahul was saying. "I seem to have heard someone telling me that he has a woman here, in these parts. A lady love. Did you meet her?"

Nomita couldn't help staring. "A lady love? No, of course not. I mean no, I don't think she was there with him. He is Guruma's childhood friend though, from when she was in Kolkata learning under Pandit Chiranjeev Mukherjee. Isn't he married?"

"Who, Deepak Rathod? Of course. He's married to Rati Mittal."

"Somebody I should know about?" asked Nomita warily. Something about Rahul's tone implied that Rati Mittal was a person whose name was common knowledge and should be well known to her.

"Rati Mittal, of Mittal Gems. She's inherited the diamond business from her father. One of the biggest exporters of polished diamonds from the country. She mostly stays in Belgium now, I believe. Antwerp. But she has offices and factories in Surat, Mumbai, New York, Singapore... She's made her firm into a world player now."

"Oh." Nomita felt a little out of her depth. "And Deepak Rathod is not... I mean he's not part of that business?"

Rahul leaned forward, smiling. Nomita knew that smile, had indeed grown up with it. It was mischievous, indulgent, affectionate, all at the same time. "They are today's business family, Nomi. Wife runs her own, very successfully. Husband runs his own, very successfully too. No clash of interests there, no buyouts or takeovers or mergers either."

"And their marriage? I mean, if she's in Belgium and New York and he is in... well, in Krishnanagar and Kolkata and Kuala Lumpur... do they have children?"

"Of course. Two. And, before you ask, also an army of the best nannies, and household help. It's so much easier to be a working mother when you have the money for excellent domestic staff. They go to school in England, I think. I can't believe you know nothing about Rati Mittal. And not much, it seems, about Deepak Rathod, either. They're out, one or the other of them, in the business pages and papers all the time. The success stories of liberalization, that's them. Ethical. The new face of globalization. The clout of New India. And it's so – *neat* – that they're married to each other."

"But not happily?" Nomita poked at the skin of her momo, and watched the plumpness of the dumpling shrink as the chicken filling came out in a hiss of steam. "I mean if he is supposed to have a girlfriend here?"

Rahul shrugged. "Who knows? If they weren't happy, they wouldn't stay married, would they? Not in today's world." He leaned forward and tucked into his own momo.

Rahul could always be relied on to expand her mental horizons. Worlds existed outside Tamulbari, outside the domain of classical music, about which she was becoming increasingly ignorant. She needed a person like Rahul in her life to perk her up, bring in whiffs of fresh air from the outside world. She felt a bit like what she did when she taught the children of Shishu Kalyan.

Remembering, she said, "I had classes in Shishu Kalyan yesterday."

"How is Pallavi doing?" Rahul knew about her attempts to get Pallavi to memorize the second line of the Jyoti Sangeet.

"That's what I wanted to tell you!" Some of the excitement, the feeling of achievement of the previous evening came to her mind again, invigorating her like the fresh breeze perfumed with the fragrance of the water that fanned them on all sides now. "She actually managed the entire second line, you know... she hummed the melody, and she was in tune, too! She was so happy! And me, too! I was so happy at her success!"

Rahul reached across the table and held her hand affectionately. "I'm glad. For her, and for you. You love your work there, don't you?"

"Yes. Oh yes. No question. I feel I'm doing something worthwhile, as if I'm, you know, making a difference. I feel as though... as though without me those children's lives will be poorer. Only a little bit, of course, since I'm only there occasionally. But even that little bit is important."

They leaned back in companionable silence, watching the river as it moved, silent yet eloquent, around them. In the distance, Tamulbari looked verdant, with the trunks of straight, leaf-tipped arrows of areca nut trees thickly screening the confusion of the town from view. Nomita wondered if Kaushik Kashyap ever felt the need to be useful, like she did. Probably not. His music never once gave a hint of any kind of self-doubt. Perhaps that was why he had risen to such heights, heights that she knew she herself would never scale, not as a performer. Not in this life.

But was it really necessary that every person who learned music should become a top-notch performer?

As far as she was concerned, she was definitely interested in classical music. But was she interested in making the sacrifices involved in becoming a top-notch performer? Was she open to having Arjuna's tunnel vision when he aimed at a target, and ignoring all the many other things that life had to offer, as a trade-off?

Nomita realized that this was the thought that had been bothering her since her return from Krishnanagar. It was a relief to be able to pin it down. But it brought its own questions.

Rahul was saying something to her. But his voice was drowned in the enthusiastic applause from all the other passengers around the launch. Melody Queen Anita had apparently finished her turn, but was not being allowed to leave. Demands for encores were coming in from all sides. The family seated at the next table was particularly vociferous in their requests.

"Please, that song from *Gangster*! 'Ya Ali,' yes, that's the one! I know, Zubeen Garg sang it, and he's a male, but I'm sure you will be able to sing it very well. Ah, yes, I knew you could. Thank you!"

Melody Queen Anita began to belt out the song, barely making it to the top notes. She was dancing along with her song, the hand holding the mike the only stationary part of her body. It was completely natural and unselfconscious.

Nomita realized that there was a lesson for her here somewhere. The lesson being, probably, that people always got the entertainer they deserved. No, that was arrogant of her. Why should she sit in judgment about what this launch full of holiday makers were all enjoying? After all, everybody's tastes in music, as in food, were different. It would be she who would be out of place here if she were to sit down with her taanpura and begin a soulful rendition of Raag Anand Kalyan. No, the lesson probably was that every musician had his or her own audience, and others, with other tastes, had no right to sit in judgement on them.

Yes, she thought, looking at Melody Queen Anita, the crooner was communicating with the audience in a way that was actually quite remarkable. There was a vibrancy, a passion in her voice, that made up for its quality. Her body danced to the rhythm of the song, her enjoyment of what she was doing was evident, an enjoyment that couldn't but affect her listeners.

Somewhat to her surprise, Nomita realized that she too was enjoying Melody Queen Anita's performance. Looking cross at Rahul, she saw that he was smiling at her.

"Not exactly Madam Sandhya Senapati, is she?" As always, he seemed to know more or less what she was thinking.

"No, but so what? Look at the way she has the crowd eating

out of her hand! Look at those children, they're copying her body movements exactly, they are with her…look at the happiness on their faces!"

Rahul looked a little surprised. "I never thought you would like her, or her music…"

"Well, I wouldn't go out of my way to attend a concert of hers, maybe. But now that we are here, eating momos and watching the Red River, why not?" she laughed.

9

The Great Day approached rapidly, the day when Kaushik Kashyap would be performing at the Saraswati Centre for Performing Arts, the best auditorium in town. Nomita found herself losing, bit by bit, her customary composure. She took the deep breaths and did the meditation exercises advised by Sandhya Senapati to calm nerves agitated by stage fright, but they did not seem to help much. Perhaps, thought Nomita grumpily after abandoning her Pranayam exercises halfway, they were only meant for pre-show nerves. Not pre-seeing of Girl nerves.

Would Kaushik Kashyap, be a difficult person? A man spoilt by overwhelming success in his field at such an early age? Well, that was what this meeting was going to be all about. Of course Tamulbari was agog with stories about his starry ways, but she knew how the rumour mills of the town worked. She would make up her mind about that later. True, in his media interviews, he didn't come across as a friendly, easy-to-know person, somebody like Rahul, for instance. She smiled to herself. But friendliness and accessibility were not the only things, though they were important, too.

In any case, it wasn't as though being a musician, a classical musician, precluded being a good man. Certainly not. In fact, it was often said that one's music, one's art, was a reflection of the kind of person one was. Look at the kind of person Bismillah Khan had been. Simple, charming, with an inner beauty that shone through his very being. Just like his music. His shehnai had played relatively simple tunes, but they had brought tears to the eyes of any listener. He had travelled the world, but the core of his life had been his music, his Allah, his Benares, and his large, extended family. He had been a caring husband, in spite of his other-worldliness. He had preferred to sublimate his feelings through his shehnai after his wife's death, rather than remarry, though it would have been greatly more convenient if there had been a woman to take up the reins of the large household.

Perhaps the great passion of any genius, certainly a musical genius, was his or her work. Bismillah, the master of the shehnai, had said, unforgettably, "By the grace of God, when the shehnai is in my hands, all the wealth of the world could be brought to me, and I'd say: get about your business, take it away." Music was a tapasya, a meditation from which no Menaka, however enticing, could sway the true Seeker.

Perhaps this was why there were far fewer women classical musicians of the stature of Bismillah Khan, or Kaushik Kashyap. True, the musical landscape did have a Kishori Amonkar here or an Annapurna Devi, however reclusive, there. But surely there were others who had had the talent to begin with? Or was it that the process of childbearing and childrearing, managing a kitchen and a household, leached away at the well of creativity? Those too were creative endeavours. No amount of recharging of that well could ever fill it up again to the level required to become a superlative performer. But for many women, that was a fair exchange.

As Pradeep and Shikha Sharma's closest friends, Rahul's parents, Bhairav and Radha Borkotoky had been taken into confidence. Shikha would need their help to ensure that the "Seeing" went off well. It was therefore inevitable that the next time they met, Rahul was full of allusions to the Expected Way for the Girl to Behave at a Seeing Ceremony.

"You'll have to look at the floor, you know," he said, his voice sober like a teacher imparting knowledge to a slow child. "You can peep at his toes, if you want to see him. At his feet, max. You can't look higher than that. His knees? Never. His nose? What *are* you thinking of? His ear? That's borderline obscene. Like looking at his crotch, which I'm confident a well brought up girl like you won't do. Haven't you seen those movies? And yes, make sure you cook a few items for him. No no, on second thoughts, don't. Who knows what will happen after he tastes your cooking. Don't worry, we'll pass off Mahi's cooking as yours. Make sure you learn the recipes. He might ask you ..." he ducked, still solemn-faced, as Nomita flung a book at him. "Walk slowly and sedately," he continued, "but wait wait, you already do! At least, compared to other people I know. It won't do any harm to exaggerate the sedateness a bit though ..."

Preparations for Kaushik Kashyap's concert in Tamulbari were paralleled in the Sharma home. The reception committee at both places wracked their brains, trying to figure out the best way to receive the Great Man. "It should be simple, but effective," said the President of the Kaushik Kashyap Nite Reception Committee of the Friends Club. "Something he'll remember for a long time."

"We'll have to receive him at the hotel where he stays," said Dr Pradeep Sharma, the unofficial but acknowledged President of the domestic reception committee. The only other member of this particular committee was Rahul, who had been co-opted to help out on the occasion. "And bring him here in our vehicles."

"Should we take along bouquets, do you think, Moha?" asked Rahul, with a straight face.

But Pradeep Sharma was too pre-occupied to grin at Rahul's joke, even though at other times, when the whole operation involved other people's daughters, he would have been the first to guffaw appreciatively.

"Hm, good idea. No, on second thoughts, no bouquets. He's sure to receive a lot of them during his stay here. Bouquets and gamosas ..."

"The bouquets that we will present to him should be aesthetically put together," the President of the Committee said. "None of your slapdash collections of tuberoses and marigolds and gladioli. Make a note ..." he waved to one of the committee members ... "we'll put in gerberas and good quality roses, maybe orchids, all colour co-ordinated, we'll get them from Kolkata."

"Won't that be a little difficult? I mean we'll have to wait for the bouquets to be offloaded, then brought here to Tamulbari, before we can present them to him ..."

The President glared at the Committee member, but wasn't too sure if he was being irreverent, or was merely mentally challenged.

"On an earlier flight, obviously," he said witheringly.

"Thank goodness we won't have to worry about where to put him up," said Shikha Sharma, frowning. "The organizers of the programme will decide that. Can you imagine, if he had come here on his own? We would have had to decide where he would stay. A hotel, or a friend's house? Of course it wouldn't have been proper for him to stay with us, not till the marriage is fixed. *If*", she added hastily "the marriage is fixed."

"He would have stayed with us, of course, Mahi," said Rahul. "I would have given up my room for him..."

"With all those curly haired guitar-playing rock musicians and practically naked women on your wall?" laughed Shikha Sharma. "Oh yes, I've been to your room, while you were away. Your mother wanted to show me something there... Would staying there have been appropriate for a Prospective Bridegroom? That too, a Prospective Bridegroom who is a classical musician? What if the sight curdled his creativity for Raag music?"

"I would have ripped off all of them, even Bob Marley, from the walls. The Supreme Sacrifice, Mahi, nothing is too much for our Nomi..."

The dilemmas of the Hospitality Committee were greater. Tamulbari was a small town, though it did have several good hotels. Not five star deluxe, but comfortable. Clean. One or two were strategically situated on hilltops overlooking the river, and the view was worth a fortune. But would that be enough? Or should one of the better-off members of the organizing committee host him? If so, where would his retinue be accommodated? For like all star musicians, Kaushik Kashyap was not coming alone. Besides the mandatory accompanists of tabla and taanpura player, he would also have, with him, his Secretary.

"Why does he need to bring his Secretary with him?" an ignorant member of the Committee had wondered. But he was quickly put in his place by the other, more knowledgeable members, who assured him that among stars of the stature of Kaushik Kashyap, this was routine. The Secretary accompanied him everywhere, and Tamulbari could count itself lucky that it was situated comparatively nearer to Kolkata, where the star lived. The great man himself never spoke about arrangements, or indeed money matters, with the organizers of his concerts. He left that to his Secretary.

Indeed, the organizers of the Kaushik Kashyap Nite were thankful that the student that he was bringing along with him would double up as taanpura player. That was one fare, one accommodation expense spared. Often, a performer would bring along one or even two of his students, and it was expected that the organizers would foot the bill for them too. Sometimes, the students were even more demanding than the main performer, and would complain loudly about the smallness of their rooms or the food provided by the organizers.

The Food Committee of the Kaushik Kashyap Nite was in a tizzy. For musicians and dancers, indeed, most stars in the performing arts were notoriously demanding about their food requirements. Not all, of course, not the Ustads and Pandits of old, or those who considered themselves performing artistes, rather than prima donnas. Still, since Kaushik Kashyap's Secretary had sent ahead a list of food items that the maestro liked, loved, was indifferent to, and downright disliked, it was assumed that the maestro was a fussy eater. He was allergic to mushrooms, liked mutton, that is, goat's meat, not lamb or sheep's meat, cooked in a certain way. Kosha Mangsho, it was written, was his favourite, though of course he didn't expect to eat much of that mutton dish outside his home State of Bengal. Fish, especially river fish, he loved, as he did sweet curds. Dry fruits were a must for him, for he began his breakfast with a handful of mixed nuts, almonds, pistachios, cashews, preferably brought in from abroad. He hated vegetarian meals, and though he liked the "Western" vegetables such as cauliflower and tomatoes, the mere whiff of such things as lady's fingers and gourds was enough to ruin his *mizaz* for the day.

There was no wine list attached, but it was felt prudent to keep some handy, as well as hard liquor, so that the great man could "relax" after the rigours of the show.

At home, more or less by default, Shikha Sharma was President of the all-important Food Committee. Kaushik Kashyap would have a meal here, of course. Probably dinner, the evening before the show itself. He would be arriving the day before, so there would be plenty of time.

"Do you think his flight might be delayed?" she asked Rahul, who was being pumped for suggestions.

"Even if it is, it won't be that long a delay. I mean, he'll make it in time for the meal, don't worry. So what happens? Moha and I go to the hotel and whisk him off and bring him here? Will that be possible? I mean what about those people who are with him? His tabla player, and, I've heard, his Secretary and student?"

Shikha looked gratefully at Rahul. "Thank you Rahul, I had forgotten they would be there. Yes, I'll have to keep that in mind when planning the menu. They'll come too, of course, it would look very rude otherwise. You'll take charge of the transportation ... Now, about the menu?"

"Look what I've got for you, Mahi!" interrupted Rahul, flourishing a piece of paper. "A Xerox of the list of the kind of food he eats, and doesn't eat! Don't ask me how I got it. You don't want to know."

"He sent a list?" asked Shikha, wonderingly.

"He sent a *list*?" shrieked Nomita, sitting nearby.

"No no, it's not how you think. It was his Secretary," soothed Rahul. "Part of his duties, obviously. A routine thing. Perhaps his employer doesn't want to be food poisoned. Perhaps he's had bad experiences in the past with food. I mean when you're a globetrotter like that, perhaps it's mandatory. I mean, not everybody in Japan may realize that he isn't into raw fish. The organizers in Korea may not think that he won't like their snake fry. Frogs legs may be on the menu in France, snails in Italy... no, I like it, it's a useful thing to send a food list ahead of time. Saves embarrassment later."

"Tirna is too polite to tell me her son's likes and dislikes. But this list saves us a lot of trouble, anyway," said Shikha practically. "Let's see it."

She frowned at the list. "Dry fruits every morning. Well that won't apply to us I expect. We'll have fresh fruits, of course ... mangoes are very tasty now. Litchis ... Luckily he's not a vocalist. Otherwise the list would have been even bigger. No pickles, nothing cooked with curd, all those taboos about foods affecting voices that one hears about ..." She rolled her eyes. "Thank goodness Sandhya isn't into all that. Nomita eats and drinks practically everything, even ice cream and pickles, though not just before a show."

It was, reflected Nomita, bad enough inviting a classical music star to your home for a meal. Most were fussy eaters, her own Guruma and, from what she had heard, her Guruma's Guru being exceptions. When that star was a "Boy" coming to see the "Girl" over a meal, the whole thing became even more fraught with all kinds of complications. For tradition demanded that he, and his entourage, be made much of. Since eating and food were such large components of hospitality, it was imperative that the meal he was to be given be impressive, if possible, even lavish.

But "No need to go overboard, Ma," said Nomita. "I mean, let's just have the kind of food that we have for a normal dinner party."

Rahul looked at her. There was a glint in his eyes that she couldn't identify, even though she knew him so well. "What, and risk getting his show all messed up? Mahi, make sure you don't give him any of your bitter gourd. I know it's famous throughout Tamulbari, but no, not this time. His Raag in the Kaushik Kashyap Nite will be without any sweetness ... sorry, sorry, yes, I know that was not in good taste. No, I'll be serious, I promise ... Yes, I was wondering, what about entertainment? I mean how do we keep him busy till our Nomi makes an appearance?"

An Entertainment Committee was hastily constituted, nobody having thought earlier that entertainment would be necessary. "Rahul, you better be in charge," said Shikha distractedly.

"Is that wise?" asked Nomita. "Rahul, none of your music on the CD player. No, wait, I'll be in charge. I'm the heroine of this girl-seeing thing, I'll very well choose the kind of music that's to be played when they are here ...."

Classical musicians were usually and famously touchy about

others' music. She would have to make sure that no other sitar artiste's music was played in their home while he was here. Should she play his music, then? Probably not. He was not visiting their home as a star performer but as a man looking for a suitable wife. It was going to be tricky to keep a balance between appreciating him as a world class musician and making sure that he did not mistake this appreciation of his music for some kind of desperation on their part. They were no doubt the "Girl's" side, but that did not mean that they would have to cringe and scrape and flatter falsely.

It was confusing, as Rahul pointed out when she tried to express her thoughts about dignity, and self-respect, and self-esteem, to him. Shikha had left, and they were alone.

"Let me get this right," said Rahul. "You have no objections to pandering to his ego as an artiste. But you do have strong objections to pandering to his ego as a prospective groom? Is that it?"

Nomita laughed, but it was an uneasy laugh. "Of course not. That's not what I mean. Well," she admitted, "sort of. Okay, to avoid all misunderstandings, let's not refer to his stature as a musician at all. No need to praise his last CD, or talk about his radio programmes. He's probably used to all that anyway. And on no account are we to talk about my music. I'll have to tell the others, too. We'll talk of other things."

"The weather? Yes, always a safe subject... no, don't get angry, I'm serious... !"

The Entertainment Committee of the Kaushik Kashyap Nite was having an easier time. "He probably won't want to move out during the day of the function itself. All musicians like to rehearse, and so on. His return flight on the day after the programme is quite early in the morning, so we won't have to think of something to entertain him for the day."

"What about the evening of his arrival?" a Committee member wanted to know.

"He'll want to rest, I suppose."

The Kaushik Kashyap Nite General Committee was having a difficult time of it as the date for the show approached. The members kept getting calls from little known "friends" and slight acquaintances, all of whom were putting in discreet requests for free tickets to the show. This was common and something that they had anticipated.

At home, it was decided that it would be proper form to invite Sandhya Senapati and Tridib Barua for the dinner. Besides Rahul and his parents, nobody else was to be invited. A gala dinner at this point was not deemed suitable.

As for the Stage Decoration Committee of the Kaushik Kashyap Nite, as D-Day approached, they were all, to the last man and woman, greatly stressed. They were well aware that they were in a way the interface between the audience and the artiste. Momentous questions needed answers: What colours should the stage be decorated in? What sort of decoration should they go in for? Flowers? How high should the dais be? What about the banner at the back, what should it say? What language should it be in? Assamese, of course, but also English perhaps? And of course there must be an inaugural lamp, to be lit by the Chief Guest. And for God's sake, they told each other, don't forget the matches, and the candle, with which the dignitary would do the actual lighting. They remembered other occasions when these vital things had been forgotten and how the audience had jeered and hooted in amusement.

Besides, they were also in harge of the sound although the actual job of looking after the all-important sound system had been outsourced to a well known company which would be doing the modulation, the balancing of the instruments, the mixing between the base and the treble etc. But if, for some reason, the sound came out tinny, or if there was static during a jhala or a keening sound during an alaap, it would be the Stage Decoration Committee on whose head the blame would ultimately fall.

At home, while there was no Decoration Committee there was the all-important question of what Nomita Would Wear. Shikha herself hadn't thought of this aspect of the whole thing till Radha brought it up.

"It's extremely important what she wears at a meeting of this kind," assured the banker who had dropped in after work, a couple of days before the event. "Where's Nomita? We need to discuss this."

"Now that you bring it up, I agree. Nomita's gone to Jhankaar, she has a class there. I wonder if she's thought of something herself."

As they waited for Nomita to return, they spoke with horror about occasions they had heard about. Remember that Girl who had emerged in such a short skirt that the Boy hadn't known which way to look? And that other one who had come out in tight-tight trousers. You would think she had deliberately wanted to jinx the whole thing. Of course Nomita could be relied upon not to do something like that. She hardly ever wore anything else besides mekhela sadors, saris and salwar kameezes anyway. Still, they decided that Nomita would be best "seen" in a sari, that deep midnight blue one that set off her colouring so well. Her shoulder length hair, straight and sleek, was, along with her expressive eyes, her greatest asset, and was best left open. Nomita never used much makeup, but perhaps on this occasion, the services of a beautician to "do" her face could be hired. After further discussion, it was decided that it might be asking too much of Nomita to do that. Some jewellery, none of that wooden or terracotta stuff she was so fond of, but perhaps earrings and necklace, of the purest gold for nothing less would do for a ceremony of this importance.

Nomita herself had decided, however, to "come out" in a normal, everyday cotton mekhela sador, with normal, everyday make-up, light jewellery, perhaps those stone studs that she liked quite a lot.

10

A large black car, its tinted windows rolled up, drove up to the Jhankaar Music Academy at the same time that Nomita entered through the gates. This was unusual. True, people from all over the country, country and sometimes even from across the border came to Jhankaar to meet one of the two musicians in peripatetic residence there. Journalists and media people often came for stories and interviews. But they rarely drove up in anything this fancy. Nomita stepped aside as the chauffeur walked around and held the passenger door open. To her surprise, Deepak Rathod got out. He greeted her warmly.

"How lovely to see you again, Nomita. How are you?"

They walked up to Jhankaar together. The other students who had gathered at the entrance looked curiously at them, but did not come up.

"Is Sandhya at home, then? She must be, I suppose, since you have come, I guess to meet her. For a lesson? Perhaps this is not a good time, then ... but I was passing through, and I thought I'd drop in."

"Guruma must be in, I'm sure. Yes, there she is ..."

Sandhya Senapati had probably seen them approaching, and she came out of the front door of the part of the house that was their residence. The other door led to Jhankaar. The students continued to look curiously on.

"Deepak, what a lovely surprise! Come in ... Nomita, you too ..."

But Nomita shook her head. "No, Guruma, I'll sit in the class, go over the raag that you gave us last time ..."

"I'm sorry, I'm keeping you from your work. I was just on my way to the other gardens, and passing through your town..." Deepak sounded apologetic.

"You must have something...something cold, come in..." To Nomita, she said, "Just tell the others to wait. Maybe you can practice that tricky bit in the Sloka. I won't be long."

Deepak Rathod smiled at Nomita. She noticed the grey at his temples, and the light sprinkle of white in his hair. "How is your music? Wonderful, I'm glad to hear that. Well, we'll meet again sometime soon, I hope."

"But you must come to the Kaushik Kashyap concert. It's happening the day after tomorrow," said Guruma, smiling at both of them. Shikha had already given her the invitation for dinner. She had also been told about the real reason for the invitation to Kaushik Kashyap. But Sandhya Senapati said nothing about all that as she gently urged Deepak Rathod, "I don't know if you've heard him, but he's really wonderful. Try to make it, you won't be sorry."

"With a certificate like the one you've just given him, he'll be nothing less than superlative. Yes, of course I've heard him. You can't live in Kolkata and be interested in Shastriya Sangeet and not hear him. All right, I'll see if I can come. I'll try. Will you be performing?" He turned to include the student. "Or you, Nomita?"

"No, it's a Kaushik Kashyap Nite," said Guruma. "He's the only performer. Unless they get a politician for the Chief Guest. He'll be a performer too of course..."

Deepak Rathod laughed, then said, "What a pity. Well, I'll try, certainly. I would have loved to have listened to you..." – he made a point of including Nomita in his glance – "again."

What a polite man, how courteous, thought Nomita as she walked to the knot of students outside the door.

"She'll be late?" asked Rupa. Nomita didn't see her face, but there was something about her tone of voice that made her look up at the plump woman.

"A little, she has a guest. She's asked us to practice that bit in the new Shloka we're supposed to sing next week."

"A guest? That was Deepak Rathod, wasn't it?" Panchali observed.

The cynical curl of her lips left Nomita wondering. Why was she so upset about a delayed class?

The shadowed room was cool and welcoming as usual, its walls lined with rows of musical instruments waiting for hands to bring them to life. Nomita took down a taanpura, and began to strum it, preparatory to tuning it. But it seemed that the others, Geeti, Shrabana and Indrani too, had things to say.

"Deepak Rathod, so that's him!" Indrani's tone also implied something more than just a routine observation.

Nomita looked up at the woman's face. There was a glint in her eyes that she couldn't decipher.

"He's good-looking isn't he?" The same tone was echoed in Shrabana's voice.

"Looks! What are looks after all? Guruji is better looking, much better looking than him. But there's something about Deepak Rathod that's more than looks..." Sujata, not normally given to discussing people, also joined in.

"Money, of course," Rupa said promptly. "What he has is money, and it shows."

"You know him? All of you?" Nomita asked, looking around at the women gathered on the mat on the floor. "I hadn't known of his existence till the other day, when we went to Krishnanagar for the function. He was there..."

"Of course he was there." Panchali's voice was firm in its assertiveness. "If Sandhya Senapati is singing, can Deepak Rathod be missing from the audience?" she finished with a rhetorical flourish.

"What do you mean?" asked Nomita wonderingly, the taanpura lying forgotten on the mat.

"Mean? I don't mean anything..." Panchali said, but her voice still held its sneer.

It was Rupa who stepped in, emboldened perhaps by the fact that all the women there, except Nomita, seemed to be in tune with her way of thinking. "Don't you know then?" she asked, her voice mock-kind as she looked at Nomita, the acknowledged favourite of Guruma Sandhya Senapati.

"Know what?" But Nomita already knew what the innuendoes were about.

"About their relationship..."

"They're old friends, aren't they? Their friendship goes back to when he was in college, and she was a student under Pandit Chiranjeev Mukherjee, in Kolkata." She looked up at the wall.

"Of course, of course," Rupa waved her hand deprecatingly. "Friendship. What a convenient word. Do friends spend their nights together, I wonder?"

Nomita felt a rush of anger, but she kept her voice quiet. "What do you mean?"

It was Sujata who spoke next. "Nomita, haven't you heard the rumours? It's well known that our Guruma is having...a relationship... well, to put it mildly, what I mean is those two are said to be having an affair."

"Affair?" For a singer, Panchali's spiteful voice was gratingly unmelodious. "That's *really* putting it mildly. A *torrid* affair, more like. Everybody knows about it. And now he's begun to come to her house, that too in broad daylight! Of course he must know that Guruji is away and won't be back till tomorrow."

The words, the tone of voice, strengthened the feelings of distaste in Nomita's mind. She had always disliked Panchali and Rupa, and wasn't surprised to hear them speak like this. But the others... Of course she didn't believe them. There were any number of people who were ready to misinterpret relationships to suit their own perspectives. Deepak's and Sandhya's was a beautiful friendship. Nomita was convinced it was nothing more. What they had was something that was precious.

"I don't really believe you," she said quietly.

"It's true, you know," said Shrabana. "Even at that function last week, when you went with her to Krishnanagar, I mean, I heard that she spent the night with Deepak Rathod, in his house, not in the hotel at all."

Nomita looked at her, speechless.

Of course, put like that...but of course it wasn't true. That was not how it had been, certainly not. She was not surprised that the news of Sandhya Senapati's visit to Deepak Rathod's tea garden bungalow should have reached here. After all, this was not a big city, where people enjoyed a degree of anonymity. This was a much smaller place. And in any case, people such as Sandhya Senapati and Tridib Barua were celebrities here and it was inevitable that their relationships, should be discussed.

No, Nomita was not surprised that the news of Sandhya Senapati's visit to Deepak Rathod's house after the function had reached the students of Jhankaar. It was the interpretation that amazed her. How could a simple thing like a visit to an old friend's house be misread and misconstrued in this way?

"But this has been going on for years, I'm surprised you know nothing about it," sniffed Panchali, with the satisfied air of one who has dropped a bombshell. "He sponsors all her programmes in Kolkata, I've heard."

"Sponsors? What do you mean?" Nomita felt disloyal to Guruma even to be asking this question, but Panchali's glittering eyes had a mesmeric effect on her.

"Don't you know?" Rupa prepared to fill in the gaps in her knowledge.

Nomita knew she should stop Rupa and the others from continuing, but she could feel her own face frozen in amazement. Impossible to get any word to come out of her mouth at this moment. In any case Rupa was already in full flow.

"...how do you think our Guruma gets so many programmes in major cities like Kolkata, Delhi, Mumbai? Because she's good? Because she's an A grade radio performer? But tell me, aren't there dozens of other performers equally good, with similar grades? Performers who live in the cities themselves? Why would the organizers of the functions invite a woman from the boondocks so frequently? No, of course you don't know..."

Rupa stopped for breath, but with barely a pause, Panchali took up the narrative.

"It's well known, silly," she preened. Her gloating voice dripped with the satisfaction of One Who Knows About the Inner Workings of the Classical Music World. "That Deepak Rathod sponsors all her programmes. That means, the organizers don't have to pay her a paisa. All expenses are borne by his company, what's it called, yes, "Rathod Enterprises," I think. Transportation, fees, everything... Hotel stay, too... but that's only a sham. She actually always stays at one of his houses in Kolkata, or Delhi..."

"But he's clever, that Deepak Rathod." Rupa broke in, a look of mock admiration on her face. "The man sponsors Guruji's programmes, too. So that people don't suspect him of..." she allowed her voice to trail away, in keeping with the proprieties.

"It's standard practice, Nomita," said Shrabana kindly. "I mean, you do know that big corporate houses sponsor musicians in this way, don't you? It's their way of promoting classical music. They get advertising space at the venue in return..."

Panchali and Rupa snorted. Unbelievably, the sounds came out in unison. "In this case, of course, he gets something more... in return."

Nomita found her tongue at last, the acid in their voices acting as a spur. "My goodness, you two know a lot about the workings of the Classical Music world, don't you?" she asked. "When did you learn all this? While you were supposed to be practicing your lessons? Of course it's understandable that you are so interested in Deepak Rathod. He's good looking, isn't he? *And* rich."

Without waiting for a reply, but noting with satisfaction the irate expressions on the two women's faces, Nomita took up the taanpura, and began to tune it. Her mind was not in it however. She was angry, and believed very little of what her co-students said. How could they speak so... so *profanely,* yes, that was the word, about their teacher? A Guru was to be revered, to be talked about, with veneration. All traditional musicians touched their earlobes in deference whenever they spoke their Guru's name.

But was it true? A small, clear voice made itself heard over the turmoil in Nomita's mind. Her hands, on auto pilot as they went through the motions of tuning the taanpura, slowed almost to a halt. Remembered half-glances exchanged over her head, recalled nuances and tones in their voices, filled her mind. And where did that leave Tridib Barua? The immensely talented, greatly successful, gentle, Tridib Barua? As handsome as Kartik, the god of War, he was regarded as the perfect spouse, the wonderfully supportive, caring partner that any classical musician could hope for. There was an understanding between the couple, Nomita had seen it herself. There was respect for each other's music, a rare enough phenomenon in the cut-throat world of classical music. Besides, Tridib Barua was that exceptional man, and an even more atypical artiste, one who did not feel threatened by another's success, even if that other was his own wife. *Especially* if she was his own wife.

She shook her head slightly, angrily, trying to dislodge the thoughts from her head. Her hands resumed the tuning, but they too were angry. Screwing the peg down on the instrument to tighten the wire, she broke the rule of doing it kindly, softly, so that the wire did not feel the pain. With a squeak of protest, it snapped in two, twanging unmusically as one piece ricocheted against Nomita's palm, painfully.

"Shit." She rarely used the word, but Nomita was unaware that she just had, as she examined her palm. It was already bleeding, the broken end of the wire embedded right in the centre of her palm. Grimacing, she pulled it out carefully. The blood began to flow faster.

At least the wire had only pierced her palm, that too comparatively lightly, she thought, it could have caught her eye or slashed her cheek. Angry with herself for getting so distracted by a piece of gossip that she had broken a string in the taanpura, she sucked her palm to staunch the flow of blood.

She hadn't noticed Guruma come into the room, but there she was, standing near her with a look of concern on her face. The other students, quiet now, were peering at her over Sandhya Senapati's shoulders, looking, thought Nomita with annoyance, as innocent as though they hadn't just been discussing their revered teacher's love life a few moments before her entrance.

"I'll bring the Dettol, that looks a little deep," said Guruma and went out again, unaware, no doubt, of what had just been said about her in the room. Or perhaps she was just unconcerned?

11

Friday morning came, bright and sunny. And hot. In spite of the fact that it was June, there was, surprisingly for Tamulbari, no rain yet. Usually at this time monsoon clouds rolled in from the Bay of Bengal, flooding the land but also cooling it.

"Well, that's put an end to monsoon Raags tomorrow," thought Nomita grumpily. She had slept badly the previous night, and was now irritated. It was normal practice for musicians to play the Malhars and the Meghs and the Deshes, the Raags of the Rainy Season during these monsoon months. But if it was going to be as clear and bright tomorrow as it was today, Kaushik Kashyap would have to play something else. Unless he was like that pompous vocalist who had "graced" the stage of the Saraswati Centre for Performing Arts last year. It had been dry and rainless on the day of his performance, too. In the auditorium, in spite of the air conditioning, the audience had been very uncomfortable. Beginning his concert with a Miyan ki Malhar, he had announced grandly that his renditions of these immortal rainy season Raags always brought rains. He had interspersed the alaap of his recital with anecdotes about how an open air January concert had had to be abandoned because he sang Goud Malhar on request. Large black clouds had appeared from nowhere then, and soaked the audience even before they had had time to run for cover. To Nomita's irritation and everybody else's gratification, he had performed very well after making these smug statements. And when they had stepped out of the auditorium, it had, indeed, begun to drizzle.

Strange, she reflected, calming down as she showered and dressed, that she still thought of Kaushik Kashyap's approaching visit as that of an artiste's, and not of a prospective bridegroom's.

The phone rang. She could hear her mother talking. After a few minutes, she came in smiling, with the cordless in her hand. "It's Tirna. She wants to speak to you."

For a disoriented moment, Nomita found herself thinking that Kaushik Kashyap had called off the "Seeing", and had delegated his mother to tell the Girl's Party about it. But no, her mother wouldn't be looking so happy if that were the case.

"So, how are you feeling?" Tirna's voice was rich and warm, as usual.

The friendliness of her voice made Nomita smile, too. Suddenly, she felt much better. Happy, almost. Certainly she was now prepared to view the whole thing in perspective. "Fine, I'm just fine," she said. Would Kaushik Kashyap's mother think that the happiness in her voice was because she would soon be meeting her son? She didn't care.

They talked of other things, the weather, and how hot it was. Kolkata was boiling, too, and Kaushik, his mother said, found it difficult sometimes to acclimatize after his engagements around the temperate zones of the world. Thank goodness for air conditioning, though that was not too good for the instruments...

"How's your singing, Nomita?" asked Tirna."Riyaz going all right?"

It was a routine question, but it warmed Nomita. If Kaushik Kashyap was anything like his mother, there would be no problem, absolutely none. Which mother of a Boy about to "See" the Girl would have enough empathy to call up and ask about the thing that mattered the most in her life?

Almost as soon as she put down the phone, her mobile rang. Rahul. "So, how are things? Big day today..."

"Rahul!" As always, it was a pleasure to hear his voice. And how kind of him, characteristically kind, to call in the morning, when he knew that she was likely to be feeling, if not downright nervous, then certainly uneasy.

"You going to school today?" he asked. He knew how important it was for her to be with her students.

"Of course. Classes are in the afternoon, so why shouldn't I?"

"Shouldn't you be at a beauty parlour or something?" The teasing was back in his voice. "That's what Girls do when Boys come to 'See' them!"

"How would you know? You've never been invited to See anybody…"

"Hm, you sound jealous of my gender. Typical female thing, I forgive you. Bye now, I have to organize my clothes. Do you think he'll approve of my black T, the one with the picture of the Living Dead? No? What about the one that says Sauce Ka Boss…I'm Different? Or the other one, 'I feel like a Nucking Fut.' No, I suppose you're right. We don't want to spoil the maestro's mizaz with my T shirts. Okay okay I'll do as you say. A plain white shirt…he'll think he's coming to a funeral or something, but I'll do as you wish. You don't want me to wear churidar kurta, I suppose? Let me tell you, I look quite devastating in that outfit. No? What a pity. Hmm. You don't want me in competition with the Boy, I guess. What! No jeans? But I don't have plain trousers… All right, I know it's you he's coming to See, not me. Of course. Right."

The darkness of her morning mood now completely gone, Nomita settled in for her riyaz. She found it calming and uplifting. By the time she finished, and went in for breakfast, she was her usual self.

Shikha Sharma had taken leave from school, and was moving round the room plumping up cushions. Pradeep Sharma had not yet come for the meal. She turned around with a welcoming look when her daughter came in. "Lots to do, I've asked Minu to stay overnight, it'll be too much for Rina alone…" The two helpers were already bustling around, cleaning and polishing. Parties and get-togethers were quite common in the Sharma household, but this was different. There was an urgency, a sense of importance about the way the work was being carried out. It spoke quite clearly of the fact that this was no ordinary dinner party that was being organized.

"You'll be going for classes today?" It was a statement, more than a question, tinged with a mild request for her daughter to change her mind, if possible.

But Nomita was firm. "Yes, I will. You know I hate missing classes, and those children will be disappointed if they can't go through the songs for the concert. It's just a few weeks away now. I'll be back well in time, don't worry!"

The bright faces of the students and their enthusiastic, toothy smiles and greetings warmed her heart as she entered the large room where music classes were held. She was glad that she hadn't stayed at home, having her face made up or her hair done and getting the jitters in preparation for the visit of a Prospective Bridegroom. Their eagerness at sitting down for lessons made her smile, too.

The Tamulbari Public School was preparing for the Annual Concert, which was still several weeks away. But the concert was a large project. Though the Tamulbari School was definitely academics-oriented, it did have a good extra-curricular calendar. Sports, art and music were given space within the school hours, which was a huge concession in this town where parents and students otherwise chased marks with grim and ferocious determination. Besides, teachers of these extra-curricular activities were not looked down upon by the others, such as those who taught Mathematics or Physics, as an inferior breed. They were given as much respect as anybody, indeed, sometimes even more, for it was recognized at the Tamulbari Public School that music and art and sports did play a very important role in the overall life of the child. For this, Nomita was happy. Indeed, as an ex-student of this same school, she had been given a lot of importance because of her musical talent. On the day of the Annual Concert, especially, she had shone, and had basked in the glow of the praise of her peers, her teachers, and the audience. And now, as a teacher in this school, she was happy that she was given a more or less free hand to teach that difficult, almost unteachable subject, music, in the way she deemed fit.

This year, she had composed a musical drama, revolving around a family of Raags. The parent Raag, Shri, was mother to Purvi, Basant and Puriya Dhanashri. Shri's personality, like the Raag she embodied, was sober and beautiful. Each child had a distinctive musical personality, reflected in the mood of the Raag and the composition. The storyline itself was simple, involving a lost kitten, who had music tuned to the frisky Raag Adana as its signature tune whenever it appeared on stage. The children, increasingly worried, hunted around for their pet, singing out their thoughts and worries in the Raags that they represented. There was also a helpful and serious policeman who sang soberly in Raag Durbari, and a rain cloud who sang in Raag Megh. It was the rain cloud who spotted the kitten clinging helplessly to the topmost branch of a tall tree as it passed over the neighbourhood where the children stayed, and informed them about it. The story ended happily, with the kitten rescued by the policeman and all the characters singing a melodious sequence of the Raags they represented. The USP of this little drama was that the characters would be acting out the pieces and singing themselves. No lip-synching was going to happen. Nor would the singers be relegated to the wings, invisible behind the black panels, or in the pit. The characters were chosen for their singing voices, and their ability to hold a tune. The drama teacher was working with them in his class to get the body language and expressions right. Basically though, this show was Nomita's responsibility and effort. She had got the literature teacher to write out the lyrics in Assamese, and had spent considerable time and effort composing the music to go with the storyline and the Raags. She had told Sandhya Senapati about it, but had not had time yet, to get her to listen to it. Of course she would invite her for the performance. She only hoped Guruma would be in Tamulbari at that time. Meanwhile, the drama had already acquired fame throughout the school as a wonderful concert-in-the-making, with the other teachers dropping by whenever they were free to listen to its progress.

It was a delight, as always, for Nomita to teach these eager-faced, bright-eyed, fresh-voiced children. True, some of them could not carry a tune, a couple of them were even tone deaf. When the song demanded a note in the upper octave of B Flat, for instance, little Sewali would be unable to go beyond the fifth note of the middle octave. But these were the challenges that Nomita enjoyed. She had solved Sewali's problem by getting her to keep time to the songs with a small tambourine. For though she had no voice, Sewali, Nomita had discovered, had an impeccable sense of rhythm. The singers who formed the chorus – that is, a large number of students – would in any case be visible throughout the performance, as they would be standing by the side of the stage. And Sewali, with her tambourine, would be right there in front, proudly keeping time. For if Sur, melody, was one wing of music, Taal, rhythm, was the other. Without Taal, as without Sur, the bright bird of music could not soar. Nomita had explained this to the class, and the covert sniggering among the children when they heard Sewali's unmusical voice had stopped immediately. Indeed, she was now envied for her special place in the chorus, and also the way she got to play the little tambourine, with a one-minute solo piece that Nomita had devised, when the kitten pranced around while exploring the garden.

Besides, there was the satisfaction of hearing, and seeing the musically inclined children grow in front of her eyes. Debojit, the young boy who played the policeman, was doing full justice to his songs, all tuned in the difficult Raag Durbari. It was a delight to discover, at the beginning of each class, that he had been practicing diligently at home. This was reflected in the way his voice showed so much more flexibility from class to class, and the way he was able to reach notes at both ends of the scale, higher and lower, more easily each time she heard him. A resonance was beginning to be heard in his voice, too, the timbre was changing to a more musically rich one, all in the last three months that they had been practicing. Nomita knew that he was not particularly good in his studies, but in her classes, he shone. Today, he was better than ever, adding grace notes to the Raag in a way that enhanced its beauty greatly. She was seriously thinking of asking his mother to get him to take music lessons at home. Or she could send him to Guruma, or Tridib Barua though neither Sandhya Senapati or her husband normally took students this young. Potential students needed to have a stronger knowledge of the basics of music before they themselves began coaching them. Still, the boy was enormously talented. Maybe they would make an exception.

Besides, there was Koel, living up to her name and singing like a bird in Raag Megh. She was getting deep into the essence of the melody. Today, as she sang her songs as the cloud that spotted the kitten on the tree, she really did bring a whiff of the fragrance of rain into the room. Wonderful!

She noticed the body language of the children as they sang. It was spontaneous, untaught, and for that reason, it revealed a great deal about the children's attitude to music. Most of them kept time to the beat with either a foot or a finger. Some swayed slightly as they sang, in subconscious imitation of the rise and fall of the melody. A few stood stiffly, as though they were at a parade. They were the ones who were likely to be more talented in spheres other than music, in art perhaps, or in mathematics. Those children who were good at sports were more aware of the rhythmic side of the music, and their bodies reflected this. Perhaps it was the physicality of sports, and the fact that they were comfortable with their bodies, and aware of them, that made their limbs and heads keep time in this way. Nomita was gladdened to see an expression of intensity, of involvement, in the eyes of all the children. They were very much into the music. No boredom in her classes.

But best of all was the feeling that she was creating an activity for them that all of them enjoyed so much, even as it honed their talents, and made them work together as a team, with a common goal. It gave her a warm feeling whenever she thought that years later, even if these children never sang another note in public ever again, they would remember these music classes with fondness and joy. They would forget her name and be unable to recall her face. But they would definitely remember these classes and even these songs if they tried hard enough. They would learn to appreciate other songs, other melodies set to Raags. And the music would be with them always.

Teaching music, especially to the very young, was very different from teaching history or mathematics. A lot depended on whether the pupils had an ear for music. In each class that she taught at the school, there were, at the most, six or seven out of the thirty or forty who had that voice, that musical intelligence. They were the ones who were a joy to teach. But drawing out the music from the ones who were not that good was, for Nomita, also a pleasure, probably because the children themselves loved the music they were creating so much.

Smiling at them at the end of the class, responding to their enthusiastic "Thank You Ma'am's" as they filed past, she became aware that it was just a matter of a few hours now before Kaushik Kashyap came – was brought – to her house. She had forgotten about it while she had been with the children. She wondered if his flight had arrived on time, and whether the drive here had been without incident. Instead of coming to the smaller Tamulbari airport, his flight would be landing at Guwahati. Something to do with the timings, she had heard. An hour saved, for an artiste of Kaushik Kashyap's stature, was an hour that could be invested in riyaz and practice.

She found her mother in a tizzy at home. "The student, the one who is to play the taanpura with Kaushik, you know. It's a woman!" she said ungrammatically, though her meaning was clear.

"So?" asked Nomita, though she was a little surprised, too. Normally, it was the male students who travelled to outstation destinations with the Guru if he was a man. Propriety dictated that a girl student should not go out overnight with her Guru and his team of tabla players and maybe even toadies, all of whom were likely to be males. "I mean, that hardly makes a difference to our plans, does it?"

"No no, the student is a woman – girl – from Italy. A foreigner. I was wondering if she would need special food, you know. Remember that foreign student of Tridib Barua's we had once? What a fuss he made about his food, wanting pure vegetarian, no onions even... really, I hope this one is not like that."

Nomita remembered the occasion. The student, a lanky American with dirty toenails who had dressed in kurta pyjamas too short for him, had decided to turn vegetarian with a vengeance, laying off not just meat, fish and eggs, but also garlic and onions. Since he had not informed them of his food preferences while accepting the invitation, the dinner had been a fiasco from both his and his hostess's point of view. Even the vegetables and daal had had onions and the dessert was an egg-based one. He had had to make do with plain chapattis sprinkled with sugar.

"How do you know?" asked Nomita, sitting under the fan.

"Rahul. He's in touch with the Reception Committee." Shikha Sharma smiled at the memory of Rahul's dry voice on the phone. "And do they have problems, the Reception Committee I mean!"

"What's the matter?"

"Well, they had thought that they could economize by putting the student and the tabla player in one room. That's what's normally done, isn't it? But now that they are of different genders, they are having to organize another room. The Sona hotel is booked solid anyway, so they're having problems."

They smiled together companionably, contemplating this small misfortune of the Committee. Thank goodness it wasn't their problem.

"Anyway, Rahul has promised to find out if she's veg. We don't want a repeat of that fiasco."

Rahul. Thank goodness. Suddenly, she wanted to talk to him.

Back in her room, Nomita called him on his cell. The music that was his call tone this week was very unlike what the guest of honour of the evening was likely to have on his. "It's my life…" screamed some voices for several seconds in Nomita's ear before Rahul's voice came on.

"Nomi, is that you? I'm doing some detective work right now; I don't have much time to talk to you…" His voice was a dramatically hoarse whisper.

"What about the food habits of the student?" A thought came to her. "Where are you?"

"At the hotel, where else? Talking to the Organizing Committee, trying to get an interview with the Food Committee. Wow, you should see this place. It's crawling with chamchas. All those kurta-wearing men with soulful expressions. Of course they're all here to get a look at the Italian student. That's pretty obvious. She's quite a looker, I hear."

"Is that why you're there so early, as well? To catch a glimpse of her? I thought you were supposed to fetch them only at about eight?"

"How can you say such a thing? I'm hurt.... No, I'm going home right now after I find out exactly how many people have come, and who eats what. I promised Mahi. Anyway why did you call? If you want to know if I've met your Kashyap yet, I haven't. They're guarding him like he's the Prez of the United States or something. Okay, see you in the evening then."

Nomita found herself wondering about the foreign student. The *beautiful* foreign student. Well, that was something that she would have to learn to cope with: over-enthusiastic fans, fawning students, men as well as women. Of course the relationship between a Guru and a shishya, a teacher and a student, was supposed to be sacred, inviolate with the teacher being the parental figure, in all senses but the biological. Figuratively, emotionally, artistically, it was as though she were born of the Guru's loins. Indeed, the shishya was sometimes more to a Guru than one's own child, for the best of them were the receptacles through which his artistic immortality was assured. The lineage was always apparent in the way the student fashioned an Alaap, or played a particular Raag. Yet these bonds were sometimes broken, the forbidden incestuousness of the relationship ignored by human frailty. In any case, what did students who came in from other cultures understand of the nuances of the Guru Shishya Parampara? With a conscious effort, Nomita controlled her galloping thoughts. She had no right yet to allow jealousy to rear its head in this way. After all, Kaushik Kashyap was nothing to her just now, except an artiste whom she admired greatly. Besides, every relationship between a man and a woman did not have to end in a romp in bed.

However, Nomita's mind continued to toy with these thoughts despite her best endeavours. Of course foreign students were a badge of success these days and many classical musicians flaunted their students for the more one had the more they added to the artiste's stature. For teaching was considered a hallowed activity, more respected, sometimes, than performance.

The thought that Nomita had been trying to shy away from

crystallized in her mind with sudden clarity in the shape of a question. What did it say about a man when he came to see a girl accompanied by another, not related to him?

The question was actually irrelevant, she thought, smiling to herself. For Kaushik Kashyap was not an ordinary person. He was a Star. And he was coming here as a Star performer and it was silly to forget this, even for a while. Tirna had probably picked her as a prospective bride for her son hoping that she would be able to understand the imperatives that drove Kaushik Kashyap's behaviour. And here she was, letting her thoughts run in a predicatable way even before she had met him. Smiling, Nomita put on the CD player. Sandhya Senapati's mellifluous voice filled the room with its soft cadences.

Nomita, touching Guruma's and Guruji's feet as she welcomed them into her home that evening, was struck, once again, with Tridib Barua's startling good looks. She had, indeed, rarely – if ever – met a man this handsome. Tall, broad-shouldered, with perfectly proportioned limbs, torso and facial features, his was a presence to which every eye was naturally drawn, wherever he went. The greying at the temples added to his good looks. He was not a young man any more. And yet, neither his face nor his physique had been corrupted by the physical and mental stresses and strains of life, or the demands and fierce competitiveness of his profession. Next to him, Guruma looked almost plain. And yet Sandhya Senapati was no mean looker herself. The other men in the room were of course no competition, though Rahul, with his vitality and vigour, had his own attractiveness. Nomita was comforted by his presence.

"You look nice, Nomita," smiled Sandhya Senapati. She didn't say more, but Nomita was cheered by her words. She knew it was her Guruma's way of instilling confidence in her.

Shikha Sharma had diffidently mentioned the real reason for Kaushik Kashyap's visit to their town to Guruma and told Nomita later that Sandhya Senapati had sounded surprised to hear this. But she had had only good things to say about Kaushik Kashyap, whom she knew slightly, having performed at the same venues on various occasions over the past few years.

"I had assumed a person like Nomita would choose her own husband," she had said softly into the telephone. "I mean…she's a different generation from us, and it's what is done these days, isn't it?"

"No, she always wanted us to choose a boy for her…" Shikha Sharma hadn't added that her daughter had probably been influenced in this by her Guru. She knew that Sandhya Senapati would be embarrassed at hearing of how her student's regard for her spilled over from the domain of music to other spheres of her life, and that Nomita looked on her Guru's marriage as a kind of ideal.

Rahul and Pradeep Sharma left soon after to fetch Kaushik Kashyap and his party from the hotel.

They chatted of this and that in the interim, their ears cocked for the sound of wheels in the driveway outside. Radha moved around with Shikha Sharma, helping her place the plates, and the cutlery. The maids could have done it, but Shikha seemed unable to sit still.

"You know the little play I am doing in school, Guruma?" Nomita was determined to keep the conversation normal.

"Yes, how is it doing?" asked Sandhya Senapati, interested.

"Well. The children are catching on to the Raags so well, I'm impressed. I want you to come to the show, if you can. I mean if you have the time."

"I'll make the time," assured Sandhya Senapati. To her husband, she said, "Nomita is in charge of a lovely project. A drama, a musical actually, where all the songs are in Raags. And each character will symbolize a particular Raag. They'll have the names of those Raags, too! Isn't that a good idea?"

"Wonderful!" said Tridib Barua, smiling. His voice was the sound of a deep, mellow temple bell. "Am I allowed to see it, too?"

"Of course Guruji, how can you think… I'll be delighted…"

"There they are," said Shikha Sharma, her voice tense. Nomita wanted to go up to her, stroke her head, and tell her, "It's all right, Ma, it's only Tirna's son. Don't worry. Nothing will happen if it doesn't work out, why are you so worried?"

But there was no time. The group of people was already being ushered into the house. Introductions were being made, murmurs of recognition and smiles and small, polite laughs were in the air. Everybody was being introduced to everybody else, pride of place being given, of course, to Guruma and Guruji. Her turn hadn't come yet.

Nomita looked not at the prospective bridegroom, but at Rahul. He stood behind them all, taller than the other guests. He caught her eye. He gave her, not the cheerful grin that he always greeted her with, but a quiet smile, tinged with some emotion she could not identify. She half smiled and only then turned to look at Kaushik Kashyap.

"... And this is our daughter, Nomita," finished Pradeep Sharma, trying not to sound as though this was the climax he had been building up to, though of course everybody knew it was.

She folded her hands in a Namaste, taking care to make it a polite greeting and not a subservient one.

Her first feeling was one of shock. The man was quite short, hardly taller than her, actually. This hadn't been apparent in the TV or print ads. But he had mesmeric eyes that looked straight into hers, as he said, " Ah, I have heard so much about you from my mother."

She was taken off guard by his statement. She hadn't expected this greeting, though of course it was quite possible that it was true. But his voice! It was thin, without substance almost. She realized that those TV ads must have doctored the sound during their voiceovers. She was so used to the resonance in the voices of the singers around her that she had almost forgotten that there existed people whose voices were not necessarily their best feature. Well, he was a sitar player, not a singer, she must remember that. His hair was neatly tied back in a ponytail. Ponytail! Neither his music nor the ads in which he had featured had prepared her for a ponytail. True, she had known he had longish, curly hair, but a ponytail! Stray locks, dark and curly, had escaped from the rubber band. She made a conscious effort to tuck away responses that came tumbling to her mind. She would think about that later. True, artistes such as Hariharan sported ponytails, but a pure classical artiste... and more importantly, a potential husband. A ponytail needed some getting used to. Yes, she repeated to herself, she would think about it later.

There was the usual bustle as they found seats for themselves. Kaushik Kashyap, she noted, did not sit till Tridib Barua and Guruma had done so. Nomita was surprised to find herself lucidly analyzing his behaviour even as she herself finally sat down, as far away from him, as possible. The other men who accompanied him were affable, simple people. Saurav Sen, the tabaliya, and Kamal Basu, his secretary were, she was sure, quite unaware of the real reason for Kaushik Kashyap's visit here. They thought this was one of the usual courtesy visits that out-of-town tours always involved, as part of the package, almost.

But it was the Italian girl, Lucia, who was easily the most riveting personality in the group. Tall, slim, with the face of a Madonna, she was indeed a striking beauty. She had the looks of a successful model. The bloom on her skin, the faultless planes of her oval face, her eyes, were perfect. Her hair was the same shade as Boticelli's Venus. She followed her teacher around the room, quite without embarrassment of any kind, with long, striding steps that had her near him in a moment. And even when she was standing right next to Kaushik Kashyap, her enormous green eyes never left her Guru's. Dressed in a perfectly fitting black silk churidar kurta with a gold dupatta, she talked little, and when she did, it was in an English that was tinged with a fascinating European accent. Her hands seemed to move of their own accord when she spoke, illustrating her words with little waves. Nomita immediately felt dowdy, and at a severe disadvantage just being in the same room as her, even though she knew that the simple clothes she was wearing herself made her look all right, too.

She remained quiet while around her, the conversation began on its usual predictable route.

"Warm weather, yes, isn't it? Is Kolkata hot too?"

"Ah, I wouldn't really know...just got back from Europe. The weather there was beautiful though. Amsterdam was warm, sunny..."

"Where did you have your concerts this time?" Guruma's interest was professional, but Nomita was curious in a more personal way. Rome, Florence, Milan, and then Berlin and Amsterdam...What she wanted to know was if Lucia had accompanied him on that tour, too. Stupid question. Of course she must have. She would have been around to show her Guru the glories of the Eternal City, the beauties of her country, her continent.

The talk turned to music, and performances abroad. Thank goodness Guruma and Guruji were here. They were the ones who were keeping the conversation going, really. The rest of them were a bit out of their depth at this moment. All this talk of concert halls, of audiences in the West being better than those in India…

"…they really listen with such attention, it's wonderful." Kaushik Kashyap was waxing eloquent on foreign audiences. "Not like here, sometimes one has to request them for silence…"

Guruma demurred. "Well, it's true that they listen quietly. But I don't know about you, I quite enjoy the, what shall I say, the *boisterousness,* of our audiences. I like the way they express their appreciation, you know, with applause, sometimes in all the wrong places. I find it rather lovable, in fact."

Tridib Barua added his voice to that of his wife's, "In fact I find the Western audiences a bit boring." He remembered Lucia's presence in the room, and added, "I mean it's very commendable of course that they are so keen to learn our music, and about it. But the energy, the vibes one gets from performing at a large music conference in Pune, for instance, or Kolkata, now that's something else indeed. True, people walk around, talk among themselves, even eat chips and colas. But then that's the way it's always been, hasn't it? We've been so much more relaxed about our audiences. It's only now that we demand their complete attention. At all times, whenever they are in the auditorium."

Kaushik Kashyap smiled, and said, "Perhaps you're right. We must remember that their audiences are used to the performances at their small soirées and big, lavish opera houses. Closed spaces. Whereas our performances often took place in open fields, in temple courtyards, in large durbars…yes, I see your point."

Nomita, listening and analyzing, found herself approving. So, star though he was, Kaushik Kashyap's was not a closed mind. It was polite of him to yield the discussion to the older performer. Probably he did not even agree with him. But that was beside the point.

"How is the hotel?" Pradeep Sharma asked a safe question.

It was Kamal Basu, the Secretary, who answered. He was a small, busy looking man, who achieved the almost impossible feat of carrying both a smile and a frown simultaneously on his face. "Not so good, I'm afraid. There's been a bit of mix-up..." The frown deepened, almost, but not quite, edging out the smile fully.

There were murmurs of concern. But Kaushik Kashyap put an end to his Secretary's complaint. "No, it's all right. Not five star, but it's comfortable enough. The place has character..."

Hmm. That's nice of him too, thought Nomita.

She turned around to look at Rahul. Like her, he had hardly spoken throughout. In fact, thought Nomita, a smile coming to her lips at the notion, it could have been Rahul who was the bridegroom-to-be, sitting quietly and observing her, the bride-to-be, while all around them, people talked of other things.

Rahul smiled back at her, encouragingly. She wondered what he thought of Kaushik Kashyap. He would tell her soon enough, of course, but she wanted him to like the man. Kaushik Kashyap was charming the people around him. True, he didn't talk much, and when he did it was always related to music. But she herself had spoken not a word throughout. It seemed she wasn't expected to, anyway.

Shikha came in and announced dinner. In the general movement towards the dining room, Nomita found herself standing next to Kaushik Kashyap. Or had he engineered it that way? She wanted to say something, or ask some question, but couldn't think of anything. He must think her quite dumb.

"What a lovely room this is," he said to her, easily. "I must tell my mother. She told me about your beautiful home, of course. She gave me strict instructions to make a note of everything..."

She smiled at him, her eyes almost level with his. She was grateful to him for giving her this conversational cue, that too in such an easy manner. "Thank you. The credit is Ma's entirely. How is your mother? I've not seen her for a long time, though we do talk on the phone often. In fact she called this morning..."

"Yes, she told me. So, will you be at the concert tomorrow?"

Nomita was surprised. "Of course. I mean...everybody in Tamulbari who is interested in music will be. And also people who know nothing about music. I mean, to attend your concert is turning out to have a kind of snob value..."

She shouldn't have said that, she thought, immediately agitated. Almost her first words to him, and here she was, sounding like a chamcha already. But the words had slipped out unawares, and anyway they were true.

Thankfully, he seemed not to have noticed. In any case, he didn't let what she had said colour his words or his expression, which remained unchanged. "I hope you have good tickets? You didn't have to *buy* them, did you?"

"Well, it's okay, we often do..."

"No no, wait..." He called out to Kamal Basu, "Tell the organizers to give Nomita three, no five passes to the best front row seats for tomorrow. No, not front row. Second row. We don't want them to get a crick in the neck looking up at the stage. Second row. Make a note of it." He turned back to her, and added, "I hope you'll be able to re-sell the tickets you bought. If not, let me know..."

It was a buffet dinner, so they were spared the worry of who to sit near whom. But like many other musicians who had visited them over the years, Saurav Sen was palpably not going to be at ease at a buffet dinner. Shikha and Nomita quickly organized a table for him and Tridib Barua, so that they could sit and eat. It was necessary to serve them their food, and Nomita busied herself with this. Between the sesame chicken and the fish tenga, she noticed that Rahul and Kaushik Kashyap were deep in conversation. Lucia was predictably at Kaushik Kashyap's side, her dramatic looks even more apparent now that she was standing. But she didn't seem to be adding much to the conversation. Even though she had a plate of food in her hand, her eyes were fixed, inevitably, on her Guru. She was a good few inches taller than her teacher though, indeed, she was almost as tall as Rahul, and that was saying something. Well, it wasn't Lucia's fault that she was so rivetingly good-looking, thought Nomita. She wasn't eating much either by the look of it, though she wasn't vegetarian. She turned back to Tridib Barua courteously and gently ladled some more fish tenga on his plate. Quelling her irrational irritation, she decided to be nice to Lucia when she got a chance. She wondered what the two men were talking about. They didn't seem to want her with them at all.

"Thank you, Nomita, I really can't eat any more." Tridib Barua's mellifluous voice was kind, as always. "Now go and eat something yourself, Majoni. You haven't touched a thing..."

"No, that's fine, don't worry about me." She wondered whether Guruma had told her husband the real reason for Kaushik Kashyap's visit to their town. She must have, of course... but Guruji was a person of refined sensibilities, and he would hardly bring it up himself, unless the topic was already being discussed.

Guruma, standing nearby, came across to them. "Yes, eat something, Nomita..." She glanced at her husband, and said, "The fish is fantastic, you've tasted it?"

"Nomita's looked after me wonderfully, I've eaten everything twice, I think." Guruji's smile was mild, as always.

Whenever Nomita had seen them together, she had been struck by this tenderness between them. If that was what happened when two musicians settled down together, she was all for marrying one. She glanced across involuntarily to Kaushik Kashyap, now talking with her father in another part of the room. Would they have this between them, if they were to get married?

Deepak Rathod, she thought with a sense of vindication, was obviously not a threat to Guruji at all. Those were just small town rumours that were going around. Sandhya Senapati's career was an unusual for Tamulbari, and they would not understand a relationship of deep friendship such as she and Deepak Rathod obviously shared, independent of her fulfilling marriage to Tridib Barua. Just seeing Sandhya Senapati and her husband together, gave her a sense of happiness, separate from all the other complex emotions she was experiencing at this time.

Determined to be an excellent hostess, and as broadminded as Guruji in the matter of friends she went up to Lucia with the bowl of salad. She asked brightly, "Can I give you some of this? You're not eating a thing!"

Kaushik Kashyap was standing nearby, talking to Rahul's father now. He turned to the two women and said, laughing, "Lucia never eats much. Isn't it, Lucia? I tell her she needs energy, lots of it, in order to play the sitar. Playing a large instrument like that one needs stamina but of course she doesn't listen."

Lucia smiled, and pushed back an auburn curl from her face. "No no, I eat enough. I put on weight in this last month…" She waved a deprecating hand at her willowy body.

She avoided looking at Kaushik Kashyap. In any case, she was adding up all the positives of his behaviour, and personality. She would dwell on the worrisome aspects later. Impressions were crowding her, even though she was confident that nobody in the room would notice that she was covertly observing him, even as she busied herself serving others. Like the perfect guest, he was making himself charming to her parents, her Gurus, to her best friend Rahul, and his parents. The thinness of his voice was already beginning to surprise her less. A couple of hours was all it had taken for her to get used to it. His fingers were long, the nailbeds oval shaped. Sitarist's fingers, sensitive to the slightest quiver of sound in the instrument below them. She could see the callouses on them, the fingerpads that had thickened over the decades that he had been playing. His fingers had two rings. One was large, with a flashing stone. It had to be a diamond. The other was a wire contraption, the plectrum that would be used when he played. Many sitarists, she knew, kept this mizrab on their little finger even when they were not playing.

Nomita found herself looking again and again at his fingers. They had surely bled when they were tender, as a child. But now music, and not pain, was what he felt when he played for hours at a time. He carried himself confidently, so that after the first surprise, his lack of inches, too, ceased to matter. His hair…That, now, would take some getting used to. She noticed that in its ponytail, his tresses were wavy and thick.

The guests did not stay very long after dinner. One by one, they left, Kaushik Kashyap and his entourage first, then Guruma and Guruji. Rahul went with Kaushik's group to drop them off at the hotel. His parents were the last to leave.

Nomita, seeing them off, wished she could discuss the evening with Rahul. She had hardly spoken a word to him in the last few of hours. But Rahul would be going straight home, and not dropping in this evening again. What a pity. She felt a sense of disappointment as she helped her mother clear up.

12

As was expected, the Kaushik Kashyap Nite drew a full house. The organizers were gratified that their tickets were completely sold out. In fact, there were many who clamoured for more tickets, but it was impossible to accommodate them. Extra chairs, uncomfortable plastic bucket-like affairs, had been put in the aisles and along the sides of the auditorium, at the back and even in front, right below the stage itself. The people who sat there would have to crane their necks uncomfortably to see the artiste. Yet people thronged the ticket counter, asking for admission. Finally, a hassled but exultant President of the Friends Club decided to allow them in at a discounted rate. There was standing room only at the back of the auditorium, but the latecomers were happy even with that.

Nomita, sitting beside Guruma in the second row, was astonished. Never before had she seen such thronging crowds in a classical music concert. It was more like a Sonu Nigam Nite, or perhaps a Jagjit Singh Evening.

"These are all classical music lovers?" she asked, amazed. "I mean – I thought I knew most of them in Tamulbari. But I know very few people here!"

"They must have come from different places." Guruma smiled, calm and content even though her own recitals never drew such crowds. "The Committee spent a lot on publicity, I believe. And he's such a famous artiste, it's but natural that people want to hear him. In fact it's unusual, very unusual for him to come to a small town like ours." She didn't add the words, but Nomita understood very well her meaning. He would hardly have come to Tamulbari if it hadn't been for Nomita. Of course it was different for Sandhya Senapati and Tridib Barua, because they lived here. But even their concerts in Tamulbari were limited these days. Mostly they performed in venues outside the region.

Much of the local press, she knew, had already gone over to Sona Hotel that morning, to interview the young maestro. Kaushik Kashyap had told Shikha Sharma that he would be busy because Kamal Basu had lined up several interviews for him. It had not been necessary for him to add that the afternoon would be devoted to pre-show preparations: a bit of rehearsals, a bit of meditation.

But even though the small number of classical music lovers of Tamulbari was swamped by the tidal wave of fans who had come in from other places, they were certainly all present there. Several of Guruma's and Guruji's students came up to where they were sitting, touching their feet and greeting them.

The complimentary tickets had arrived that morning, courtesy the Kaushik Kashyap Nite Ticket Committee. Instead of going through the embarrassment of asking them for a refund, Nomita had gifted the tickets she had bought to Shishu Kalyan. No doubt Silsila, Pallavi and Prabha were sitting there with a teacher somewhere in the crowd, waiting excitedly for the programme to begin. Her parents had come, too, but were sitting a short distance away, along with Rahul's parents. Of Rahul himself there was no sign. Indeed, she had not heard from him at all that day, though she had tried calling him up several times. She wondered what he was doing, where he was. It was unusual for him not to call up at least once during the day when he was in Tamulbari.

Deepak Rathod had come, after all. He was a seat away from her, next to Guruji. The two men, sitting side by side, reminded her of the conversation at the Jhankaar Music School the other day. Here was Guruma beside her, calm and serene as ever, quite unfazed by the fact of her legally wedded husband sitting right next to the man who was rumoured to be her paramour. Surely she would have felt a stir of unease, of guilt, perhaps, at this point, if this had been true? And surely Tridib Barua would have had some inkling of the affair? But both of them had shown only uncomplicated good cheer when

Deepak Rathod had come up and sat beside Guruji. "See, I made it!" he had said, and Guruma, smiling, had replied, "You won't regret it, you know." Guruji too, had added, "It would have been bad if you had been in town and missed this concert. This artiste is well on the way to being one of the greats. Vilayat Khan, Ravi Shankar, Ustad Halim Jafar Khan ... the way Kaushik Kashyap is performing these days, he will soon be at par with those all time greats ..."

Unstinted praise, that too from one who could be construed as a rival. But both Guruma and Guruji were like that. Back-stabbing and jealousy were so common in this field that it was indeed refreshing to find two people who had the generosity to acknowledge talent, genius and greatness in others.

The thing about so many other classical musicians, thought Nomita, watching the arrogant profiles of several of them as they sat in the auditorium, was their staunch belief that the whole world owed them. It was as though they, and they only, were the designated keepers of the flame of culture, of the "magnificent tradition of our ancient past", of the "glories of the golden phase of our history." This belief gave them an air of disdain, which they cultivated carefully.

Kaushik Kashyap didn't seem to possess such airs, such condescending manners, but perhaps he was just on his best behaviour. She would certainly have been put off totally if, on top of the ponytail on his head, the diminutiveness of his height, and the lightness of his voice, he had also had a condescending manner.

The hall was bursting at the seams. The air conditioners were humming busily against the June temperatures, but already the body heat of the almost two thousand strong crowd was making the auditorium uncomfortably stuffy.

Certainly people had come to listen, but also to be seen. Looking around, Nomita picked out the faces of those whom she knew to be music snobs. They were there, in a more expensive seat than they could afford, looking sober and serious already, as though something of great import was about to happen, something to which the rest of the people in the auditorium were not privy. They talked among themselves in solemn tones of what Kaushikji had said about the people of Tamulbari ("such a very musically advanced town..."). Their deliberately restrained manner reinforced their pose of being In The Know. Impossible to contradict them, to even ask, "How do you know these things?" Proximity to the great star was implied in the gravity of their body language. It was hinted, though not actually said, that Kaushikji was in touch with them.

Nomita, listening, could hear snatches of conversation swirling around her.

"Kaushikji's just back from that tour of Europe. Hariji and Shivji were there too, and also Rashidbhai."

"Hariji was saying the other day that the best concerts are happening in the West these days, not in India at all."

"How can they happen here? Amjad Saheb was talking about the same thing. He's been given such honours in the UK, an honorary doctorate and whatnot, what is there in India? It is our good fortune that he chooses to stay here and play at some concerts, which we can attend."

The "Ji" syndrome, Nomita noticed with suppressed amusement, was in full swing all around her. It had been Rahul who had first brought it to her notice, some years ago, when they had attended a concert together.

"Why do students of classical music use 'Ji' so much? After all, 'Ji' is not to be found in their own languages. It is borrowed from Hindi..."

"It's to show respect, isn't it?" Nomita had asked.

"Is it? It seems to me that the use of 'Ji' in their conversation is to show off their familiarity with the big names in the field of music. Familiarity that is real, or invented. It's actually name-dropping in another form, at least for these people."

Listening to the people behind her, she was reminded of that conversation. She took a quick peek at the speakers. They looked vaguely familiar. She smiled at them, to show that she was not someone who gave herself airs because she was a radio and TV performer and was seated beside two well known artistes. They smiled back in a controlled and distracted manner. Yes, thought Nomita, they conformed to type. They were earnest-looking young men, thin, with hair gelled – no, not gelled, *oiled* – down the sides of their heads.

In spite of the heat outside, the three of them were wearing printed cotton scarves. In Tamulbari, this type of scarf was worn not just as protection for the throat, but also as a kind of label, to show that they were a breed apart from the rest of uncreative humanity.They were probably singers, students of vocal classical music, whose ambitions were greater than their achievements. They had not yet realized what was already apparent to others, that they would never become the kind of stars that they aspired to be. They would be competent enough, and pleasant to listen to over the local radio or at small-town concerts. But the fame, the adulation, and the big money that they saw heaped on the leading lights in the field, their jet-setting, glamorous lifestyles, would never be theirs. At this stage of their lives, though, they still harboured dreams of making it big. They invested in expensive concert tickets in order to live up to their imagined reputations. In five years, maybe seven or eight, their heads would come down from the clouds, and their feet would touch terra firma again. Till then, the "Ji" syndrome would be in full flow on their lips.

At the other end of the spectrum, there were those who already had supercilious expressions on their faces. They were getting ready to damn the performance, preparing their phrases for later, when they would be discussing the recital on the way out of the hall. These were the ones who believed that to praise was in some way to concede that they were callow beginners merely. Their aim was to get listeners to believe that they knew so much about music that they were beyond being impressed by the artiste before them, so what if it was Kaushik Kashyap himself.

There were so many nuances, so many rules that one had to keep in mind when interacting with people who were into the practice of music in Tamulbari. It was dangerous, for instance, to become so mellow after listening to a recital, that one became unwary. To say, after being rendered incautious by the beauty of the music, to one's neighbour, "Now that was wonderful, really wonderful, wasn't it?" was to invite all kinds of attitude on one's unsuspecting head.

"Hm. Yes, not bad." Damning with faint praise was an art that many in Tamulbari had mastered. "She may even make it to a B in the All India Radio grade system."

Several rows to the right of the hall were reserved for the Press. Normally, during classical music concerts in Tamulbari, these rows were filled more with hope than actual journalists, print or electronic. Today, however, the seats were overflowing. Some camerapersons were standing in the aisles, their heavy equipment poised on their shoulders. Photographers were already fiddling with their cameras, in preparation for the moment when the maestro would begin his recital.

Besides, Nomita noticed, many of the town's glitterati were out in strength. To be Seen at a concert like Kaushik Kashyap's was part of their social calendar. Their presence at this concert also signalled Kaushik Kashyap's stature. Nomita would have thought that nobody less than Chaurasia or Grammy Awardee Vishwa Mohan Bhatt or Amjad Ali Khan or Ravi Shankar himself would be able to drag them away from their kitty parties or mahjong evenings. It was an indication of Kaushik Kashyap's fame and stature that he had been able to pull in this category of people to his concert.

Looking around, Nomita noticed people whom she knew by face, vaguely, but whom she had never seen at a classical music function here. There were plenty of music lovers, she noticed. But they were not the kind who usually attended a Hindustani Shastriya Sangeet event. There, in the corner, two rows behind hers, she saw a group of long haired young men. Their clothes – black Ts and slashed jeans – were at variance with what would have been expected at a place like this, when it was usual for the audience to dress "up" a bit, as befitting the formality of the occasion. Their faces, under their stubble, though, looked vaguely familiar. Nomita realized that she had seen them on the local TV channels quite often. They were members of Voodoo Child, a very popular rock band that, she had heard, was making a name for itself across the country.

"All kinds of people here," she observed to Guruma, the surprise she felt evident in her voice. "Even rock bands..."

Sandhya Senapati smiled. Down the line, Deepak Rathod, who had heard the comment, leaned forward and remarked, "Being a rock musician does not necessarily preclude an appreciation of other musical genres. But can the same be said of all those who practice Classical music? I wonder..."

She would certainly have expected Rahul to be here, commenting irreverently on the goings-on. She wished he were here. Maybe he was, hidden somewhere in the seething crowds. She began to take out her cellphone to contact him, but was interrupted by an announcement...

"Good evening. Welcome to this evening's programme of Shastriya Sangeet. May we request you to maintain silence, so that the solemnity of the music that we will be hearing is not broken? Also, please switch off your cellphones..."

Hastily, Nomita did as she was directed. In any case, she should be concentrating on the stage before her, on what her would-be spouse would be playing, rather than thinking of another person, even if that person was only Rahul. Her best friend. Still, she couldn't help wishing that he was here beside her right now, sitting in Guruji's place. And was Guruma wishing at this moment that she was sitting next to Deepak Rathod? Who knew? Nomita stole a glance up at Guruma, but nothing could be discerned in the habitual calm of her expression.

The Friends Club had decided against having preliminary artistes to precede Kaushik Kashyap. This was unusual, but practical. After all, people had come to listen to the maestro and it would be stretching their patience to make them wait. The curtains opened to an empty stage, decorated beautifully with out-of-season flowers. The raised dais, with its scattered bolsters, was covered with crisp sheets of pristine white.

The announcer told them that the President of the Friends Club himself would inaugurate the programme by lighting the lamp.

"No politician, now that's great," said Deepak Rathod, smiling down the line at the three people sitting to his right.

The lamp lighting was over in a few moments. The President made a brief speech, in which he mentioned that the show was for charity.

And, they would be pleased to learn, Kaushik Kashyap had waived his own fees, so that more money could be used for this laudable purpose.

Thunderous applause greeted this announcement. Nomita joined in politely.

"And now, ladies and gentlemen," said the announcer, as the President concluded his speech, "we present before you . . . ."

One by one, the accompanying artistes came in. Each was greeted with enthusiastic applause from the audience, and welcomed with garlands and gamosas by the Reception Committee. The loudest and most enthusiastic applause was, predictably, for Lucia, Kaushik Kashyap's foreign student, she who had generated, in the last thirty hours, almost as much talk and speculation as had her Guru. The people of Tamulbari, even those who had little interest in any kind of music, were gratified that a foreign lady had actually set foot in their little city. Yes, a true blue Mem, with green eyes and reddish hair, just like, Angelina Jolie! And so tall! Most of the men in the audience, and each and every one of the women present, were appreciably shorter than the beautiful foreign lady. Indeed, Lucia, though just a student of Kaushik Kashyap's, had, unknowingly, generated by her mere presence in this town, a spate of ticket sales. At the last minute, she had pulled in listeners who would otherwise not have stepped into a concert of Classical music at all. Now, looming over the President of the Kaushik Kashyap Nite Committee, but managing to look graceful nevertheless, she inclined her head and accepted the gamosa. A girl came up and, with some difficulty, garlanded her with marigolds and tuberoses.

One by one, the accompanists settled into their allotted places on the white-sheeted dais. Saurav Sen took his place behind the tablas to the right of the space kept for the main performer. Somewhat to the disappointment of the young men in the crowd, Lucia positioned herself towards the end of the white sheet, for after all she would be playing the taanpura at this show.

Nomita noticed, once more, the way Lucia walked, as she went across the stage to her seat. Her stride was easy and free, the span of the steps quite long. Nomita was aware that she herself took even smaller steps than usual when she was before an audience. There was a kind of roll to Lucia's gait that came from swinging her legs from the hip as she walked, a gait that was unencumbered by a personal history of cultural or sartorial bindings. With her auburn fall of hair framing her Madonna-like face, she looked stunning.

The Stage Management Committee had, Nomita noticed, been advised by someone who knew the requirements of classical musicians on stage. They had refrained from getting a fat, comfortable and soft mattress, and had instead left the raised dais under its white sheet covered only by a thin carpet. Too plump a covering would dampen the sound of the instruments, and make the playing of the tablas difficult. With a slight shock, Nomita realized that the two accompanists were wearing colour co-ordinated clothes. Maroon kurtas, with white salwars, set off by a long white dupatta in Lucia's case. The front buttons on their kurtas gleamed and glistened under the bright lights, adding to their glamour.

Another question entered Nomita's already teeming mind. Would Kaushik Kashyap co-ordinate his clothes to that of his accompanists? Okay, to Saurav Sen's too, but more to the point, to Lucia's clothes? If he did, they would look like a bride and bridegroom, posing before photographers at their wedding reception. Pushing aside that thought, Nomita tore her eyes away from the fascinating figure of Lucia, and focussed instead on Saurav Sen, who, she noticed, had put something on his face that made him look a good couple of shades fairer than what he had been last evening at their house. Make-up? Her mind baulked at the idea, but Nomita had to acknowledge that it wasn't talcum powder, the white stuff that male musicians often put on their faces before appearing on stage. Probably some light coloured cream that "brightened" the complexion.

Kamal Basu, the Secretary of what Nomita was beginning to think of as the Kaushik Kashyap Company Private Limited, was also requested to come up onto the stage. This was not exactly routine but perhaps the demands of hospitality required him to be felicitated too.

The audience clapped dutifully, though not with the same fervour as it had done for Lucia or even Saurav Sen.

In any case, the audience was waiting in an expectant hush for the Maestro himself to appear. The MC began to deliberately build up the tension, as he read out in a dramatic voice the many triumphs of the great Kaushik Kashyap himself. The names of his Gurus, his musical coups across the world, and how honoured they were to have him in their midst, in spite of his extremely busy schedule... Pride of place was given to his Grammy nomination, which took precedence in the list even over his Padma Shri. Finally, in a voice that, in its drama and controlled excitement implied a roll of drums and a crash of cymbals, he said with a flourish, "And so here before you, ladies and gentlemen, is the Great Maestro himself, the One, the Only... Kaaaausheeek Kashyaaaap!"

The sitarist entered the stage briskly, hands folded in a Namaste, smiling slightly. Both Lucia and Saurav stood up again and remained standing till Kaushik Kashyap was seated. The sitarist took his time to do this. He stood on the dais before his sitar, hands held aloft in a Namaste over his head, acknowledging the surging applause before him, acknowledging too, the standing ovation of the crowds as they got up spontaneously, to give this artiste the warmest welcome they could.

Should she stand up, too? Taking a quick look behind her, Nomita saw that everyone was on their feet. On their row, too, most of the people were standing and applauding enthusiastically. So should she get up? In other circumstances, she would certainly have done so. But now, she felt an awkwardness, a kind of shyness. Of course nobody in this place, except Guruma and maybe Guruji, knew about Kaushik Kashyap's true intention in coming to Tamulbari. It was only when Guruma and Guruji, and Deepak Rathod stood up, smiling and applauding, that Nomita, too, got to her feet.

The man certainly had a magnetic stage personality. He was dressed in purest white, the silk of his kurta gleaming with a pearly opalescence under the lights. The large ring winked at them, scattering the light into small rainbows every time he moved his hand. His hair was still pulled back in a ponytail, but from here, below the stage, it looked as though the man had a conventional haircut. He looked fresh and rested, and, she noticed thankfully, hadn't put make-up of any kind, or even talcum powder, on his face. Or perhaps he had, but so expertly that it wasn't apparent to the audience. The auditorium lights had been dimmed, but he indicated to the technicians in the well below the stage that they should be put on, so that he could see the audience. This gesture brought on an even stronger wave of applause as the hall grew bright again.

Garlanded now and with several gamosas on his hand, Kaushik took the microphone from the MC. "Thank you, thank you so much!" he said in impeccable English. After all, he was a new generation classical musician, one who toured the world, but more importantly, one whose mother was an English teacher herself. Indeed, he had had, Nomita remembered, his formal education at La Martiniere's, and held a degree in physics from Presidency too. No wonder his English was so good, uncharacteristically so for a classical musician.

She focussed on his accent because, by doing so, she almost succeeding in ignoring the strangeness of his voice, its thin, almost piping quality, which was accentuated by the microphone now. Nobody else in the auditorium, it seemed, was disturbed by this feature of his voice. All around her, with shining eyes and mouths slightly agape in adoration, people were hanging on to his every word.

"I am really touched by this reception. This is my first visit to your beautiful town, but I have heard so much about it from others, other musicians and also my friends, that I insisted on coming here when the opportunity arose. The audiences here are legendary, I have heard..." This bit was routinely spoken by all visiting performers, but the audience could always be depended upon to fall for the bait. They clapped vigorously now, flattered smiles lighting up their faces. "Yes, this is the first time I am here, but hopefully, not the last..."

Kaushik Kashyap spoke a few more words in similar vein, but the sudden upsurge of an even greater tumult in her mind made Nomita unable to concentrate. Not the last time he would be here? What did he mean? Obviously the hallfull of listeners took it to mean that he would be coming to Tamulbari again on a professional basis, to perform. The hall resounded with applause once more. But was there a hidden meaning to this, something that involved her?

By the time she had recovered her composure, Kaushik Kashyap had sat down before his instrument, and was running his fingers over it. In a moment, he was transformed from the crowd-pleasing performer, a person with a Private Secretary, to a serious devotee of Saraswati. His expression, though still pleasant, was unsmiling now. His concentration was totally on his instrument. Nomita noticed the built-in microphone on it which added a rich dimension to the sound. A few last micro-turns of the tuning knobs to adjust the pitch, and he was ready to play.

Lucia, on the taanpura, was already strumming its strings. The two electronic taanpuras before him hummed a steady drone. A hush fell on the crowd. One by one, the last rustlings of paper, the final coughs, the concluding whispers, died out. The performer's concentration, and the drone of the perfectly tuned taanpuras, created an ambience that was ageless, dating back to those times before proscenium stages, before lighting and sound systems, before the advent of paying audiences. The music spoke its own language, calling out to something within each listener.

It was Marwa that he played first, that contemplative melody that never failed to induce a sense of pensive thoughtfulness in even the most restive, or uninformed audience. It was a difficult Raag to perform. But when well done, the Raag could bring calm to the high strung, and peace to the edgy. Within minutes of the opening Alaap, Kaushik Kashyap's music entered the minds of the listeners.

Gradually, he built up the tempo. It was a full fledged recital that he was giving them, thought Nomita, not one of those truncated ones that artistes from the metros were prone to offer, cursorily, when they came to small places like theirs. If he had not been performing free, Kaushik Kashyap would have earned every paisa of his no doubt astronomical fee. All the years of mental and physical discipline and toil that had honed his art to this level of perfection were apparent in his every stroke, in every carefully-thought-out phrase and note-sequence. They were coming spontaneously from him, yet they carried behind them the weight of a huge amount of musical thought.

After half an hour or so, Saurav Sen joined him grandly, with a complexly patterned nine-cycle flourish that was greeted by the audience with enthusiasm. As both artistes settled down to explore the intricacies of rhythm, tempo and melody, it became apparent that they were very much attuned to each other's thinking. Each kept his individuality intact, yet each bowed to, and showed keen respect for the personality and music of the other. Saurav Sen was an accompanying artiste, in the sense that the tabla player always followed the main player. Yet Kaushik Kashyap, Nomita noticed with a kind of happiness, or was it pride, gave the tabla player every courtesy, even while always, indisputably himself remaining the primary artiste.

Little rivulets of melody within the main stream danced independently to their own beat cycles, coming down, each time, on the Sam, the first and most definite beat of the cycle. She registered Kaushik's flashing hand over the body of the sinuously curved sitar, its gleaming strings arching to keep up with the kind of melody that he was coaxing out of its body. The diamond on his finger was a blur of light now, but even then, it was less incandescent than his face. His hair was a halo as he approached the very pinnacle of melodic and rhythmic climax. And yet, even at this pace, there was present, contradictorily, a sense of calm. It was not frenzied, this pace, though it could well have deteriorated into agitation.

It was evident that now there was no thought in his mind other than the music he was making. Kaushik Kashyap's prowess made each listener respond just the way he wanted them to. Through his music, he manipulated the feelings, the emotions of the hallful of people before them, urging them to moods of tranquillity or grandeur, of passion or romance. It awed Nomita to think that he could do this so easily, without effort, and seeming, always, to be unaware of the effect of his music on the minds of the people before him. Or perhaps "manipulated" was too strong a word. Like other musicians, he was perhaps unaware now of his effect on the minds and emotions of others.

Finally, in a complex cycle of twenty seven beats repeated nine times, the Raag was brought to its conclusion. Applause, deafening and whole hearted, erupted all around Nomita. People were on their feet again as they were freed from the spell, clapping, then roaring out their approval.

On stage, Kaushik Kashyap and Saurav Sen mopped the perspiration off their streaming faces, smiling. Nomita, freed too from the spell, glanced at both of them, then, inevitably to Lucia. Throughout the recital, the student had kept a steady drone going on her instrument, never once allowing her own personality to intrude, not even with a well-positioned "wah" or appreciative "Kya baat." Indeed, it was a measure of Kaushik Kashyap's success that even that part of the audience who had been initially lured to the concert by the presence of a "foreign artiste" on stage had forgotten all about her during the recital. So, too, had Nomita.

Now, however, Kaushik Kashyap turned and smiled at Lucia. It was, Nomita saw, a smile that any Guru could give a student while on stage. A professional kind of look, which had in it an element of paternal feeling, too. But no, wait, was there more in his glance than fatherly sentiment? Hm.

A Khamaj Dhun filled the hall with a different kind of emotion. From the prayer-like meditativeness of the Marwa, the emotions in the minds of the listeners changed to that of playful romance. But there were layers in his Dhun, just as there had been layers in his Marwa. At one and the same time, Kaushik Kashyap played at different levels, appealing both to the cognoscenti and the uninitiated. Every note, every phrase, was dripping with "Ras," that indefinable quality that was a blend of perfect tune, pitch, and evocativeness. The air was now redolent with the wistfulness and lighthearted romance of the Khamaj.

It struck Nomita again that adept musicians were experts at manipulating the emotions and sentiments of their listeners. Kaushik

Kashyap seemed to play as knowledgeably on the heartstrings of the audience as he did on the strings of the sitar itself. Would this skill spill over to other aspects of his life too? The thought came unbidden to her mind, surprising her with its suddenness. Or was she mixing up the two Kaushiks in her own mind – the one who was here as a star performer and the one who had visited their home last evening?

Another Dhun followed, a lighter melody based on Des. Romantic, but full of longing. This was the Raag of separation, of Viraha, and also a rainy season Raag. There was now a poignancy in his phrases, reviving in his listeners long-dormant memories of lost loves, bitter-sweet pangs. Was the performer feeling the same way as were his listeners? Nomita wondered. Was he then a romantic at heart? Or was he just a consummate artiste, a master who knew exactly which shruti, which microtone and which grace note evoked a specific feeling in his listeners' minds? How could she find out during this brief visit?

"Thank you, thank you so much." He spoke to the audience as he retuned a few strings swiftly for the next leg of his programme. "What a wonderful audience you are, you make me want to keep on playing..."

Manipulation, skilled PRO or not, it didn't matter. The hall erupted in a roar of applause. Lucia, behind him, leaned forward and said something in his ear. What was it? Certainly the posture had an intimacy that seemed to exclude all else around them. What could it have been? She noticed that Kaushik responded to whatever she had said with a smile. He leaned back and said something to her, inaudible to the rest of them though the mike was still on before him. Of course it was probably something as mundane as "The taanpura needs to be retuned, will you do it or shall I?" But why smile while saying it? In any case an Indian student would never have taken the liberty. He would have proffered the instrument deferentially to the Guru to retune, respecting the etiquette that mandated the Guru tuning the instrument rather than the student. And of course no Indian student would presume this level of familiarity with any Guru on stage.

Her own Guru was commenting on the recital to her husband

and friend and student in her usual generous way. "Wonderful, truly wonderful. He's moved streets ahead of any other performer I know. His technical mastery is something else, but even that, I would say, would be maybe something to be expected in a man at the prime of his youth. He has the vigour, the energy. But I never expected such tenderness from him, such an emotive level of playing. And his thinking! Unique, yet absolutely uncompromisingly in keeping with the Shastras...!" Nomita had never heard such effusiveness coming from her teacher.

Guruji nodded. In his beautiful, low pitched voice, he added, "Yes, he's improved tremendously since the last time I heard him, at the Sawai Gandharva Music Festival in Pune, I think it was. Though he was amazing then, too..."

Leaning across, Sandhya Senapati said, "Deepak, what do you think?"

The man turned to her and smiled, including both Guruji and Nomita in his glance. His even teeth flashed whitely against the dark of his skin. "I found his tunefulness quite wonderful. After all that's the basis of all melody, isn't it? The rest of it, the structure of the Raag and the superstructure of the emotive or thinking process comes later. Though his grip on the concepts of each melody embodied in the Raag is highly impressive, too."

Nomita was surprised. He spoke like a musician himself. Perhaps her expression spoke her thoughts. Guruma, smiling, said, "Deepak's understanding of music sometimes leaves me surprised, too."

And where, wondered Nomita, remembering the conversation at Jhankaar the other day, where did that leave Guruji? But Tridib Barua still looked his usual quiet self, as he glanced first at his wife and then at her friend, nodding in agreement with what they said.

People were sending up little slips of paper to the stage with requests for particular items. Somebody wanted a Bhajan, somebody a Piloo Dhun, another wanted the melody that had won him the Grammy nomination. Good-humouredly, Kaushik Kashyap played the Bhajans and the Dhuns, saying with a smile, "Sorry, for the Grammy nominated melody, you will have to buy the CD! Or maybe

I'll come here another time to play it for you! This is a classical music Nite..." he nodded expressively to the banner behind him..."so please, not this time!"

The man certainly had perfect stage etiquette. Many artistes were not aware of how each word, each gesture, contributed so much to the total performance, even above and beyond the recital itself.

"I would have thought somebody would have asked for a Malhar?" he asked during a pause. "It's the rainy season, after all." He paused, and added impishly, "You are safe with me. I promise I won't bring in floods with my Malhars..."

The crowd roared its approval, as though this was a rock concert, and not a classical music one. Laughing, Kaushik began a short piece of several monsoon Raags strung together. Megh Malhar, Sur Malhar, even the more sober Miyan ki Malhar. They evoked the patter of rain, the gusts of moisture-laden wind. It was welcome, this rain that he suggested so skilfully, bringing relief to the parched land, and bringing the soaring temperatures down to bearable levels.

There were more requests after this. The audience was certainly getting its money's worth, and more. The concert, billed for about two hours, had gone on for over three, and still the audience was clamouring for more. More Dhuns, some melodies based on river songs from Bengal, even a short kirtan followed.

Another pause. "I am having a wonderful time. Are you?" he asked, redundantly.

"Yes yes yes" chanted the crowd, lapping it all up. Nomita tried to imagine Guruma or Guruji interacting with the crowds in this manner, and failed. Indeed, she could not even imagine herself doing this. Soon the man would be taking off his kurta and throwing it into the audience, like a rock star. She wished, again, she could share this thought, uncharitable but amusing, with Rahul.

Once more, the sounds of the sitar filled the auditorium. It was a Raagmala this time, a garland of different Raags, strung together expertly on the cord of a basic melody. This, they realized, was going to be the final piece, for the first lines of the Raagmala were based on Raag Bhairavi, the melody that signaled the end of the programme.

It was a polite way of saying, "No more, this is the last bit of my programme today."

She noticed his face, his body language. Along with the changes in the tenor of his music, his physical aspect, too, had altered during the course of his recital. Like all communicators who used any kind of performing art as a medium, Kaushik, too, used his body to add to the dialogue he was creating between his audience and himself. Even though, as a sitarist, he held a heavy instrument, he did not allow that fact to hamper the use of his hands to add drama to his recital, or to make a point. During the Marwa, his gestures had been much more controlled. But as the mood of the music became lighter, and the rhythmic cycles livelier, his gestures became more flamboyant. He continued to sit in the uncompromisingly classical stance of the sitar player. One leg was tucked under his seat, the other bent in such a way that it provided a resting place for the instrument itself, with the sitar at the prescribed angle across his body. Indeed, the fact that he was still comfortable in this demanding posture, with none of the shifting and fidgeting that one saw in lesser performers, spoke in itself of the long hours of riyaz that he had put in over the decades. But now he allowed his torso to move forward a bit as he, along with his tabaliya approached Sam, the starting point of each cycle, and its climax. It was a graceful motion, hardly perceptible unless one looked out for it. But it showed his one-ness with the rhythm and tune that was flowing out of his mind, through his fingers, to the instrument, and through its strings, to the minds of the audience. He allowed, whether consciously or unconsciously, his hands, too, to become more expressive, more dramatic. The diamond swooped and glittered in arcs as his arm flew up just after landing on the Sam after a particularly intricate sequence of several cycles, set to complex beats.

The audience, released from the seriousness of the previous pieces, and now relaxed, prepared themselves for this final change in the tenor of the recital. It was, unashamedly, a lighter piece, with bits of contemporary airs from folk tunes, even popular hit songs, swimming in and out of the sea of melody.

The two of them, Kaushik Kashyap and Saurav Sen, were enjoying themselves now, smiling and nodding as they playfully matched melody to rhythm, tempo to tune. Their body language was now much more flamboyant, their heads nodded in unison as they arrived at the Sam in each cycle. Kaushik, she noticed, was playing up to the crowd, now. His hair fell in curly locks around his head, swivelling enticingly with each swing and nod. With a sense of detachment, she noticed, too, that he held his pose for a split second longer than strictly necessary every time he returned to the main melody on the Sam. The ring sparkled as he ran his fingers through his loose curls. Was that, too, a calculated pose? Maybe. She glanced at the two artistes who flanked her. They would never do any of this during their own recitals, but they were smiling, enjoying the music and appreciating what Kaushik Kashyap was doing to the garland of melody.

Nomita's mind wandered now, as it had not done in the earlier parts of the recital. She glanced around and behind her. If, suppose, the next time this artiste came to Tamulbari to perform, it was as a son-in-law of the town, what would her, Nomita's own reaction to it be? Would she look around the audience with so much anxiety that she would not be able to actually appreciate any of the music herself? Would she look around triumphantly every time he landed unerringly on the Sam, as though it was she, in some way, who was responsible for the exactitude of his rhythmic exposition? Or would she morph into one of those obnoxious Star Spouses who put on airs and demanded all kinds of comforts from the poor hassled organizers wherever she went? A fan placed just so before her. A flowerpot that formed part of the stage décor removed because it was interfering with her peripheral vision.

Ha, that would be fun.

She was aware that she was smiling, but that was all right. All around her, people were listening with smiles on their faces now. She wondered if Kaushik Kashyap was aware of the way his audiences responded to him. There was a palpable bonding between the man on the stage and the people in the auditorium. Of course all artistes, to be successful, needed to connect with their audiences. Guruma,

Guruji, even she herself... It was this ability to take audiences along as they performed that formed the core of a successful performance. But with Kaushik Kashyap, it was something more. Much more. It was as though he had created a bamboo bridge, deceptively fragile, unbelievably strong, that swayed in the storms of melodies around it, yet held firm, allowing communication between both ends.

And then it was over. Huge rounds of applause again, as the three on the stage stood up with deep namastes. It was on this scene that the curtains fell on the Kaushik Kashyap Nite.

13

A bomb dropped on Tamulbari's musical world: Kaushik Kashyap had changed his plans!

"He's going to stay on a full day longer than scheduled, do you know?" said one of the earnest, scarf-wrapped students of music to another. His air of triumph at being In the Know about the plans of the maestro were, on this occasion, overlaid with genuine astonishment at this sudden change of itinerary .

"Can you imagine?" A heavily made up middle-aged woman asked the paunchy man by her side. "A busy man like that, deciding to stay on in this place. I wonder what he sees here?" Mentally, she made up her mind to upgrade a couple of notches this town in which she had to unfortunately live.

The announcement had come over the mikes after the curtains had come down, the announcer sounding surprised and gratified in equal measure. The artiste would stay on longer than planned. But no reason for this extension of stay had been given. Certainly, no extra musical programme was planned.

The organizers of the Kaushik Kashyap Nite were in a tizzy. Cancelling tickets, getting new ones, re-booking the Sona hotel rooms for some more time, past the usual checkout time. Of course it was a coup of sorts, something they could talk about with boastful airs for a long time to come. But the work that was involved in re-organizing the man's schedules was not going to be easy.

Nomita focussed on the crowds around her so that she would not have to think of the implications of this change in Kaushik Kashyap's plans. She waved and smiled to several people she knew who were filing out of the auditorium, and murmured, over and over, "Yes, fantastic, wasn't it?" to the vaguely familiar faces that overtook her.

But the question could not be avoided once she got home. Her parents were already there, having returned immediately after the show, while her own return in Sandhya Senapati's car, had been delayed because so many people had wished to speak to them as they came out.

"I loved the way he played, what do you think?" asked Shikha Sharma, almost as soon as Nomita entered. She was not an acknowledged connoisseur of classical music, and she was therefore quite unselfconscious about commenting on a performance by such a respected maestro in such lay terms. In any case, this sentence was just a way to get the conversation going, the main thrust of which was going to be,

"So, what do you think? Made up your mind yet?"

But of course she couldn't ask her daughter that question so baldly, not right now, though she was longing to. Instead, after a few exclamations all around about the fine performance she asked, "He's going to stay on one more day. Well, for a few more hours, actually, in spite of all the hype and excitement in the hall about how he's extended his stay for a whole day. Instead of going by the morning flight, he's taking the evening one. "

Nomita looked questioningly at her mother. "Yes, he called, asking whether you had been at the concert. It seems your cell was switched off? Yes well, I told him of course you were, sitting right there in front with your Gurus, in the seats provided by him. I think he had rather expected you to go around backstage after the performance. You know, to congratulate him, or something."

It was of course the done thing, an expected ritual. Members of the audience often went backstage after the concert to felicitate the artistes, and show their appreciation. But it had not occurred to her to do so, firstly because neither Guruma nor Guruji or even Deepak Rathod had seemed at all inclined to take part in that ritual. In any case, she would have been far too self-conscious to do anything of the sort. But it seemed he had expected to see her there. Hm. What did that signify?

But there wasn't time to ponder on that now. Shikha Sharma was still talking. "Anyway, he wants to know if he can take you out tomorrow..."

She looked at her mother, dumbstruck.

"Where?" she managed to ask finally.

Horrifying visions of herself and Kaushik Kashyap sitting in total silence opposite each other in one of Tamulbari's trying-hard-to-be-posh eateries leapt into her mind. The word that the great sitarist was actually eating out in their town would be out, and soon newspaper and TV journalists would be surrounding them as they sat with their momos and chowmein, trying to look pleasant and happy as they stared at the lenses bristling in all directions. She felt her mind going blank with shock at the picture that rose before her.

"I don't know. Why don't you call up and ask yourself?" her mother said with an edge of irritation in her voice. The arranging of one's daughter's marriage was always a stressful affair, no doubt, but in this case it was compounded many times by the fact that the "boy" in question was such a well-known personality. "It was you he wanted to speak to, not me, naturally."

"Okay okay, sorry for asking," soothed Nomita. "Did he give his number, or do I go through the hotel PBX or switchboard or something...?"

"No, better not do that. I do have his number somewhere...yes here it is." She produced a slip of paper and added contritely, "Sorry, I shouldn't have snapped at you like that. But seeing the kind of effect he has on his audience has unsettled me a bit, I think. I mean, I hadn't realized he was...so good. Such a star. So popular, so, so *idolised,* yes I think that's what I mean, by the people." She patted her daughter's arm kindly, and added, "He seems a very nice person, though, doesn't he? As an individual, not a star, or performer. Not that I'm putting pressure on you or anything..." she clarified hastily, "I'm just stating my opinion, that's all, independent of what yours may be..."

Pradeep Sharma, audience to this dialogue between the female members of his family, chortled. "Your mother's being careful, Nomi. She wants you to make up your own mind, she doesn't want to influence you in any way! Not that you would be, would you?" His laugh was kindly, but his words were perceptive.

Nomita only smiled in reply.

Minutes later, on the phone with Kaushik Kashyap, Nomita felt a sense of unreality as his thin voice said, "Yes, I was looking for you. I didn't see you in the auditorium, actually I hardly ever see anybody or anything around me when I'm playing. But later. I was looking for you later."

How could a girl, a small town girl at that, not feel gratified? He wasn't giving her much of a chance to keep a level head.

"But I was thinking, could we go out somewhere tomorrow for a bit?"

"What did you have in mind?" She did sound stiff, even to herself, but it was too late to recall the sentence.

"Well, I was told that you have a beautiful river here. Maybe a boat ride? It can be organized, I believe."

"Of course."

Times, meet-up details were discussed and finalized. It was only after putting down the phone that Nomita remembered her schedule for the next day. She had classes in the afternoon with the children of Shishu Kalyan. A twinge of regret made her wonder whether she should reschedule the trip, maybe cancel it. He hadn't asked if she was otherwise engaged.

But of course this was a special occasion. So perhaps it was okay for him to assume that she would drop everything and come with him for the river cruise he had suggested.

His Khamaj dhun played in her mind, its melodic phrases repeating themselves as she got ready for bed. Intermittently, she tried to call Rahul, but a recorded voice on his cellphone kept repeating that he was out of range. Where could he be? Out of range? She wondered whether she should ring up his parents in their home to find out, but decided against it. In any case, she wanted to sleep.

But it would be nice, she thought, if Rahul could come along on the boat ride tomorrow. After all, his people would surely be there, Saurav Sen and Kamal Basu and the beauteous Lucia. She should have a friend with her, too....

She fell asleep with the thought of Rahul, and the melody of Khamaj on her mind.

What should she wear? Sari, mekhela sador, salwar kameez? Remembering the other boat ride with Rahul and his friends, she decided to dress in Western clothes. She looked different in the mirror, she thought, much slimmer than she normally did in her Indian wear, either in the layers of the sari or the fullness of the mekhela sador or the volume of the kurtas and salwars. She was pleased with her image, and decided to let her hair loose. This was her one act of rebelliousness. She was a small town girl and probably the jetsetting maestro was well aware of the effect that his music, his glamorous lifestyle, would have on her. True, no doubt the effect was unintentional, but how could the adulation, the hype that surrounded him always, fail to impress a mofussil mind like hers? What chance did she have, she with her mediocre music, and small town upbringing, of refusing a Boy as Suitable as Kaushik Kashyap? Was it fair, this Seeing? How could she refuse a man like this?

Had this been his intention, then? To present himself in the best possible light, so that there would be no question of a refusal? "Small town girl refuses Kaushik Kashyap's proposal of marriage." How terrible the headlines would read. People would wonder.

No, of course she was over-analyzing.

Her mind was in tumult, but she greeted the man himself quite calmly. He was waiting for her at the jetty. He was dressed in his usual kurta pyjama, the embroidered off-whites looking cool under the hot sun. It occurred to Nomita that perhaps he never wore Western clothes at all. They would probably be less suitable for his small frame than these Indian clothes that lent an air of romance and glamour to his personality. Her small act of rebelliousness went unnoticed, it seemed. At least he made no comment, and his smile remained untouched by any doubts about the sartorial tastes of this potential bride.

They were not alone on the boat. She had not expected to be, for he would have to bring his entourage with him.

"Didn't see you last night!" exclaimed Saurav Sen (cheerfully) and Kamal Basu (smilingly/frowningly) as she came up the gangplank. "But of course I was there. Right up there in the second row, with my Guru." She thought it would be redundant to add "You were great," and so instead she said, "We are so proud of our river here. Do you like it?"

"Beautiful, beautiful, I feel like I am back in the land of my parents, East Bengal that is now Bangladesh, you know," said Saurav Sen, jovially. He leaned over the railings to take in the vast expanse of the river, and began to sing a Bhatiali, the river song from Bengal, softly.

Hiding her momentary panic with what she hoped was an appreciative smile, Nomita listened to the tabla player. He was certainly good, and in this ambience, with its wide riverscape fringed by low hills, his strong, tuneful though untrained voice sounded as though he really might be a boatman poling his way upstream to his home, making his journey less tedious through melody.

But no, it was going to be okay, she would not be asked to sing, at least not today, not on this boat. No need to panic. These were all professional musicians, and they knew, perhaps, that another professional or semi-professional musician like her, would not be comfortable bursting into a song on demand.

There weren't too many people on the boat. Just the artistes from Kolkata, and a few of the Organizing Committee members of the Kaushik Kashyap Nite. Apparently they had been waiting for her to board the little boat, for she felt the engines throb beneath her, and the boat glide out from the jetty.

"Let's go up, to the top…the view is great there. Lucia is there too…" Kaushik turned to his secretary, and asked, "Coming up, Kamalda?"

"No no, you go ahead, it's first-class for us here…" the man answered with good cheer. He looked less hassled now, though the worry line between his brows still remained.

The ladder going up to the small top deck was definitely difficult to negotiate. But Kaushik Kashyap, though solicitous, did not extend a hand to help her up. "Careful, I hope you can climb up... we can stay down here if it's a problem..." he fussed. But perhaps he was too traditional to help a woman he barely knew, up a ladder on a rolling boat by steadying her with his hand. Even though the woman might, one day, be his bride.

But she managed, aided by her more practical clothes today. Kaushik followed her up the ladder to the top deck. She noticed, as she waited for him to come up beside her, that he placed his hands with unusual care on the railings guarding the ladder. Well, of course. It would be second nature to an instrumentalist like him, a person who earned his living by his hands, and indeed, owed his very identity to them. Doubtless they were heavily insured, as was the norm these days with performing artistes. Even a small cut on the ball of his finger would mean the cancellation of several concerts, shows that had been scheduled weeks, months ahead of time. His hands were beautiful as they rested on the rail of the ladder, with the winking ring catching the bright sunlight all around them. Today, too, he wore the mizrab, the cage of wires on his little finger, the ring-plectrum that created a waterfall of melody from the strings when they were stirred. She wondered what it would feel like to have those hands on hers. Would that ring of wires on his little finger bite into her flesh when he held her, perhaps?

She glanced quickly at his face. Had he read her thoughts? She caught his gaze. Climbing the last rung, he came to stand beside her with a smile.

It was truly beautiful here. It was just a small space, really, enclosed by a railing, with a few chairs scattered here and there, and a canopy overhead. But the view of the river that was now spread out all around them was quite breathtaking. The fresh wind on her face had an exhilarating feel.

Lucia was standing at the railing, with her face to the wind too. Her auburn locks flew around her face as she turned around with a smile when they came up. "How beautiful it is here!" she said, the accented English adding to her allure. She tried to add some more praises, but apparently her vocabulary was not up to it. Shrugging her shoulders, she left it to her hands to do the talking. They made complementary gestures while she said, "So... so... you know..."

"Yes, isn't it?" agreed Kaushik Kashyap.

Nomita returned her smile, she hoped warmly. It was difficult to feel very cordial now, at this moment. She immediately felt dowdy again next to Lucia's Pre-Raphaelite beauty, though it was the Italian who was dressed in traditional Indian clothes, green this time, to match her eyes, she supposed.

Surely now Lucia would see that she was a kabab mein haddi, a hindrance to a tête-à-tête between two almost betrothed people, and move gracefully down the ladder, leaving her and Kaushik Kashyap together? But what would they talk about in that case? At least now, between the three of them, the conversation moved forward at a normal pace, though running along predictable and un-scintillating lines. The beauty of the surroundings, the wonderful Tamulbari audience, how sad they were to be leaving this place, but what to do, they had to catch a flight to Tokyo that very night.

That very night?

Yes, that very night. "Actually, I've told Ma to pack a case of fresh clothes for me and send it on to the airport through one of my students there. I'll reach Kolkata airport at about nine at night, and the Japan flight leaves at two in the morning. No point going home, is there?" Kaushik Kashyap smiled, the locks escaping from his ponytail adding to his charm.

Once more, Nomita could not fail to be impressed by the weight of meaning of his postponed departure. She wondered what she should say to acknowledge the fact that in spite of being a small-town girl, she was aware of its significance, without sounding crass. But while she was hesitating and wondering, the moment passed, and then it was too late to say anything. In any case, the foremost question in her mind was: Would Lucia be going too?

"Sauravda and Kamalda will be going, too?" she asked, instead.

"Yes, of course. Lucia too," he added, as though he had read her mind.

The Botticelli painting smiled. With the hills behind her and the blue of the river all around, she did look like Venus rising from the Sea, though dressed quite respectably in green, concealing clothes.

"I'll be moving on after that, back to Milano," she added.

"You travel a lot, don't you?" asked Nomita, addressing Kaushik Kashyap but including Lucia in her question.

His long fingers grasped the railings of the boat as he leaned out to look at the water below. With smooth, confident strides that were in no way hampered by her flowing clothes, Lucia went to his other side, echoing his gestures and actions as she too, peered down at the water.

"It's the modern musician's fate, isn't it?" he asked, straightening up and looking at her now. His eyes were almost the same level as hers, just an inch or so higher, maybe, even though she was wearing flat heeled shoes. But his shoulders were broad, an instrumentalist's shoulders, and his long slender, fingers could only belong to a tabla player, a sitarist or sarodist. "Previously, right up till my Guru's Guru's generation, maybe, it was the other way round. The musician never travelled so much, because he was supported by a King, or a Prince, or at the very least, a zamindar. He would just need to go to the court, at times, to present his songs. I have heard my Guru speak of those long ago times when all *his* Guru had to do for days on end was sit at home and do intense riyaz. On the first of the month he would present himself to the treasury officer and draw the money he was entitled to. And when he did sit down at the court, with his accompanists, his patron would always enquire solicitously about his health, his mood, his mizaaz, before requesting, in the most courteous terms, for a particular Raag to be played, if he felt upto it. These days, of course, it's just the opposite. Nobody asks about the performer's mizaaz anymore. In fact, it's we, the performers, who have to take into account every nuance of the audience's mizaaz, its mood. We have to be expert psychologists, you know..."

Flanked by two women, the disciple and the practically-betrothed, it was perhaps inevitable that Kaushik Kashyap the maestro should speak as well as he did. The refreshing breeze whipped away his slight voice almost as soon as it was out of his mouth, but the words were enough to put an adulatory look on Lucia's face. She glanced at Nomita, perhaps to include her in the swell of emotion that she was no doubt feeling. But though Nomita was impressed with Kaushik's words, Lucia's expression fuelled irritation instead. In any case, she herself could hardly be classified in the same category as a simple student. All right, a beautiful foreign Venus-type woman, but a beginner-student nevertheless. She began to feel combative, and argumentative.

"But then today's musicians, at least the successful ones, are much better off than those of the past, aren't they?" she asked, careful to keep her voice low. Certainly her voice, a trained classical singer's voice, was much better than either of her companions' on this top deck. Without being snooty about it, she was confident that being musicians, they would be aware of its aesthetic appeal. "I mean, even those Kings and Princes and Nawabs and whatnots who had a retinue of musicians, even for them, it was more a status symbol than a love of music, actually, wasn't it? I've heard it said that many of them kept their musicians' quarters filled up in the same way that they filled up their harems. If there was a famous beauty, or a renowned singer, the potentate would not rest till he had the beauty and the musician in his power. The beauty, if lucky, would receive the King's favours once a year, maybe less, till age got to her. And the musician, if lucky, would get his salary at regular intervals. But usually the ruler would be too pre-occupied with matters of state, and wars, and famine, and pestilence, to actually listen much to him. At the most, he would be brought out and flaunted when important visitors came to Court..."

There, I've offended him, and I may as well get off the boat now, because this arrangement has gone as far as it's going to get, she thought. She noticed Lucia's look of faintly scandalized shock, but couldn't bring herself to glance around at Kaushik Kashyap.

His laugh, though, came quite readily, surprising her and nipping her combativeness in the bud, just as she was beginning to warm up to her topic. "That's a thought," he said. "Those Kings and Nawabs may have been at par with a company executive type of today, who attends a Classical music concert for its snob value, though he understands nothing." He put his arm around Nomita's shoulder, and added, "That's a new idea. We tend to glamourise the past so much, we often forget the tumultuous history that this music has gone through. We should perhaps acknowledge the fact that the music today owes almost as much to the revivalists of the twentieth century, Pandit Bhatkhande and D.V. Paluskar, as it does to those numerous musicians and theorists who developed the form over centuries."

She tried to keep her mind on what he was saying, focussing on his words so that she could pretend that his arm around her shoulder, his faintly cologne-scented proximity, was of no significance to her.

"The reach, the global interest in our music today is something that the Ustads and Pandits of the past could never have dreamed of," he added. "Yes, perhaps you have something there. Musicians may be having it better today, at least in some ways, than they ever did in the past."

"Technology. It's all because of technology," she said, remembering a conversation she had had with Rahul some time ago. The hand had been withdrawn, making it easier for her to think. "The voice, the instruments, they have such a finite reach. It's because of technology that we can amplify their range so much, so that audiences around the world can now listen to them. Through CDs, through satellite radio, electronic media... And even on a stage now. When performances were held in open fields, the sheer power and strength and stamina needed to "throw" one's voice was quite enormous. Even the training was different...voices had to have strength, in order to be heard by the person sitting in the last row of the makeshift auditorium in an open field. They had to compete with the sound of mooing cows in the next field, of people coming and going. But today we demand, and get, silence in the halls. But Indian music was never performed to a silent audience in the past, was it?"

"No, you're right, it never was. Our audiences were always noisy in their appreciation, quite definite in their dislikes..."

"And instruments. Is it a coincidence that instruments like the santoor, with their soft and silvery tones, have only gained popularity after the microphone became compulsory in all performances? The built-in mike you have in your sitar, now that has changed the style of playing so much. And in fact women vocalists - they could never come to the fore when power, rather than softness, was the pre-requisite for a good performance. In addition to social restrictions, of course."

Was she talking too much, that too holding forth with opinions that were contrary to wisdom received about the history of Classical music?

But Kaushik Kashyap had taken up the thread of the conversation, and was developing it in his own way.

"Actually, technology has helped women musicians immensely, in more ways than one. Do you know that when the gramophone companies began their studio recordings decades ago, the established South Indian musicians did not go to record their music. They felt it beneath them to do so. They said that they did not want to be heard in the barber shops and the marketplace, which was what would happen if their recordings were to be played over the radio. It was the Devadasis, the temple musicians, who seized this opportunity, and went in to record their music, which they had been traditionally performing anyway."

"Devadasis. Yes, women have always been more practical and pragmatic. Even though the Devadasis believed they were wedded to God, and in fact were offered to God by their families, it was good that they made the most of this earthly opportunity. No ego hassles, either," she laughed.

His stories were quite interesting, she noted, though so far they had only talked of music. In the meantime, she felt a certain satisfaction that the role of the Botticelli painting in this conversation had been a dumb one. Perhaps it was time to be polite?

"Don't you think so, Lucia?" she asked.

The adoring look was still in place, and the student said, predictably, "Guruji always has such interesting ideas."

Guruji? It was *her* idea, well Rahul's actually. Though, to do him credit, Kaushik Kashyap seemed to have a more open mind than did most classical musicians, many of whom were notorious for not being receptive to new thoughts.

14

It wasn't till the next morning that Shikha Sharma, awkward but determined in her role as Mother of Girl Being Seen, asked Nomita the expected question: Well, what did you think?

After returning the previous afternoon from the boat ride, Nomita had behaved in such a "normal" manner that even her mother, looking searchingly at her face throughout dinner, had failed to detect any sign of her daughter's preferences. She hadn't returned starry eyed, in a pink cloud of romance, but she hadn't been annoyed, or irritable, or even pensive, either. True, she had always known that her daughter was a level-headed girl. Indeed, her interest in classical music, and frequent stage appearances had probably deepened this tendency of Nomita's to be a steady girl. She was not known to flights of excitability, and was, Shikha sometimes thought, just this side of being staid. Indeed, in temperament, Shikha sometimes thought, her daughter was closer to her Guru, the tranquil Sandhya Senapati, than to her mother.

Now, waiting for her daughter to answer, Shikha looked at her as a stranger might. Medium height, curves in the right place. Not rail thin like some of her own senior students in school. Not size zero, but well-proportioned. She knew her daughter felt fat next to some girls of her own generation, but that was only in the mind. Long black hair that fell, straight and gleaming, down her shoulders, to her back. Her most striking features were her hair and eyes. It was as though all the vibrancy, the restless energy of youth had been gathered from all parts of her being and were now concentrated in her eyes. Her movements were calm. Her hands, with their long, tapering artistic fingers were rarely used to gesture, or gesticulate. It was only while she was performing on stage that her left hand moved in accordance with the swaras and taans and meends she was executing. Not like that Italian girl's hands the other night, who used her hands to such striking effect when she spoke. Perhaps she should have been a dancer, instead of a sitar player. She was beautiful, that girl, with such expressive hands and body language. But then, Shikha observed with a dispassionate eye, Nomita had a way about her that was quite eye-catching too. Graceful, controlled, but hinting at hidden depths.

Nomita replied, deliberately contrary, "Great! What a wonderful artiste! It was a fantastic experience, his show. Really, he's more than lived up to his reputation."

Her mother rolled her eyes but said patiently, "... And?"

"And. Yes, that's the big issue." Nomita's voice and expression were both sober now. "Actually, there's nothing to say No to, is there?" she said reflectively.

"So... ? I mean what will I tell Tirna?"

Nomita's thoughts seemed to be following their own line. "A fantastic musician such as Kaushik Kashyap - one can see the brilliance of his future. In fact his present is already brilliant. He's well on his way to becoming well known all over the world, isn't he? No wonder his mother is being so careful about who her son marries. A talent like his needs not just support, it needs domestic understanding, harmony, in order to blossom fully. And of course he's a nice person, he'll be a good provider materially, as they say. I guess he's already much richer than anybody I know. Of course he'll always be on tour, or busy with programmes, but should I be quibbling about small things like that? Probably not..."

"You'll be busy with your own music, your own career, won't you?" pointed out Shikha Sharma. "I mean that's the idea... both of you being in the same line, like your Gurus, can only help. It can be a symbiotic relationship. After all nobody expects you to be like those wives of Ustaads and Pandits in the past, tending to home and hearth all by themselves. His background is like yours, both of you went to similar schools. Your interest in music is much more than a hobby, it's a passion for both of you. Not that I'm forcing you to say yes, or anything," she added hastily, "but I'm just pointing out why we've come so far on this thing now."

"Yes. It's yes, of course," said Nomita unexpectedly. "It was yes all along, wasn't it? Wasn't it more or less understood that I would say yes? This meeting was just a formality, wasn't it? I mean he's a wonderful artiste, a nice person, with proper manners, a brilliant career laid out, good family. That's what matters in these arranged marriages, isn't it?"

"I wouldn't know. Mine was an arranged marriage, true, but it was decades ago. Things have changed now." Shikha placed a hand on her daughter's arm and said gently, "Nomi, you know you can say No. If you want. Nobody's forcing you to anything. There's no pressure, none at all."

Unexpectedly again, Nomita smiled broadly. "Of course. I've always known that. But don't worry, it's yes. A good, proper, wholehearted yes." She gave her mother an uncharacteristic hug, and said, "You worry too much. Bye now, I must drop in to Shishu Kalyan and school."

As usual, Silsila and the others, Rafique, Pallavi, Seema, Prabha, were delighted to see her. Social norms had not yet taught them to tone and temper their emotions. Or rather, the toggle in their minds that taught people these things had not been switched on yet. They moved delightedly towards Nomita, awkward and clumsy. Silsila, strapped to her wheelchair so that her body would not slump over, waved in her usual uncoordinated fashion from a distance.

"Did you go to the concert, then?" Nomita asked, getting ready with the harmonium to take the class that was cancelled yesterday.

"Yes!" The enthusiasm of the reply made her smile.

"We saw you sitting in front," added Rafique, his speech slow even though he was greatly excited. "You didn't see us though."

"I'm sorry. Did you like the music?"

Heads nodded, vigorously. "Pretty music. Pretty. Pretty." Their lack of vocabulary was more than made up for by the enthusiasm of their gestures.

Back to teaching the same two lines of music, patiently, again,

Nomita couldn't help wondering what Kaushik Kashyap would say, how he would react, if he were to see her now. True, both of them, Kaushik Kashyap and Nomita, had taken music as their professions. But their practice of it was so different! Pure music, as a sadhana, a tapasya, even as entertainment, was less important to her than was Classical Music as therapy.

Performing on stage was satisfying, no doubt. But as she smiled encouragement at Rafique, Nomita realized that her teaching gave her a sense of achievement that no amount of praise from an appreciative audience could ever replace. And yet, she remembered, that this passion of hers had found no mention in her conversation with Kaushik Kashyap on both the days they had met. In fact, she realized, they had not spoken of things relating to her, personally, at all.

Not that she had much time to mull over these questions. She had work to do. School, and then, what she had almost forgotten till that moment, Kamal Basu's request to her just as she was getting off the launch yesterday, "Please, could you do me a favour? Kaushikji gave a lot of interviews in your town. And there was a big Press turnout at the show, too. Normally I ask the organizers to send me cuttings, but well, could you just look out for them and send them on to me? Thank you, that's very kind of you."

Tamulbari's papers, all of them, had really gone to town on the Kaushik Kashyap show. Instead of relegating the concert to a Friday report in the culture pages, most of them had featured the story on the front page either as the anchor or the second lead. A beautiful coloured picture of the three musicians on stage brightened the front page of the *Dainik Tamulbari*. The yellow lighting gave it a brilliance that was heightened by the black backdrop. Kaushik's picture had come out extremely well. His long fingers on the sitar were positioned slantwise across his pale kurta on which diamond buttons flashed. His face, presented in profile, with tendrils coming out from his ponytail, suggested a kind of other-worldliness, an immersion in his music that was confirmed by the intensity of expression in the half-closed eye that was visible. The diamond on his finger was a bright point of light. Saurav Sen's hands were a blur above his tablas, but Lucia's picture, behind them both, had come out quite clearly. She looked ethereal and also exotic. The picture was captioned: "Sitar Maestro Kaushik Kashyap immersed in music before a record crowd in Tamulbari."

"Kaushik Kashyap praises Tamulbari audience," said the *Tamulbari Tribune*, continuing, "The maestro, who has performed in most of the important music capitals of the world, said that every artiste needs a knowledgeable and perceptive audience in order to give of his best. He gave credit for his own brilliant performance to the informed and sensitive audience of Tamulbari, whose feedback during the show was largely responsible for enthusing him to give of his best."

"Smaller town audiences are best, says renowned maestro," boasted the *Tamulbari Herald* on the front page, continuing inside, "Attributing the success of his extremely well-attended concert to the enthusiasm and sensitivity of the Tamulbari audience, the sitar star, speaking to this correspondent after the show, said that it was always a pleasure to perform before audiences in the smaller cities across India. People living in big cities no longer have time for the pursuit of serious music. It is in the smaller cities like Tamulbari, therefore, that the flame of classical music is still being nurtured."

One or two mentioned the Raags he had performed. A couple of others talked of his style and the sweetness of his tonal presentation. Several mentioned Saurav Sen and his excellent tabla support. And though normally, the taanpura accompanist never found mention in reports of this kind, all the papers, without exception, made it a point to state, "The stage was graced by Pandit Kaushik Kashyap's student, Lucia, who came all the way from Italy to accompany him on the taanpura on the Tamulbari stage." They made it sound as though Lucia had flown in just for this specific concert from the distant shores of her homeland, which some papers also said was USA, others UK, and one Sweden. Still, the basic fact was there, proudly presented in print before the world: not only had an artiste of the stature of Kaushik Kashyap played in their town, a foreigner, too, had come onstage before them.

Smiling at the simple pride of the papers, and the naivety of the readers to whom they catered, Nomita set about cutting out the articles, keeping them carefully aside to send on to Kamal Basu later. She took out the last paper, the *Saptahik Janambhoomi*, a respected weekly, and skimmed through the article on the concert.

The piece contained, not the usual star-struck pronouncements about the sitar player, but a reasoned, sober and sensitive analysis of the whole programme. Nomita was impressed. The critic seemed to know his job.

"Kaushik Kashyap is one of those rare musicians of our times who is in touch both with the traditional and the contemporary. He can please a modern audience, anytime, anyplace, without seriously compromising on what the Shastras have said about the essence, and the manner of presentation of Raag. There are, for instance, distant echoes of Western ideas of harmony during his presentation. But even while he dexterously weaves these into the fabric of the Raag he is playing, he never compromises on the traditional learning that has been imparted to him by his Gurus. He knows that the musical sensitivities of a modern audience, exposed to world music at the flick of a switch, are very different from those that his Guru's Guru had performed for. He knows perfectly well that speed brings an exultant rush of feeling to the hearts of his audience. He gives them that speed, and that resultant rush, without compromising on the melodic and tonal qualities of his music. Each of his musical phrases is carefully wrought, without losing its spontaneous appearance. Each is capable of standing, sparkling, on its own. But each is also part of a greater design, a grandly built structure. Few musicians of our times have this talent. He has the temperament that those stalwarts of the late nineteenth century are said to have had. He has the broad vision of a world traveller, and this is heard, always, in his music. But he is fully aware that he is who he is, Kaushik Kashyap the Grammy Award nominee, because he brings to the table a strong rootedness in his own culture, an uncompromising sense of musical values. It has been said of Kaushik Kashyap that "he has an 18th century DNA combined with a 21st century motherboard." This critic fully agrees.

"One looks forward to more Kaushik Kashyap concerts in Tamulbari in the near future. This, if rumours are to be believed, is quite likely to happen, because he is engaged to be married to a local girl."

Nomita had to re-read the last paragraph several times before the weight of it sank in.

How long would it be before her name, too, became public knowledge in Tamulbari? She began to feel hemmed in, suffocated. She stuffed the columns quickly into a large envelope, then paused. She took up the envelope again, and fished out the *Saptahik Janambhoomi* piece. Without looking at it again, she tore it up into little pieces, and flung them all into the tidy in the corner of her room.

15

At the Tamulbari Public School, rehearsals for the Annual concert were moving ahead quite according to schedule. Extra time had been given to Nomita for her rehearsals. But for some days now, there had been a problem with Debojit. His voice, shaping up so well, was becoming increasingly hoarse. The boy, disconcerted, kept clearing his throat, even while singing, but the frayed edges of his voice did not get better. He faltered on the higher notes, and an inaccuracy of tone crept into the midrange swaras, too. Probably he was over-practicing at home. Delight in the discovery of his own talent, was probably making him over-enthusiastic about practice.

"You need to rest your voice a little," Nomita had told him. "It seems to be getting strained."

Debojit had stared back glumly at her, but nodded. Through his growing expertise in his ability to carry a tune, he had been finding himself, as well. He was a quiet boy with a tendency to portliness who had not yet developed the defence mechanism that most overweight schoolboys usually wore as armour. He had not yet donned the comedian's mask. Though not actively disliked by his classmates, his company was not usually sought out by them, either. He had no special friends, no "gang" that he belonged to. But in recent weeks, his increasing skills as a singer had enhanced his prestige in the school. His confidence had been growing as a result, and his classmates were discovering in him a kindness and helpfulness that they had not suspected he possessed.

Today, his voice was in even worse condition than usual. It was in fact becoming quite unpredictable, even while speaking. His normally clear speaking tones, this morning, had changed suddenly to a shrill piping that had evoked titters from the others. He had not yet got over that, when, next time he spoke, it came out like a bellow.

With a sinking feeling, Nomita realized that her star singer's voice was breaking.

She should have seen this coming, she thought as she listened to him attempting the middle notes of the Durbari that was his signature tune. After all, he was of the age when he would be prey to the hormonal hurricanes of adolescence.

But Debojit's role, and his singing, was integral to the success of the play. Opening day was just round the corner. How could she replace him? Besides, she had noticed the way he had blossomed as a result of the success he was savouring in her classes. It would be heartless to take the role away from him now.

Perhaps there was a temporary remedy, something she could do to keep his voice on track for a few weeks, without straining it permanently. She would have to ask Guruma, or better, Guruji, about it.

The *Saptahik Janambhoomi* was a widely read journal in Tamulbari, and its review of the Kaushik Kashyap Nite was much discussed. It was inevitable that the last line created the most interest. For all readers, it was a surprise, a pleasant one. It was also a matter of pride for them that Kaushik Kashyap had chosen a local girl as a life partner. Who was it? Nobody had a clue, though conjectures were rife.

"It must be some girl who's lived in a big city, probably his hometown. Kolkata," opined one group. "He's a sophisticated man, a globe-trotter with an English Medium background, he won't go in for a girl with a small town mentality. Yes, the girl may be from our Tamulbari, but she's probably working in Kolkata somewhere now."

Many were in agreement with this view, though others thought differently about the details. Gradually, over adda sessions, several alternate profiles of the girl were built up, each one so vividly that it was almost as though she was there in her various avatars before them, fully fleshed out.

"A working girl? Unlikely." This from one of the older musicians of the town, Shankar Babu, a lean, dhoti-clad music teacher who was in the habit of flaunting his purported closeness to musicians, past and present, to his pupils as well as their guardians and parents. Sipping on the tea provided at the home of his students after lessons, he held forth.

"A musician needs family support, first and foremost. Especially a classical musician." Not averse to placing himself in the same category as Kaushik Kashyap, he effortlessly slipped into the first person plural. "We are creative people, different from say, those who work in banks. Or teachers. Or doctors." He said "different," but what was meant, and implied, was actually "superior to." He took another loud sip from the tea before him, signifying his satisfaction with the brew by sighing a long "aaaah."

"After all, we, the creative people of this place, this country, are responsible for upholding its culture. Its values." For a few moments, he sat contemplating the enormity of the responsibility placed on his shoulders. Fortifying himself for the magnitude of the task with a large bite of samosa, he continued, "Yes, the girl will have to understand that. She cannot expect the musician to be at her beck and call."

But there were others who had different opinions about the kind of girl who would make a fit wife for Kaushik Kashyap. They cited the example of Shalini Devi, the efficient wife of the sarod player Pandit Devadutta Roy. She was the one who handled his programmes, she was the one who acted as his Secretary, fixing engagements around the world, juggling dates, bargaining for higher fees, more perks, better hotel rooms, first class air travel. Yes, they agreed, that was the kind of wife a modern musician needed.

They talked of how it was not unheard of for Shastriya Sangeet performers to have two women as Significant Others in their lives. One was the wife whom they had married when still at the lower rungs of their careers. A girl from their native village or small town, usually, she was a docile, submissive woman, content, indeed happy to remain with her husband's extended family, looking after in-laws and relations and children while her spouse toured the world. She was gratified with the pregnancies that occurred at regular intervals, and wore them as badges of honour. Nobody had the heart to tell her of the Other Woman in her husband's life, the one who lived with him in that swanky apartment in Toronto, or maybe Mumbai, the one who held the keys to his career advancement. No, she did not have children, at least not from the musician, nor did she want any. The heady feeling of being the real power behind the throne was much more satisfying than a mere maternal instinct could ever be. And indeed, this Other Woman became accepted as the Real Significant Other in due course of time. His needs, he would say to himself in justification, had evolved. He had seen the world, and he had grown in stature and sophistication. He needed a woman by his side who understood not just music, but also the cut-throat competitiveness of his world. Indeed, when it came to a toss-up, the need to understand his music was not as necessary as the need to understand, negotiate and ultimately manipulate the competitiveness of his surroundings. As for the little woman back home in the village... well, she was illiterate, and what did she know of the world anyway. Besides, the New Woman in his life did not insist on marriage, or even, indeed, think of it. It was a convenient situation for all concerned.

But of course Kaushik Kashyap, said this group of analysts, would not want his first wife to be like that. An educated musician from a good family wanted an educated, smart person who would make her husband's talent her career.

Not much of this was echoed, though, at the Jhankaar Music Academy. Unlike the prevailing opinion in the rest of the town, the Academy's students preferred to disbelieve the news. Among themselves, they dismissed the whole thing as nonsense.

Panchali, Rupa, Geeti, variously buttonholed with questions along these lines by different people, tried not to show too obviously their gratification at being thus asked. It gave them an added sense of self-importance. But in sober and serious voices that were befitting their status of being Persons in the Know, they would give non-committal and largely irrelevant replies.

"Ummm. So you've heard of that too?" or "Actually, that's probably why he came to our town in the first place, isn't it?"

And when urged to give them the identity of the betrothed, they looked mysterious, and replied, "No, please…don't press me. I mean…if it got out that I revealed the girl's name, Kaushikji will get really annoyed. He wants it kept a secret, still."

There was a flurry of movement as Sandhya Senapati entered the room, her very presence seeming to bring down the temperature of that hot afternoon which the old, slow-moving fans overhead had done little to alleviate.

For almost two hours, they were busy, preparing for another group recital that was to be held the coming Saturday. It was to be another invocatory song, not the Mangalacharan during which the chandelier had detached itself from the ceiling of the stage, but another shloka, glorifying the role of the Guru in the life of the student. Their invocation song was to open the Golden Jubilee celebrations of a local college, and it was therefore deemed appropriate for the occasion.

Gurur Brahma, Gurur Vishnu,
Gurur Deva Maheshwara,
Guru Sakshaat ParaBrahma,
Tasmay Shri, Guruvay Namaha…

Yes, reflected Nomita. She reached the Gandhaar of the Taar Saptak, and held it steady for a long eight beats, alone, her voice soaring above the others as they moved down to the same note a full octave below her. Yes, they were sounding good together, even though their natures and musical ideas, as individuals, were so disparate otherwise. This was Guruma's own melodic composition that they were singing, though the hymn was ancient. She had incorporated elements of harmony within the musical structure, giving it a rich fullness and body.

She was reminded of Debojit, and his voice, made unpredictable by the exigencies of adolescence. She would need Guruma's advice on this problem, since she herself obviously had no experience of it.

She waited for the others to leave after lessons.

"Ah, poor boy, he must be quite embarrassed!" sympathised Guruma when she learned of Debojit's problem. "But do you know, that's not something I know much about," she smiled. "I'll ask your Guruji how *his* Guru handled it..."

She was a traditional woman, never taking the name of her husband aloud, always referring to him as "My husband" or "Your Uncle" or "Your Guruji," depending on the person she was talking to.

"But I was going to ask you something after class anyway...." She paused, and added, "There's to be a concert, a monsoon festival in Kolkata next month. In the last week of next month, actually. The Borsha Utshob."

"Ah, Haren Das..." remembered Nomita.

"Oh yes, you had met him, I had forgotten. Anyway, they've invited me to perform there. I was wondering, would you be interested in coming along? As supporting singer, they will pay your travel expenses, of course..." She smiled at her student, and added, "I don't know if Kaushikji will be there, but from the point of view of your music, it will be wonderful exposure for you. To listen to the performances of great musicians is a sure way to grow yourself."

Next month. It was impossible to remain untouched by excitement. Was this because she would get to meet Kaushik Kashyap again? Or was it because this would be her first performance on a stage outside this region, in a big city, in fact in a city famed for its rich classical music culture? All right, as a supporting vocalist, but still...

Would it be possible? Quickly, she calculated. Yes, by the last week of next month, the Tamulbari Music School's show would be over. She could certainly take leave.

Sandhya Senapati smiled at the excitement in her pupil's eyes, and her enthusiastic "Yes, of course!" If she thought this enthusiasm came from the probable prospect of seeing Kaushik Kashyap again, she did not mention it, though his name, Nomita realized, was still very much in her Guru's mind. What she did say, however, was:

"The sounds of the sitar from Kaushik's concert are still in my mind. It was fantastic, wasn't it? His Raagdari was superb..."

Nomita nodded, but wondered. How could she turn the conversation from the music to the man? She realized she wanted her Guru's opinion on the player himself. Sandhya Senapati, who had seen so much more of the world than she herself had, she, who was acquainted with the person, and had met him on several occasions backstage after or before performances... what did she think? As for herself, the music and the man were too mixed up in her mind. She could hardly trust herself to make any kind of unbiased judgement. He had come to Tamulbari as a star, and try as she might, she had become, admittedly, a little star-struck herself. Not by his persona, but by his music. Yes, Sandhya Senapati would be able to advise her on Kaushik Kashyap's real nature, and what being married to him would mean, in practical terms.

But she could not bring herself to ask. Indeed, there seemed to be nobody with whom she could talk about this, nobody who understood what being married to a musician in today's world was like.

They had been walking out of the hall, talking more like sisters. Nomita remembered to pay the ritual obeisance by touching her Guru's feet just in time, as Sandhya Senapati was turning away towards her own part of the house, and Nomita was moving towards the gate. She felt the softness of Sandhya Senapati's hand placed on her head in blessing. Did everybody feel like this when an elder blessed them, or was it something that only she did? A sense of calm seemed to flow out through Sandhya Senapati's hands and some of her habitual tranquillity settled in benediction in Nomita's mind.

She stood at the gate, waiting to hail a rickshaw or an autorickshaw. It was already a little dark outside, and the heat had subsided somewhat, though the humidity was still palpable. Several rickshaws, pedalled by skeletal frames passed by, but each one of them had portly passengers comfortably ensconced in them. The autos that came down the road simply ignored her, even though several were empty.

She was wondering whether she should start to walk when a bright yellow car slowed, then stopped before her. The door to the passenger side was opened welcomingly, and a warm voice called out, "Nomita! What are you doing here? Want a lift?"

Nomita peered inside. It was Sheila, her smile as bright as though

Nomita was her closest friend. "Are you going towards my house? I don't want to make you go out of your way..." she began.

"Just *how* out of my way will a detour to your house take me?" Sheila laughed, her hair dancing joyously around her face. "Our Tamulbari is hardly that big. Come on, I'm on my way home anyway, a bit early for a change."

Nomita slid gratefully onto the seat. The cold air inside was immediately invigorating. "How have you been?" asked Sheila, sending the car speedily into the stream of traffic again. "And yes, what were you doing there, standing at the gate of that old house?" She thought for a moment, and asked in some alarm, anxious that she might have been tactless, "That's not your house, is it?"

"No no," Nomita reassured her, laughing. "That's my Guruma's house. And the Jhankaar Music Academy. Where I take my lessons. I was waiting for a rickshaw or auto..."

"You don't drive?" asked Sheila, turning around and staring at her, oblivious to the traffic swirling all around in the dusk.

At Nomita's rather shamefaced "No..." she replied immediately. "But you must learn. You work in a school, you need to get around. Get yourself a set of wheels, nothing like having her own wheels to give independence to a girl. You can start with a second or third hand car, it costs hardly anything these days, and loans are so easily available..."

Once more, Nomita got the feeling that Rahul's friends were from another planet. None of the musicians she knew, certainly none of the women musicians, ever spoke of the need for her, Nomita, to enhance her independence by buying a car.

Sheila, mistaking Nomita's thoughtful silence for umbrage, placed a hand on her arm and said contritely, "Sorry, don't mind me, Reza is always saying I talk too much. Anyway, how have you been? Any big shows lately?"

"No no, I don't mind in the least, you're probably right, I should learn to drive myself around, instead of depending on others always. Starving rickshaw wallahs or snooty auto drivers, or somebody at home..."

"Take driving lessons, properly, not from a relation but from a school. I took mine from the Safe Driving School, I'll give you the address if you like. I had thought I'd get Reza to teach me, but after the first lesson we almost ended up divorced. The beast that lurks in the breast of every husband goes on a terrible rampage when he's asked to give driving lessons to his wife, that's a well known truth..."

"I don't have a spouse, and my father's too busy, I think I'll take the address of the driving school from you," said Nomita to Sheila now, laughing. "How's Reza? And the others, Ranjita and Jimli?"

"Fine, we're all fine. We all met the other day, last Saturday, yes, had a lovely get-together. Rahul was there, too. He can really set the floor on fire, that guy. Pity he's got this virus now, and laid up in bed."

Nomita, trying not to sound surprised, asked, "Virus?"

"Yes, don't you know? He's got some bug. High fever..."

Ah. So that explained Rahul's silence. But it was strange that he hadn't called to tell her of it. She was suddenly impatient to see him. There was so much to discuss with him, so much to talk about.

16

Back home, Shikha Sharma was waiting in some excitement for her daughter to return.

"So many calls for you, I feel like a Personal Assistant," she said in mock complaint, her expression betraying her happiness at these developments. "Who? Well first there was Tirna, wanting to talk to her prospective daughter-in-law after I told her that your response was a Yes."

"I'll speak to her later. In fact, I might even meet her, sooner than you think! Guruma has asked me to accompany her to Kolkata for a function."

"Really? That's nice. Maybe you can shop for your trousseau there," said Shikha matter-of-factly, ignoring the several stages in between that would need to be negotiated, dates to be fixed, ceremonies to be organized, before the practicalities of buying a trousseau could be embarked upon. "Sandhya Senapati has really excellent taste, she can help you, then I don't have to be there with you…"

"Who else?" asked Nomita, trying to steer her mother back to the matter of telephone calls. "Rahul?"

"What? Oh, calls for you. No, it wasn't Rahul. It was Kaushik Kashyap from some faraway country. I suppose I should stop thinking of him as Kaushik Kashyap. But it feels strange to call him Kaushik right away. Maybe he has a pet name or something. I must ask Tirna. Anyway, he wanted to speak to you."

"Oh."

"Yes, it seemed he called your cell, but it was switched off or something."

"It must have been while I was with Guruma. What did he say?"

"Say? To me? Well he was polite, he said he enjoyed the dinner here greatly. It seems his luggage was lost on the plane, but that girl, what's her name, Lucky, Lucy, yes Lucia, she got him some clothes from the shops so he's all right now."

Tirna Ghosh must have given her cell number to Kaushik Kashyap, for she did not remember doing so. But she had no idea how to contact him. No, wait, Ma had his number. She herself had spoken to him on it on Saturday, how could she have forgotten? Should she call him now? She couldn't decide.

Rahul's cell, too, was switched off now, though Shakuntala responded when Nomita called the landline. Yes, she said, Rahul was better today, but he was still in bed, asleep, and his fever hadn't left him completely. Should she wake him up so that he could talk to her? Nomita told her not to bother, and hung up. Poor guy. He must be really unwell. When that happened, he was usually a bad patient, she remembered with a smile. She made up her mind to see him that very evening.

She had barely replaced the receiver when the phone rang again. It was Tirna, her rich contralto warm with affection. "I am so happy, Nomi... I can call you that, I hope? Nomita is beautiful, but a little long... well, Nomi, I wish I could meet you in person right now, I'm longing to hug you."

Whatever ambivalence there might have been in Nomita's mind about Kaushik Kashyap, his manner, his dress, his lifestyle, she felt nothing but affection for his mother. Indeed, it was impossible to remain unaffected by the kindliness in her voice. For a fleeting moment, Nomita recalled her son's thin voice. But she quickly pushed the fact away as being disloyal, now that she was, it appeared, betrothed to the man. With a smile in her own voice, she replied, "In fact, we'll probably be meeting, maybe sooner than we both thought. Guruma has a programme in Kolkata, she's asked me to accompany her... yes, sometime next month."

"That's wonderful, it really is. Rana hasn't met you, he's been asking me all kinds of questions, here, speak to him..."

Before she could prepare herself to speak to her prospective father-in-law, a normal male voice came on the line. She had never met Rana Ghosh in person, but knew, from her mother and from Tirna herself, that the man was a creative person who worked in Advertising. He was also a poet. As she listened to his words in her ear, she imagined his face. Most likely he wore glasses, and of course he would have a French beard, greying now. And a ponytail. Yes, probably there were two ponytails in the family, though his would be a salt and pepper one. Though why had she thought of his voice as a "normal" one? "Normal", as opposed to his son's slight voice? Quickly, she pushed the thought away again.

Rana Ghosh sounded formal, at least compared to his wife, and cautious. Well, that was natural. After all, he was speaking to a girl he had never met, a girl who was going to be his daughter-in-law, the wife of his only son, his only child, in fact.

"Yes, I think – hope – to meet you soon. In Kolkata itself, yes."

"I'm looking forward to meeting you," he said formally, and handed the phone back to his wife.

"Let me know as soon as you decide on the dates," said Tirna, the excitement in her voice making Nomita smile again. "You must of course come over..."

Replacing the receiver, Nomita couldn't help thinking of the inequality of the relationship. Shikha would hardly be able to speak to her son-in-law with the same degree of informality as Tirna was already doing with her to-be daughter-in-law. And it was not just a question of gender. For her father too, would certainly not be able to speak in the same informal way with his son-in-law. A son-in-law, in general was never spoken to in a bantering or frivolous tone. And when that son-in-law was a Star, a Maestro, it was unlikely that Pradeep Sharma would ever be on back-slapping terms with his only child's spouse.

On her way to Rahul's house, she thought of the one and only occasion she had met Tirna. She was tall and heavy set, but with such a pleasant expression on her face that any person meeting her for the first time was immediately captivated. Her short iron-grey hair was neatly cut in a swept back style. Her sari had been crisply starched and ironed. She had looked very much like the schoolteacher she was, and one would hardly have thought that her only child was a musician by profession. One would have expected her children to be college professors, perhaps, or IIT graduates, or working in IT companies in Silicon Valley. She had come to Tamulbari for a teacher's conference, and Ma had brought her home. Indeed, Tirna Ghosh had dropped into their home several times during the week long conference, and had even stayed the final night with them. Neither Nomita's parents nor Nomita herself had been aware that Tirna's son was Kaushik Kashyap, the sitarist whose music was so frequently heard on the World Space set in their home.

"How well you sing, my dear," Tirna had told Nomita on the day of her departure. She had heard Nomita at her routine riyaz as she was getting ready to leave. "You're really good, in fact."

Nomita had smiled her thanks, taking the compliment in her stride. But Tirna had surprised her by asking, "Who is your Guru? And your Gharana?" Unless they really knew something about classical music, most people's compliments stopped at "How well you sing." To ask the name of one's Guru and Gharana implied a serious interest in, and knowledge of music.

"Guruma is Sandhya Senapati. Hers is a mixed Gharana, but based mostly on Patiala with a bit of Kirana."

"Sandhya Senapati. Of course, she lives here, doesn't she? I've heard her in Kolkata, several times. She has a wonderful mizaz. Her temperament is so calm. She sings the Sandhiprakash Raags beautifully, the dawn and dusk melodies that are so tranquil. They merge with her nature, perhaps. Well, you're in good hands."

"You must be interested in music to know about such things as Gharana, then?" Nomita had asked at the breakfast table that day.

"Oh, greatly." Tirna's voice had been brisk. "I go to as many concerts as I can, luckily Kolkata is a Mecca for musicians during the season. I remember hearing your Guruma's Guru too, many years ago. Pandit Chiranjeev Mukherjee. He was very good, even towards the end of his life when excesses of many kinds were beginning to fray his voice. Sandhya Senapati was his favourite student, though temperamentally I imagine they must have been very different."

"Kolkata in the season…" Nomita had said wistfully. "I love our Tamulbari, but sometimes I wish I was in Kolkata, so that I could listen to all the music there."

"It's a very competitive place for a musician, but then competition is essential for growth, isn't it? Are you serious about your music, or is it just a hobby? All right, a serious hobby?"

The question had been asked with a kind of intensity that Nomita had found a little surprising. "Of course I'm serious. I teach music, I'm taking regular lessons, I perform on stage, on radio, on television. Music is what I do."

"Ah." Tirna Ghosh had been silent for a moment. When she spoke again, her voice was carefully neutral. "My son is a musician too. A sitarist. It's what he does, too."

"Really? Who is his Guru?" Nomita asked, in the expected way. To ask the name of one's Guru was to ask about one's musical identity. Classical musicians introduced themselves on the strength of their Guru's name, it was their lineage, and, in musical terms, their family name.

"Pandit Om Prakash Mishra," Tirna had replied. She had hesitated a moment again, and added, "His name, my son's name, is Kaushik Kashyap, his stage name."

The word "name" thrice in the same sentence would have been inappropriate when applied to somebody else, perhaps, but in this case it was quite seemly. The other three people around the table had gaped at her in jaw-dropping amazement. They would not, perhaps, have been more surprised if she had informed them that her child was the President of the United States of America. In any case, during the week that she had been in Tamulbari, Tirna had never given any previous hint of being the mother of an International Star.

After the first surprise, Nomita had felt a sense of embarrassment. Kaushik Kashyap, the Grammy nominee, the person who was taking Indian music to such great heights worldwide was her son. She was used to a much higher standard of music than what she had overheard that morning during Nomita's routine riyaz. She tried to remember what it was she had sung behind the closed doors of her room. Guruma was teaching her Patdeep, yes, she had been practicing the Raag in the morning, but in an inexpert way. After all, it would take her some time to master the more minute details of the Raag. She had forgotten about the visitor in their home, forgotten that her voice could be heard beyond the closed door. With her tongue tied in sudden awkwardness, all she had been able to manage had been "Aah..."

Tirna Ghosh seemed to have read her thoughts. "A melodious voice has its own beauty," she had said, endearing herself for ever to Nomita. "Yours is beautiful. You have great musical sense too, I can tell." Some people spoke words of supposed admiration about a singer's voice because that was the only thing good about their music, and they couched their words in such a tone that there was no mistaking the fact that they were damning with faint praise. But the way Tirna said it; there was no offensiveness in her sentence. It was a word of praise, pure and simple, and Nomita, understanding her intent, smiled, at ease again.

They hadn't spoken of music, or Kaushik Kashyap at all again that day. Tirna Ghosh had left for the airport, and the three of them had gone off to their various chores. Meeting up at dinner again, they had talked about Tirna's friendliness, her unassuming nature, especially in the light of her being the mother of a musician who was so well known. "Such a level-headed person, I'm so happy we met. I do hope I get to see her more often. I want us to become good friends. She's extremely intelligent, also," her mother had said.

The two of them had kept in touch. Telephone calls were routinely made, news exchanged. Shikha, on her way to Cuttack for another conference, had stayed over in Kolkata with Tirna for a couple of days on her return.

"What fun we had," she told her daughter happily on her return home. Nomita had sat on her parents' bed, watching her mother unpack, happy in her happiness. "She called some of her friends over, we had a lovely time. New Market, Gariahat, she took me to all the shops. We had a great time haggling." She took out a packet and handed it over to her daughter. "Here, she sent this for you."

It was a cream coloured Kantha silk sari, heavily embroidered. "It's beautiful! But tell me Ma, did you meet him? Kaushik Kashyap, did you hear him play?"

"Tirna's son? No, he's away in some place, Singapore I think she said. Some conference on Eastern Music. He's giving a lecdem there."

"Oh. That's disappointing."

"Yes," agreed her mother dutifully, though Shikha had actually enjoyed herself too much at Tirna's home to think that she was missing an opportunity to hear a great musician practicing in his natural habitat. To console her daughter in her disappointment, she added, "I saw his rooms, though."

"What good is that?" Nomita started to laugh.

"No, I mean it's the room of a musician all right. Tirna's is a very large flat, actually they are two adjacent flats made into one. Very spacious. One wing is Kaushik Kashyap's entirely. His bedroom is small, but the rest of the place was like a museum when I saw it. Full of sitars and tablas. Tirna told me he collects old sitars, and she took me into the special room that houses them. There were several there, in specially- made racks that had strange shapes. I mean they didn't look like today's sitars at all. Apparently he's hunted out existing models from all over the world. He got an old piece from Lahore when he was invited by the Government of Pakistan to play there. Now he's heard that there is an instrument that's a kind of forerunner of today's sitar sitting in some remote village in Afghanistan, and is trying to go there to have a look and if possible bring it back. His mother is worried, after all, no mother wants her son to go to Afghanistan right now, when things are so unstable there."

"I can imagine…"

"There were large laminated photos of him playing all over the world, or being felicitated by important people the President of India, the PM, and also leaders of other countries. And tablas, surmandals…really, just entering the place made me feel the air was full of music, though of course there was no sound from them at that time. You would have loved the place. Maybe some day we can go together..."

A month or so later, Nomita had returned home to find her mother waiting for her in the drawing room. She had followed her daughter to her room, not saying a word, but with an air of suppressed excitement.

Nomita had been surprised. But her mother had waited till she had had her cup of tea before saying, carefully, "Tirna rang up today..."

"Really? How is she?" As usual, the mention of the older lady brought a warm feeling. "It would be lovely if she comes here again..."

"Actually, she had something important to discuss," her mother had continued in the same careful tone. "She...in fact..." she stumbled over her words, then collected herself, "what she said was, she wants you...that is, she has given a proposal of marriage."

"For whom?" Nomita had been genuinely puzzled.

"For you, of course. And her son. She wants you as her daughter-in-law."

Nomita had been too surprised to answer immediately. "Why me?" she had asked finally. "And what about her son? He's not seen me, he's not even heard of me." She had started to laugh. "Come on, Ma, this is the twenty-first century. Marriages don't take place like that, especially the marriage of a well known musician like Kaushik Kashyap. He travels so much, he's sure to have a girlfriend somewhere. Or maybe he's so busy he won't want to get married now. You can't just arrange a marriage like that! Surely your friend – much as I like her – should be aware of it."

"That's exactly what I told her," Shikha had exclaimed. "But it seems her son is now in Kolkata, and she has spoken to him about you. He is quite ready to settle down, but he's far too busy to woo and wed a girl himself. His mother's choice will be his, she said. And you are her choice."

"What?" Nomita had stared at her mother for a moment. She had started to laugh again. "You're serious? And she's serious? What about me? Where does that leave me?" She had started to laugh harder at the sheer preposterousness of it.

"No, wait, don't laugh. Of course it's not what you think. Tirna herself told me to tell you to think it over. There's no pressure... it is your choice. You can meet him if you wish, that can be arranged, either in Kolkata or in Tamulbari itself. In the end, this whole thing hinges on your decision, yes or no." She had put a hand on her daughter's arm, and said, "Nobody's pressurising you, not Tirna, certainly not me or your father. All I'm asking is that you give it some thought. You're an intelligent girl, think it over. There's no hurry..."

"And he? Won't he want to 'see' me, the 'girl' of his mother's choice?"

"No, he's confident of her ability to choose a fine girl, he told her. But he is ready to be 'Seen' by you."

"What?" The idea had struck her as ridiculous, and she began to laugh again. Her mother had joined in. "You mean the great Kaushik Kashyap will sit and wait in a hall for me to come in, to examine him, look at him from all angles, ask him to speak, test his nature, his character, his intelligence, his general knowledge, his earning capacity... and then meekly and humbly wait for my decision... Ma, what are you saying?"

The two of them had laughed even harder at the picture that Nomita had created, that of a Swayamvara with a single candidate. After a few moments though, Shikha Sharma had sobered sufficiently to say, "Don't be ridiculous, Nomi, it's not going to be like that. He always has invitations to perform at cities around the country. He can arrange to perform in our Tamulbari, it will be a camouflage. Nobody, or very few people, will actually know why he is here. And don't forget, after all he's getting on, he's in his middle or late thirties now, soon he will be deemed to be a crusty old bachelor, too old for the matrimonial market. He probably is never long enough in one place to actually get attached to a suitable girl, or for a suitable girl to get attached to him."

"That sounds awful, the way you put it..."

"It's most likely to be true, though. He's always on the move, as you know. He must have had his share of puppy romances by now, what with adoring fans probably flinging themselves at him every time he plays at some major Conference. But at the end of the day, every man wants a stable family life, take it from me, no matter how successful he is. A normal life to come home to..."

"Ma, you sound like those mushy romance novels..."

"Don't sidetrack me now. No, I can understand that he's left the choice of a girl to his mother. Actually, men who do that are quite canny. It's not just Kaushik Kashyap or musicians or artistes. Why do you think the institution of arranged marriages has survived so long, why do you think it's flourishing now? Look at internet marriages, sites like, what was it, marriagedotcom, I believe. After all they facilitate arranged marriages, don't they? And they're flourishing, Radha was saying the other day. Her colleague's daughter got engaged to a person she met on the site, and they seem to be Made for Each Other. Love at first sight, or love and romance leading to marriage is only one way people get hitched. And if you come down to it, how long does the starry-eyed phase last anyway? After that, to successfully negotiate the domestic grind, the couple have to have so much more than just romance to see them through."

"*Just* romance, Ma? But yours was an arranged marriage. What do you know of..." she started. But Shikha Sharma interrupted her.

'Yes, ours was an arranged marriage. But it's been, I would say, a successful one. It had, providentially, all the ingredients that a successful marriage, arranged or otherwise, needs. Your father and I had a peaceful, easy pre-marriage time, yes, with some romance too, believe it or not. A calm romance, of course, not a torrid one, within the structure of the arranged marriage. There weren't any Romeo and Juliet hurdles that we had to cross. Our families were very alike... middle class, with the same values, educational levels, aspirations, their economic backgrounds were the same..."

"Is that all it needs to have a successful marriage? It sounds so... tame. A little boring. Similarity of values, of economic aspirations."

"It's not 'all', but it's a very vital part. We're all shaped by our environments, and much of what we are is a product of our environmental inputs."

"What about the stars, the moon, ghazals playing softly, music wafting in the breeze..."

"You're a singer, create your own music. Two musicians, one as great as Kaushik Kashyap, should surely be capable of that!"

"Ma, stop looking so pleased with yourself for being so clever!" But Nomita hadn't been able to help laughing, herself.

"No, seriously," Shikha had sobered down and added. "It's not, of course, a question of Kaushik Kashyap's fame, or his wealth, that makes this proposition attractive to me and to your father. His mother is a teacher, his father a professional, he himself has had the same kind of education as you. You'll be able to relate to each other. But even more important, you have the same passion, the same interest in music."

"Though we're at very different levels..." Nomita had felt bound to interject.

"That's not the point. You know, I've seen, and so have you, many talented girls unable to pursue their interest in music at all seriously. Oh, it's nothing to do with being 'allowed' by the husband, or his family to do it. Those days have more or less gone, though I suppose there are vestiges of that disapproval still around, of women not being allowed to sing in public."

Nomita nodded. She knew well enough how easy it was to throw in the towel in the face of the myriad, subtle yet inexorable demands of domesticity. No matter how supportive the family, it was not easy.

"But," continued Shikha warmly, "with a family like this, it's not likely to happen. They know very well the demands of the profession. Just look at your own Guru. How well adjusted they are, one can see in the glow on Sandhya Senapati's face that she's content. And both have been growing in their respective professions, it's not as if one has sacrificed his or her career for the other..."

"That's of course true. But what about all those other women musicians who married other musicians? Ultimately they had to put their own musical careers on the back burner. There's that Irfaan Khan, the Hindu vocalist who converted to Islam and got himself a new name so that he could leave his first wife and marry Shahana Begum. She was at that time at the top of the music world. Who knows what happened in their domestic life, but now one hardly gets to hear her anywhere. And even if she's asked to perform somewhere, Irfaan Khan insists on singing with her, in Jugalbandi. Nobody wants to listen to his raspy voice, though we would all love to listen to a full fledged recital by her. But that's too high a price to pay... So the world has been deprived of her music, too." Nomita pointed out.

"Well...true. But that Irfaan Khan's mother wasn't a working woman, he probably was never exposed to the idea of women earning their own money, or women actually earning more than their husbands. With Kaushik Kashyap this won't be true, of course."

"I suppose so..." Nomita had answered doubtfully.

"In any case, Tirna will be well able to choose a suitable girl, a *very* suitable girl, for her son. She's a capable woman, intelligent. Besides, she's is such a *nice* person..."

"Nobody's doubting that, Ma." She had hesitated, then added, "Well, give me some time. I'll think about it, let me just get used to the idea first. Tell her that..."

Over the next few days, in fact, Nomita had thought of little else. Her mother had not, during that time, brought it up again, but Shikha had known, by the look in her daughter's eyes, that she was indeed giving the matter serious thought, and had refrained from interfering.

There was nobody in Nomita's circle, people she met during the course of her day, or people she was friendly with, with whom she could discuss this astonishing proposal, or examine the idea in all its dimensions. It was only Rahul with whom she could open up sufficiently to talk about it. She had called him up in Bangalore to discuss it.

"Do you know...have you heard about Kaushik Kashyap? He's a sitarist..." she had asked. After the routine questions about what each of them was doing at that time had been asked, and replied to, she was suddenly a little diffident.

"Hmm Kaushik Kashyap? Yes, I've heard of him, I mean one sees him on TV quite often, isn't it? That guy who does that ad for that airline? "My sitar travels with me, creating music... and we travel by Excel Air. Musically." Something like that..."

"That's right," Nomita had recalled. She herself had mostly, for the last few days, thought of him, as a musician, and a potential husband, but she realized again that Kaushik Kashyap was also, among other things, a star, with a worth that advertisers paid good money for, probably crores. Crores! Suddenly, Nomita realized that if she did marry Kaushik Kashyap, she would be a rich man's wife. That was another angle...

"Anyway, why do you ask?" Rahul's voice had broken into her tumultuous thoughts.

"He's... actually, no, his mother, who is a friend of Ma's... she... well she thinks I might make a good daughter-in-law."

"You!" Predictably, Rahul had hooted with laughter, his voice echoing mirthfully down the line. She had waited till he had finished. With a sigh of mock patience, she had continued, "Are you done?" She hadn't been able to keep the laughter out of her own voice, though.

"Sorry sorry, I didn't mean to insult you. The idea of you as anybody's daughter-in-law..." he had begun to laugh again. Behind him, she had heard the sounds of Bangalore traffic. He had been on his way back from work, he had said, he had been working late. She had suddenly wanted to be able to see him, meet him face to face that day, so that they could talk over this momentous matter that had cropped up in her life.

"That also involves being somebody's wife..." she had said.

"Yes. This guy who advertises Excel Air?"

"He's a musician, Rahul. A star. He got a Grammy nomination some time ago for his fusion disc," she had said, patiently.

"Ah... he's the one? I've heard the CD. He's good, Nomi. Very good." His voice, she remembered had been more serious. "He wants to marry you?"

"His mother. She's the one choosing a girl for him."

"What's wrong with him, can't he choose a girl himself?" But he had immediately added, "Sorry, Nomi, that wasn't what I meant. Just something that slipped out…ignore it. Well, what can I say? But… wouldn't you want to meet him before you make a decision? I mean, even if he is fine with the idea of seeing you for the first time on the wedding day?"

Exactly. He had put her thought, nebulous in her mind till then, in clear focus. "Yes. Of course. I'll have to tell them that I can't make up my mind till I meet him. But he's a star, a famous person…will he agree?"

"You always were a pathbreaker, Nomi," Rahul had said approvingly. "Even in kindergarten, you refused to accept that two and two made four. I remember you insisted for a long time that two and two made two… But no, seriously Nomi, you can't marry anybody, without at least seeing him. Okay, if you want an arranged marriage, I suppose nobody can stop you. But at least talk to him, meet him. If he doesn't want to, you'll have to say you do. You're a modern woman, aren't you? So what if you are singing melodies and lyrics composed hundreds of years ago? You have to remember that you don't live in that age. All that pining for the absent lover, the male-centric stuff in those lyrics you sing, the glorification of the absent male lover, you've evolved beyond that, surely? Insist on a meeting, that's the way to go. Make up your mind after you've met him."

"Yes, certainly, I definitely will," she had said, her voice full of resolve. One step at a time, and this was the logical next step in the path before her. "It's not about the money, though, Rahul. I mean I'm not agreeing to this just because he's very likely a rich man. You know that, don't you?" It was important to her that Rahul should understand that if she did marry this man, it would be because of things other than his wealth.

"But actually, Nomi, it's a very practical thing, to marry someone who has money."

"Come on Rahul…"

"No listen to me, hear me out. Don't interrupt. One minute…" He paused, and once more, Nomita could hear the Bangalore street noises, mingled with voices in a language she did not understand. Kannada, probably. He came to and from office in a car pool. Yes.

Rahul seemed to be speaking to the driver in Kannada, a language she had not realized he knew.

"Okay, Nomi, I was going to say: if you are serious about your music, you have to marry someone who has money. No, don't interrupt. Classical music, is not paying at all, unless you are in the upper echelons. But how many can be a Shiv Kumar Sharma or a Vishwa Mohan Bhatt or Amjad Ali Khan? And didn't Bismillah Khan himself live in poverty, bordering on penury? Look at all the performers around you. At your level, how many can support themselves? If you hadn't been living at home, if you didn't have your teaching job, would you have been able to sustain yourself with your music only?"

Of course what he was saying was true. Still, it rankled.

"Family support, whether from parents or spouse is crucial, Nomi, in your line. Not just for artistic consonance, for a meeting of minds. But also for the money. You'll have to live, survive..."

"Rahul, the way you're saying it, it sounds awful. I am not going to marry anybody based on his income, you're not being fair Rahul."

"But I'm pointing out a truth. If you were to marry a struggling musician, both of you would either starve, or look around for other jobs to work at. Or more likely, you would begin to detest each other, after all how long would you be able to sustain a marriage based on music only? Hmm? Tell me that?"

"If... *if*, mind you... if I were to marry Tirna Ghosh's son, it would be because of his music, because of what he is, not because of his money," she had said sulkily.

"Of course. You're far too impractical to be a gold-digger. But if you find you like him enough to marry him, and the marriage succeeds, his income will play a huge role in the success. Money will smooth over any small niggles you may have. Of course I'm practical. Always have been. Bye now, think over what I've said. But make sure you see him first, talk to him..."

It had been a good idea to call Rahul, she had thought. He had a way of going straight to the heart of the matter that made complex problems seem easily and simply soluble. Today, with his logic, he had made the whole exercise seem like one of those cut and dried matrimonial deals that one heard about. Still, she had admitted grudgingly to herself as she put down her cell, he had a point. Guruma and Guruji were well known musicians. Though their income was not enough for anybody to call them wealthy, it was enough to make them quite comfortably off. The house they lived in had been inherited, but it took money to maintain. And yes, they had their students, and their teaching, which fetched them additional income. But would she ever be able to reach Guruma's level in music?

Of course what Rahul had said made sense. It was well known that the successful young practitioners of dance and music in the Classical mode were all either from upper-middle-class or rich business families. In dance, especially, it seemed that one needed to be the daughter of a person with at least five large factories in order to guarantee artistic survival. Or the wife of a Foreign Service employee, or at least a civil servant with a guaranteed income and lots of domestic support. Or they were from the traditional Gharanas, which was its own support system. Look at Ayaan and Amaan, Amjad Ali Khan's two sons. The kind of support they were getting from their parents was unimaginable for a person in her own situation.

Strange, she had thought, she had just finished talking to Rahul, and she was thoughtful. Usually, she was always laughing as she hung up. He made her smile even on her most serious days. Sometimes, she knew, hours, even a whole day would pass without her actually laughing, or even smiling. Not smiling in the polite mouth-stretched-to-say-hello-Namaste-how-good-to-meet-you way that was expected of her, but really, *feelingly* smiling. She couldn't see herself sharing much of a joke with her co-students in Jhankaar, in fact it was quite dangerous there to make a witty remark in passing. It was quite likely to be misconstrued, or reconstructed in a way designed to give offence when repeated to another person. With Rahul gone, her relationship with Sandhya Senapati, though that of a Guru and Shishya, was probably the closest she now had in Tamulbari. Yet there was still that inevitable distance between them, which made her diffident about broaching the subject with Sandhya Senapati at this point.

She wondered, now, walking to Rahul's house and recollecting that evening when she had called him for advice, what kind of sense of humour Kaushik Kashyap would have. It had not occurred to her to think of this before. Would they laugh at the same jokes? Would they laugh together at all? Or would he smile only at those music-related jokes that musicians, especially successful musicians, were prone to relate? They did this usually when they were surrounded by their students and chamchas and toadies, so that they could be sure, that there would be uproarious laughter from their listeners.

She remembered one such joke that she'd heard from Giridhari Kapoor, a visiting flutist from Delhi. It was about a music teacher trying to get a girl who was a sincere student, but tone deaf, to sing the notes of B Flat with at least some degree of accuracy. He had asked her to faithfully reproduce through her voice, the notes of the scale on her harmonium. What he hadn't known was that one of the keys, the note Ma, was faulty. Instead of producing melody, it only gave out a hissing sound when pressed. To his horror, at her next lesson the girl sang "Sa Re Ga *Fiss* Pa Dha Ni Sa, Sa Ni, Dha, Pa, *Fiss* Ga Re Sa." Nomita had not been able to manage more than a weak and forced smile at this, even though all around her, the other students were practically rolling around in merriment, exaggerating their mirth, and already making mental notes of how they would relate this joke from the very mouth of Pandit Giridhari Kapoor to their acquaintances later.

Probably Kaushik Kashyap would be too busy to joke with her, she thought resentfully. He would always be travelling, or practicing, or maybe shooting for an advertisement for some product totally unrelated to music. Maybe...um...maybe tandoori chicken? Or Prawn, or Hilsa? "I travel so much, I miss the Malai Curry of home. I always eat Prawn Malai Curry at this restaurant when I am in Kolkata."

She realized she was smiling. She should tell Rahul about it, she thought, then caught herself up short. This was no way to be thinking of a prospective husband. And of course she should not discuss him in such a derogatory manner with anybody, even if he was her best friend.

But here she was, in front of Rahul's house.

17

Rahul was in bed, wrapped in a sheet, even though it was quite hot inside the house. The room was not silent, nor would Nomita have expected it to be. Music belted out from the TV, its energetic images contrasting with the supine form on the bed. She had to speak up in order to be heard.

"He's asleep?" she asked Shankuntala, who had brought her up.

"Gone off to sleep again, I suppose. He had very high temperature some time ago, though it's coming down now. Poor boy, he must be feeling quite ill…"

The bundle on the bed stirred. Rahul's face, flushed and puffy under his unruly mop of hair emerged from under the covers. In all the years that Nomita had known Rahul, almost a lifetime, she had never seen him look like this. Vulnerable, in need of caring. Strange. "Vulnerable" was not a word she would ever have associated with Rahul, not even when they had both been in nursery school.

"Rahul! You look ill! Why didn't you tell me? I was wondering what happened to you…"

He sat up in bed and smiled. "Couldn't. Can't, even now." His voice was a hoarse croak.

"Oh I see. Hm. Lucky you're not a singer… !"

"Lucky I'm not at work, though," he mumbled.

"Don't talk, you sound awful, you'll strain your voice," fussed Nomita.

"No, that's okay. I was beginning to feel my voice might become fossilized if I don't get to use it." He coughed, cleared his throat, and continued in a stronger voice. "What's that you've got there?" He eyed the package in her hand. "Something for this poor invalid who's wasting away to a shadow..."

"Chicken soup. It's good for your cold, and your throat..."

"Chicken soup for the soul..."

"What?" She didn't understand his reference.

"Nothing... I'll explain some other time when my throat is better. Pour me a cup... wow, lovely aroma, a flavour to die for..." He sipped on the soup, and rolled his eyes in appreciation.

"Got you some momos too... from that place you like... here, have them while they're still warm..." She placed the container with the half-moons of steamed, chicken-stuffed dough on the table beside his bed.

"Florence Nightingale! My saviour!"

She laughed, and looked around the room. It was familiar to her, but every time she entered it, she was taken by surprise, all over again. The huge posters on the walls, of musicians whose names she did not know, gazed down at her, totally unlike the musicians she was familiar with in looks, clothes, and instruments they carried. The music system was silent at this moment, having yielded to the DVD that was playing through the TV, but she could well imagine that the sounds pouring out from the speakers when turned on would be something that those people on the walls would have created.

Rahul's TV screen was full of images of young male musicians, oblivious to all else but the music they were creating. The room reverberated to the sound of their music. Nomita particularly noticed the deep, vibrating beat of the drums.

"Who's the drummer?" she asked, as visuals of the person behind the large electronic drumset flashed on and off in a montage, cutting into and out of pictures of the guitarist, the vocalist, and the screaming fans.

"Ah yes, you've hit the spot. I'll make you a rock music fan yet," said Rahul. "You've noticed him, haven't you?"

"I've noticed his music. It's – how do I put it, I've listened to so many rock bands in your room, but his drumming is different. The sound, that's different, also."

There was something in the beat, the way the rhythms were executed on the drums that seemed to reach into the blood coursing through her veins.

"Watch his playing... here, there's a drum solo coming up. They'll show just him in closeup..."

Sure enough, the camera zoomed to the platform at the back of the stage where the drummer was seated, surrounded by a plethora of equipment. From this angle, she could only see one arm, but that arm was everywhere, moving over the drums, up and down, side and out, touching them swiftly, yet powerfully, to create a continuous rill of reverberating beats.

Gradually, though, she became aware of something else.

"Why are they showing him only from this camera angle? I mean, both the drummer's hands are making music, why aren't they showing his other arm?" she asked. It was disconcerting to watch just the one arm flying around the arc of toms around him.

"That's because he doesn't have any."

"What?" asked Nomita.

"He has just one arm. He lost the other in an accident, long ago."

"What?" she asked again, in a different tone this time, of disbelief.

"It's true. It happened when this group, Def Leppard, was still quite young. Three hit albums had already come out. Pathbreaking, they were. They're from Sheffield. UK, the birthplace of Heavy Metal. They were hugely successful already when their drummer was involved in an accident. Rick Allen, he was only twenty-one at the time. He lost his arm. His left arm."

"Ahh!"

She tried to imagine how it must have been. A young, highly talented, committed musician, losing one of the two limbs without which no instrumental music was possible. He must have thought that this was the end of the road for him.

"But the group waited till he recovered. There were of course any number of offers from other drummers, to fill the gap. But they waited. And when he was able, he gradually took the first steps to playing again, this time with one arm. Of course he had to work hard, to get the remaining limb to do the work of two. But he had talent and motivation and soon he was performing onstage with his group again ..." Rahul closed his eyes for a moment, and coughed, clearing his throat. He added, "From his music, it's impossible to make out that he has an arm missing, isn't it? Of course his kit is customized, he uses his feet a lot more than other drummers, but still, I don't know how he does it, how he compensates ..."

"No, not compensates," said Nomita slowly, blinking. "He's lost a limb, but he's gained something else, and it shows in his playing. He knows that there is humanity in humans, that true friends give more than anyone expects ... Yes, and this knowledge has enriched him, and it shows in his music ..."

"Missed you these last few days, Rahul," she added, turning back to the patient on the bed. He paused to offer her a momo, acknowledged her refusal with a surprised raise of his eyebrows, and continued to bite into them.

"Really. The concert was really good, you would have enjoyed it ... I looked for you everywhere, tried you on your cell ... We went for a boat ride the next day ..." She perched on the edge of his bed and leaned across to pour him another mugful of soup.

"We ... ?"

She was suddenly diffident. "Umm ... the artistes from Kolkata. And of course Lucia ... It was good."

"Ah. Not a twosome then? You and Kashyap?"

"Your voice is better already, see, the soup is working its magic." She decided not to avoid the issue. "No, it wasn't a twosome. It's not time yet for a twosome. There were people from the Kaushik Kashyap Nite, and his secretary, and also the tabla player and his student."

"And you. His prospective bride?"

Rahul waited for her to answer. He looked at her, his mouth full of bits of chicken, but there was something, an intensity in his eyes, that made her look away.

"Yes. I said yes." Her voice sounded inaudible even to herself, so she added, louder, "Well, I mean, of course I said yes."

"Of course." Rahul continued with his chewing. But he extended his hand and said, formally, "Congratulations. I am sure you will be very happy. You deserve it."

"Thanks, Rahul... I..." Suddenly her voice shook, and she was aware of tears forming in her eyes. She blinked them away, thinking, there's always something about a wedding that brings out the sentimental side in everybody. Why else would she be feeling this way at Rahul's words? Rahul, her best friend, the person she was most at ease with... If I'm this mushy now, what will happen later, during the ceremony itself? Deuta will have to build a ditch to drain the waterworks from my eyes to the Red River.

"Khura will have to connect a large pipe from your eyes to the river at this rate... !" Rahul observed. His voice was still hoarse. She sniffed, then laughed. It was quite normal for both of them to think the same thought, carry the same images in their minds, at the same time. That was what made them such good friends, she thought.

"Here, take my handkerchief. No, on second thoughts don't. Germs. We don't want you with a voice like mine..."

"That reminds me... I'll be going to Kolkata!" exclaimed Nomita, a bubble of happiness rising at the thought.

"Naturally. I expect you'll be living there after your marriage..." Rahul's voice was neutral. "Or maybe in California, since Kashyap spends so much time there..."

"No no, all that is..." she waved an impatient hand later. Much later. Nothing is decided yet. No, what I meant was, I'm going with Guruma. To sing!"

"Wonderful. Great experience for you professionally. Will Kashyap be there?"

"I don't know. This is not related to him. It's to do with Guruma and me, it's just incidental that Kaushik lives there."

But a violent bout of coughing had overcome Rahul, and he didn't seem to hear her words as he bent over, coughing painfully.

"Sorry," he gasped, after it was over, his face flushed with the effort.

"No no, *I'm* sorry," she said, contrite. "I shouldn't have made you talk so much. There, go back to sleep now... I'm off. I'll call in the morning..."

"How did you come? It's quite dark..."

"Walking. Don't worry, it's not that late."

"You really should learn to drive," he wheezed. "Give me a call after you reach home."

"Right. Bye. Take care."

Going back, through the gradually emptying streets of Tamulbari, she thought of Rahul, whom she had left popping the last momo into his mouth. Always, since they had been children, she had felt safe when she was with Rahul. As they had grown up, this sense of safety had deepened, and it had had very little to do with his six-foot frame and strong build. Rather, it had been his basic sense of decency, his sense of caring, camouflaged under an easy camaraderie that had strengthened this feeling in her. She was sure that the other girls in his life felt the same way. For it was impossible for a woman to remain friends for long with a man unless there was this basic sense of mutual respect between them. She always enjoyed those rides home with him, filled with discussions and easy arguments.

She remembered an evening. She smiled at the memory as she switched off her cell after calling Rahul that she had reached home safely.

They had been in college still, she in BA English Major in a local college, but he in Bangalore already, studying Computer Engineering. He had come home for the holidays, she remembered, and they had slipped easily into the slots that they had been in before he had left. He would accompany her to the programme she was featuring in, and either stay till she was done, or go away, and return to bring her back when her turn was over. She had been grateful for his presence, for going for a performance was never easy, in logistical terms. There were the bulky instruments to be packed into the cars, the delicate and large taanpuras, two of them usually, needing special handling. There was also the heavy, scale-changing harmonium which Guruma had herself got for her on one of her trips to Kolkata. Its weight was such that Nomita, even now, staggered back when she tried to lift it. Rahul always hefted it with a smooth movement though, and he would take it up to the greenroom if nobody else was around to do it.

After one of those programmes, Rahul, driving her home, had asked, "Why do you call yours a solo performance?"

"Because it is," she had replied, trying to balance the large resonator of the taanpura on her lap.

"But it isn't, actually, is it?" Rahul had asked.

"But..." He had her attention now.

"All the classical musicians I've seen performing say theirs is a solo recital. Look at you, for instance. Today you had Srinjoy on the tabla, Rekha and Kalpana on the taanpuras, Biren on the harmonium and Bidyut on the violin. So there were five people on stage besides you. Six altogether. How is that a solo performance? Sometimes when it's a bigshot, there are even more people. Those "samajhdars", or what do you call it, those people who don't play anything or sing either but just sit behind the maestro and say wahwah at appropriate intervals..."

"The maestro needs them to psych himself into the proper frame of mind. Mizaaz, you know. Disposition. Mood." She tried to keep the giggles out of her voice.

"Whatever. But what I want to know is why is it called a solo performance? Sometimes the names of the tabaliya and the harmonium accompanist are not even mentioned. The poor taanpura players are routinely left unnamed."

"No no, today I had specifically asked the announcer to give their names..."

"That's an exception. But otherwise, all these people are there up on stage for the same time as the main performer, and they're not sitting idle, either. Even those "samajhdars", appreciators, whatever you want to call them, I've seen them sometimes at performances by the really old maestros in Bangalore."

"You go to classical music functions in Bangalore?" she had asked, surprised.

"Only the North Indian ones, not the Carnatic, I don't understand them. I go when I'm homesick. Anyway, to get back to the topic..."

"You never sound homesick. On the phone. And you're always having such an exciting time there, it seems..." Nomita had interrupted. "Plays, theatre, music groups like Scorpions I think you said..."

But Rahul had refused to digress. "No, let me finish. Even those samajhdars have to work really hard. After all they are on stage, people are watching them. The performer keeps glancing back at them whenever he executes some difficult phrase. Their wahwahs have to be sincere, or at least sound sincere, their appreciative nods have to have just the correct touch of drama and truthfulness. They have to be ready to forward the glass of water whenever the performer indicates, usually with a lift of the eyebrow only, that he is thirsty. I once saw one holding a spittoon while the aged maestro hawked and spit into it. And yet the samajhdar's name was not mentioned by the announcer. I would say his role was as difficult as the violin player's..."

"Hm. I'll have to think about that. Yes you're right. I wonder why it's called a solo performance. Got it. Yes. It's because the main singer or musician performs, and the others follow. The harmonium and violin players echo, follow what the vocalist sings, though of course they are at liberty to add their own embellishments, within limits, of course."

"But the tabla? They have to be creative in their own right, don't they?"

"Yes, but...the pace, the tempo, is set by the vocalist or instrumentalist. Always. The tabla player never does that." She felt quite pleased with herself for managing to best Rahul at least once in discussion. "The other performers are indispensable, but they are secondary. Which is why there is this convention that a more proficient accompanist will never play with a lesser main artiste. Obviously Zakir Husain will not play with me, because he's cuts above me. He will not 'follow,' it will be I who will be left limping after him. See?"

"Doesn't seem fair, though," Rahul had said. "They shouldn't be called 'accompanying artistes,' I feel..."

"Don't worry, some of them make much more money than the main artiste. After all, they accompany many artistes, and though they get less than the main performers each time, the amounts add up because of the number of artistes they accompany! That should make you happy for them. I know for a fact that Srinjoy made more than me today, because he accompanied two other artistes. Of course for my show he made only half of what I did, but on the whole..."

"Maybe you should have taken up the tabla, then," Rahul said, expertly avoiding a pothole.

"A woman tabla player. Yes, perhaps..." She had leaned back, careful not to upset the delicate equilibrium of the resonator on her lap. "Yes, why not. Another Anuradha Pal. Striking a blow for women's emancipation as well as bettering my economic condition, all in one go..." Giggling, she had added, "But maybe I would have become masculine looking...muscular, with broad shoulders. And my hands would definitely have been roughened."

"Anuradha Pal looks feminine and pretty, though," Rahul had pointed out.

"Hmm . You've seen her?"

"On TV. And pictures. She dresses very well, looks nice..."

"Yes, she does, doesn't she...?" In case Rahul thought she was envious of his praise of this woman tabla player's looks, she added, "She's really attractive, isn't she?" Nomita had thought for a few moments, and added, "Why is it that there are such few women tabla players? Why is it still such an overwhelmingly masculine domain?"

"Because women are poor in mathematics!" Rahul had said, smugly.

"Really? Who said?"

"Name a world famous mathematician who is a woman? No? Can't think of any, offhand? See what I mean?"

"That means nothing, I don't know the name of any world famous male mathematician either. In any case, playing the tabla is much more than mathematics," Nomita had pointed out.

"But knowledge of mathematics plays a very important part in the teaching of the tabla. In fact all Indian percussion instruments need a lot of mental counting." Sometimes Rahul's "insider" knowledge of the finer points of classical music surprised her.

"What is needed is arithmetic, Rahul, not mathematics. And women are good at that, no argument." She had paused, then whipped out her trump card. "All the arithmetic teachers in our school were women, don't you remember? Right from kindergarten. Two plus two, eight multiplied by three... that's the kind of calculation that is needed in playing the tabla. Cycles are doubled, tripled, while still, all the time, maintaining the tempo of the base cycle... And also, to be a good tabla accompanist, you have to have sensitivity, you have to anticipate what the musician is going to do next, you have to adapt your playing to the different styles of the main performers that you accompany, vocal or instrumental..."

"And in any case, women don't have the stamina, the physical strength, to play the tabla," Rahul had ended complacently, as though Nomita hadn't spoken in between.

"I wonder if that's true, though," said Nomita thoughtfully. "I mean if women can run the marathon, and play power tennis, surely they should be able to build up enough strength to play the tabla? The practice required is rigorous, no doubt, but then so is the practice required for sport."

"You may be right," Rahul had conceded unexpectedly. "In fact for example look at the gap between the prize money in international tennis in the men's and women's sections. But the money for women's tennis is catching up with that of men's. Hmm. Maybe it's historical, then? I mean women weren't allowed to perform in public anyway, it wasn't perceived to be a 'proper' thing for women of 'good' families" to perform on stage. And accompanying a male singer on the tabla would be a double whammy. A rousing scandal, twice compounded? Something like that?"

"There's also the hierarchy thing," mused Nomita. "It's still very strong..."

"Yes, you had told me about it... Sandhya Senapati's stories about her problems with getting a good tabaliya during the earlier part of her career..."

Nomita remembered how Guruma had smiled wryly, as she had recounted the travails of those days, how hierarchy in the world of classical music was indeed a very strong force. She remembered too, how much, but not all of it, was age related, and it was all part of what was expected. An older accompanist rarely sat down on stage with a younger sitarist or vocalist, even though he was very good. But with women, even accompanists who were younger often avoided being on stage with them. It was all done delicately, no doubt, but it was unmistakable.

And when it came to a young girl such as Sandhya Senapati, hugely talented no doubt, but an upstart in the sense that she belonged to no established Gharana, no traditional family of professional musicians, there had been problems. In her twenties, Sandhya Senapati had been a luminous performer, lighting up the stage with her music as well as her presence. But her very youth had worked against her. None of the established tabla players of the day had wanted to sit with her on stage, for to play with a young person, and a woman at that, was seen as doubly demeaning by them.

"Guruji used to be very distressed, poor man," she had said. "Pandit Chiranjeev Mukherjee was unused to this kind of behaviour on the part of accompanists. Oh it was subtle, no doubt, nothing crude or overt about it...but over a period of time, it became increasingly apparent to Guruji that things were different when it came to a woman performer. The best tabla players of the time – Pandit Ram Kishore Pandey, Ustad Tanveer Ali, the best regarded sarengi players of the age, Pandit Bhola Choudhury, Zubair Khan – would cancel previous appointments in order to accompany Pandit Chiranjeev Mukherjee on stage. They would fall over themselves to satisfy the maestro's every whim, for he was at the top of his powers then. To accompany him at the Gandharv Sabha, or the All Bengal Music Festival, was high honour, and there was intense competition among the best of them for the privilege.

"But when it came to accompanying me, the same rules did not apply. Of course in the beginning I did not merit accompanists of the stature that Guruji did. But even the second rung players, with whom I was certainly at par in those days, shied away from accompanying me. Oh, they would throng Guruji's house, no doubt, waiting for a chance to sit with him at practice, waiting for the opportunity to impress him, so that he would tell the organizers of his next few functions that he needed this tabaliya, and that sarengi and harmonium player, to accompany him. But when it came to playing with me, they would suddenly remember that they had been booked for a programme on that very evening. 'So sorry Guruji, extremely sorry, but what can be done? This programme in Burdwan, (or Srirampore, or Asansol or any other small town whose cultural life was not easily verifiable from Kolkata in those days) is a nuisance, but what to do? I am committed to it. If you command me, I will of course cancel it, nothing can be more important than obeying your wishes…" But of course Guruji could not do that. Cancelling a programme is one of the greatest acts of unprofessionalism on the part of musicians, and can only be done in the case of death in the family or serious illness. And even those tabaliyas and harmonium accompanists who were, at that time, several rungs below me in proficiency, even they were reluctant to come on stage with me. But your Guruji tells me he never faced this problem. There were any number of accompanists, of his standard, who were vying with each other at any point of time to avail of the chance to travel with him, appear with him on stage, no matter how far the venue, or how small the remuneration, or also, how unimportant the occasion.

"Of course things have changed now, at least from the gender perspective. But only changed. They haven't got rid of that mentality totally, at least that's what I feel."

She remembered now that Rahul had his own take on that. "Maybe it has something to do with male bonding. You know, the corporate thing, the old boys' network, kind of transferred to the musical domain," he had offered. Warming up to the theme, he had added, "After the stress of a function, comes the high of achievement. Doesn't it? Everybody wants to celebrate. A drink or two in the hotel room, a sense of camaraderie... none of which is possible if the main performer is a woman. And even if there's no tippling, there's this male fraternity thing."

"I don't agree, Rahul, I think it's just a gender issue like so many other things. Women performers were equated with dance girls, who solicited even as they danced and sang. And a woman accompanying a performer on stage is perhaps seen to be in a similar light. That's why maybe there are hardly any of them around." She had paused, then added, "If I ever have a daughter, I'll make her a sarengi player. A woman sarengi player! The world's first!" she had finished dramatically.

"It's the nails..."Rahul had said calmly, unimpressed by her earthshaking pronouncement. True, sarengi players, as far as anyone knew, were always male, usually of a certain age, for this was recognized to be a "dying instrument." There were few new students who came to learn under a Guru, for there were instruments that could be mastered much more easily, compared to this notoriously difficult one. So what if the sarengi's voice was acknowledged to be the closest approximation, world wide, to the human in intonation and timbre? As an accompanying instrument, as well as a solo one, it brought out the throbbing pain of the human condition in a way no other could do. The sufferings of the harsh desert land to which it traced its origins were immediately evoked when the bow was placed on the strings of the short, squat instrument. But the hours that had to be spent daily on rigorous riyaz, before the sarengi began to sing under the maestro's fingers were notoriously long. It demanded a lifelong commitment, and also sheer physical pain, literally blood and tears, before it began to respond to the player's fingers in such a way as to moisten the eyes of the listener. The tips of the nails of the fingers of the playing hand of dedicated sarengi performers were always worn down to the quick, for there was no intervening plectrum or pad between the player's fingernails and the rough gut strings of the instrument. The protective callouses that gradually formed on the fingers gave some relief from the pain, but just a week away from the instrument would bring back the sensitivity, and the excrutiating pain, when the first note was played again.

"Cosmetic reasons," Rahul had said infuriatingly. "You know what the fingers of sarengi players look like. Gnarled, calloused, thick yellow nails that are ground down to the base, almost. Which young girl is going to start on the instrument knowing that her hands and fingers are soon going to look like that? The sarengi player's hands age so much before the rest of the body. No, your mythical daughter is not likely to take up that instrument, even though you want to strike a blow for women..."

Nomita had rolled her eyes exasperatedly, but hadn't risen to the bait.

"In fact," Rahul had said, warming up to his theme, "now that I think of it, cosmetic reasons play a huge role in a woman musician's choice of instrument. Seen any women flutists lately? No, of course not. They don't take it up because playing it would make their cheeks puff out... not so aesthetic, is it?"

"Haven't you heard of the Sikkil sisters?" Nomita had asked irritatedly. "Wonderful flutists, Carnatic style. And they don't puff out their cheeks, they play with their lips. And they have such attractive stage personalities..."

But Rahul had steamrolled on, pretending not to hear. "Or the shehnai. Heard any women shehnai players? No, I thought not. Naturally, girls don't want to spend their working lives puffing out their cheeks... Or the sarod. How many women sarod players do you know? Very few. It's the same problem with the nails, the fingers. The sarod is a long and heavy instrument, without frets, it needs to be played with the fingertips which become calloused in no time."

"God, Rahul...!"

"Or wait, there's another reason, I mean in addition to all this!" he had continued, his eyes gleaming, "there may be another aspect to it. It's all about that area where men have acknowledged superiority. I mean, no question..."

"Rahul, there is no such area, you know it perfectly well."

"Of course there is. Strength, brute strength." He had preened, comically exaggerating the movement. "That's the reason. How can a woman lug around an instrument as heavy as the sarod? It's just not possible…"

"It's obvious you haven't heard of Shireen Daruwalla," Nomita remembered retorting, as sarcastically as she could. "A woman sarodist." Even as she said it, though, she had felt the feebleness of her point.

"One swallow does not a summer make, Ms Nomita Sharma. The bulkiness of these instruments is probably the reason – well, one of the reasons" he had conceded "that women don't take them up. There are many more women violin players, after all, than there are women rudra veena artistes. The violin is small, light, portable. Weight, and strength, are also probably the reasons you have hardly any woman harmonium accompanists. Those scale-changers of today, like the one you have, are real monsters, aren't they? Accompanists in any case don't get the kind of treatment that the main artistes do, they are expected to lug around their own instruments, at least in the early stages of their careers. I notice you can't walk very far with your own harmonium, you need male help…!"

"Rahul, I'm going to scream if you don't stop this instant."

Rahul had grinned in a pleased way. He had barely listened as Nomita fulminated. "You know very well it has nothing to do with looks, or strength," she had said. "It's a gender issue, a very sad thing. Daughters were never taught music in traditional Gharanas, you know that, because they would take the knowledge to a rival Gharana after marriage. And today, the traditional teachers are more comfortable with male students, though I admit this doesn't apply to everybody. And instruments like the Rudra veena and the Shehnai and Sarengi are dying out because of their sheer difficulty. I mean, which boy would opt to spend large chunks of his youth blowing at a mound of sand on his hand, or a dish of soapy water? That's the training shehnai players get in the beginning. The soap bubbles have to come out all the same size, exactly. The sand has to form a perfect crescent in the palm of the hand. That's how they are taught breath control. Leave alone girls, which boy, for that matter, goes in for that kind of agonizing training these days? It's so much easier to press the keys on an electronic keyboard, adjust the panel knob to 'sitar' and play it. No raucous notes, just clear melody from day one. Of course it's a different matter that the suggestiveness of the instrument, the special timbre, is lost. Bismillah could bring tears to the eyes of the most unschooled listener with a single phrase of his shehnai. The keyboard can replicate the same musical phrase, easily, but where is the emotion, the Bhav, the Ras?"

She had become quite passionate.

"And as for accompanying instruments, haven't you seen the new cases that musicians use for their instruments? Nifty fiberglass affairs, totally padded for protection. The tablas are put in a kind of fiberglass tower, one on top of the other, and what's more they have very efficient wheels. The same thing goes for the harmonium, the sarod, the sitar. Brute strength is a neanderthal concept, a highly overrated virtue in today's world. Male muscles are irrelevant. And in any case, not all instruments are as heavy as the scale changing harmonium. The ghatam, for instance. A clay pot, so light, a child can carry it, yet capable of the most intricate percussion. But you don't have women players. It's a gender thing, I tell you."

Rahul had grinned. "Of course it's a gender thing, but not in the way you mean. Ghatam players rest the pot against their bare bellies, their upper bodies are bare. This gives more resonance to the sound of the instrument, I think they use their bodies like a resonator. Wonderful. But then how can a woman do that? I don't see a woman taking off her Kanjeevaram and her…ummm…undergarments to produce the same sound! Maybe in a nightclub, but in a staid classical music concert…!"

"Rahul!"

"It's still as easy as ever to rile you, I notice," Rahul, had said, infuriatingly. His grin had been wide as he brought the car to a gentle stop in front of Nomita's house, and had added, "We'll continue this debate another day."

Actually, thought Nomita later as she lay in bed listening to Shiv Kumar's familiar santoor on World Space, actually, the way one drove one's vehicle was more or less an extension of the way one walked. Remembering the argument with Rahul in the car had brought the question of being driven around to mind. She thought of the ride home from Jhankaar with Sheila. Moving through the world, negotiating the traffic, or the people in one's path, on wheels or on one's own two legs... surely the two couldn't be that different. A person who walked timidly would surely drive timidly. Other drivers would bully him on the road, crowd him into a corner, overtake him from the wrong side. He would be intimidated into driving for miles behind a truck billowing black clouds of exhaust fumes, and would arrive at his destination blackened and despairing, but not raging.

Or would he? Maybe not. Road rage was quite likely to overtake the timid person once he or she was behind the wheel. All the suppressed wrath within would come boiling out like lava on a fresh volcano, destroying everybody in his path with his rampaging anger.

Hmm, yes. She couldn't change the way she walked, not yet, but she would change the way she moved around town. Her parents both drove their own cars, but Nomita had never picked up the skill. It was perhaps a reflection, again, of her profession. She knew no woman classical singer who sat behind the wheel. Guruma had a chauffeur, and lately, Tridib Barua, too, had begun to prefer being driven around to driving in the snarly Tamulbari traffic. It was as though the traditions that were part of the classical music heritage pulled the devotee and the performer into the past. There was no reason why she should not drive herself to work, or to functions, instead of waiting around for rude auto drivers to fleece her or for skeletal rickshaw pullers to shakily practice their poor road skills on her.

She would start from the very next morning, she resolved, she would ask her father to start giving her lessons. Or maybe, it might be a better idea to enroll herself in a driving school, perhaps the one that Sheila had mentioned: Safe Driving School. Her parents would be surprised, for she had never shown the slightest interest in acquiring a skill that most other girls of her age, had these days.

Perhaps, once she acquired independence of movement on Tamulbari's streets, her walk would change, too for a walk was a reflection of one's personality, after all. Maybe her walk would be like Jimli's or Sheila's, brisk and confident, with long strides.

18

Over the next few days, Debojit's voice got rapidly worse. It now became quite apparent that it was not going to be possible for him to carry off the important role of the policeman in the play. Not unless some drastic measures were taken. Nomita did not know what palliative to use to repair it, or at least mend it temporarily till the concert was over, after which it could go the way nature dictated, till it finally stabilized in a different register.

Sandhya Senapati, true to her word, had asked her husband about the best way to deal with the problem of a breaking voice in an adolescent boy. Tridib Barua had come to her next class himself, and waited till the end to talk to Nomita alone.

"It's a normal thing, of course, but it has to be handled sensitively," he had said, his own low pitched voice resonant with latent melody even as he spoke these words. "On no account must the boy be allowed to strain his voice. On no account. If he puts any strain on it... if he tries to reach for a note that is not within the range of his breaking voice right now – the damage caused to his vocal chords will be permanent. His voice will crack, and it will remain like that, cracked and discordant and untuneful, for the rest of his life."

This sounded alarming.

"Actually, why don't you bring him over, and I'll see what I can do. His scale, the pitch at which he sings now, will have to be changed. Probably lowered for a while. But that will need sitting with him for some hours, testing his voice, its register, its present range..."

Nomita was surprised. An artiste of the stature of Tridib Barua would hardly be expected to look at the problem of an unknown boy's cracking voice. But then she had always known him to be a kind man.

"Nomita's got another problem on her hands," added Sandhya Senapati. "Her concert is coming up, and this boy, Debojit, has an important role. Lots of singing, in Raag Durbari, na?" she asked, turning to her student.

"And I can't bear to think that the boy may be deprived of his role. He was blossoming so well, singing and acting also... in fact his whole personality was changing, he was becoming so much more confident. He'll be shattered if his role is taken away. But what can be done? The concert's only weeks away, we can't wait for his voice to settle."

"No," agreed Tridib Barua, "In any case, the whole process might take a year, or more."

The Kolkata programme was just a few weeks away. Nomita's lessons with Guruma were now centred on the forthcoming event. These were the lessons that she took from Sandhya Senapati, by herself.

"I was thinking of some Raag that has a touch of the monsoon, since it's going to be in the middle of the rainy season. Nothing heavily into the Malhar group, not Megh Malhar or Miyan Malhar, you know, those Raags that are associated only with the rains. I mean, the other artistes are sure to perform those Raags, it's expected. Pandit Ashutosh Ghosh, for instance, he's more or less specialized in those Malhars. After all one only gets to perform them at this season. Sur Malhar, Ramdasi Malhar, the lot. It will be a treat to listen to them."

Nomita, playing the perfectly tuned taanpura softly, smiled. All these names – Pandit Ashutosh Ghosh, Ustad Rashid Khan, Pandit Ajoy Chakravarty, Vidushi Kishori Amonkar, Ustad Asad Ali Khan, Shahid Pervez, Ashwini Bhide, Amjad Ali Khan – they were names that were so deeply embedded in her consciousness that she tended to forget that she had never actually met, or even seen, any one of them. But one or the other's voice, or instrument, was always playing in her room.

Once more, she felt a sense of happy anticipation. A live performance always brought a different dimension to the whole musical presentation. The sterility of the studio was replaced with the living, vibrant presence of an audience.

But Guruma was speaking again, her voice so soft against the melody of the taanpura that it seemed like a song, even though she was only instructing her student.

"... so I was thinking, what about Des? It's a monsoon melody no doubt, but not one of those "obvious" ones. Or maybe Jaijaiwanti. Miyan Malhar would have been wonderful, obvious or not, but I always feel that female voices are not suited to it. A good baritone does wonders for the loops and meends of Miyan Malhar, bringing in the effect of dark, heavy-bellied rainclouds on the horizon. I wish I could have heard Tansen perform it!"

Nomita smiled at the picture that Guruma's words evoked. The durbar of the Emperor Akbar in its heyday, the Navratnas, the Nine Jewels, sitting in the court, and, amidst the ornate carvings of the Durbar Hall, the immortal Tansen himself presenting his newest creation, Miyan Malhar. Miyan as in Miyan Tansen, and Malhar for the melodic family from which this Raag was created. Outside, the clear skies darkened as his voice swooped and dipped, bringing in little ripples of cool air into that summer-heated court. Then, as the taans gathered speed, the breeze freshened, and drops of rain, scattered at first, but swiftly gathering intensity, spattered the roof. To the mesmerized listeners, melody and monsoon merged into one as the heavens opened up to welcome the creation of this composition celebrating rain.

And later, this very rainy season melody became his rescuer, his saviour. If only she could have been present when, at the instigation of courtiers jealous of Tansen's bright star in the court, the Emperor requested him to sing Raag Deepak. Akbar himself was a tool in the hands of these envious people, for he had no idea of the terrible consequences that would be unleashed by his order. But Tansen knew fully well the intent of his enemies who were behind this order. Preparing to perform the incendiary Deepak, he also instructed his daughter in Miyan Malhar. And so, in front of the full Darbar, to the horror of most but joy of a few, the fieriness of the Raag Deepak caused the musician's body to be enveloped in flames. But just then a sweet but assured voice began the alaap of

Miyan Malhar from behind the purdah that screened the women who were witness to this scene. Such was the power of the Raag, and such the prowess of the performer, that within minutes, rain clouds had gathered, and the heavens opened up to pelt down rain. The maestro, burning with the flames generated by Deepak, rushed out to the courtyard, where the rains poured a benediction on him, and on the earth all around.

What a lovely legend, thought Nomita, as the images ran through her mind. So loaded with meaning. Even constant repetition hadn't succeeded in making it a cliché for her, not yet.

"All the compositions I've heard in Des are about love in the time of the rains. I mean, besides, of course, that ad in Bhimsen Joshi's voice. The usual bandishes in Des are more often than not sung in the female voice, aren't they? At least the ones I've heard, though there are lovely instrumental numbers too," remembered Nomita. She hummed the well known bandish that Malobika Kanan's mellifluous voice had immortalized,

Beet Jaat Barkha Ritu
Piya Na Aaye Eri...
The rains have come, the rains have gone,
But my beloved has not yet come home...

At the Tamulbari Public School, there was no way, now, that the calamity of Debojit's voice could be disguised. Tridib Barua had just come in from a concert in Pune when she took Debojit to him. When she had called him that morning, he had said, "Ah yes, the boy you had told me about. Yes, bring him in this evening, you don't have much time left for your concert, do you? I should be back by about four, so around six in the evening will be fine for me. Will that suit you? And him?"

She hadn't been aware of his absence from town when she had visited Guruma, just the day before. But of course Sandhya Senapati rarely spent lesson hours talking of her spouse, or his travel schedule. "You had a programme," she said, more as a statement of fact than a question.

"Yes, last night. In fact I left the dais at four AM, and came straight to the airport. I'm waiting for the flight now."

But when Nomita, with a nervous Debojit in tow, met him at the appointed time, Tridib Barua hardly looked sleep-deprived. True, he had had a bath, and was wearing a fresh kurta pyjama, but there was no trace of tiredness in his face, or voice. She wondered at his stamina. Tridib looked kindly at the boy as he rose from touching the Guru's feet. Debojit's new-found confidence had been on the wane after the crisis with his voice. Now it seemed to be at an all-time low.

"Cracking voice? It happens to all of us. Your Nomita Ma'am is a fine teacher, but when it comes to changing voices, obviously she's lost. Girls don't have all the drama about voices that we men do." He smiled gently, and said, "Right, let's start. We'll need the harmonium today, Debojit could you please just bring it here before me…yes, thank you. Now let's see."

Over the next two hours, Tridib Barua devoted his full attention to the boy sitting cross-legged before him. Nomita, sitting quietly at the side, marvelled at the man's ability to immerse himself so completely in this most basic of musical tasks, finding the correct pitch for Debojit.He could certainly have delegated the job to a senior student. But then Debojit's self-esteem would not have received the same boost as it was now getting. The boy, at ease now, was once more the confident singer that Nomita had coaxed him into becoming over the last several months of practice.

"Yes, so," said Tridib Barua, without glancing at Nomita. His whole attention was focussed on the boy before him. "So I think now, at least till this concert is over, you will have to sing in B Flat. Or perhaps lower, in A? Yes, better make it A, to be on the safe side. Let's see now, yes, this is your scale. Let's try the song on this pitch, shall we? How does it go… ?"

Now that the whole pitch of the song had been lowered appreciably, Debojit sang it with confidence again.

"Wonderful," said Tridib Barua, smiling. In his cream coloured kurta and immaculate churidar, he looked like the handsome god, Kartik. But he himself was totally unaware of his appearance, focussed as he was on Debojit. "Great. Sing it with a swing... and on this pitch, you really sound like a policeman, a musical policeman. But don't sing loudly, just do it in your normal voice. Too much volume will make your voice crack up again..."

He turned to Nomita, whose worry was clearly written on her face.

"I know what you're thinking. How will you synchronize his pitch, his register with that of the others now? Isn't that what you're worrying about?"

"Yes. The rest of the concert is in C sharp, the maximum I can lower the pitch without effecting the sound quality is one note, that is, C. If Debojit's songs are suddenly in A, it will not sound good at all..."

"But it will, if you bring in a bit of lead music. Like..." His fingers flew swiftly over the harmonium. Magically, a melody in C sharp dissolved into a series of rills that swooped and swirled in descending spirals till it came to rest on the tonic of the A scale. From here, the melody picked up, and then, suddenly, it was playing the Raag Durbari, in which all of Debojit's music was composed.

"And you do the reverse when you need to go up from his melody to the main one. Understand?" He gave a brief demonstration, coming to rest on the tonic of C sharp. He made it look and sound easy, but of course that was only because his sensibilities had been honed to a fine point by years, decades of practice. Nomita closed her eyes and committed the aural effect to her memory.

Debojit was beaming as they prepared to leave the room. "It will be all right now, won't it, Ma'am?" he asked trustingly.

Nomita smiled. "I think so. Just make sure you don't use your voice too much till the concert comes up... don't shout or even talk very much. Take care."

"I will," he promised, and she knew he would.

Placing the harmonium back on its shelf, she asked Tridib Barua, "Is Guruma inside? I don't think she knows I am here... I'll just go and pay my respects..."

"No, I don't think she's back yet," he said, looking at his watch.

"Oh, she's out? She has a concert, does she?" Nomita was surprised, for normally she knew Guruma's concert schedule quite well, and she hadn't been aware of one this evening. Sandhya Senapati usually did not go out for such things as social visits and shopping, not in the evenings, which were devoted to concerts, or lessons, or riyaz.

"No, not a concert. She's gone out with her friend... Deepak. Deepak Rathod. You met him at the Kaushik Kashyap concert?"

She looked sharply at his face. But his face was quite unworried. Tamulbari was a small town, and both Sandhya Senapati and Deepak Rathod were well known faces here. Their going out together was sure to raise comment. Surely, she thought protectively, they should be more careful? There was no anonymity here, tongues would begin to wag. They were already wagging. And why was Guruji so unaware of it? Even if their relationship was totally innocent and above board, even then, small town conventions dictated that they should not go around together, since both of them were married, with spouses waiting at home for them.

"Ah... where have they gone? I mean..." she sounded like Rupa or Panchali to her own ears, so she hastily amended it to: "I wanted to ask her something, about that trip to Kolkata we're scheduled to make you know... I thought I might meet her here now..." she ended lamely.

"They're at the riverside, I think. They were planning to take the ferry to see, experience the sunset on the river." His voice was as quiet as the scene he was describing. "Actually I haven't met her after coming back at all... she had gone out already."

This was worse. A husband coming back after several days' absence, only to find his wife gallivanting across the scenery in the arms of another man. Well, maybe not the arms, exactly, but that was what everybody would say. She realized that she was thinking like Rupa and Panchali.

"And yes, your Kolkata trip. Sandhya told me about it. You're looking forward to it, I suppose?" he smiled at her.

"It will be my first performance outside this state, you know. And I've never performed at such a huge Conference... I mean of course Guruma will be the main singer, but as a supporting voice..."

"Of course," he said soothingly, putting at rest her fears that he would think her uppity, concerned only about her own small role in the forthcoming concert, when she was after all going to be only a supporting voice to Sandhya Senapati. Such an easy man to get along with, she thought. Such a *good* man, she realized, and was surprised at the thought. "Good" was not an adjective that came easily to describe most of the people she met. Intelligent, lively, fun, talented, concerned… most of the people she met had lots of positive qualities. But it was Guruji whose presence and personality brought this adjective automatically to her mind. A good man. A man whose wife was taking his goodness for granted? She shook herself mentally, and, touching Tridib Barua's feet, took her leave. Other people's marriages were always a mystery, and when those other people were her Gurus, it was best not to allow her own thoughts to walk along those paths.

Guruma herself brought up Nomita's visit to Tridib Barua when they met for lessons. "Your Guruji told me you had come. That boy, Debojit, he has talent, your Guruji was telling me. I hope things become okay for him. Not much time left for the show, is there?" She didn't mention either her trip to the river, or Deepak Rathod. Though both were uppermost in Nomita's mind, she too, did not bring them up.

Nomita loved these lessons when she was alone with Guruma. It was not just that as Sandhya Senapati's most advanced student, the level of the lessons was pitched higher but also that the interaction between them when they were just the two of them, brought alive the historicity of the musical heritage that they shared. She felt she herself was the inheritor of a treasure that had come to her down the ages.

Guruma never withheld anything. She obviously believed in the Sanskrit saying that it was no shame to be defeated by one's son, or one's student. She laid out all that she knew, all that she had to give, in front of her students, according to the level of skill they had acquired.

There was that other thing about Guruma's teaching, her patience with the most inept of students. Sandhya Senapati thought nothing of spending hours more than the stipulated time with the girls and boys under her tutelage, constantly repeating the lines till the student finally got the hang of it. She was, in that sense, a New Age Guru. Till a generation ago, the Gurus, especially the traditional, Gharanedar ones, were notorious for the methods which they used to teach their wards, usually their children, or nephews. They would rise for early morning prayers, or Namaz, according to their religion, but make sure that their wards also rose with them. These were often children, little more than seven or six years old, the age at which training traditionally started. If these sleep-deprived tots delayed, they thought nothing of hitting vulnerable parts of their bodies, their ankles or their knuckles, with a cane or stick, till the child got up. They saw to it that they were kept busy with music all day long, with a break for school. But Nomita sometimes wondered: was it worthwhile to be an artiste of legendary calibre, if, in the process, that artiste had never experienced childhood? Today, these methods would probably be considered to be child abuse. Of course those were different times, the sensibilities were different, and the maestros of that era were recorded countless times speaking proudly of the tortures that had been inflicted on them during their training period. They wore them as badges of honour. It was all done with the child's best interests in mind. But things had changed, and thankfully neither Sandhya Senapati nor Tridib Barua even dreamed of using the notorious teaching methods of the past.

Listening to Sandhya Senapati, Nomita once more became aware of the way her personality and her music melded so beautifully It was the spaces, thought Nomita, listening to the leisurely unfolding of the Alaap, the introductory movement that set the mood of the piece. The spaces, and the silences. The calmness came to a large extent because of them, but they came so naturally to Sandhya Senapati that they seemed to be, again, an extension of her personality. True, her taans were fast, as fast as any woman vocalist, at par with Kishori Amonkar at her best, or even Parween Sultana, the doyenne of the superfast taan. But she sang them effortlessly, with subtle spaces between the phrases of even the taans, so that the tenor of quietude was not disturbed even during the swift portions of the recital. She had trained her accompanists to play subtly, in consonance with the serene Raags she sang so often. Her own surmandal was a whisper, an almost imagined zephyr that played within the portals of the Raag, accenting rather than disturbing the vast arches of stillness that she built, highlighting the spaciousness and the quietude.

This was a riddle, thought Nomita. How could one use sound, and yet create an aura of quietness? Yet Guruma did it time and again.

The air resonated with melody as Sandhya Senapati sang the phrases that defined Des. These were the notes, laid out, baldly, for all to sing, or play. But it needed a musician of exceptionally high calibre to be able to evoke the very essence of the Raag so effortlessly. The grace notes, the meends, the pauses, the silences that seemed, and indeed, now were, effortless, had actually been won through a great deal of sweat and toil. Nomita could not help the involuntary nod of her head in praise as she listened to the air around her prickling with the mood of the Raag.

"You were right the other day," said Guruma now, her speaking voice not breaking the spell of the melody. Nomita continued to strum the taanpura. "Most of the bandishes, the traditional lyrical compositions in Des are about separation. Love. Viraha. Since the Ras, the emotion that this Raag is meant to evoke is that of separation and longing in the time of rains, obviously there's not much that can be done about that. But for this programme I have a composition of my own... It's not about the longing of a woman pining for her lover."

Nomita looked at her cassette player, and checked to see whether it was working. Sometimes she missed large chunks of a lesson because for some reason the cassette player had stopped recording. Today, however, it was moving along nicely.

"I thought, why have the predictable? Why only a woman pining for a man? I mean... a man can pine for a woman too, can't he? Look at Ranjha, to what lengths he went to be near his beloved. How come we don't have any compositions in Khayal showing the man's point of view, of the longing that comes with the pangs of separation?"

"Maybe these compositions were there, and now they are lost," offered Nomita. "After all, till a couple of centuries ago, this was an oral tradition. Compositions have come to be written down only comparatively recently. It is more than likely that these were lost because of the path that classical music itself took in those preceding years. I mean, when compositions in these romantic Raags were sung by the Kotha women, obviously they would have had to cater to the male gaze. Their customers were male, they could not give the male viewpoint."

"You could be right," said Sandhya Senapati. "Anyway, even though I wanted to create a couple of stanzas from the man's point of view, I realized that it would seem incongruous if I sang it on stage. The audience is just not ready to take a woman singing out the despair of a man when he is separated from a loved one."

Nomita couldn't help smiling. "I see what you mean. It's okay when the genre is a ghazal. A man can sing of the fickleness of woman, about maikhaney, and shama, and parwana, and all those other conventions that come with the genre. That's why, barring greats like Begum Akhtar, the best ghazal singers are men. But in a Khayal, it's different. It's always the woman's point of view, isn't it?"

"Or nature. Or perhaps God, a Deity. Those are acceptable. Always have been. I thought of a devotional song, but then I didn't want to get into the Radha-Krishna cliché either. So I've been working on this composition. The whole song is a metaphor. I've tried to show the earth as a woman, the monsoon clouds as a male lover."

She picked up the book where she wrote her lyrics, and began to sing.

Sandhya Senapati often sang her own compositions. Indeed, Nomita had noticed that of late her Guru had become increasingly restless and dissatisfied with the traditional bandishes, the lyrics that both evoked the mood of the Raag, and were also the four-, six- or eight-line poetic pegs that were used to hang the melody on. And while melody was unchanging, the poetic content was sometimes a cause of dissatisfaction, for the Nayika of the sixteenth century was very different from the girl of the twenty-first. And the sensibilities of both singer and audience had changed greatly, especially if the singer was a woman. Sandhya Senapati often gave traditional bandishes a miss if they contained a heavy dose of words such as "Rasiya", "Baalam", and all those other monikers for "Beloved", or rather, "Male Beloved." She often composed her own lyrics, using the vocabulary and poetic conventions of the traditional ones, but a different set of images altogether.

Today, her composition was a masterly blend of earthly romance and a worship of nature. It took the diverse elements of romance and a love of the environment and seamlessly blended them into a composition that resonated at different levels. The symbolism was not heavy-handed, and was in consonance with the lightness of touch of the whole. Yet the lyric was quite capable of standing on its own merit, as a modern poem, instead of being merely a hook on which to hang the complexities of the Raag. In this, as in several others of Guruma's recent compositions, the poem was not just a bow to the inevitable requirement of words that a vocalist needed. It was a beauty in its own right. Nomita, listening to the bandish, was amazed. Guruma is a poet as well as a musician, she thought, not for the first time. And she is that unusual person, a classical singer, a woman classical singer with a contemporary sensibility of what womanhood in the twenty-first century is about. A classical vocalist who works with material that has come down to her through generations and centuries, but is moulding it according to contemporary thought. This, she knew, was a rarity in the music world.

As she left Guruma's house after lessons were over, Nomita wondered whether she would not have liked to sing "Beet Jaat Barkha Ritu…" on this particular occasion. She didn't yet know Kaushik Kashyap's plans, but what if, as the curtains opened, Nomita were to see his face right there in the front row? But then of course this particular lyric would not be very appropriate, for the next lines said "Piya Na Aaye Eri…" My beloved has not come. Whereas he would be there, very much so, right in the front row. Well then, another lyric of love, perhaps? Hindustani classical music had no dearth of women celebrating and welcoming their beloved's advent into their spaces.

Kaushik Kashyap – she really should stop thinking of him by his stage name – had called once or twice. She couldn't help feeling gratified that in spite of his strenuous schedule, he made time to call her.

"Why?" Rahul had asked when she had confided her feelings to him. Long distance, because he had left Tamulbari a few days ago. They were speaking on the phone, he from faraway Bangalore and she from the comparative coolness of her bedroom. "Nomi, you must realize you are engaged. To be married. Of course he should call you. So what if he's busy? Aren't we all?"

"True..." Nomita had admitted humbly, seeing the logic of what he was saying immediately.

"You must stop thinking of him as a star, Nomita, and begin to look at him as your prospective husband."

"Oh, absolutely..."

It wasn't going to be easy, though. The phone conversations between Europe or Japan and Tamulbari had been static-filled affairs, with their voices echoing emptily down the thousands of miles between them. Inevitably, the "How-are-you" and "Fine-what-about-you?" had not been sustained very long. She had in any case forgotten to ask Kaushik Kashyap - Kaushik - whether he would be in Kolkata at the time of her function.

But at least the man was making an effort. *Some* effort, she could imagine Rahul's exasperated voice correcting her. Would this much have been enough if her fiancé had not been a star? Would she have been happy, gratified with just this occasional phone call after they were engaged? Would she, in fact, have even agreed to an arranged marriage of this kind, with hardly any opportunity to know the groom, if she had not been a little star struck? A little in love with the man's music, much before she actually met the man in person?

Probably not.

She wondered how it had been with Sandhya Senapati and Tridib Barua. Now, of course, they listened to each others' music as appreciative listeners and were also, she knew, each others' most sensitive and honest critics. Indeed, to have an in-house critic in the form of a dearly beloved spouse who was also a practicing musician was a wonderful thing. But then Guruma and Guruji had been almost at par when they had got engaged. Both had been well known performers in their own right, and it was as separate performers that they had grown, in their highly individual ways, to their present stature. Whereas there was this gap – this chasm, almost, she thought in sudden despair – between Kaushik Kashyap's level of artistry and hers. She hoped Kaushik Kashyap would not deem it necessary to come to see her on stage with Sandhya Senapati if he was in town. In fact it would be good if he were not in town at all, and she could interact with Tirna and Rana Ghosh without the distraction of a fiancé hovering around.

She tried to hide the smile that came with the thought. Were all arranged marriages like this? If the "boy's" mother was as nice and friendly as Tirna undoubtedly was, was she, the potential mother-in-law, more of an attraction than the "boy" himself? Was marriage, then, essentially a bonding of women of different generations, with the husband a necessary… well, nuisance? No, not nuisance, of course not, not in that sense, but… a necessity that had to be tolerated?

In the smaller towns and certainly in the rural areas, the concept of the joint family was common. And all those bandishes that she herself sang, all those swoon-songs that the Raags were set to; did they not evolve through the nights of longing that the wives of merchants experienced when their spouses were away for extended periods on business? The lyrics she herself sang were full of references to the joint family. She hummed one under her breath…

Payal More Baaje…
Aila Piyu More Mandar
Ek To Dar More Saas Nanadiya
Dooje Deuraniya Jaage…
The anklets on my feet jingle with joy
My beloved has come home.
I fear his mother and sister will hear its sound
And yes, his brother's wife, too…

In fact, come to think of it, the lyrics were teeming with references to family. Even though they were four-line or at most eight-line affairs, mothers-in-law, sisters-in-law, brothers-in-law, fathers-in-law, were standard presences in them. They each had a fixed role, even though, usually, the Beloved was absent, or at best, a just-arrived or about-to-depart presence. The in-laws were all perceived to be in adversarial positions, all ready to put the Nayika firmly in her place. These were allotted roles, and the people in these compositions never moved away from the slots assigned to them.

Thank goodness Guruma had a contemporary sensibility. Thank goodness, too, Guruma was composing her own lyrics for the Des. Guruma, in spite of being so traditional looking, and being so rooted, was a woman of her times, and was creating a repertoire of lyrics more suited to today's young woman. Starting out with the compositions that she had been handed down by Pandit Chiranjeev Mukherjee, she had, over the years, slowly begun to sing bandishes, lyrical compositions that were her own.

Playing, or singing in Kolkata for the first time was, for a Hindustani Classical music performer, a definite landmark. Especially if the performer was from a place which, on the Shastriya Sangeet map, could be considered the boondocks. But even other artistes, those from Mumbai and Pune and Lucknow, considered it an honour, and a challenge, to be invited to perform at one of the several prestigious venues in Kolkata during the musical season.

Guruma had sent in Nomita's name to the organizers of the Borsha Utshob as her seniormost disciple, who would be providing her vocal accompaniment during her programme. The organizers had immediately and courteously replied, on a sheet of cream coloured paper with a flowery letterhead printed in Bangla and English, that she would be most welcome, and indeed, the organizers would be happy to bear the cost of her transport and hospitality, provided of course Sandhya Senapati booked her ticket immediately, so that they could take advantage of the lowest-priced ticket available. The extra money that could be saved could be used to pay for the transport of another group of performers. They also clarified that they had asked all artistes to come by one of the economy airlines, or by train.

This anxiety, thought Nomita when Guruma showed her the letter with a smile, was not misplaced. She had heard of several artistes, usually middle-rung names but also smaller fry, who deliberately delayed buying their tickets till the very last minute, throwing organizers of the concerts into a tizzy, and their budgets irretrievably into the red. It was no doubt a status symbol kind of thing for the artistes, who could boast about their supposed supremacy to the other artistes in the concert in a roundabout way by saying, "Ah, they paid you five thousand rupees for your ticket from Mumbai to Kolkata? Round trip? Hm. They paid me…let me think now…" Making a show of trying to recollect the amount, they would say, with mock vagueness, "Twelve thousand. Yes, twelve thousand, wasn't it, beta?" to the chamcha who accompanied the artiste. "Twelve thousand for the round trip. For each one of us."

Guruma, and also Guruji, of course were above all this. It would never occur to either of them to ever think that there could be this kind of "ticket-pricing politics" being played out in the Conferences that they attended.

Guruma wrote back immediately, and also explained that yes, she would certainly buy two tickets in a low-cost airline. This time, she had asked Nomita to help by buying them online. Neither Tridib Barua nor Sandhya Senapati were net savvy, though they had students who were more than happy to maintain their websites, answer their emails, or buy their tickets online for them. Yes, two. She planned to ask Soumeen Dutta, the noted tabaliya from Kolkata to be her tabla accompanist, and Prabal Mishra to accompany her on the sarengi. She would also pick one of the several top grade harmonium accompanists who lived there. She had spent many years with her Guru in Kolkata as a student, and was familiar with the accompanying styles and idiosyncrasies of most of the top-notch tabla, sarengi and harmonium accompanists. The organizers wrote back gratefully, for after all the price of three tickets saved was not a small sum of money. They offered her, in appreciation, the accommodation of her choice within a specified range.

Guruma, receiving this latest missive, opened it after Nomita's lesson with her.

"Where would you like to stay, then?" she asked. "They've enclosed a sample list of hotels. But a hotel is a hotel, a box kind of a thing, no matter how deep the carpet, or how springy the bed. A house is always better, na? I still feel inhibited practicing in a hotel room, even now. I feel I'm disturbing the people in the next rooms, though of course I know quite well that the sound of their TVs drowns out that of my riyaz, any day."

"Guruma, whatever you say, I hardly know any hotels in Kolkata. Somewhere near the venue, I suppose."

"Gauri Sabhaghar, that's the venue. It's very centrally located, so there'll be lots of good hotels around, that won't be a problem at all. But..."

Nomita looked questioningly at her.

"Deepak was saying he will be there at the time of the Conference. He wants us to stay there, at his house. It will of course be very convenient, it's in Ballygunge, not too far from the venue, we can go and listen everyday to the concerts. And if we stay in a hotel, naturally the organizers will only pay for one, maximum two nights. I was thinking... maybe we could take in the whole Conference, all seven days of it. And maybe a couple of days more, before and after – we can take in more concerts if there are any at the time. It will be wonderful exposure for you, and of course great for me, too. Some of the best performers will be there. I haven't heard some of them live, for years. This will be a fantastic opportunity. It's polite to take in the work of one's colleagues, see and listen to and feel what they are doing, their latest ideas and thoughts. It's a courtesy that we should extend to each other. In any case this is otherwise the lean season, there are fewer concerts being planned. I'm free during that time anyway. So what do you think?"

Staying in Deepak Rathod's place. Of course it would be so much better to stay in a home, anybody's home, than in a hotel. And Deepak Rathod... "What a wonderful idea! Yes, we'll do that, I'm so looking forward to it." She wondered if the home also housed the wife. She would have to ask Rahul , when they spoke in the evening.

She would be expected to at least drop in at Tirna Ghosh's place. Kaushik Kashyap's place. She remembered that she still hadn't told him that she would be going to his hometown. She resolved to do so, immediately.

She could never connect to his phone. Maybe it was the roaming, maybe a small town like Tamulbari just did not have the sophisticated technology needed to connect with someone who was in Florence one day, Milan the next, and Rome the third. She went, that evening after dinner, to the PCO round the corner, and, under the inquisitive combined gaze of three other customers in line behind her, plus the PCO operator, she tried the number many times, but failed to get through.

"Okay Ma'am let me try..." But in spite of the PCO operator's confident words, he too failed to connect.

"It's a Kolkata cell number, isn't it?" He examined the first digits and spoke with the authority of one whose life's work was to make sense of all these numbers that identified one's means of telecommunications.

"Yes...but it's on international roaming, he's somewhere in Europe now..."

The boy looked at the numbers, then at her with new respect. People making international calls from his Public Call Office booth were very common, hardly worth commenting on. But this was probably the first time a person was trying to get through to somebody on international roaming. The person who was being called must be rich, he thought. It needed a tidy packet, to take calls on an Indian cellphone in 'phoren' countries. "Let me try again..."

But Kaushik Kashyap was unreachable that evening. Perhaps he was at a concert. Perhaps he was with Lucia, giving lessons of course. She scolded her small town thoughts into order before they strayed into the arena of speculation. Perhaps he was too busy composing something for his next fusion album, something that would bring him even more awards and accolades.

Back home again, she called Rahul instead. As usual, his voice on the phone, "So Nomi, what's up?" lifted her spirits immediately. So what if her betrothed was unreachable. There was Rahul, her best friend, who was always there for her. Rahul, whose friendship had been her constant companion ever since she could remember. Rahul, whose closeness geographical distance had not managed to dim. She remembered that he too was due to head West. For a few years. She shrugged, mentally. Well, most of her income would be swallowed up by phone bills, there was no help for it. Unthinkable that she would curtail these calls, these impulsive hellos, throughout the day. He too, called her whenever he felt like it. Of course there was the cheaper option of the internet, and email. But there was nothing like actually hearing the voice of the person one was communicating with. She would have to learn how to Skype, she thought, remembering what Rahul had told her about it. Marriage to Kaushik Kashyap was hardly going to change anything, as far as her friendship with Rahul was concerned. After all, they were all in the twenty-first century now, and if she could be so calm, so matter-of-fact, about Kaushik globetrotting with Lucia in tow, then surely Kaushik too, would just have to take in his stride the fact of her friendship with Rahul.

"Guess where we're staying in Kolkata?" she asked. She knew he would understand that she was talking about the Borsha Utshob function.

"Kashyap's house?" he asked immediately.

"No no, of course not, it wouldn't be proper, Rahul." She did not doubt that he would be able to detect the irony in her voice immediately. "Besides, there's Guruma, I have to stay with her. We'll need to practice..."

"Taj Bengal? Oberoi Grand? You sound excited. Maybe Shonar Bangla? "

"Don't be silly, Rahul, this is a classical music concert, not a rock show or a Bollywood binge, remember? Guruma is highly respected but classical conference organizers are hardly as rich as those bringing in Mallika Sherawat to entertain the drooling masses. No, we'll be staying in Deepak Rathod's house! For a week! Maybe more! I'm looking forward to it! Really!"

"Wooo, you're not joking?" Rahul's voice sounded even more excited than hers. "Deepak Rathod! He has a penthouse apartment in Alipore..."

"No, in Ballygunge, I thought?"

"And a mansion in Ballygunge. That's the family place. Not to mention dwellings in Mumbai and Delhi. And one or two abroad, I think. Thailand or was it Indonesia, if I'm not mistaken? Nomita, I wish I had stuck to those tabla lessons when I was small..."

"Tabla...?" But even as she repeated the word, Nomita began to smile. She knew what was coming.

"Yes, I could have gone as your tabla player, you would have prevailed on Sandhya Senapati to take me along, wouldn't you..."

Nomita laughed. "It's a mansion, did you say?"

"Nomi, what world do you live in? His homes feature in the lifestyle magazines all the time. His interviews are always appearing in the pink papers. He's quoted extensively in *India Today, Indian Express,* and not just in the business pages either. He's supposed to be one of the faces of New India. And really, it's not fair that you, and your Guruma, who are part of Old India, are going to stay with him! It should have been me!"

"Hah, Old India, are we? What do you mean?"

"Well...ummm. Traditional, that's what I meant."

"Are we?" Lately, Nomita had often felt the same, and the thought had depressed her. To be traditional, in her mid twenties, was that a good thing? It sounded so boring. She should have been part of the New India at her age, bringing vibrancy to tradition, instead of merely continuing the tradition through her music.

She listened absently to Rahul chattering on about Deepak Rathod's excellent talk at an Economic Conclave that had been televised live. For a moment she saw herself morphing into the long line of those women whose images were ingrained in her mind. Kesarbai Kerkar, Gangubai Hangal, Girija Devi, Begum Akhtar, Shobha Gurtu. Wonderful musicians all, but all of these venerable ladies had, during their time, been at the cutting edge of modernity. Of course they had continued the tradition in their music, but in their lives, they had been feisty feminists, going where few women had gone before, making sure that the way became easier for people like her to follow. To perform on stage in those days was a new and difficult thing to do. And here she was: instead of breaking boundaries, she was the embodiment of tradition.

She chafed at the thought.

"I was reading an interview of his just last night where he said his favourite musician is Sandhya Senapati. You know? In fact, I thought the interview gave a hint of something going on there. Is it true?"

"Some of those interviewers are very narrow-minded it seems," said Nomita primly. "They still think a friendship between two people of different sexes must end with a frolic in bed. I don't know what papers you read, Rahul, but they seem to be little more than gossip rags..."

"Ooops, sorry, only asking. Can't imagine your Sandhya Senapati having an affair, that's true, she's so proper and virginal, but one never knows..." Rahul sounded unrepentant and cheerfully irreverent.

"A friendship between two people of opposite sexes, no matter what their ages, is quite common. We don't have to mistake a friendship for lust, or romance, or even love, do we? A friendship is a friendship, and if spouses are comfortable with that, why should others bother? A friendship, Rahul, surely you, of all people, should know that such things happen...?"

Nomita paused to take breath before continuing her harangue, most of which was only half jocular.

Uncharacteristically, Rahul didn't rush in to fill the gap. After a couple of beats, he asked, "Why me of all people?"

"What?" She was momentary confused.

"You just said that. 'You of all people.' Why me?" His voice over all those thousands of kilometres was suddenly different. Cautious. Quieter.

But Nomita noticed this only peripherally. "Well, because you have lots of friends, friends who are boys and friends who happen to be girls, don't you? Ranjita, Jimli, Sheila. Me. Nobody would point a finger and suspect you of having a romantic liaison with any of the girls here. And friendship, in itself, isn't it as valuable, maybe more valuable even than romance? It's not necessary to keep talking about, umm...to keep *affirming* friendship, because it's there. A friend is not easy to find, Rahul, and harder to keep. I think friendship is more complex, more permanent than romance. Friendship is a long distance race, romance is a sprint. Romance is not long lasting...I mean it's good while it lasts, but it never lasts long, does it? Look at the rate at which divorces are happening..."

"Am I hearing these tirades against romance from the girl who is...umm...betrothed to the great Kaushik Kashyap? And what is this talk of divorce-shivorce from the lips of a soon-to-be-bride? You sound too...practical...for a girl who's just had her marriage fixed with a TV star." Rahul's tone was back to its usual bantering. Maybe she had imagined the change earlier; in any case the lines across all those kilometres of ether were unreliable.

"He's not a TV star, Rahul, you just say that to irritate me, he's a famed classical musician. One of the foremost of his generation. *The* foremost, some say. By the way, I really should look at his website. I suppose he has one?"

"Everybody does. Except you," pointed out Rahul. "Shall I..."

Nomita remembered the website. It had occurred to her, suddenly the other day, that she hadn't looked at Kaushik Kashyap's – no, Kaushik's – website. She wondered at her oversight now, and resolved to look it up as soon as possible. She hadn't yet done so. Why hadn't she looked at the website before he had come to Tamulbari for the concert? Or even later, when she was "officially betrothed" to him? It had just never occurred to her.

She had no doubt that a jet-setting star like Kaushik would have a website, updated at regular intervals by one or a group of his students. Or perhaps, he would do it himself. Rahul had once told her that it was quite easy to put up a website, provided one knew how to go about it. He had offered, many times, to put one up for her.

"See how your programmes will multiply, Nomi! Exponentially!

We'll have you jetting around the map before you can blink!" he had said. "I'll do it for you in no time, just give me the details you want put up. And a picture, we want a good picture of our Nomi with her taanpura..."

But Nomita had demurred, feeling suddenly shy about it. "No, Rahul, thanks. I'm still at what is called the 'District Level,' or at most the 'State Level.' It will be redundant, because the organizers of classical music concerts in this State are totally ignorant about the Net anyway."

"You're probably right. Most of them seem to be old fogeys, I mean, sorry, 'People of a certain age,' aren't they? There are hardly any young people in the organizing committees of the concerts you've been performing in, I notice. If you're fifty you'll be considered a spring chicken in those circles, I guess... Still, no harm in trying..." Rahul had urged.

But Nomita had not agreed. She felt that it was a kind of advertisement of oneself, or at least of one's skills, to do so. Was putting up a website a kind of extended "self-promotion"? She knew many people, even in Tamulbari, musicians who she thought, quite objectively, to be less skilled than her, who had their own websites. There were performers who routinely sent their updated CVs to the committees of the music conferences. Sandhya Senapati did not need to do it, for she had a full itinerary anyway. She was quite sure, though, that Kamal Basu did it for Kaushik Kashyap, on a larger scale than she, Nomita, could even imagine. The man had a global reach, and also global ambitions, and he would need to advertise globally.

19

Stage rehearsals, dress rehearsals, final rehearsals. It was all quite exciting, not just for the participants, but also for the teachers who were organizing the whole show. It was of course acknowledged that this musical production was Nomita's baby, more or less, though she was helped by Sulekha, the dance teacher, and Sunil, the theatre teacher. Still, music was the backbone, the foundation on which the whole structure rested.

It was amazing though, thought Nomita as she stood in the first row of the school auditorium, watching the final rehearsal of "The Adventures of Kareena Kat," how free of stage fright these children were. The smaller the child, the more he or she took it as a game to be enjoyed, a wonderful, fun event. They stood in their roles, as trees, hills, flowers or clouds, quite alert to their cues. After all these months of practice, their singing was effortless and tuneful. Kareena Kat sang her way through her role in Raag Adana in a way that brought out the friskiness quite wonderfully.

The older ones were, in comparison, a little self-conscious, less at ease in their costumes, which they kept looking down at, and smoothing, to begin with. Gradually, though, they too were caught up in the joy of the performance, and things went easily, and effortlessly.

Debojit sang beautifully, but that didn't rid Nomita of her worries about him yet.

Now that Nomita had realized that Kaushik Kashyap would certainly have a website, she couldn't wait to have a look. As soon as she connected, the home page rolled in, beautifully conceptualized. On the gleaming background was a large picture of Kaushik playing the sitar. The camera had captured him at a moment when he was probably playing the alaap of a sober or majestic Raag such as maybe Malkauns. The expression on his face was serious, his eyes were focused in the distance, as though he was so immersed in the thought process of playing the music that he was unaware, unconscious of the photographer. His hands, one of his best features, with their long fingers, were placed on the gleaming instrument, whose metal frets caught the light. The ring sparkled, capturing the viewer's attention. From this angle, his ponytail wasn't apparent, though his curly hair seemed to be slicked back.

Of course it was a carefully chosen picture, maybe even a posed one. Still, it was impressive. She analyzed it critically, not as a prospective spouse, but as a web designer. It would appeal to both the Eastern and the Western. The ponytail, which would perhaps have antagonized organizers of such Conferences as, say, the Gandharv Mahasabha, or others in Pune or Jaipur, was diplomatically kept invisible. Yet the colour scheme of the home page, even the kurta that he wore – a shade of creamy gold that was the exact shade of the lettering on the page - was such that it would immediately catch the eye of the casual Western visitor to the site. There were three other, smaller pictures at the bottom of the home page, each in different poses, in different kurtas.

A thought crept into her mind. Did the sitar, that instrument which earned him his living after all, did that gleaming instrument look like a prop, rather than the focus of the picture? She quickly quashed the thought.

She clicked on the links. CV, with pictures, beautifully outlined in little oval frames, of Kaushik Kashyap playing in different poses. Accompanied by the traditional tabla, and also with Western musicians, in fusion. The prestigious venues at which he had played, all over the world were on another page. The fact that he was both a highly regarded classical performer who played within the tradition, and also a frontline fusion artiste, was highlighted. His many awards were listed in a beautiful scrolly font on another page. These included the "Most Promising Artiste" at a Sammelan in Mumbai years ago, when it had been Bombay, and he had been a teenager. The "Kal Ke Kalakaar" award, "Tomorrow's Artiste" at a Conference where his talent had been marked out, this when he was still a callow youth. The Padma Shri. Padma Shri! She hadn't known he was a Padma awardee. No, wait, she knew, but had forgotten. She remembered now that it had been listed at the concert. How could she have forgotten such an important honour? It just showed how stressed she was about the whole thing. The website mentioned also that he was one of the youngest recipients of this Government honour, probably the youngest as far as Classical music went. There was of course the mention of his Grammy nomination.

Remarks and excerpts from the reviews of the most well known music critics of India formed the content of another page. She turned to another link, where his addresses, email as well as geographical, and his phone numbers were given.

She sat back, dazed. On an impulse, she googled his name. Kaushik Kashyap. Fifty-six thousand eight hundred and thirty-two entries about him existed in the ether. She scrolled down the page, and looked at a few. They were all about his concerts, where he had played, what others had said about him, the reviews that well known journals all around the world carried about him.

And this was the man she was going to marry! A Padma Shri! Did girls like her marry Padma Shris? This was the man, in fact, who was already her fiancé! She felt out of her depth, as though the solid earth had slipped from beneath her feet.

She called Rahul immediately. As soon as he said, "So Nomi, what's up?" she wailed, "Rahul, I've been looking at his website! Kaushik Kashyap's! I'm going to marry a Padma Shri!"

Rahul chortled uninhibitedly. Nomita waited for his merriment to subside. Listening to him, though, she felt her anxiety drain away. She began to smile. Finally, in a voice still edged with laughter, he said, "So what will that make you? A Padma Shrimati?"

She could feel the giggles begin. Suddenly, though they were divided so immensely by space, it was as though they were in primary school again, making surreptitious fun of the teacher together, careful that nobody noticed their shared mirth. But even while she was chortling down the line, her delight fuelled by the sounds of Rahul's hilarity mirroring her own, a newer feeling crept into her consciousness. It was a feeling of...unease. Yes. Uneasiness cut off her jollity in mid-laugh. Wasn't it disloyal of her to laugh, that too with Rahul, about something pertaining to her fiancé? Even though, she tried to rationalize, it was the concept, the idea, which was provoking all this hilarity, rather than anything against the man himself.

Still. Pradma Shri, Padma Shrimati. The thought triggered off gales of laughter again. It wasn't just this particular not-so-good joke, it was the shared memory of all those occasions when they had guffawed together, when shared chortles, mostly surreptitious, had strengthened the bond between them. Those memories reinforced the humour of this moment, as they always did, sending the two of them into gusts of merriment quite out of proportion to the humour of the joke itself.

"This is ridiculous," gasped Rahul finally.

She could see his face in her mind as he spoke, his laughter-flushed face. His eyes would be crinkled up, maybe watery after this prolonged bout of merriment. His head would be thrown back, a capable-looking hand holding his cell to his ear. Rahul's hands were not like Kaushik Kashyap's, or Guruji's. They were engineer's hands, a little knotty already, but competent looking, even though he was an IT person, not somebody with a hard hat supervising construction in the open air. His voice was a familiar comfort, though she wished, suddenly, that she could be sitting opposite him in some newly opened Momo Palace in Tamulbari, discussing the nuances of the plateful of crescent-shaped pork-filled steamed dough, whether the covering was too heavy or too thin or just of the right thickness to hold the juices and the herbs and the meat safely inside.

"Okay, have to go, keep me informed about the Deepak Rathod thing. The mansion. And the wife, don't forget the wife. She's quite a somebody, in her own right, as they say. And if you can pick up a tip or two on how he made it so big, don't forget to call me. By the way, guess what, there's a new momo place in town! It's near HSR Layout and it's much better than that place near Brigade Road that had a monopoly, more or less, all these years. Still, it's nothing like our Momo Ghars and Momo Palaces... Bye now, take care..."

After all these years, she had stopped being surprised by the fact that quite often they thought the same thoughts, though there seemed to be no apparent logic to why a particular subject suddenly occurred to both of them at the same time. No doubt he, like her, was at this very moment thinking of the way, several years ago, they had together graded the momo outlets that kept springing up around their town.

"It's an art, finding the right momo place," he had explained when they were still in college. "You don't want to waste too much time ploughing through plates of indifferent stuff before arriving at the perfect momo. The trick's in the small print, of course."

Nomita remembered having looked derisively at him. But he had continued, unfazed, "See, the name can be anything, Momo Ghar, Momo Hut, Momo House, Momo Palace, Momo Palace-on-Wheels which, by the way, is what they have named that new cart at the market crossroads. It's the smaller print on the signboard that gives you the clue. If it says "Momos also available here," give the place a miss, even if it is a Momo Palace. The perfect momo needs dedication and concentration. The chef – that is, the urchin doing the cooking – should not be distracted by having to rush here to turn out a plateful of chowmein, and run there to stir a pot of chicken corn soup. If the small print says "Momos sold here," you can give it a try. It means that they concentrate on making momos, though they also, if required, turn out other stuff. But it's the signs that only say "Momo Cabin" or "Momo Cart" that turn out the best momos. No small print under the name, because it's unnecessary. They do only momos, and there's always a bamboo steamer full of the freshly made stuff. That's the place to go to."

Ringing off, she realized that all these thoughts of momos had made her hungry for some. But who would she go to the corner Momo Hut with? She decided to send Rina to get some, instead, though of course the actual way to eat them would be to take them off the steamer as they appeared, and pop them, piping hot and chilli-paste smeared, onto one's salivating tongue.

She wondered if Kaushik Kashyap was a momo addict. Probably not. Hardly anyone outside this region was one. Maybe she would have to give up her love of it, or keep it alive only when she came to Tamulbari, and Rahul too, was in town. This mournful thought so depressed her that she called Rina over and asked her to bring across two platefuls of momos from Momo Hut, and yes, that would be her dinner today, she wouldn't be eating anything else, thank you.

Padma Shrimati. She tried not to giggle again.

Rina arrived with the momos. Gloomily, thinking now of Lucia, she bit into one. Today, even the luscious slurp of the juices bursting out of their doughy skin on her tongue failed to cheer her up as she contemplated the fact that Lucia of the astonishing pulchritude was even now in close proximity to her fiancé, in who knew which place in Europe?

She finished the last one, guilt already eroding the pleasure her tongue and mouth had just received. Ten momos in one go! She visualized them going straight to her hips, which were already, she thought, of proportions to rival those statues on the Khajuraho temple walls. Probably, she gloomed, she was now at least double the size of Lucia. Never mind. She had been chosen by the Mother of the Boy, and it was anyhow well known that mothers liked their sons' wives to be well-nourished types.

Her cell rang, and she picked it up with one hand while licking off the last of the chicken shreds on the other. It was a number her cell did not recognize.

"Nomita?" said the pleasant voice at the other end, in response to her "Hello?" "This is Deepak." He paused a beat, and added, "Rathod."

She liked that pause, the natural humility which did not assume that she would recognize him as soon as she heard his voice for the first time on the phone. Though, of course she had, at once, for she was sensitive to voices.

"Of course Deepak, how lovely to hear you. Where are you? In Tamulbari? Or in your tea garden?"

"No, I'm out of the country actually. In Indonesia, on some work."

"Ah." She was getting more calls from outside Tamulbari these days than from the town itself. All her friends were long distance ones, it seemed. What did that show about her, she wondered briefly.

"Anyway, tell me, how are you? Good. Music going well? Riyaz? Great. Your voice sounds lovely as usual, even on the phone. One can always tell a trained voice – it has a kind of resonance. What's the word? Jowari. You have it."

"Thank you, Deepak, nice of you to say that." Genuine praise about the quality of her voice gladdened her more than praise about her appearance. How did Deepak Rathod know that? Or maybe he didn't, he was just being his usual nice self. There was no indication that this was a call from Indonesia, no echo or the gap between the saying of a word and the hearing of it that signified great distances. "You're in…" she quickly tried to recall those long-ago geography lessons… "Djakarta?" she asked tentatively.

"Yes, I arrived yesterday. I'll be here for some days, but I'll be back soon. In time to listen to you in Kolkata."

"Oh, that's nice." She meant it. They wouldn't have to stay in a house without its owner while in the Ballygunge place. They wouldn't have to make conversation with his wife whom she hadn't yet met of course, a stranger who was likely to be very different from her husband.

"Yes, actually I called to tell you, you're most welcome to stay with us, I mean I don't want you to think of yourself as an appendage to Sandhya or something, I look forward to your company there…"

He was nice, he really was. They talked a little bit of this and that, Nomita confessing that she was nervous and excited at the same time, and Deepak telling her not to worry, she and Sandhya sounded so good on stage together. He made her feel as though she was almost the main artiste, though her role, they both knew, was just a supportive one.

She felt much more cheerful after the call, more positive and looking forward to the Kolkata trip again.

It was good, really good of Guruma to take her on this trip. Actually, these days, the practice of having a vocal support was seen to be a kind of admission of being defeated by age. Most musicians did not take a vocal or instrumental support – a student who would fill in the gaps, play or sing the composition while the main artiste got his breath or stamina back – till they were of a certain age.

Sandhya Senapati was like the old Gurus, in this way. Stage exposure was a sine qua non for a student's growth And so besides performing at the smaller functions, it was necessary for a musician to get used to the experience of singing in vast auditoriums. And in any case, the accompanying, though not as challenging as a solo performance, was no easy thing, either. It needed a certain level of competence and imagination, and a deep understanding of the Guru's mizaaz, or temperament.

She realized she was referring to Deepak Rathod in her mind through his first name. Whereas when she thought of her fiancé, it was as the lengthy "Kaushik Kashyap" which was, in fact, not even his real name. Weeks after their marriage being fixed, she was still thinking of him by his professional name. She really should break out of this, and call him... what? Kaushikji? That was too cloying, as though she was a student, or worse, a chamchi. Of course many traditional wives of classical musicians did call their husbands "ji," but Nomita baulked at it. In any case, the "ji" suffix was never used in Assamese nor in Bangla. So what should she call him? Should she coyly invent a diminutive, like the wife of the famed violinist, Shekhar Singh, who called him by the ridiculous sounding "Shekhoo?" When a perky young journalist had asked Shekhar Singh at an interview if she could call him "Shekhoo" too, she, had been firmly put in her place by the musician, who had said ponderously, "No, that name is only for the use of my wife. You can call me Shekharji like everybody else."

And then, at the Tamulbari Public School, it was time for the final show.

Nomita, watching from an unobtrusive seat, felt a sense of exhilaration, and joy. It was a success, true, and she was responsible to a great extent for it. And considering that these children had known, and still knew, very little about Raags, she felt she had been a success as a music teacher. These children would remember this concert all their lives. It would be a warm and joyful memory, embedded in their minds, to which they could return again and again to recapture some of the feelings of this evening, and indeed, of the many days spent in rehearsals and practice. She hoped that she had sparked some interest in classical music in at least a few minds besides Debojit's. Perhaps, later, several of these children would learn to appreciate the wonder and beauty of this music.

She could see, from the way both Guruma and Guruji were leaning forward slightly, and smiling, that they approved. That was the accolade she wanted, and she was gratified when, once or twice, she saw Guruma's lips forming a spontaneous "Wah," and her head nodding synchronously in appreciation.

She wished Rahul could have been here. They had gone to this school together for over twelve years, and now, even though he was in Bangalore, he kept in touch with what was happening in his old alma mater through her. He would certainly have enjoyed the show, and praised her efforts in his own way. She had sent invitations to Ranjita, Jimli, Sheila and Reza, and she was glad to see them there, in the middle of the auditorium, looking happily at the happenings on stage.

The audience was enjoying it. True, this was an audience of parents, mostly, and guardians, with a sprinkling of grandparents, too. They would naturally be partial to any play or dance drama these children were in. Unlike the audiences that Nomita faced, they were all predisposed to think that this was one of the best productions that they had ever seen, in their entire lives. Most of them knew nothing about classical North Indian music, and were rather overwhelmed that their little tots were actually performing Raags. The announcement at the beginning had explained the concept of putting suitable melodies, encapsuled in specific Raags, to embody the main traits of the character who sang that song. It was a new idea for Tamulbari.

The auditorium was bright with flashbulbs. Not journalists, but parents who were capturing the moment for eternity, and for doting relations in distant parts of the world. In a professional production, the show would have been preceded by stern injunctions not to take pictures, because that would disturb the artiste. Here, the reverse was true. It was wonderful to see the pride on the faces of the parents as they walked to the side of the auditorium, careful not to block the view of the people sitting behind them, to take a picture of their little Nisha as a flower or Vedanta as a tree on stage.

She hardly ever felt this sense of exhilaration in her own performances these days. Was she jaded already, then? Jaded at twenty six, with so much still undone, so many peaks of musical excellence left unscaled?

And then it was Debojit's turn.

The interlude music began. It twirled and spiralled down in melodious phrases to the lower pitch, yet so subtly that hardly anyone in the audience was aware of what the actual purpose of this music was. She could imagine Debojit at the wings, impatient and slightly edgy, but confident, waiting to come up, singing his Durbari, while the rest of the cast looked at him with deference. He was after all the figure of authority in this production, and indeed, in his small sized white police uniform, complete with whistle and épaulettes, he looked quite impressive. And there was the baton, of wood but with ivory tips, which he twirled about impressively and quite effortlessly even as he sang his piece and strode about the stage looking for the lost Kareena Kat, and trying to fix the problem.

She glanced at Guruji and Guruma, sitting in the front row. Tridib Barua, recognizing the music, was leaning forward slightly, looking towards the wings to catch a glimpse of his protégé. He was like a father… in fact he would have made a wonderful father, she was sure. Incongruously, the thought flitted into her mind… Wonder why they don't have children? Professional commitments, too busy? Lifestyle problems? Or medical reasons? Or…

And then the musicians began to play the first few bars of the Durbari. This was Debojit's cue. And yes, it was going to be all right now. His voice, today, was in fine fettle in this new scale of his, it had the ring of authority of a policeman in its depth and its resonance. Both Tridib Barua and Guruma looked at her, smiling. She was aware that she was smiling, too. Nomita felt her spirits lift. Her nervousness vanished, and she settled down to enjoy the rest of the show.

The praise, the words of congratulations for her at the end were heart-warming. She was used to praise after her own programmes, but this was different. Parents were actually queuing up to meet her, even though she had thought she was sitting unnoticed in her place. Many of them she already knew, not so much by name but as the parents of her students.

Rana's father, a muscular man who looked anything but musical, said in his booming voice, "I must congratulate you, Ms Sharma, I don't know much about music, but this was really good. You got Rana to actually stand up on stage and sing… he's hardly ever in the same place at home for more than two minutes at a time, he's so restless, I know you must have been very patient and understanding with him…"

Sharmishta's grandmother held her hand and said, "It brought back memories of my own school days. But we had readymade plays and musicals in those days. Mostly Western ones, sometimes maybe something from Tagore. What you've done is wonderful, dear. To compose all this yourself, and then get these children to perform… nothing short of a miracle!"

But it was Guruma's and Guruji's words of praise which moved her most.

"Teaching is the noblest profession, Nomita, never forget that," Tridib Barua said. "It's obvious you're excellent at it. The show speaks of your talent for teaching music. It's not something everybody can do… Debojit is a highly talented boy, and I'm going to take him as my student. That is if you, Nomita allow me."

"That's really wonderful… I can't wait to tell him!"

"You've done marvellously, Nomita" he continued, his voice low pitched and warm. "Very creative, and so well executed! Wonderful, Nomita, really wonderful. You should travel with this show to other places. These children are good...you've made them good!"

Guruma glowed, as though the compliment was directed at her. She put her hand on her student's arm and remembered, "By the way, Deepak called from Djakarta, regretting he couldn't be here. He sent his best wishes."

"Thank you, that's so nice of him..." She turned back to the queue of parents and guardians waiting to speak to her.

20

The porter saluted them smartly and opened the leaves of a gate that looked like black Belgian lace. The house came into view.

It was, as Nomita had expected, a beautiful house, set in a leafy lane off the busy main road. Rahul had told her it was a mansion. The house's white, colonnaded porticoes and large bay windows pointed to its history. Unlike many of Kolkata's crumbling heritage buildings, this one was beautifully maintained, luminous in its setting of green lawns and immaculately tended borders that spilled over with bright flowers, all enclosed in high white walls that kept out the noise and the roadside pollution. Bougainvilleas arched the porch, and trees of a medium height shaded the house from the rays of the sun. The green of the lawns was echoed in the shutters on the deep windows on all three storeys of the house.

It's not a mansion, though, thought Nomita, relieved. Thank goodness. It's a neat size, not big enough to be a mansion. Or intimidating enough. There was an air of grace about it, and a welcoming look that imbued the house with a friendly aura.

The gardener came up to them, his weathered face creased in smiles, his hands gnarled from a lifetime's work with the soil.

"How are you, Dadamoni, *kemon acchho?"* Guruma asked warmly, addressing him affectionately as an elder brother. They discussed his arthritis and the fact that even the venerable Suttons in Russell Street had become a very unreliable supplier of seeds these days. It was only then that they moved on, to the cool, shaded interior of the house. The salaaming bearers, liveried and respectful but not obsequious, led them to their rooms on the first floor. Shaheb was away, and Memshaheb was not in town either, they informed Guruma, but of course Shaheb had told them to prepare the two rooms for them. Guruma they knew quite well, and she, too, was evidently quite at home here, asking an elderly bearer about his grandchild, and a young one about his wife. They stepped in to gleaming floors of red oxide. Nomita had expected marble, and was pleased. The ceilings were high, and the fans that hung down had long poles on which whirred the large-bladed devices, cream coloured, sparkling clean and quite efficient in spite of their age.

They already knew, of course, that Deepak was not in town, but would be in from Djakarta at dawn next day. As for Rati Rathod, no, Rati Mittal, she too was away, in Brussels, where she had an office. But she was expected soon, maybe even this week, if her work permitted.

The Borsha Utshob, the Rainy Season Festival, was not as old as some of those other classical music conferences of Kolkata, several of which had a hoary history like the Dover Lane Concert, the ITC Sangeet Sammelan, the Gunidas Sangeet Sammelan, the All Bengal Music Festival or even the Kolkata Jazz Festival. But it was already a very popular one.

This was in large part due to its being scheduled right in the middle of the rainy season. Traditionally, practical problems had made it difficult to hold elaborate music festivals during that time. True, the monsoons had always been celebrated in song and dance, poetry and drama, throughout the history of the arts in the subcontinent. But the holding of a Conference to actually celebrate the season when it was still in progress was a different matter. For one thing, it couldn't be held in the open air. With so many top notch artistes heralding the rains through Raags specifically created to celebrate them, it had been considered pragmatic not to hold a large conference under the skies at that time.

And so the Borsha Utshob took advantage of technological progress by using the Gauri Sabhaghar, the spacious Centre for Performing arts, a centrally air conditioned venue to keep the audience in comfort in this hot and humid season. Advanced architectural designs had enabled the builders to erect huge halls where the view of the proscenium stage was not marred and blocked by pillars to hold up the roof. Large enough to seat more than two thousand, it fitted the bill for holding a Borsha Utshob perfectly.

It was a measure of the wealth of the organizers of the Borsha Utshob that they could rent the hall at all, though it was also true that the Committee in charge of hiring out the hall gave classical musical functions, and especially the Borsha Utshob, deeply discounted rates. They said this was their way of supporting the arts. But it was also, undoubtedly, a good way of adding a touch of perceived class to the hall, which, otherwise, had to be perforce hired out to organizations holding such things as Talent Contests for Bollywood Dance Troupes.

Most importantly for musicians, the sound system and the acoustics of the place were renowned. So too, were the placing of the lights, for which reason dancers, and the light designers who were part of any good performance, dance or drama, were always happy to perform at the Sabhaghar. In this solidly built hall, the sounds of Kolkata's boisterous monsoons did not disturb those who savoured the melodies associated with it and even when the Miyan ki Malhar on stage brought on a deluge that turned the road outside into a raging river, the Sabhaghar, raised high above street level remained aloofly dry, even as the ground floors of neighbouring houses began to resemble water bodies.

In spite of the short term of its existence, the Borsha Utshob, always held in the last week of July, had become a fixture in the musical almanac of the city. Music aficionados of Kolkata always pencilled in that week in their calendars, keeping it free from other cultural appointments. There were many who also, in fact, actually took leave from work during that week in order to attend the music programmes that went on till late each night. The schedule was always fixed so that the final night fell on a Saturday. The programmes went on till Sunday morning, and ended much after the buses and trams of the city began once more to ferry Kolkata's public around the city.

True, there had been a time, years ago, when "whole night" was the time frame that organizers of these functions aspired to. Since they were held in winter, dedicated audiences in those days would leave their homes well wrapped in mufflers and monkey caps, even if the venue was an indoor one. Music was one way of celebrating winter. And, for those audiences, taking out their heavy woollens even if the temperatures were mild, was another. They would unwrap their home-made snacks during the gaps between artistes, and sip from Thermos flasks full of spiced tea and strong coffee to keep them alert till the last strains of Bhairavi faded out the next morning. To be able to stay up on consecutive nights like this, leaving all responsibilities for later consideration, was deemed to be the sign of the true connoisseur, a mark of the real lover of music, a person who was truly "cultured."

It was, of course, the audiences that had the musicians hooked on Kolkata, the famed and feared audiences, who could make or break a budding musician with a single comment during the performance. They were notoriously difficult to please, but they were also famously knowledgeable. The audiences here were a confident lot, aware of their own deep and hard won knowledge of the genre, and unwilling to be intimidated by any starry airs that musicians put on. Indeed, all performers wore a cloak of humility, genuine or false, when they came to Kolkata. Tales of the irreverent comments of the audiences were rife, striking nervousness if not fear in even accomplished performers.

The Borsha Utshob began the next day, but there was no time to relax or look around the place. Appointments had already been made well in advance with Soumeen Dutta and Prabal Mishra, the tabla and sarengi players, and Sanjoy Karmakar, the harmonium player, and they were due to come in at five for rehearsals. Guruma's programme was on the third day, at perhaps the best time, eleven at night, the slot when the audience had settled in nicely. The restiveness that came from the day's happenings would have calmed into composure and a receptive frame of mind. It was also the time for the more serious Raags.

The accompanists arrived on the dot. They greeted Guruma warmly, and discussed the latest happenings in the musical world of Kolkata while the bearers brought in tea and snacks.

"Lovely tea, thank you Keshto," said Guruma to the bearer, sipping the fragrant brew.

"The tea is from our own gardens, of course," said Keshto, his turban bobbing up and down with pride. "This is the best Darjeeling. I remember you preferred it to Assam, last time. We have the Coonoor and Ooty ones too, if you want..."

"No, this is perfect, it's really nice of you to remember, thank you so much," smiled Guruma.

"But do you know, Sandhyarani, about Paritosh? Yes, the tabla player who used to accompany you in Panditji's house?" Soumeen Dutta touched his earlobe briefly as was the custom, to signify respect when he referred to Chiranjeev Mukherjee.

Sandhyarani. Soumeen Dutta was almost elderly, certainly he was not young. He used the name with affection, in a way nobody in Tamulbari did. Once more Nomita was reminded of Guruma's strong roots in this musical community. She wondered why she had settled down in Tamulbari, when she was so much at home here. Well, what kind of a thought was that! Tamulbari was home, that was where she had settled down in happy and harmonious matrimony with Tridib Barua. Besides, Kolkata was hardly that far away from the valley of the Red River these days. Barely an hour by one of the numerous flights out of Guwahati.

"... Paritosh, I don't know what got into him," Soumeen Dutta was saying with relish, "has now suddenly upped and made a fusion album with some group from Germany-Shermany. Fusion? Confusion! At his age. All right, the tabla bols he's put in there sound OK. I'll grant him that. But *ki bolbo aami*, what can I say, he's actually stooped to playing the dholak, the dhulki there. OK, the dholak is fine as a folk instrument, nobody can deny that. But he's a classical tabla player. A senior tabla player like him, the prized student of Therekwa Sahib, why is he compromising his dignity like this? For cheap fame, what else? And some chance to play at some concerts abroad..."

Obviously neither Soumeen Dutta nor Prabal Mishra or Sanjoy Karmakar believed that fusion music was creative. She noticed

Guruma glance at her with a strange expression. Why? What was it? Suddenly, it clicked. Of course, she was engaged to be married to a musician who was famed for his fusion music, over and above the classical stuff. Guruma was perhaps worried that Nomita would be hurt, or offended. She felt like reassuring Guruma, but didn't know how to interrupt the accompanists, who were even now in full flow, expressing their contempt for those who stooped to play fusion. She should tell Guruma sometime that she didn't feel as though she was engaged to Kaushik Kashyap yet. And she was hardly going to spend the rest of her life, after marriage, flying to the defence of her husband's music when somebody criticized some aspect of it. One couldn't please everybody, she shrugged mentally, it was hard enough to find out how one could please oneself, and then follow the path that would bring oneself some happiness.

They had of course brought along their own electronic taanpuras, for no musician, big, medium or small, ever travelled anywhere without them these days. She had thought they would practice today with one of these. The Borsha Utshob would no doubt provide them with ladies taanpuras of the required pitch on the day of the function. She was surprised, therefore, to see Keshto come in again, this time with a large long object. Even though it was covered in its cloth wrapper, it was obvious that this was a taanpura.

"Thank you Keshto..." Guruma took off the wrapper to reveal the instrument inside. She strummed the strings, and tuned them swiftly. The instrument itself glowed with a patina that only age could bring to seasoned wood. The sound was sonorous and mellow, the sound of an instrument that had been weathered and aged through years, decades, of being used, and played, lovingly.

"Keshto, you look after my instruments so well! This sounds better and better every time I come here!" She touched the burnished wood and gleaming resonator with her palms, then placed them reverentially to each of her eyes in turn, then her forehead. Turning to Nomita, she said, "This is a Miraj taanpura, the best kind. Guruji had it specially made for me, and brought it back himself from the instrument maker who lived far away, in Maharashtra. He would go by train to the place, while it was being made, he would even go by bus and car if he was in Pune or Mumbai for a show. It took quite some time, some years actually, before it was done to his satisfaction. It was a strenuous journey, but he would go to see that it was being weathered properly, even though he was not too strong on his feet at that time. He personally supervised the making of it. He knew quite a lot about making taanpuras, too, you know. I wish I had learned something of that from him. Now it's too late. He chose the gourd, making sure it was the right size for me. And the wood for the neck, he stayed with the taanpura maker and made sure it was well seasoned…"

There was a hesitation in Guruma's voice. She turned her head away, and bent over to fine tune the strings again, but Nomita had already seen the moisture in her eyes.

"Shall I bring the harmonium and tablas too, Didi?"

"No, no need Keshto, since Soumeenda and Prabalbhai and Sanjoyda have brought theirs, we'll use those. Maybe tomorrow… My surmandal, too, we can bring them all out tomorrow."

"Ah, we had forgotten you have your instruments here, Sandhyarani," said Soumeen Dutta, tuning the instrument as Guruma strummed. "For me it's all right, my tablas are not heavy, and certainly no vocalist keeps a spare sarengi for Prabalbhai. He has to carry his own. But Sanjoy finds his instrument heavy these days."

"Tomorrow, when we sit for rehearsals, don't bring the tablas or harmonium. In any case the last time I used my instruments here was, when, a month, two months ago?"

"You had come in April for the Raagmala programme I think…"

"Yes, that's right, that's when I used them last."

Nomita tried to banish the questions that had popped into her head as they began their rehearsals. So Guruma kept her best instruments, her most cherished pieces, here in Deepak Rathod's home, rather than in Tamulbari itself. Well, in a way it made sense, of course. After all the best programmes were here, and one had to go through Kolkata anyway in order to access cities such as Hyderabad or Chennai or Bhubaneswar when there were programmes there. And this house was so large, and so empty of inhabitants, that obviously space was no constraint in keeping them in prime condition.

Still…

And weren't there children in the marriage of these two big industrialists? Yes, Rahul had said there were two. Away in England, studying. They were not in this house right now, that was for sure. She realized that there hadn't been any words about Deepak Rathod's children in any conversation she had had with him. But now that she was in his house, the question of children began to bother her, unaccountably. And Rati Mittal, how would she feel when she came home and found that two women had taken up temporary residence in her heritage home?

But the melody began to take over as all five of them settled down to their practice, banishing the questions from her mind. As Guruma developed the Raag, the accompanists, too, got into their stride. It was obvious that there were many years of past rehearsals, and stage performances, between them. Non-verbal cues between the five of them passed effortlessly as Guruma, with a glance at the others, speeded up the tempo, or began another sequence. There was no need for any of them to praise each other even after rehearsals were over. Only a quiet "wah" from Soumeen Dutta, a "Khoob Bhalo" from Prabal Mishra and a "Besh" from Sanjoy Karmakar showed their appreciation.

The rehearsal had been good, Nomita knew, even her own part in it. It was amazing how a higher level of accompanists raised the whole standard of the performance.

Haren Babu dropped in as the accompanists were getting ready to leave. It was a courtesy call, but there was cordiality in the way Guruma welcomed him and served him tea herself. It was almost as though she was the lady of the house, thought Nomita watching, she was so much at home here.

They went to bed early. Nomita's room, next to Sandhya Senapati's on the first floor, was large by today's standards. Certainly the surrounding apartment houses were unlikely to have rooms this spacious. Three long-stemmed ceiling fans stirred the air busily, as she feel asleep.

Their host arrived at dawn the next day. Nomita, coming down for her breakfast, saw Guruma and Deepak Rathod laughing together in the dining room. Still smiling, they looked around at her as she entered.

"There you are Nomita, how lovely to have you with us," smiled the host, getting up for her. "So. I hope you're comfortable in that room? Good. How are things? Rehearsals?"

"Yes, we've started that. It's a different level altogether here, isn't it?" Nomita answered.

"Probably. Don't let it bother you. You'll be fine. Here, come and sit down, this upma is quite good, I believe. And that Radha Ballabi… my favourite, you must try it."

What a nice man, Nomita thought again, as they sat down to eat.

That evening when they got ready to leave for the performances it was raining heavily. The programmes were scheduled to begin at seven, but Deepak said they should start early, even though the Gouri Sabhaghar was not far at all. As they negotiated the flooded streets of the city, it was obvious that this had been a good plan. Inside the white walls, the emerald lawns and bright flower borders gave no clue of the havoc the rain was creating outside, but as soon as they crossed the lace-like black iron gates, the chaos was apparent. Already, when they started out, the streets were ankle deep in water. Rush hour traffic slowed and then came to a crawl as they moved at snail's pace. Before their eyes, the water around them rose alarmingly.

"Should have brought the Qualis," said Deepak. "It's a higher vehicle…" Indeed, the water had now risen, in a matter of minutes, to the level of their doors in the low slung car.

"This whole concept is quite decadent, actually," said Deepak, once they were inside the auditorium. It had taken them forty-five minutes to cover a distance that was usually completed in fifteen. Here, there was no hint of the floods and confusion outside. The sounds of the traffic snarls and the anxieties of the people who had been left stranded by the flash floods were now shut out, as though they belonged to another planet. Moving up the sweeping curved staircase, past the marble counters selling snacks, they reached the auditorium, their feet sinking into the lush carpets. The coolness of the place welcomed them into a different world as the Committee Members, recognizing Sandhya Senapati, ushered them to the front rows reserved for artistes who would be performing at the Utshob. They sank into their seats in the middle of the third row, and settled down.

"Decadent?" Guruma had smiled, perhaps she had heard Deepak's ideas before. But Nomita was interested. "How?"

"Well, here we are, all settled in to celebrate the rain. While outside, we've just seen what the rain is doing. Hardly a cause for celebration. We are here in an ivory tower, ready to listen to yes, extremely beautiful music, but what about the masses outside? The suffering people?"

"The masses? And you, a capitalist, are worried about them?" Nomita wouldn't have said this to him even last month, but she was now almost as much at ease with him as she was with maybe Rahul. Or maybe it was Kolkata's atmosphere, red even in these capitalist-tinged days, which made her speak in this way.

"Ha, I like a girl who argues," said Deepak approvingly. "Sandhya hardly ever does. She just ignores me when she doesn't agree." He looked at Guruma, seated between student and friend, and smiled at her. Turning to Nomita again, he said, "But wait, what gave you the idea that capitalists don't care for the masses? Forget those outdated ideas of exploitation and whatnot. We are job creators, creators of wealth. Families depend on us, children go to school because of us. Do I sound as though I'm bragging? Well, I'm proud of what I do. But yes, this musical celebration, beautiful though it is sure to be, seems decadent to me. Kind of like fiddling while Rome is burning. Though here it's the exact opposite, the fiddling will be done while Kolkata is drowning."

There was a gleam in his eye as he said it. His voice was quiet, as usual, but his face was bright with feeling. Nomita realized in a moment of epiphany that the quietness of his voice was habitual. It came from power, perhaps. He did not need to raise it in order to get things done. It was power, not years of riyaz, which imbued his voice with such an attractive tonal quality. Pleased with her sudden insight, Nomita laughed, and said, "We'll continue this argument later. Art versus life. It's quite a tangled subject..."

"Actually," said Guruma, amusement in her voice, "the whole thing is rooted in the history of the music. Much of the Raag music we have today came from the folk songs of UP, Rajasthan, places that are much drier than Kolkata or our own Assam. No fear of floods there. At least there weren't, all those centuries ago, when the melodies began to evolve and refine into what would eventually become Raags. Naturally for a person from those places the rains would have a different connotation than for somebody in, say, the upper part of our Assam." She turned to Deepak and said, "Near Krishnanagar, for instance, where you have one of your tea gardens. Floods and heavy rains are so routine there that they don't even merit a discussion, let alone a Raag."

"I bow to your superior knowledge," said Deepak as he settled down deeper in the upholstered seat. He looked around the almost full hall. They had come well in time, even though they knew their seats would have been kept for them. But it would be the height of discourtesy to come tramping in after the artistes had begun their performances. "I come here as much for the ambience and the audiences as I do for the music," he continued. "The three are inseparable, actually."

"You come every year?" asked Nomita, impressed. After all, he was a busy man, here today, on another continent tomorrow.

"Well, not for the whole Conference, though I would love to do that sometimes, too. But certainly if I am in town, I make it a point to drop in for a few hours."

"You've improved over the years, Deepak," smiled Sandhya Senapati. "I remember the time it was difficult to get you to attend any classical music conference. Only the bait of having some agile beauty dancing on stage could get you to come at all..."

Deepak laughed. "Remember the time Mona Sharma came to dance here?"

"Mona Sharma, the Hindi film actress? What did she dance? Not a Bollywood number?"

"No, thankfully, she didn't." Guruma took up the story, her voice full of laughter. "Actually, she is a trained Bharata Natyam dancer, and she was invited in that capacity. She was quite good, too, I remember. But you should have seen Deepak here. As soon as he found out that I would be performing in a Conference that featured Mona Sharma on the same evening, he became so eager to come with me, so interested, suddenly in Shastriya Sangeet!"

There was something boyish about Deepak Rathod's grin. "I remember that very well. But you know the sad thing. Mona Sharma came to dance at a conference in Kolkata just a few months ago. I happened to be free, so I went to watch."

"Isn't she past her prime now?" Guruma asked.

"Her figure certainly is. She is quite – ummm – corpulent. Of course her dance mudras and expressions are beautiful, but a dancer must have a fit body, it's the minimum requirement. The poor girl was practically booed off the stage. The backbenchers said things like *"O Didi, ektu VLCC tey enrol korey ashoon!"*

His Bangla was naturally fluent, for he was a native of this place. They laughed as much at the story as at the expression on his face as he related the remark about the dancer being asked to shed weight at the VLCC chain of fitness centres.

"Better not snigger till my own show is over, though," said Guruma. "Who knows what they'll shout?"

"Actually I enjoy the remarks quite as much as I do the music in these Conferences," he continued. "Especially if the artistes are the pompous types, you know, the ones with starry airs. Kolkata audiences take the hot air out of prima donnas pretty fast. Remember the time," he turned to Sandhya again "when that vocalist, what was his name, began to give repetitive melodic patterns on the single note, Sa?"

"Long time ago, Deepak, I'm surprised you still remember it…" Guruma was laughing, too. She turned to her student, and said, in fluent Bangla *"Dada, egiye cholun, egiye cholun, kichoo bhoi nei, ekhaney millennium paar hocche, aapni ki oi Sa tei roye thaakben?* It was one of those concerts in December 1999 to celebrate the coming millennium. The singer was very repetitive, no doubt about it. It was really funny though the way the backbenchers, the ten-rupee-ticket boys, exhorted him to move on, because the new millennium was coming, and the singer was in danger of being left behind in the old one! They are very irreverent, these audiences."

"Kolkata's always been very good to you, though, Sandhya, hasn't it? You've been performing here ever since your student days, and they've always been very appreciative. The reviews you get are always excellent too..."

Sandhya Senapati held up both her hands, showing her crossed fingers. Smiling, she said, "I hope...this time too." She looked across at Nomita and said, "I want this experience to be good for her. Of course you'll probably be settling down here, in Kolkata after your marriage. You'll be performing solo at all kinds of venues, I hope. But I want this first time to be an experience to remember... Performing in your hometown is one thing, but performing in a metro city, where you are an unknown face, is totally another. The audiences listen to you objectively. But in Tamulbari they already have expectations, they have already judged you at numerous other concerts, they have listened to you since you were a small girl, still in frilly white frocks."

If she married Kaushik Kashyap, this would be her world, thought Nomita, looking around. She would be able to listen to these recitals whenever she felt like. This time, she was here as Sandhya Senapati's supporting artiste, her senior student. If she got married to Kaushik Kashyap, she would be here as the wife of one of the brightest stars in the musical firmament. If? But she was committed to that already, she remembered. It wasn't a question of if, but of when. *When* she got married. No doubt, with constant exposure of this kind, her music, too, would improve. The prospect was pleasing, but she hoped she would be able to find a school like Shishu Kalyan where she could also spend her mornings teaching children like Silsila and Pallavi.

Guruma, of course, was already a part of the musical scene here. Nomita had never seen this side of Sandhya Senapati in Tamulbari, where she and Tridib Barua were two bright but more or less solitary stars of their calibre on the classical music firmament. There, at functions, Guruma was unfailingly polite to the people who came up to greet her. Here, however, there was a camaraderie between her and many of the artistes, which reminded Nomita again that Sandhya Senapati had spent a good many years in Kolkata, and indeed, was very much in touch with the people here. In fact, she seemed to have more friends here than she did in Tamulbari. Indeed, thought Nomita now, suddenly perceptive, Sandhya Senapati's life there must be a lonely one. True, she had her husband, but his profession demanded constant travel, as did hers. In fact, over the last few years, it seemed to Nomita that she herself was the closest that Guruma had to calling anyone a friend there, in Tamulbari. Whereas here, in Kolkata, there were, besides Deepak Rathod, so many others with whom she shared that camaraderie.

So why, wondered Nomita again, did Sandhya Senapati shift to Tamulbari? Of course she married Tridib Barua, but his work, too, took him out of that town very frequently and they could easily have settled down in Kolkata. Surely Tamulbari, so cut off from the mainstream of classical music, was a kind of exile for both of them. A self-imposed one, surely? Of course their careers were going well but they would be much better known if they'd settled in Kolkata. And they would have friends here, whereas in Tamulbari, as far as Nomita could make out, they lived a fairly restricted life.

The evening of their performance was cloudy and muggy, but thankfully it did not seem likely to rain. Nomita and Guruma had spent the day in some last-minute practice. Not much, because it would overstrain the voice, just enough to keep it honed and open. Keshto and the other help already knew that on the day of a programme, Sandhya Senapati's food had to be light. Deepak started out with them in the Civic. Sandhya Senapati carefully carried in her lap the taanpura that her Guru had so lovingly made for her, refusing all offers by the waiting bearers to carry it down to the car.

"No air conditioning, right, Sandhya?" asked Deepak, sitting in front with the chauffeur.

"Please. If you don't mind. The strings are so delicate, I don't want too many changes of temperature. As it is these air conditioned stages play havoc with the tuning, especially if the greenrooms don't have air conditioning. Luckily this venue is good that way…"

Nomita's cell rang. It was Rahul.

"Do your best, Nomi, that'll be more than enough. How are you feeling?"

It was not that she was nervous, exactly, but it was the first time, after all, that she would be on stage in a Conference as large as the Borsha Utshob and Rahul was aware of that…

She laughed, suddenly feeling some weight lift from her mind, a weight she had not even been aware of. Softly, so as not to disturb Guruma and Deepak as they spoke among themselves, she said, "Fine, Rahul, wish you were here, too. I mean what an ambience, what a hall… I'm sounding like a dehati, a village yokel, but really, the Conference itself is so wonderful. I'm getting to listen to all the best artistes here."

"And now they'll get to listen to you. Great. Let me know how it goes…"

Both Guruma and Deepak smiled reassuringly at her as they walked backstage, to one of the several greenrooms.

"I'll be sitting in our usual place, then, all the best to both of you," said Deepak, making his way to the auditorium

She would have felt intimidated by the huge expanse of stage that lay in front of her, if it hadn't been for the warmth of Guruma and Soumeenda, Sanjoyda and Prabalbhai as they waited in the wings. The screen had already been drawn, the instruments had already been set in place. It was the custom at this Utshob for the artistes to walk onto the stage as their names were announced. The three men went in, smiles and Namastes ready. They walked to the front of the stage, and accepted the bouquets that were presented to them, before settling down on the white-sheeted space on which their instruments rested. Somewhat flustered, Nomita realized that her own name was being called out.

"Nomita…" encouraged Guruma quietly. Quickly, Nomita bent down and touched her feet, before stepping out onto the parquet floor. Rounds of applause greeted her, but of course this was just the politeness of the audience. She received her bouquet, and made her way to her own space on the sheet, behind the vocal accompanist's mike. She picked up the taanpura that had been carefully tuned back in the greenroom, checked it for sound and pitch, and began to pluck its strings.

It was all right. She felt the nervousness drop away from her as the familiar drone of the taanpura filled the stage, the auditorium. A huge round of applause greeted Guruma as she appeared onstage. Her steps were graceful and small, her hands were folded in a Namaste, her smile was serene and beautiful.

Nomita could feel that this audience was predisposed to like Guruma. Unless they bungled up the whole two hours that they had been allotted, the Kolkata audience were already fans of her music and this positive vibe helped the artistes to scale up their own performance. Many of them had been listening to Sandhya Senapati since she was a student with Pandit Chiranjeev Mukherjee. Nomita could feel the audience before her settling down, looking forward to a recital by a girl they had watched growing up, and coming to musical maturity.

Guruma, after the last and final microtuning of the instruments, began to strum her surmandal. But instead of beginning her alaap, she said, in Bangla, "Nomoshkar. It is always a pleasure to come before you, the learned audiences of Kolkata. It is an honour that I am invited here so frequently, and in appreciation of that honour, I am placing before you a composition, melody as well as lyrics, that I have specially created for this Utshob. It is in Raag Des but the sensibility is contemporary..."

Guruma waited till the applause had died down. She continued, "I can truly say that it is you, the Kolkata audience, along with my Guru's teachings, who have shaped my musical sensibilities. As a young girl, when I performed on the stages of Kolkata, you were kind enough to shower me with your love and encouragement. Today, the wheel has turned full circle. I bring before you my student, Nomita Sharma, who will be giving me vocal support. It is her first time before you, the audience of Kolkata. She has come with me all the way from

Tamulbari, where we live... I am sure you will give her the same love and affection that you did, to me, and indeed still continue..."

Bemused, Nomita realized that the sound of applause that rolled up from the auditorium was for her. The lights in the auditorium were still on, and she could make out individual faces from where she sat. Guru Usha Sabhlok, who had just finished her violin recital, was in the first row, beaming encouragement. The critics of the well known journals whom she had been introduced to in the preceding days were clapping their hands, and smiling in parental fashion at her. She looked around for Deepak. There he was, sitting in his usual seat, third row, not clapping, and smiling only slightly. But in spite of any absence of physical stances or gestures signifying encouragement, Nomita read the expression in his eyes. "Give it all you've got, Nomita!"

She stood up, and with hands folded in a deep Namaste, acknowledged the applause.

And then, once seated, there was no time to think of anything else. In automatic response to the sound of the taanpura, she focused on the music. She was playing the taanpura that Pandit Chiranjeev Mukherjee had had made, so lovingly, for his best student. And now here she was, keeping the continuity, playing the same taanpura that Chiranjeev's hands had touched so many years ago, the instrument his mind had conceived and his affection had brought into existence, here she was, the well loved student of *his* best loved student.

The weeks of rehearsals they had spent on this new creation of Guruma's were paying dividends now. There was no time to think of other things, but it was always possible to know from small cues about the audience reaction. The coughs, the whispers dwindled, to be replaced by quiet "Kya Baat" and "Wah!" The whole performance was going smoothly, to a greatly appreciative audience, and each one of them, Prabalbhai and Soumeenda and Sanjoyda and she herself were adding their own inputs. Yet they kept those inputs within the parameters set by Sandhya Senapati, who took them forward, note by note, phrase by phrase, through an ever-increasing tempo, till at last, with a series of silvery taans spanning a full three octaves, the Khayal came to an end. Barely waiting for the applause to die down, she started on a thumri, and then went on to the Kajri they had rehearsed. These were monsoon songs, based on Raags, but in a tempo and with embellishments that made them lighter than the Khayal she had sung before. Finally, the famous Meera Bhajan

"Barase Badariya Saawan Ki..."
The clouds of Saawan are pouring rain,
The rain of Saawan, the rain that gladdens my heart...
My heart beats faster in the month of Saawan,
Through the crash of thunder, and the flash of lightning,
I hear the footsteps of Hari approach...
Meera's Lord is He who holds aloft the mountain in his palm,
Bringing peace and joy to the land around...

The air of devotion as Guruma sang this was palpable. All the people in the audience were familiar with this composition, but Guruma's voice and her mind imbued it with an emotion that always moistened the eyes of listeners. The quiet in the auditorium erupted into applause as they finished. There were requests for more songs, bhajans and kajris and other short pieces, but Guruma, with folded palms, smilingly declined. "Next time," she spoke in Bangla again, "I will surely sing all this for you next time. The time allotted to me is over, it is time for the next artiste, Iqbalbhai and his sarod are waiting in the wings...Thank you so much..."

The curtain scrolled shut. They were free to relax their postures now.

Deepak was already in the greenroom by the time they collected their instruments and walked there, their progress slowed by people who wanted Guruma's autograph, her blessings, to be photographed with her. Many came up to touch her feet humbly. To Nomita, they said, "Your vocal support was wonderful, really. So when are we going to hear a solo from you?" He waited in a corner of the room, his head tilted a little, and a small smile on his mouth, as a crowd milled around Sandhya Senapati. Finally, after the autograph seekers and fans had left, he came up, and said, "You get better every time I hear you, Sandhya."

Guruma turned her face up to him, her eyes sparkling, an incandescent smile on her face. "You think so?" She reached out a hand and held his momentarily, "Thanks, Deepak."

It was the first time that Nomita had heard Sandhya Senapati respond with anything other than a murmured "Thank you so much," "I value your blessings..." to the numerous compliments that came her way after every recital. Today, her voice and expression gave away much more than usual. Deepak's opinion, his words of praise, seemed to hold more meaning for her than did the compliments of the music critics who had come backstage to wish her.

"...and Nomita, you were wonderful," these critics were saying. "Such balanced support. Really. Not intrusive, but not diffident either. And your voice, it's just wonderful. Not too high pitched. Warm. Beautiful. Just right. I can't wait to hear you in a solo programme..."

After the concert, back again in Deepak Rathod's drawing room, Guruma asked in her usual soft way, "Could I please have a cup of tea?

Keshto assured her it would be no problem and bustled away.

"Tired?" asked Deepak.

"You know how I feel after a major concert. Not tired, really. Drained. And... relieved."

"Relieved, Guruma?" asked Nomita.

"Of course, relieved. Why, are you surprised?" she smiled.

"A little," Nomita admitted. "I mean I would never have expected..."

"Music is a performing art. Stage performances of music, like dance, give you no second chances. It's like sport... anything can go wrong in a concert. A slip of concentration for a fraction of a second, and you cannot catch the Sam as it comes round in the cycle. Or your voice is just that bit off on a note in the upper octave. Or there is that lack of co-ordination between the supporting musicians. Or the sound system acts up. The 'cooing' of the mike, we used to say. So many things...yes, it's always a relief when a concert is over without any bungles. "

Sandhya Senapati smiled slightly as she said this. Nomita, listening, was struck again by her humility. No, humility was probably not the word for it. Humility implied a kind of conscious act, a kind of awareness of one's own talent and ability. Guruma's was a much more natural thing. The performer's ego never intruded in the interaction that took place in the auditoriums around the country between audiences and Sandhya Senapati.

The tea arrived, and Nomita, sipping the brew from their host's garden, immediately felt restored.

"You carried it off well, Nomita," said Guruma, reaching for her second cup. "The support was wonderful, so steady, and yet you put in those creative bits of your own."

She took another sip, and continued, in a voice that was almost dreamy. "Every audience is different. Today's audience was different from the one we will be part of tomorrow, even at the same Conference. It's not just about being made up of different people. The same people, even those who were present today, will have different expectations, different needs."

"Needs, Sandhya?" Deepak's voice was quieter than usual.

Sandhya Senapati turned to him, her eyes lustrous. "Needs. We all have them, don't we Deepak? All kinds of needs. But..." she paused, and turned to look again at Nomita, "here I'm talking about an audience's needs. The needs of the people who make up the audience, at a particular point of time. My job as an artist is to fulfil that need, or at least some part of it, through my work on any given day."

"What kind of need... ?" Nomita had never thought of audiences as having needs. They were there, before her, a composite entity that needed to be musically satisfied. But that implied need, she supposed.

"So many kinds. The need for a voice that suggests, hints at half-forgotten memories. Or in the case of instrumentalists, the need for a skilled hand, or mouth, that brings to life that particular instrument. The need for an intellect that structures a melody and gives it form, so that it is becomes a story, a narrative. But most of all, I think audiences have a need to be put in touch with their emotions, through art."

"You're right," said Deepak slowly, though Nomita hardly dared to breathe, leave alone say a word. Deepak's voice, too, was low. "It's art that makes us aware of our feelings again. Different forms of art, for different people. It's music for me, classical Hindustani music, though for others it could be jazz, or opera, or traditional music. We lose sight of our feelings ... art puts us in touch with it again."

"And Indian classical music is in any case more than entertainment," pointed out Guruma. "It's a spiritual journey. The more you listen to it, the more you get engrossed in it, the deeper you find yourself in a sacred place. It gives you something that is beyond the rituals of organized religion, it takes you to a different space."

"Right. Like church music in the great cathedrals of Europe. The high, vaulted ceilings, echoing and enhancing voices lifted up in purest devotion. Of course the hymns are not sung with an audience in mind. But no listener, even an atheist, can remain unmoved by the beauty, the emotion ..."

Guruma took another sip, and continued, looking at Nomita now, "Audiences have this need, even if they don't know it themselves. A good performer has to fulfil this need of theirs. And don't forget that performers, too, have their needs. Don't we?"

"Yes ..." said Nomita slowly.

"As an artiste, I have a need. So does the audience. I try to find a space where we can meet during my performances. So that they can go away with their needs, or some of them at least, fulfilled ..." Guruma's voice seemed to float over them.

But ...

"When I think of my need, as an artiste, I don't think of audiences in the same way as you do ..." said Nomita, slowly. She closed her eyes, trying to follow a thought.

"Yes ... ?" Guruma's soft voice was questioning.

"I mean ... what you said about audiences, their needs. I think of Silsila, of Debojit ... they are my audience, not these knowledgeable connoisseurs. Of course it's a different experience performing before this kind of crowd, don't get me wrong, it's exhilarating. But..."

"I know what you mean," said Guruma.

Nomita opened her eyes, and found both Deepak and Sandhya Senapati looking at her.

"Yes. When Silsila listens to me, every muscle of her twitching body seems to want to rush towards me. Her eyes tell me that her mind is listening. She's getting something from my music that other audiences cannot. She, and Pallavi, and others like them. They are my audience. Yes." She looked with wonder at the two people before her, amazed that she had not known this about herself all this while.

"You have a special gift, Nomita..." said Guruma. "Something that is precious, and probably more valuable than what the rest of us are doing. To be in a position to help people who need it, that..."

"No, it's not a question of what is more valuable, what is not," said Nomita firmly. "In the end, it is, I think, a question of different audiences, different kinds of people needing the artiste, and the artiste communicating with them in a way that, as you said, meets some need of theirs, too."

"You are right," said Deepak. "As we grow older, and experience more of life, the fault lines, the cracks, become more and more difficult to ignore. We are all in search of healers, in different ways. A good musician is a healer, music itself the medicine. And I'm not talking of the "Raag as Medicine" kind of thing. I am talking of the whole, the holistic perspective, if you like...."

Keshto came in, announcing dinner. They talked no more of this again, but Nomita went up to her room with a feeling of quiet euphoria that was only partly connected to her satisfaction with her own stage appearance that evening.

21

Even after their own function was over, Nomita listened to the rest of the Utshob with a learner's ear. Guruma occasionally pointed out certain aspects of the Raag that was played, or sung, so that at times it was like an extended lesson.

"Notice this Jaijaiwanti," she would say as a singer from the Kirana Gharana performed the Raag. "It's performed differently from the way our Gharana does it. The style of the Gharana is such, that's why the effect is somewhat different. Shastriya Sangeet is more than entertainment, more than being just sweet sounding. It has a philosophical component, an intellectual input. The ideal listener is one who knows exactly what inputs, philosophical and intellectual, the artiste is putting in. It's a journey, a lifelong one, for the artiste, but also for the committed listener. Both grow in ideas and appreciation over the years."

All Shastriya Sangeet performers wore traditional clothes when on stage: kurta and dhoti or churidar by the men, and heavy saris by the women. But even though the women wore saris, Nomita noticed the way they walked. Young or old, there was a confidence in their gait, a big-city energy that could not be hidden even by the yards of heavy silk wrapped around them, over petticoats that were sometimes almost as bulky. But these were mostly women who had travelled the world and were untrammelled by the weight of tradition. As they came up to the dais after their names were announced, there was a briskness in their walks that showed, unmistakably, that they were modern, working women, even though they worked with music that was traditional. There was a simple confidence even in the gait of the senior women artistes. Nalini Mishra of the Benaras Gharana, for instance. She came in smiling onstage, her red bindi huge below her snow white hair, matching her paan-reddened lips, her face like a stay-at-home grandmother's. But her walk to the front of the stage from the wings was not the limping, arthritic pace one would have expected of her, going by her appearance and the way she pulled the pallu of her sari around her back and over her right shoulder in the traditional manner. Her pace even in that space was brisk, her shoulders pulled back, her back straight, though her hands were folded in a humble namaste and her head bowed to acknowledge the crowd's applause.

And there were the younger performers, Tarini Shiva from Mumbai, Shreya Goenka from Jaipur. Their walks were the walks of young working women anywhere in the country. There was grace in their stride, and feminity, but also purpose, confidence, and assurance. Their walks reminded Nomita of Sheila and Jimli back home. No doubt away from the stage, they dressed as young people everywhere did, in jeans or trousers or shorts or skirts. Onstage, they sat in the time honoured stance. The instrumentalists sat with the sitar or violin in the way that had been taught to them by their Gurus, the tried and tested method that would cause least fatigue during the hours of riyaz needed every day. The vocalists all sat cross legged, a taanpura or surmandal on their laps, their right hands raised to play it, and their left faithfully shadowing their voices through gestures.

Nomita wished that she could have gone to one of these great conferences earlier. Perhaps when Hari Prasad and Shiv Kumar and Bhimsen were in their prime, or earlier, when Ravi Shankar's sitar and Amir Khan's amazing voice and V G Jog's violin, which he lovingly called his "behela" and of course the one and only Bismillah ushered in the dawn on various occasions with their own spiritual renditions of Bhairavi. Bismillah, the shehnai, and Bhairavi, with the sun peeping over the eastern horizon at some open air venue, the chill air warmed by the strains of the shehnai. Or Jasraj, chanting "Govinda Damodar, Shri Krishna, Gopal," in a rare duet with L Subramaniam on the violin, the sheer bhakti in his voice bringing tears to the eyes of even the most hardened non-believer in the audience.

But: "That's just nostalgia," Rahul said matter of factly when she mentioned it to him on the phone, next day. "Twenty years later you will have the same feeling about today's artistes. In any case, you musicians should be thankful for technology. Recordings of the musicians of the past sixty, seventy years, at least tell you something about their music."

"True," Nomita agreed.

How wonderful it would have been, she thought, if Tansen and Swami Haridas or, nearer home, Shankardeva and Madhavdeva could have been recorded, for posterity. Or would it? Would they have been able to live up to the mythical stature that they enjoyed now? In any case, they were, in musical terms, what a story teller would be if he or she lived before the invention of the written word. Their art would be ephemeral, confined to the here and now, more evanescent than the morning dew. For after all sound was perhaps the most fleeting of mediums through which to capture one's art. More fleeting, even, than the sand sculptures created painstakingly on the seashore, those palaces and portraits that were washed away by the incoming tide, unless technology came to its aid and extended its life through recordings.

The organizers of the Borsha Utshob had taken pains to curate as varied a collection of instrumentalists, vocalists and styles as possible. As evening after evening passed, Nomita was amazed at the sheer variety of artistry within the broad field of Hindustani Shastriya, North Indian Classical. The differences in temperament, in cerebral inputs, in Gharanas, in cultural factors, among the artistes themselves all contributed to the wide variety of music on offer.

There were instruments she had never actually seen before, though she did have the music in her CDs. The Rudra Veena, for instance. She was as amazed at the depth, the grandeur of its sound, as she was at the sheer difficulty of playing it.

Indeed, the variety and richness of the musical instruments over the seven days was in itself amazing. Sarod and sitar, the two staples of North Indian Instrumental Classical, were of course well represented. There was Santanu Patwardhan on the flute, and also

Amitabh Banerjee, and the styles of the two were so different that the audience never felt a sense of repetition. There were several violinists, three of them women. And here was Vishwa Mohan on his path-breaking guitar, which he had named Mohan Veena, heralding the rains in Kolkata with a rare variety of Megh, even though his instrument itself had originated in places where the monsoons were an alien concept. And, in a coup of sorts, the organizers had managed to get both Bhajan Sopori and Shiv Kumar Sharma on the santoor, both from Kashmir, both with the same instrument in their hands, but creating, amazingly, such varied atmospheres with their music! And the esraj, once pronounced to be a dying instrument, but very much alive on the Gouri Sabhaghar stage, producing sounds that seemed to float over their heads from a different era.

And the accompanists, too, were of a standard that astounded. There were tabaliyas who echoed the main artiste faithfully, providing a strong yet aesthetically pleasing rhythmic support, while yet showing flashes of genius in their own playing. The harmonium and the sarengi players, all men, echoed the main vocalist so faithfully that it was like listening to a reiteration in another medium. But even within the framework of the echo, they put in, each one of these accompanists added their own inputs, their own little tonal or rhythmic signatures, so that what the audience heard was not a clone, but an individual.

"It's the range of voices that we're hearing that fascinates me," Nomita confided to Guruma as they sat on the fifth day after a throbbing recital by Ustad Mushtaq Khan. "I mean, each person's voice is so individualistic, each person's ornamentation so unique. Even though so unique each one is singing a monsoon Raag, it's as though they are singing totally different things!"

Every singer's voice is shaped by so many influences, and anyway our training accentuates the individual within the framework of the tradition. Besides, there are many things that contribute to the individuality of the voice. Diet, for one. Climate for another. Have you noticed how classical singers from Pakistan, for instance, have such a high pitch? It's their dry climate, and the diet. Wheat based.

But when the climate becomes more humid, the pitch is lowered. It is said that when Bade Ghulam Ali Khan Saheb shifted from Lahore to Kolkata, his voice, over the years, settled on a lower pitch. Naturally the style of singing on a lower register differs greatly from singing in a higher…"

There were the gestures too, varied enough in this Utshob to enrich Nomita's collection. The beginners with their timid, close-to-the-body hand gestures, the confident, aimed-at-the-cameras gestures of those were approaching the peak of their careers, the restrained, but expressive gestures of those who were well into middle age, with their contributions to music over the decades acknowledged by all. Even the instrumentalists, she noticed, had got into the habit of using dramatic gestures, especially during the speedier portions of the recital. The audience always erupted into applause at these moments, appreciating both the music and the drama. Camera persons positioned themselves along the wall as these spurts of theatre took hold, and captured the pictures of the artistes that would later appear in the review columns of the culture pages of the main papers and journals of Kolkata. *Desh, The Statesman, The Telegraph,* the critics of these journals and more were all sitting in the front row, not nearly as exuberant as the audience behind them, but appreciative, all the same.

Deepak, sitting beside them for several of the performances, noticed Nomita's interest in the gestures. Or perhaps he did not, but had a hobby of his own, collecting them. In any case, next morning, while they were sitting on the verandah of his house sipping tea, he brought up the topic himself.

"I always wonder about the hand gestures of the artistes," he said, as Keshto poured the amber liquid from a plump white traditional looking teapot into equally traditional looking matching cups with diagonal swirls. "I mean, are you trained in them, too? There seems to be a kind of common language that the gestures speak."

"Of course there is," said Guruma. She looked pretty in a pale peach mekhela sador. The bougainvillea shading the veranda dappled her face lightly with shade. "A common language, I mean. Just as there is a common language of the music we perform. But no, I don't think any Guru actually gives lessons on hand gestures. It's not as if this is dance. But the way the hand is used, it's almost a dance in itself."

"The lady who sang the Megh yesterday, Shipra Bose, her hand, her face, her body, everything seemed to echo what her voice was expressing. It was a subtle kind of dance.Not exactly a complete dance, but a kind of embryonic dance, you know? The seed of a dance, with all the leaves and branches and flowers and fruits of a full fledged dance curled up, within the tightness of the gestures themselves. True, the musicians do not move around the space of the stage, but their feet are always tapping out the rhythm, their hands are making complete signs, their facial expressions reflect the song..."

"That's perceptive of you, Deepak," said Guruma. "No, we are never taught gestures, but we imbibe them from our Gurus. Right, Nomita?"

"I suppose so..."

Deepak Rathod was a person who seemed to notice everything. "See the Pandit's mudras?" he whispered to Nomita as Ratan Choudhury of the Gwalior Gharana began his recital next evening. "They are almost as expressive as his voice, don't you think? I always wonder whether these hand gestures and pleasantness of facial expressions have become so integral to the performance only in the last few decades."

Nomita looked questioningly at him.

"You know, after photography and video recordings have become so popular. I remember hearing people say that the old maestros, singing with wads of paan tucked inside their cheeks, made rather hideous faces while singing. Contortions, you can call them. They were quite unaware of the picture they presented, it seems."

He refrained from using the word "spectacle," but it was obvious that in his irreverence he would have used that word if Sandhya had not been there.

"Not my Guruji," responded Sandhya Senapati, turning back to them after acknowledging the smiles of the people across the aisle who had recognized her. "He always told me to be careful not to make faces. Once I got into the habit, he said, it would be difficult to stop. Of course he was ahead of his time in a way... he was born and was taught in a different era, but he grasped the strengths and nuances of today's media and technology much before many of his peers did. Today of course contortions are not seen at all on stage..."

"But some rather sweet gestures are still around, thankfully. Things haven't yet become all boring and homogeneous in this field. Some time ago I heard Amit Choudhury's recital..."

Both Guruma and Nomita looked questioningly at him.

"Ah, you haven't heard of him. He's more famous as a writer, he's written several novels, but he's also a competent classical vocalist. He has that old gesture of putting his hand to his ear while he sings. You hardly see that these days, though it was very common about thirty, forty years ago, wasn't it?"

All three of them smiled companionably at each other.

They went prepared to stay up the whole night on the last evening. By then, Nomita was on nodding and smiling terms with many of the regulars at the Utshob, people she had seen around her, in the auditorium, for all the seven evenings. They exchanged comments during the slots when one artiste left the stage, and another prepared to begin a new recital, behind the drawn curtains. They were all, it seemed, incredibly knowledgeable.

"Was that a Desh Malhar he played?" asked a dhoti-clad gentleman, leaning across to Guruma during a pause in Ashutosh Banerjee's sarod recital.

"Yes"

"I'm asking because when I last heard this Raag, oh, about fifteen, twenty years ago, the meends, the glides, were played in a different way. It was an esraj recital by Pandit Shivendu Bhattacharjee. I remember it as clearly as though it was yesterday."

"Well, maybe," said Guruma thoughtfully, "the type of instrument being played makes a difference to the glides and so on. The character of the Raag is bound to change if the instrument is different, isn't it? And an esraj is after all very different from a sarod, na?"

"True, very true, Sandhyarani." The gentleman nodded, satisfied.

"That's Amrit Saha, the well known critic, he freelances. His columns are held in great esteem," whispered Deepak, leaning in from beyond Guruma. "He was a great friend of Sandhya's Guru, I believe."

Melody and rhythm reached a crescendo, instruments and voice bringing a profusion of monsoon Raags, rare as well as those that were often heard, to the audience. Midnight came, and went, but the auditorium remained packed.

"Nobody will leave now," said Guruma when Nomita commented on it. "No buses, no trams, the metro has stopped. And those with cars have parked them in safe places, or their chauffeurs have taken them home, and will come, like Deepak's, in the morning, to take us back..."

"Some people form a group and buy a single ticket. A kind of consortium. See that seat there?" Deepak Rathod indicated a place down the rows, "have you noticed how the people sitting there keep changing? It's an expensive seat, a good one. Probably five or six people have chipped in to buy the season ticket. They have decided on who will take in which slot, at which time of the evening. The next person gets ready to take the seat after an item is over... This 'relay audience' system is quite common in Kolkata."

And finally, it was the last item, the shehnai. Bismillah had passed away a few years ago, but this was Ustad Shiraz Hussain, now the worthy occupier of the slot that the former had vacated.

The moving notes of the instrument, resonant with emotion, brought in the dawn, with yet another variant of Malhar. The audience listened, no trace of weariness on their faces, though some eyes were red from lack of sleep. But there seemed to be no lack of concentration in either the performers or the listeners.

And then, at last, it was Bhairavi, the Raag that greeted the morning, and said good bye, the Raag that signified an ending, but also a beginning. Even though this was a festival of rainy season Raags, it was mandatory that this Conference, like all others, should end with Bhairavi, the melody of sadness but also of joy, of spirituality but also of worldliness. As the final notes of the shehnai died out, Nomita found her eyes dampened by the sheer evocativeness of the melody.

22

Unexpectedly, Kaushik Kashyap called one evening during the Festival, just as Sandhya Senapati and Nomita were about to leave for the Utshob. Nomita did not recognize the number on her cell when it rang, and she was surprised to hear his voice at the other end. It sounded faint, and was made even thinner by distance.

"Nomita. How are you? How is everything in Tamulbari?"

She had told him the last time he had called about their programme in Kolkata, but then it was perhaps a bit much to assume he would remember that. He was a man who needed a full-time secretary to keep track of, and remind him about his own programme dates and functions. To expect him to remember his fiancée's programme details, that too in a supporting role, was no doubt expecting too much.

"No, ah, I'm in Kolkata."

"Yes of course. You had mentioned the Borsha Utshob. Is Sandhya Didi's programme over?"

"Yes, it happened last evening." She could still feel the rosy clouds of euphoria drifting around her as she spoke.

"It went off well, I suppose?"

"Yes. Yes, I think so. The audience seemed to like it. The reviews this morning were very good." Maybe she should tell him about the one-line mentions that several journals had given her. "Sandhya Senapati was ably supported by her senior student, Nomita Sharma, who, with her musical sense and tunefulness made us look forward to the time we can get a solo recital of hers here." And "Nomita Sharma, Sandhya Senapati's vocal support, displayed just the right mix of confidence, initiative and deference that a good supporting artiste is expected to have."

But he was already speaking. "I haven't heard her for some time, but everybody speaks very highly of her in Kolkata. And you? What have you been doing? Enjoying the programmes, I expect?"

Had he forgotten the fact that she was supposed to support Guruma on stage? And that this would be her first time ever on the Kolkata stage? Or maybe ... wait, yes, perhaps she had forgotten to tell him. Diffidence, as usual. Was this a good thing for a girl to have with her fiancé, especially when he was in the same "line" as she herself was? Now that the function itself was over, she could look back with wonder at her hesitancy.

"Umm, yes, everything is such an eye opener. Actually yesterday I was on stage too, I mean," hastily, in case he got the wrong impression "as vocal support, of course."

Was there the tiniest pause before his reply came to her? No, it was probably the distance that caused their voices to reach each other microseconds after they spoke.

"Oh?" Another pause, while his voice echoed over the seven seas separating them. "And? How did it go?"

"Well. It went well. Guruma was excellent; I think she performs better in Kolkata than she does in Tamulbari. At least that's my opinion. It could be the climate, it's drier here, her voice is even more timbred in Kolkata. I'm of course used to singing in a support role with Guruma, I do it all the time, so it wasn't anything new for me, but I was happy. Singing in Kolkata is new for me ... it's a first, so what if it's as vocal support?"

She stopped, aware of the silence from the other end. Had the connection snapped? Had she nattered on compulsively to empty space? "Hello?" she asked tentatively.

"No, I'm here." His voice sounded thinner than ever. She could hear the echo of her own voice, a split second after she spoke, sounding in fact very much like Guruma's. "You sang as a support?"

"Yes, I mean I'm hardly good enough to sing on my own steam in a conference as big as this Borsha Utshob. People were talking about your performance here last year, by the way. "

It was true. Whenever the talk around the coffee kiosks had turned towards past conferences, one of the names that had cropped up had invariably been that of Kaushik Kashyap's. Opinion had been unanimous that his performance of Miyan Malhar had been one of the best ever heard by Kolkata audiences in living memory, and that was saying something. They hadn't been able to stop their admiration for the way he had pushed the boundaries of his instrument, the way he had incorporated the heavy curves, the meends that were compulsory for bringing out the character of the Raag, but which were difficult to play on the sitar unless one was technically skilled to a great degree.

"I see…" He didn't sound gratified or anything. Maybe he was used to compliments, after all he was hardly a callow performer like she was, pleased no end with a mention in the papers and a few compliments to her face that were probably insincere. Suddenly, she felt depressed. The clouds of euphoria had vanished without leaving even a mist behind. She realized she knew very little about the private thoughts and feelings of this man whom she was to marry, though she knew all about his public life, his life on stage.

"They were hoping to hear you play at the Utshob this year as well…"

"Actually yes the organizers had contacted me, but I was already committed to Europe. Besides, overexposure is not a good thing. I never perform at the consecutive sessions of the same Conference."

He sounded brisk and professional, leaving her feeling inadequate.

"So, you accompany Sandhya Senapati often?" he asked.

She was surprised. He had hardly ever asked about her music, though he had always been very nice, no doubt about it, on all other counts. "Yes. Quite often, at least back home. This is the first time she's brought me here, outside the state, though."

"Is that wise?"

"What?" She was confused.

"No, I mean, vocal support is all very well, but… she's not that old, she hardly needs a support, does she?"

"Actually no. She's only brought me here for exposure, obviously. For my sake, not hers."

Kaushik Kashyap was speaking again. "But that's the point. Being cast in a supporting role has its own drawbacks. It becomes difficult to get out of that slot, and start out as a performing artiste in one's own right again."

What was he saying?

"No, but…"

"Of course Sandhya Didi means well. But be careful. You don't want to be stuck in the role of supporting artiste for the rest of your life, like some people I know… It's a real danger, believe me. Try and avoid doing that in future. After all, at your age, people are full- fledged artistes themselves. People like Kaushiki Desikan Chakravarty or Sandipan Sabhapandit, for instance. So…"

She hardly knew how to reply. Instead, she said, "I didn't recognize the number you're calling from. Is this your new number or something?"

"No, I'm calling from Lucia's cell. Something's happened to mine, I can't get through to India on it."

"From Italy?"

"No, we are in Belgium this week. We have a few performances here, in a pretty place called Lasne, and another lovely place, Redu. It's known as the Village of Books. Most of the houses here are bookshops. There's a festival going on at the town hall here, called 'Music of the World', something like that…"

She was acutely aware of how well travelled he was. Of how much, consequently he knew about such things as being a supporting artiste and thereby ruining your career. Still, she couldn't help asking, "Is Lucia playing with you?"

"Only the taanpura," he replied, making her feel ashamed at the "tit-for-tat" significance of her question.

"That's what I meant, of course." They seemed to be on the brink of a squabble, an argument, that too long distance, through somebody else's phone. It took some effort, but she asked in a cordial tone, "How is she? Do give her my regards." There, she could be just as insouciant about having girls accompanying her fiancé around the world as anybody else.

Of course, she reflected later, analysing the conversation and her own reactions to what he had said, of course he thought nothing of it. Otherwise he would hardly have used Lucia's phone to call her. She felt ashamed again. Here he was, a busy artiste, giving sincere advice and taking time off to speak to his fiancée, and all she was doing was thinking negative thoughts.

"Actually, ummm...how long are you going to be in Kolkata?" he was asking now. "Ok great, I'll be there over the weekend; I'll be arriving Sunday afternoon actually. You'll be there? Wonderful, we'll meet then..."

Ringing off, she considered her own reaction to his last words. Was she happy? Why was there a sense of something similar to dismay when he had said they would be meeting? Probably it was nervousness, not dismay. Yes, that was probably it. Nervousness about the impending meeting with a fiancé who was a star in this city, a city that was his home, but not hers.

All this travelling, moving around from one place to another, one climate to another, one culture to another. Surely it would take a toll on him, and his musicianship, soon? Perhaps, like those corporate executives who lived uni-dimensional lives revolving around the sales figures of their companies, to the neglect of hearth and home, his life, one day would soon reach a plateau. Or maybe he would suffer a sudden burnout, leaving him nothing in life to fall back on.

What a thought. Nothing of the sort was likely to happen, she realized. He would be energized by the fan following, the adulation, to reach ever-higher peaks of excellence, instead.

They got back on the fourth evening to find the lady of the house in residence.

It was almost one o'clock at night, and the streets had been comparatively quiet. As they drove up past the salaaming durwan and swept up the short but wide driveway, Nomita noticed that the house was ablaze with lights. On the other nights, only the porch light had glowed dimly.

"Ah, Rati's back," said Deepak.

"Of course," said Sandhya Senapapti. Turning to Nomita, Guruma explained, "Deepak's wife. She likes to have bright lights, all the lights if possible, wherever she is."

Nomita listened to the tones of their voices, but could find nothing in them beyond the normal interest of two friends discussing the arrival of a third in their midst. She felt vindicated, though why she should feel like this was mystifying, even to herelf. After all, she was not her teacher's keeper.

They found the lady of the house sitting in the larger drawing room, talking to the help who were all lined up in attitudes of deference before her. She turned towards them as they entered, but did not break off what she was saying to Keshto.

"... so I took the earlier flight. I have a meeting in a few hours with the Industries Minister here anyway, I thought let me at least sleep in my own house for a change."

It was only after she finished her sentence that she said, including her husband, his friend, and friend's student in her glance, "So, how was the concert?"

Her voice, with its deep base notes, was a rich contralto. It was a highly individual, unforgettable one. She had a different accent from any that Nomita had ever heard, a mixture, but a pleasant one, of Indian English, British, and... what, Continental? Or, perhaps, East Asian? She remembered that Rati had business interests in Singapore and Hong Kong and Belgium.

"Ah, you're back." Deepak moved forward to his wife, and, bending down, gave her what looked to Nomita like a polite hug, which Rati returned equally politely. Well, with all the family retainers looking on, it was perhaps circumspect of them to reserve the passion, if any, for later. She was dressed, not in the power suit that Nomita had expected, but in a cream coloured, heavy silk sari, its pallu pinned neatly to her blouse. Her thick black hair brushed her shoulders. Her face was lightly lined, but perhaps that was because she had just come in from an exhausting flight. She wore no makeup, though diamonds twinkled on her ears, throat and fingers.

Guruma came forward, though she made no move to hug Rati.

But her voice was warm, and sincere too, as she said, "Rati, it's been months since we met. How are you?"

"Fine, as you can see." The lady's smile was bright, too. "Anyway, you didn't answer, how was the concert? You had your programme today? No wait, yesterday? The time zone thing makes me disoriented nowadays, must be getting old..."

"Yes, the programme was yesterday. It went off well, Rati. I enjoyed it..."

"That's the main thing... And this is?" Rati looked directly at Nomita as she stood quietly at the side.

She stepped forward as Guruma said, "Ah, my student, Nomita Sharma. She's from Tamulbari, as well. She gives me vocal support during my concerts..."

Nomita smiled, and folded her hands in a namaste. Why was she getting the feeling that they were paying tribute to a deity or something here? It was probably because they were all standing around and Rati Mittal was seated on the most elaborate sofa in the room. But she was probably just too tired to get up.

"Nomita, what a nice soft name. Like your face. Like Sandhya's face. Aren't you ever going to age, Sandhya?" She smiled at Nomita and added, "I do hope you were comfortable? Forgive me, I don't know if Deepak told you, I can't walk, you know. I shouldn't be sitting here while you, our guests, are standing..."

Trying to prevent her eyes from straying towards Rati's legs, hidden under the sari, (of course, that was why she wore the otherwise impractical sari, even for travelling, and not trousers or even salwar kameez) and also trying to keep the shock from showing on her face, Nomita said, "How can I not be comfortable? Everybody is taking such good care of us, and the house is so beautiful, anyway..."

She was nice, thought Nomita, really nice. In spite of what she had told Rahul, in spite of her own hot defence of her teacher, her own responses to Deepak's friendship with Guruma had been so stereotypical after all. She had assumed that they had "allowed" their friendship to become so much deeper over the years because of some lack in their spouses, at least in Deepak's case. She had assumed that the

Ivy League-educated businesswoman had "neglected" her husband, pursuing the goal of success in her businesses, while he pursued his. She had demonized the wife in her mind, subconsciously, and here she was, in the flesh, Rati Mittal, the poster girl of Indian success in global business, having proved her wrong. It just showed that being successful, in the cut-throat worlds of music or business, did not necessarily lead to bad manners and boorish natures.

"Let's eat here, is that all right? I can't bear getting on the wheelchair again even to go to the dining room," decided Rati. "Do sit down, Sandhya, Nomita, tell me about the concerts. I don't know much about music, not like Deepak here, but still…"

"How was the flight? The food?" Guruma's voice had its usual softness.

"Good. They're improving first class in all the airlines, I'm happy to say. It's the competition. One can actually sleep on those chairs that open out to become beds, more or less…"

"You look fresh and rested, it's amazing, you've just got in from a long flight. And you're flying all the time, Deepak tells me…"

"Yes, I have to move around a lot. That's ironical, isn't it, considering I can't actually move at all? Or hardly at all?" She laughed, but it wasn't a bitter laugh at all. It was, in fact, realized Nomita with a further shock, a happy one.

Tables were quickly shifted, and the food was brought in. It was only then that Nomita noticed the wheelchair, placed discreetly in the corner of the large room. Two women entered. Nomita had never seen them before. Obviously they had come in with Rati Mittal.

"No, it's okay, I'll manage, thank you. Go and rest, you must be tired," Rati Mittal told them. "Deepak will lift me to the chair, he does it quite well, don't you Deepak? He gets a crick in his back, though, sometimes," she smiled, patting her husband's shoulders in what certainly looked like a fond way.

As the two women went away, Nomita realized that they were Rati's attendants. So this was how she travelled the world. Still. She hadn't yet recovered from her amazement.

"You know, I'd have loved to have been at your concert, but India isn't like Europe," she said, waving aside the cutlery and tucking into her rice with her fingers. Her relish was obvious. "A person in a wheelchair always attracts stares. And even questions."

"You can hear us here, Rati, why should you bother to go anywhere else?" Guruma looked smilingly at the other woman. "I am going to have a practice session again, the tabla and harmonium and even the sarengi will be here. I can ask them to come again whenever you are free, na. I'll sing whatever you want..."

Rati leaned across and grasped Guruma's hand with her own free one. "That's so nice of you." She turned impulsively to her husband and said, "In fact Deepak, why don't we arrange a baithak? You would like that, wouldn't you?" She turned back to Guruma and asked, "I mean, if you don't mind? When are you free, let's organize it, it will be really lovely..."

Later that night, before going off to sleep, Nomita called Rahul again. "Why didn't you tell me Rati Mittal can't walk?"

But Rahul was equally amazed. "What do you mean, can't walk? She's had an accident?"

"I don't know whether it's an accident or whether she was born this way or whether it was some illness or something. But it's not recent. I mean she's quite used to being on a wheelchair, it's not a new thing for her. She even jokes about it. She has two attendants who take care of her when she's travelling."

"Really? Amazing," said Rahul. "Anyway, save up everything for when we meet, tell me everything in great detail. Rati Mittal wheelchair bound! You in Deepak Rathod's house! Strange things never cease happening, do they?"

They had already spoken after the concert yesterday. Rahul always called after an important concert to find out how it had gone, even in Tamulbari.

There were voices on the line, reminding Nomita that Rahul was working late these days.

"Ok, I'll call again, I'm going to Tirna's place tomorrow, you know. Don't want to look more haggard than necessary."

"Right, Nomi, take care, let me know how it goes." There was static on the line, and then his voice emerged from the noise, asking, "So have you met your fiancé yet?"

"But Rahul, I told you, he's not here right now..." But the static engulfed the line again, and she wasn't sure, as she slowly pressed the End Call button, whether he had heard her after all.

None of the ambivalence she had felt while talking to Kaushik surfaced in her mind when she went to meet his parents. Tirna Ghosh was as warm and welcoming as Nomita would have expected her to be. She was waiting for her as she emerged from the lift on the fifth floor of a block of apartments, looking just like she had back in Tamulbari. Nomita had come alone, in a taxi, independently. Her hosts had urged her to take one of their cars, but she had stood firm in her refusal to do so, assuring them that she was perfectly capable of going in a taxi.

"Imagine, Nomita, you've been here in our city for what, five, six days already, and we haven't met. I would have gone to hear you, of course, but we had this teacher's workshop that dragged me to Siliguri. How did it go? I read the reviews, they were all so positive. They said good things about you, too, specifically. Now that's really great, and unusual also..."

Chattering in a way that immediately made Nomita feel at ease, she led her into the apartment.

"Where is..." she hesitated, looking around the airy space, not knowing how to refer to Tirna's husband, Kaushik's father. It was too early to call him "Baba" like his son did, after all she was not actually married into the family yet, but how could she call him by name?

But Tirna Ghosh rescued her, tactfully. She must have been aware of the girl's confusion and the reason for it. "Rana?" she asked. "He's just stepped out, to a sweetshop actually..." She smiled, and put her hand affectionately on Nomita's arm. "Fresh mishtis to welcome you... anyway, here he is..."

The man who entered, with a shopping bag in his hand, was tall and thin, almost gangly. His beaky nose supported a pair of black spectacles. Of the French beard or ponytail she had imagined, there was no trace. Indeed, he did not look like the adman and poet that he was, but like a normal Bangla bhadralok, just back from the shops after getting a bit of fish and some mishti for the girl who was to be his daughter-in-law. Nomita noticed the anxiety in his eyes, and realized, with a kind of troubled comfort, that he was at least as nervous as she herself was.

She wondered whether she should touch his feet. In their home, feet-touching was not a gesture that was common, though of course in the world of music it was ubiquitous. But perhaps Tirna and Rana expected it? Or would it be too much? After all they were modern people. Still, perhaps in their culture it was expected? If they had been musicians, it would have been so much simpler. After all a junior in the line was expected to touch the feet of the seniors. It wouldn't have been awkward. She wished she had thought out this issue of feet-touching at home, but then the question hadn't occurred to her. Better be safe, she thought, and prepared to pay obeisance in the traditional manner.

But Tirna pre-empted her. She put her hand on her shoulder again, and led her to the beige sofa near the verandah at one end of the room. "Come, sit down, it's so hot, you must come under a fan for a while..."

"Did you have problems finding our place?" asked Rana Ghosh. He seemed to have overcome his initial hesitation. His voice was not in the least like his son's. It was pleasant and quiet.

In fact, thought Nomita, as she sat there talking with the two middle-aged people, neither of them was like their son, at least physically. Both Tirna and Rana were tall, though Tirna's generous proportions did not make her look as tall as she was. Rana, though, was quite lanky. She wondered how it was possible for their son to be so short.

The couple of hours she spent in their house passed agreeably. Indeed, within a few minutes of her arrival, Nomita felt quite relaxed. She was pleased to see that Rana Ghosh, too, seemed to have lost his hesitation, or was it his shyness of her? Before long, she felt as though she was visiting some friends of her parents, rather than her prospective parents- in- law.

"But why aren't you at work today?" she asked both of them as she sat eating the vast spread on the dining table a little later. It was mandatory for a first time visitor, Rana had explained gently, to eat at least four different kinds of sweets in a Bengali home. Grateful that he had said "first time visitor" and not "prospective daughter-in-law," Nomita was gamely nibbling her way through the third large koda pak sandesh on the dish before her. "I mean, you had to miss work because of me, isn't it? I'm so sorry... but then it's impossible to come in the evenings, we're out every day for the concerts, you know, and then there are the people coming in to see Guruma..."

"No no, don't be apologetic," they both assured her. "I just switched some classes with a colleague, and Rana has flexible timings at his office, it's no problem," assured Tirna. "How is your mother, then?"

They were nice. They were not creating a big issue of her arrival, and were making her feel at ease. There was nothing in this house, or at least this room, she thought, looking around between sips of tea, to indicate that this was the home of one of the country's foremost musicians. No trophies stacked up on wall units, no blowups of the artiste receiving the Padma Shri from the President on the wall. It was just an airy, aesthetically appointed space. They did not talk of the absent son for most of the time that Nomita spent there. It was only towards the end of the visit, as Nomita was preparing to leave, that Tirna said, "I'm so happy you'll be able to meet Kaushik while you are here. During the weekend, isn't it?"

Nomita had wondered whether she should mention this herself, but had felt too diffident. "Just for a couple of days, it seems?"

"That's what he said. Actually, I hadn't expected him. But it seems he has some recording in Mumbai. Besides, there's a memorial concert in his Guru's Guru's name, he has to attend that, it would be very bad of him not to. His own Guru is already here, he wants Kaushik to feature in the concert, too. So he's dropping in for a couple of days... But I don't think he'll have time to do much..."

They saw her off at the foot of the apartment block, hailing a taxi for her, and fussing, "Really, let us drop you back, it's not that far."

But Nomita refused all offers of a lift as firmly as she had Deepak. She would go back independently, the way she had come.

Independence. She was the daughter of a working mother, of an age when she should have been earning much more than she actually was. Women her age around the country were taking up responsible jobs, climbing the ladders of corporate, civil service, medical, law, and all kinds of success. And here she was, on a humble teacher's salary, that too practically part time, supplemented from time to time by her meagre earnings from the TV and radio programmes, and some concerts. Would she be able to support herself on this kind of earning? No, certainly not, well at least not in the style in which being a doctor's only child had accustomed her to. If she were to live on her earnings alone, she would not starve, true, but then her life would be one of financial anxiety.

She fanned herself with her dupatta. It was hot, but the sights of the street around her made the heat bearable.

There was a question to be faced, she realized, the question of what she would do with her life after her marriage to Kaushik Kashyap. Now that she had seen his home, met his father, yet another door had shut behind her, making escape that much more difficult. Abruptly aware of the slant of her thoughts, she pulled herself up short. Why was she thinking of this impending marriage as a prison? The metaphor of the door clanging shut had come unbidden to her mind. She should be thinking in terms of doors opening, and of the rainbows beyond them. True, it was an arranged marriage, but then in this country, arranged marriages were quite common even among those who considered themselves "liberated".

In any case, she had heard of several people, and even one of her friends, who had happily combined the latest technology with the concept of arranged marriages, and searched for partners online. Jina, who had taught Chemistry in her school till a year ago, had posted her name on a matrimonial site. Choosing among the several matches that came her way had not been easy, but then she had met nobody she could have got married to in Tamulbari itself. Finally, something had clicked between her and Peter, living in distant

Gujarat, not a Gujarati or an Assamese like her, but an Andhraite, working in a textile factory. He had come over to meet her, she had gone to his home in Hyderabad, and there they were, six months later, happily married and now even expecting their first baby in Ahmedabad. True, Jina had chosen her spouse, but the website had been the facilitator. It had been the technological equivalent of the matchmaker, who had been quite often the priest, in the older days. He had gone from house to house with a bundle of horoscopes in his jhola, praising the attributes of this boy to the family of that girl, and the home-making qualities and beauty of this girl to the family of that boy, till all the girls and boys whose matrimonial fortunes had been entrusted to him by their families had been suitably, no, excellently matched. Internet sites, today's equivalent to that long ago priest, were increasingly being used as a tool to getting the right partner, to facilitate a modern arranged marriage.

No, being in an arranged marriage in itself was not any kind of bar to independence within the marriage. All the women she knew, were, in one way or another economically self- sufficient. True, most of their spouses earned more than them, but they, too, contributed financially to the running of the household. She, having been brought up by a working mother, couldn't imagine being dependent on her husband for money, no matter how high his earnings. But what work could she do here?

She wondered whether there was a vacancy for a music teacher in Tirna Ghosh's school. Or in any other school, or institution, within easy distance of her new home. She was after all a small town girl, and unused to long commutes. Through the gap between a large white Accent and a smoke-belching Ambassador, she noticed a signboard opposite where her taxi was still firmly stuck. "City Music College," it said, in no-nonsense but not inartistic lettering. "All Kinds of Indian Music Taught Here," it continued in English, with the same message repeated below in Bangla. Cheered, Nomita sat back in her seat as the taxi finally began to creep ahead again. Surely there would be a place for her in the City Music College, or in a similar institution.

Luckily, thought Nomita, Kaushik was not going to be present for the small jalsa that Deepak and Rati were organizing the evening after the Borsha Utshob ended. He had, thankfully, some other engagement. Guruma would be performing, of course, but Nomita was to be the opening artiste. Rati had invited a small group of people. These were not just connoisseurs of music but also a few of her friends, and Deepak's, and several of Guruma's co-students, artistes who were now well established performers in Kolkata.

Talk of the visit to the Ghosh home cropped up that afternoon, over lunch. Guruma asked her, her kindness and concern tinged with some anxiety, "So how did it go?"

"They are nice people, I know Tirna Ghosh from before, she's my mother's friend..." Nomita said. She noticed Deepak and Rati looking at her, their concern evident in their faces, too. "It's not as if I was a bride-to-be visiting my fiancé's house, you know. I mean there was that, of course, but it was more like visiting, you know, my mother's friend. They are nice..." she repeated.

"Good," said Rati Mittal, smiling. "We must invite them over to the jalsa, of course. Give me their numbers, Nomita, I'll do it right away, after lunch. What a pity your fiancé won't be able to make it. You would have liked him to be present, wouldn't you?"

"Certainly not!" was the reply that sprang to Nomita's lips, but she bit it down just in time. She managed to replace it with a smile that she hoped was non-committal, instead.

"He's going to be here for his Guru's Guru's commemorative function, I heard?" asked Guruma. "But the function itself will be after we leave, na?"

"Yes..."

"After you leave? Oh. What a pity we can't move our jalsa to when he is available," said Rati regretfully. "I would have loved to have met him again."

Nomita looked questioningly at her.

It was Deepak who answered. "Oh yes, we've met him several times before, both of us. I go to concerts whenever I can, and sometimes we have these jalsas at home so that Rati can enjoy the live music.

I believe he's performed here before... several years ago, wasn't it, Rati?"

"Yes. When he was quite young. There was a fire in him even then. I mean it was obvious that he would make it big, really big. And now his fiancée is staying with us. What a small world!"

They were very kind, but she couldn't help feeling that there was something that they were holding back from her, something that she didn't know about. What was it? Or was it just her imagination? She looked at Guruma, and caught her eye. Kaushik's advice to her about not giving her vocal accompaniment came to her mind, but she dismissed it firmly. Guruma smiled at her, as she had on countless other occasions. But was it her imagination, or was there just that bit of constraint in her smile?

Were they all thinking of some girlfriend he had had in his past in this city then? After all they would know the gossip. Or was it to do with some student, maybe a foreign one, about whom there was more talk than the merely professional. It was quite likely, thought Nomita. The people around her were too kind to speak about it now that she was already engaged to the man. But there was some kind of undercurrent here.

"Wish you could be here," Nomita told Rahul when he called her late that afternoon. He knew that she was always at the Utshob in the evenings, so he timed his calls for when he guessed she would be free.

"I wish so too," sighed Rahul. "Deepak Rathod! Rati Mittal! How wonderful to be able to talk to them, face to face I mean... Deepak Rathod was on the cover of *Business Fortnightly* again this issue, you know."

She did indeed know, because Rati had shown her the journal. "Rathod in race to buy company in Europe," the headline had said. She had been taken aback, because talk around the dining table, or even otherwise, had never dwelt on that.

"Is it true?" she had asked, surprised.

"Of course. Deepak's companies are doing very well, he needs to acquire companies now if he is to really go global the way he wants...

But of course all this is very early. The journos like to speculate. It's just preliminary discussions at the moment, weighing the options, getting the valuations, that kind of thing now. "

"How does he... how do both of you... do it?" she had asked, impulsively.

"What? Acquire companies? We don't do it alone, you know ..." Rati had sounded amused. "We have extremely competent people working along with us."

"No, that's not what I meant." Nomita had hesitated, remembering the way most of the musicians she knew talked of nothing else but their work, their music. Yet in this house, where the host and hostess were certainly as committed to their work as any musician, the talk had been of so many things, not confined to work. Or maybe she'd missed something?

"What I meant was... how do you, what's the word, yes, how do you compartmentalize so well? You are obviously working, so is Deepak, but when we meet up with you it's as though you have all the time in the world for us."

"That's a wonderful compliment," Rati had smiled. "Thank you..."

Now, talking to Rahul, she recounted the conversation. "Yes, I saw the magazine, and complimented him on his looks. Very shallow of me, I think. But what to do, I know nothing of business wheeling and dealing, I couldn't comment on it at all..."

Deepak had laughed when she had said, "You look good in the picture!" Guruma was looking at the journal, and saying, "Deepak, is it wise to take over a company that has had so much labour trouble?" surprising Nomita. She had never thought that Sandhya Senapati would know anything about business. Certainly she looked as though she lived in the ivory tower of classical music, though gradually, bit by bit Nomita was getting the feeling that this was not completely true.

"Thanks, Nomita, the photographer certainly went to some trouble to see that I came out better than what I normally do." He had waved aside Nomita's protestations, and replied to Guruma, "That's the reason the asking price of the company is within our budget, you know. Otherwise we wouldn't have been able to afford it."

"Talking of looks to Deepak Rathod, the famed Deepak Rathod, when there are so many questions, so much to talk about," said Rahul now. "How... cliched. You know, like those aunties who look at your pictures at some party or wedding and say..." his tone became prim and condescending "how *nice* you look, Rahul. That's a *nice* shirt you're wearing..." Resuming his normal tone again, he said, "Now if it were me... I want to ask him all kinds of things, about this buyout he's planning..."

"Maybe you'll meet him sometime soon, Rahul. He has his business interests in our part of the world, plus he's such good friends with Guruma, he's always going over to her place..."

"Yes, that's another thing. What's your idea of this rumour that's been going around? You've seen them together so many times, you're at his house with her..."

"Also with his wife present, don't forget, by the way she's a really nice person. I had cast her in some kind of evil mould in my mind. Well, not evil, but snooty. Uncaring."

Rahul was in full flow, seeming not to have heard her interjection. "Do you think..." his voice dropped dramatically to a whisper, even though he was thousands of kilometres away and it was she who was in Deepak Rathod's house, not him, "do you think there's something going on between them? He's always going to his tea gardens in Assam. Owners don't do that, you know. Not so frequently, anyway. Several of those profiles of Deepak Rathod have hinted at some kind of, you know...."

"Of course not, Rahul, how can you think such a thing. What a... just shows you have a villager's mind. Can't you accept a friendship, plain and simple, stretching back to their student days, for what it is?"

"Ummm... no smoke without a fire, you know." He didn't sound in the least bit contrite as he trotted out the cliché.

"It's perfectly possible to have smoke without fire if the smoke is in your own dirty mind," said Nomita, more ascerbically than warranted by Rahul's banter. But he didn't mind, bless him.

23

When Nomita got up in the mornings and came downstairs she usually met Rati Mittal, looking fresh, wearing a beautiful sari, sitting in her wheelchair in the verandah.

"So, how was it last night?" she would ask, setting aside her cellphone or laptop or whatever was engaging her attention at the moment. Her smile was that of a simple hostess, not a woman with business interests across the world. "I was busy on a conference call, but I heard you come in." She would stretch out a hand, and gently pull Nomita to sit on the seat next to hers. "Who performed? Amjad Ali Khan? Ah, good, Deepak enjoys his playing and I'm glad he got a chance to listen to him again. That too in your company and Sandhya's, it must be educative to sit near her while listening to the best music there is in the country. "

There was not a trace of any emotion other than cheerfulness in her voice. Nomita felt out of her depth. She had already rearranged her thoughts as far as Rati Mittal's nature was concerned. Now the concept of marriage was undergoing a modification in her mind. This marriage was so very different from any she had seen so far. Her parents' marriage, for instance, or even, in fact, Guruma's marriage to Tridib Baruah, in spite of her friendship with Deepak Rathod.

And her own impending marriage, what would that be like? Would Lucia be a presence in their marriage in the same way as Sandhya Senapati was, in Rati Mittal's? Lucia, or perhaps another beautiful and accomplished student who was also what Lucia symbolised in Kaushik Kashyap's life? If Lucia was such an all-pervading presence, how would she herself react? Would she be able to be as matter-of-fact as Rati Mittal? Perhaps it needed the self-confidence generated by huge successes in the workfield to be able to be so nonchalant about it. Would she ever have that kind of success, that kind of confidence?

Nomita found herself looking forward to these early morning interactions with the lady of the house. Sitting on the wide verandah of the ground floor, overlooking the garden, fresh and green at this hour, with the morning sounds of the Kolkata streets coming in mutedly from beyond the walls, she found herself enjoying Rati's company, even though, she realized, she had been subconsciously prepared to dislike her. Why? Just because she herself had a warm and cordial relationship with Deepak? And Deepak was friendly, with Sandhya Senapati, whom of course she respected highly. But now, as Rati set aside the papers she was looking at, and welcomed Nomita with a smile, she couldn't help admiring and respecting Rati, and yes, liking her, too.

"Have a cup of tea with me, Nomita ..." she said, pouring out from the fat-bellied white teapot herself. "I think you'll like it, it's from your State. Actually it's from Deepak's garden ..."

"Lovely, thanks," Nomita accepted the strong and fragrant brew. She wondered if she should tell her that she had been to Krishnanagar, near one of Deepak's tea gardens, with Guruma. For some reason, she hesitated, though she realized even as she did so that it was probably not necessary to take pains not to disclose such a thing. Probably Rati Mittal knew about it all, already.

But in any case Rati was saying, "It's a beautiful place, I believe. Unfortunately I haven't been there myself yet, though I would love to. Isn't it strange? I can fly all around the world, no problem. But I find it so difficult to sit for a long time in a car. I'll have to make the journey to Deepak's tea gardens by car. They always are a long way from the nearest airport. It's the nature of the business. What a pity."

Involuntarily, Nomita found herself glancing at Rati Mittal's legs. Under the sari which she wore in impeccable folds even at this early hour, they seemed quite, well, normal. She wondered, as she had often done in the past few days, how this had happened. Nobody talked about it, not because it was something to be hushed up, but on the contrary, because it was treated as an ordinary thing. But Rati Mittal had intercepted that glance. In a voice that had no twinge of self pity or even offence, she said, "Ah, my legs. You looked surprised, that first evening, when you realized that I couldn't walk."

Nomita looked up at Rati Mittal's eyes, dark and intelligent. And perceptive. "Yes. I... wasn't expecting it."

"No, I could see that. You tried very hard not to look at my legs at that time." There was a smile in her eyes and her voice. She reached across and put a hand on Nomita's arm. "Don't look so stricken. That's a reaction I like in people." She paused, and said, "The people I am close to know I hate my condition being talked about. It is something that will arouse pity in the listener if that person doesn't know me. 'Poor thing, to be confined to a wheelchair at her age'... no, I don't want that. Deepak never speaks about my disability to others, I know. And Sandhya..."

"How did it happen?" The words were out before Nomita was even conscious of the thought.

But Rati Mittal did not seem to mind. "It's a progressive disease." She turned her gaze away, looking at the magenta bougainvillea on the white wall of the compound. "Limb girdle muscular dystrophy, that's the name, if you want to know. I wasn't always like this. I mean, not wheelchair bound, though I have known, for a long time, that this was coming. But it's not... I mean, I'm used to it. It could be much worse. The disease won't affect my mind, that's the main thing. And one of its characteristics is that it only starts later in life. For me, praise be, it put me into a wheelchair only after Raji and Dhannu were born. Our children, you know. Deepak's and mine. Rajyalakshmi and Dhananjay. I could hobble after them for a few years, I got that. Probably you'll find my head lolling to one side some years later. I insisted the doctors tell me the worst-case scenarios. But my voice won't be affected." She reached out a hand again and patted Nomita's. "I'm not a singer or anything, but I would rather keep my own voice, instead of one of those voice machines. Better option, don't you think?"

There seemed to be nothing that Nomita could say. She looked at her hostess dumbly, totally out of her depth. But Rati Mittal didn't notice. Or maybe she was too polite to let on that she had noticed.

"Thank goodness I have my work." she continued. "And my children, and family, and so many other things besides… And yes, I am happy that my brain is as alert as ever, that I can talk, plan, run my businesses. So I am happy, I give thanks to God every day. I can travel the world. I hardly feel the loss of my ability to walk. Of course a lot of it is because I have the money, but I've worked for it. True, I inherited my father's business, but the turnover today is so many times more than what it was when I first joined."

Her voice was even, but there was something in it, some emotion, that made Nomita aware that this was not something she talked about frequently.

As though conscious of her thoughts, Rati said, "Actually, I never talk about this to others. There's something in you, Nomita, you're so much younger than me, but something in the way you look at people, something in your innocence…" She looked away again, and said, "But since you really are interested… I finished my schooling as a private candidate. By then, slowly, I was able to channelize my competitiveness. I'm very competitive, you know, Nomita, I revel in it. Maybe I could have competed in the Olympics if this hadn't happened, certainly I could have run for India. That would have been a first. A girl from my background, a business background, where girls were married off at sixteen with fat dowries. But since that was not to be, I gritted my teeth and put my competitiveness to use in business. Ethical business, mind you, Nomita, that's the only way one can grow. I have made Mittal Gems a multinational, its stocks are traded in the BSE. That's the Olympic medal I have awarded myself… and I love it."

There were many questions that Nomita wanted to ask. How had she met Deepak, how did they get married, what kind of a marriage was it…? Instead, all she said was, "I have a very good friend. Rahul. He's your fan, yours and Deepak's. But even he didn't seem to know that you are confined to a wheelchair. He reads all the business papers, but he didn't know…"

"Ah, you've been discussing me," Rati Mittal said, but pleasantly.

"Well, yes, I'm sorry, but I was so surprised that evening..."

"Yes. I can understand that," she said, her voice thoughtful. "Have some more tea? It's nice, isn't it?" She poured out more of the fragrant beverage. Sipping it, she turned with a sudden smile and said, "Actually, your surprise when you saw I couldn't walk...when I saw that, I was proud. I was really pleased."

"Proud?" That, thought Nomita was hardly a word she would have used.

"Yes. It means I have risen above my handicap, don't you see? It means that when you, a girl who has heard of me through various people, Sandhya and as you said your friend Rahul – you have heard of me, my firm, my work. But you have not heard of the fact that I am wheelchair bound. Nowhere have you read, or heard, that Rati Mittal is the creator of a multi-million-dollar business empire *even though* she is confined to a wheelchair. She employs so many hundreds of people, so many people have a job because of her, *in spite of the fact* that she is handicapped herself. You don't know – you can't imagine - what satisfaction your surprise gave me that day. The same kind of satisfaction that I get when I see my name in the financial papers, with no mention made of my handicap."

"I understand," said Nomita slowly. She thought of another girl with a wonderful voice who could not sing in public unless she was strapped to a wheelchair, and said, almost absently, "I must tell Silsila about you. About what you told me today."

"Silsila?"

"Yes. My student."

"Ah. You teach music? Already?"

"I teach music to children, in the school where I studied. But Silsila doesn't study there. She can't. She's spastic. Not severely, but enough so that she can't walk, or co-ordinate her limbs. I teach also in a place where children like Silsila wait for me, much more impatiently than I wait for Guruma. Not that I am as good a teacher as Guruma is. Far from it. But they look forward to my classes because I bring to them music, and music brings something – I can't explain it – some joy, some sense of wonder, some happiness, that inspires them. Silsila is an excellent singer, but she can't stand without losing her balance. She has to sit in a wheelchair, she has to be strapped to it, otherwise her body flops about too much. But her voice is amazing. True and clear. Of course I don't teach her what I learn from Guruma. Those Raags are too complicated for her. She sings simple songs, but they have a great deal of beauty. She loads them with her feelings, you see. I wish you could hear her sometime..."

"It's enough, now, that I hear you talk about her. I know this is not a nice thing to say, Nomita, but I wish – I hope – you never become so famous or so well known as a classical singer that children like Silsila are deprived of a teacher who will bring music to their lives. It's always that one teacher, that one mentor, who makes a difference in our lives, isn't it? I remember so clearly the person who motivated me to refuse to feel sorry for myself and join the race."

Kaushik Kashyap's impending visit had unsettled Nomita. She found that she wasn't able to enjoy that evening's concert nearly as much as she was expecting to, even though the main artiste was Ashwini Bhide. Her recital was all Nomita could have hoped for, her voice as bell-like in its clarity and resonance. The Sur Malhar that she chose was one of the best that Kolkata audiences had heard in recent times, rivalling, in its own style, even the memories of the same Raag that Salamat and Nazakat Ali Khan had mesmerised audiences in this city with, many years ago. All around her, Nomita heard people expressing their appreciation of the music in softly murmured spontaneous expressions such as "Ba, ki shundor!"

And yet she could not immerse herself in the music as she had hoped, and expected. Thank goodness, Nomita thought as she sat in Deepak and Rati's reception room for the jalsa a day later, thank goodness Kaushik is not going to be here. I don't want him to hear me sing, not yet.

She wondered at her own bashfulness. She was rarely coy about performing in public, or even before an audience of two or three hundred people. As a singer, that was what she did. She was rarely intimidated by the star status of another highly revered performer, either. After all, she had sung numerous times in Guruma's music room before some well known names in the music world. So it wasn't Kaushik's stature as a musician that was causing this dread, this alarm that he would be here to listen to her sing. Of course he hadn't shown much inclination to do so when they had met, but thank goodness for that. It was just the combination, of a fiancé and a star performer, which was making the prospect of singing before him so daunting.

But it was perfectly all right that Tirna and Rana should be there in the audience, listening as she performed. The room was now transformed into the perfect venue for a baithak with white-sheeted mattresses and big white bolsters. It was a small gathering, mostly of the host and hostesses' business friends and colleagues and some musicians. Once more, Nomita was surprised, and then surprised at herself for being surprised, at the fact that Guruma seemed to know most of the people there. Of course she would.

Tirna and Rana Ghosh were welcomed warmly by Rati, sitting on her wheelchair at the entrance to the room.

"How wonderful that you could come at such short notice! But we decided to have this only on the spur of the moment."

"It's good of you to have us," murmured Tirna.

Rati looked at Nomita and smiled. "How could we not have you here when our Nomita is singing? Make them comfortable, Nomita."

There were just the two of them performing this evening, Nomita and Sandhya Senapati. Nomita enjoyed singing her brief Yaman and two Meera Bhajans before this audience. They were knowledgeable, but not pedantic. They were prepared to enjoy the music, without bothering about the "correctness" of the presentation of the Raag. Besides, they did not feel the need to air whatever knowledge they had about Shastriya Sangeet to the others, or impress. They applauded her enthusiastically at the end, and even though Nomita knew that this was not a critical or learned audience, she was gratified. It was good to sing just for the pleasure of singing.

Sandhya Senapati's choice of Raag for this audience was Chhayanat. It suited her voice beautifully, and the swoops and meends of the melody allowed a blend of emotions to be conveyed. Romance, of course. But there was also joy, and with it, sometimes, in the lower octave, a tinge of sadness. It was a deceptively simple Raag, for though it was quite possible to be technically correct during its performance, it was extremely difficult to get the exact spirit, the Ras or mix of moods that the melody conveyed. Nomita was glad that she was not accompanying Guruma on this. For once, she was seated in the audience, for the room, though large, was not big enough to accommodate too many aural inputs at one go. The taanpura was played by Guruma herself. Nomita was free to observe not just Guruma and her accompanists, but also the audience, surreptitiously, from her vantage point at the side of the gathering.

As always, Guruma's music embraced all listeners within its fold. So absorbed were they now in the music that their faces mirrored their emotions with a great deal of clarity. It was always like that when people were totally engrossed in the melody that surrounded them. It was as though their most intimate feelings floated up to their visages, pushing aside the masks that habitually covered them, the masks that had almost grown into their skins. An excellent musical performance, Nomita had noticed many times, had the power to do that.

Deepak and Rati were sitting separately, at two corners of the room. The hostess's wheelchair did not allow her the choice of sitting on the gaddi-covered floor. By now Nomita knew her hostess well enough to understand why she had chosen not to sit on one of the sofas that had been pushed to the end of the room. The act of being helped from her wheelchair to another chair made her look clumsy. But more importantly, it made her look helpless. And dependent. No doubt these were her friends all around her, people she knew very well, people she was at ease with. But she did not wish to expose the frailty of her flesh to even these people.

The Chhayanat was coming to a close; the soft sensuousness of the Raag mingling with the teasing of the lyrics, words that today had not been penned by Guruma, but were a traditional composition.

Baar Baar Kahi Haar Tumso
Kaahen Na Maano Hamari Batiya.
Jaao Jaao Tum Sang Ham Nahin Bole
Youn Hi Gawayee Hamaree Ratiya…
You've defeated me, never listening to my words,
Go, go away, I'm not going to speak to you,
Not after you've made me waste the night
Waiting…

The applause was muted, but heartfelt nevertheless. It was as though no one in the audience wished to break the spell, yet they wanted to show their appreciation. Sandhya Senapati adjusted the tone of the taanpura again, and said, "I am so happy to be able to perform here before you…it is an honour. And such a privilege that my hostess, Rati, is here. This concert is for her, actually…Rati, tell me, what would you like me to sing now…"

"Thumri. In Pilu…" replied Rati with a promptness that surprised Nomita.

It was a sad melody, made more haunting by Guruma's pliant, honed voice. The separation of souls, or lovers, or the Creator and the Created. But even then, Nomita was taken aback by the expression she glimpsed on Rati Mittal's face. There was sadness so deep, so unfathomable written on it that Nomita quickly looked away again. Perhaps naturally, her gaze stopped at the other end of the room, where Deepak Rathod was sitting, with a large takiya between him and the wall. He was dressed in a kurta and churidar today, cream coloured with chikan work around the neckline. Though his posture, as he reclined on the bolster, was an apparently relaxed one, there was a tension in his body. And on his face, as he looked at Sandhya Senapati as she sang the lover's words of the thumri, was a look of quiet desperation.

Guruma made eye contact with the audience, including everyone in her glance. Almost everyone. Nomita, her head now full of thoughts far removed from the music around her, noticed that she did not look even once in Deepak Rathod's direction. Not once. It was Rati Mittal that she smiled at, time and again, Rati Mittal to whom she dedicated the next jhoola, "I know my friend Rati likes this next song I'm going to sing, a jhoola, performed during the monsoons. She told me once that it brings back memories of her grandmother, who used to sing the folk songs on which these jhoolas are based."

Rati smiled, the sadness driven momentarily from her dark eyes by the caring gesture. But it was back again as the melodies twirled around her...

Jhamak Jhuki Ayee Badariya Kali,
Jhoola Jhoolay Nandkishore...
Dark clouds come with drumbeats near
Nanda's son sits swaying on his swing...

Did she know? wondered Nomita. Had she seen what she herself had on Deepak's face? She felt like going up to Deepak and pulling a screen across his face. It was impossible that anyone else should see what she had seen and not make out the import of it. Impossible.

On an impulse, she got up, and stood near her hostess. She would never have taken this liberty with Rati Mittal at any other time, but now she reached out and put a hand on her shoulder. Almost automatically, without moving her eyes away from Sandhya Senapati, Rati brought up her own hand to clasp Nomita's.

24

Kaushik Kashyap looked a little plumper, thought Nomita, trying not to appear as though she was staring at the man she was going to marry. Not much, just a little. His skin looked smoother, maybe a little lighter. Europe, and the company of women like Lucia, seemed to have suited him. The ponytail was neatly in place, though from the front, it wasn't too apparent.

Nomita tried to ignore it, and wondered at her strong reactions to what was after all an innocuous detail. She had tried to analyze it back in Tamulbari, and ended up as confused as ever. Did the hairstyle signify the man, or merely his lifestyle? By sporting a ponytail, was Kaushik Kashyap declaring his non-conformity? Or was he only showing his tame conformity, his timid compliance with a supposed non-conformity that was only implied, not symbolized, by the ponytail? It certainly seemed to her that he was trying too hard to build an "image." Or was all this merely too much analysis? Perhaps he only wore his hair like that because he thought it suited his face? Perhaps somebody, maybe his barber or stylist or maybe Lucia had told him that.

She was conscious of the fact that she herself was not looking her best. The taxi ride through the clogged and fume-filled Kolkata streets had been wearying. But she had insisted, once more, on going by herself, refusing all offers from Rati and Deepak to take one of their vehicles. And Kaushik hadn't volunteered to pick her up when he had called her that morning. "Can you come over?" he had asked. "I believe you know the place..."

At that hour, except for Kaushik, only the help were around. "Both

Ma and Baba had to leave for work…" he explained. "Shall we go to my living room, then?"

He led her through a passageway to the adjacent flat. There were pictures everywhere, on walls and tables, of Kaushik Kashyap in performance at various venues all over the world. Some shared space with the images of other famous faces, musicians or well-known people who had come to listen to him. A blow-up on one wall showed him receiving an award that could only be the Padma Shri from the President of the country. But there were other well known faces, leaders, businessmen, musicians, who looked out at her in his company from the walls and tables.

She tried not to look overwhelmed. In any case, Kaushik Kashyap was urging her to sit on the low divan below a window. A maid whom she remembered from her last visit came in with a tray of freshly squeezed sweet lime juice and sweetmeats. She smiled in a friendly way at Nomita, put down the tray on a nearby table, and left.

What could they talk about? She had already asked him on the phone how his trip had been, how hot it was here, how it was warm in Europe too…

"I heard you collect sitars?" she remembered, with relief.

They moved to the large room that led out from the one they were sitting in. The entrance to it was barred by a heavy wooden door that was firmly shut, and Kaushik had to use considerable force to open it.

It was cool and pitch dark in here. The door swung shut behind them, and for a moment, Nomita could see nothing. But before she could panic, Kaushik pressed a switch that bathed the room in a soft blue light.

"The room is temperature and humidity controlled," he explained, taking her arm and walking her over to the opposite wall. "Some of these instruments are really old, I've collected them from all over the subcontinent, including Afghanistan when I was there much before the troubles began."

"The sitar has exponents in Afghanistan?" she asked, trying to ignore the touch on her arm. It was a light touch, anyway, nothing remotely lover-like about it. The passion that she saw reflected in his eyes in the blue light was directed at the instruments that were ranged in specially-built racks and glass-fronted cases all around her. There were no labels, but before and around her was definitely a museum, built up over the years as a labour of love.

"Very few. But then they have the rabab, the folk instrument from which, they say, the sarod evolved. In any case at one time much of the culture of the Middle East influenced North India. And vice versa. And though some people say Amir Khusro invented the sitar in India, obviously he couldn't have just waved a wand and constructed it. He may have done some work to modify it to suit the local musical temperament better. In any case there were all the many forms of the veena that were there at that time..."

She knew much of this, of course, from her theory lessons in music. But it was fascinating to hear him talk about the instruments as he took her around. His voice seemed to have gained substance. The enclosed room perhaps had something to do with that, but it was also the passion with which he spoke.

"I have heard of another beauty in Afghanistan, but right now I've been advised against going to that country. Let's hope it's not destroyed by the time I can make it there. And this..." they had stopped before a small, almost a baby sitar, embellished with ornate designs, "this I got from a person who said his father had brought it with him when he fled from Burma. It wasn't yet Myanmar then. It came in through your part of the world, he said, through Assam, during the Second World War."

"Is that ivory?" she asked, for the ornamentations, dark beige in colour, were beautifully weathered, and different from what she was used to seeing.

"You're right," he said. She was pleased that she was measuring up. "Ivory as ornamentation on instruments is of course banned these days, sitars have that terrible raw-looking white plastic or bone. But the man who sold it to me said that his family kept elephants in those days. They used to be rich, it seemed. This sitar belonged to the man's mother when she had been alive. His father brought it to this country with a great deal of trouble, strapped to his back, as a memento of his dead wife. The ivory came from their own domesticated elephants. He wept when he sold it to me, but he said that in the slum in which he now lives there is no place for it. He sometimes comes here to see it. I allow him to handle it. He feels – you know – in touch with his past when he does that. In any case he knows the instrument has a good home now, even if he himself is almost homeless."

They moved on to the other exhibits, his hand still at her elbow. She could feel the wire ring on his finger. Engrossed in viewing the sitars, she forgot, for a while that this was her fiancé who was taking her round. In her mind, it was Kaushik Kashyap, the sitar maestro by her side now. The thought came to her head that the collection that she was viewing was, in monetary terms alone, extremely valuable. Each instrument had a history. Each was a chronicle of the life of the person, or people, who had owned the instrument, and played on it. This was also a museum of sitars that were important in themselves, without regard to whether they had belonged to a well-known performer or not. This was a museum that cherished the instruments for their own sakes, rather than the people who had once owned them.

She blinked as they emerged into the living room once more, "How long have you been collecting these pieces?" she asked, still a little dazed from the beauty and wonder of what she had seen.

"Oh, years. Decades. It began with Ganesh Babu, the person who used to make my sitars here in Kolkata, telling me once that a person had brought in an unusual sitar to sell. It was old, he told me. I didn't realize how old till I looked at it. Each age, each era has modified its musical instruments, and going by those modifications, I judged it to be at least two hundred years old. You saw it..."

"Yes. I remember..."

"It's not easy bringing these instruments in from a foreign country, even if it is a neighbouring one. Taxes, heritage issues, whatnot. And then there's the delicacy of the wood, the ivory work. They don't travel well. Besides, they're used to a certain climate, and the Kolkata weather is not exactly the best kind for musical instruments. But it's worth it all..."

His voice definitely was deeper now, weighted with feeling. It was as though he was talking about well loved people, the women in his life, perhaps, and not instruments. But before she could marvel further, in almost the same breath he asked, "It's a bit warm here, isn't it? Shall we go down to that Café that's come up nearby? It's really very new, I think. I didn't notice it last time I was here…"

Of course his bedroom would be air-conditioned, but it was out of the question, in this situation, that he should invite her there to cool off. Yes, simply cool off, not heat up. Nomita suppressed a smile, and realized that she was quite curious to see the man's bedroom. But for that she would have to be patient. It went against his sense of propriety, she realized, that he should ask her into his bedroom when the rest of the house was practically empty, except of course for the help. Strange indeed, for a man who traversed the world with women students in tow. He seemed to be more conservative than her in this matter, for she would have thought nothing of it. She routinely went in to Rahul's room, and he came in often to hers. Or maybe he thought her small town mind wouldn't be able to stand the shock of being invited into a man's bedroom.

But the Coffee Bar that they went to was cool and welcoming. Bright hued, it was vibrant with young people. The music was loud but peppy. She noticed that like her, Kaushik too did not recognize it. It sounded very much like Rahul's kind of music though, the kind that was always on his player in his bedroom.

Nomita, sipping her Cappuccino, looked at the other customers. They seemed to be mostly in their twenties, like her, but they all seemed much livelier. In fact, Kaushik too looked as though he didn't belong here, though he obviously liked the ambience and the cooler temperature. His maroon and purple ikkat kurta and white churidars stood out as much as his ponytail did, in this crowd of crew-cut young men in jeans, ornamented with iPods.

Kaushik Kashyap looked around and commented, "They call this a Café, but it's so different from the ones in Europe."

Was he being patronizing? She sprang to the defence of the Café culture in India, and said in deliberately mild tones, "No reason why it shouldn't be. Every country makes its own culture, like its music. Isn't it?" she added, to soften the impact of the words.

But he agreed with her. "Of course, I wasn't criticizing, just commenting on the difference. These are more like the American chains."

"Do you like being out of the country so much?" The words seemed to pop out without her thinking.

But he wasn't taken aback or anything. Looking thoughtful, he said, "Well, the travelling is all right if the organizers get you business or first. I never go economy these days...it's too tiring. The places where I go to perform or teach or conduct workshops are vibrant with new ideas, so I like that very much. Have you noticed that quite often in our Shastriya Sangeet gatherings, it's the same old ideas that are trotted out, intellectually speaking?"

Nomita looked at him, surprised, but didn't say anything.

"Actually," said Kaushik, leaning back on the low seat, coffee cup in hand, "actually, in so many ways, performing out of India, no, performing out of the subcontinent, is a better experience."

Nomita tried to keep the slight smile that she had carefully arranged for the last few minutes from slipping. But she felt a sense of annoyance. She remembered that he had said something on similar lines once before, on the boat in Tamulbari. This was probably a pet subject. Kaushik Kashyap was beginning to sound predictable, like those artistes who went on "foreign tours" and came back rolling their eyes at the "wonderful audiences" they encountered there, the "highly cultured" and "educated" people who were so knowledgeable about Shastriya Sangeet. There was silence in which you could hear a pin drop, the people there listened noiselessly, swaying to the beat with their eyes closed. To Nomita it had sometimes sounded like the audiences there were stoned out of their heads, but now here was Kaushik Kashyap, who was about to speak about the "quality audiences" abroad. She got ready to listen to him, but made up her mind that she would put in a tactful word about the vibrancy and learning of audiences in India, too.

But Kaushik Kashyap, it seemed, was not about to move down the track that she had set out for him in her mind. Instead, he said, with a twinkle in his eye (could she be imagining it? No, it was there. Oh, thanks be. The man had a sense of humour!)

"You know, we are spared the Invocation Song there."

"Ah... so is that bad? Having an Invocation Song?" What could he mean? Was he teasing her? After all, she was practically a veteran of Invocation Songs back in Tamulbari, surely he couldn't mean that Invocation Songs to deities were a bad thing?

"No, don't get me wrong," he said, his voice thin again, soothing. "I have nothing against invocation songs as such, in fact they perform a wonderful function. After all, you can't expect the main artiste to begin the evening's programme in India. That's not the tradition we have here. Our shows are always progressive, aren't they, with a good but lesser known artiste preceding the main one? And of course it's always good to have a singer invoking the blessings of Ganesh or Saraswati at the beginning of the programme, it's an auspicious thing, and sets the tone for the function to follow."

Relieved, Nomita looked at him questioningly.

"But you know, sometimes it's too much of a good thing." He took a sip of the Cappuccino, and continued... "I mean what if the Invocation Song goes to a desperate type?"

"Desperate type?" repeated Nomita, but she was catching on. She began to smile, waiting to hear the rest of the story.

"Well, you know. The type who's desperate to get a function, a platform, any kind of platform, just so that he or she can strut her stuff, you know. Of course I know that all the organizers, especially of major programmes, give strict guidelines to their artistes about the time limit. But have you actually seen anyone sticking to the limit?"

"Well... rarely," admitted Nomita, laughing.

"Right. If it's a well known performer, the musician tries to get away by shaving a few minutes off the time... if he was contracted for two hours, it's the rare A Grade performer who will perform for two and a half hours. Me included. But if the performer is lower down the rung, you can bet your last rupee that he will perform for longer, sometimes much longer than he was told to. If the organizers said,

"Keep the invocatory song to ten minutes, no more," both parties know they mean fifteen minutes. But the performer usually stretches it to twenty."

"Not us," said Nomita, laughing. Kaushik Kashyap could tell a story well, she thought. "We always stick to our time... well, almost always..."

"You do invocations?" he asked, raising an eyebrow.

"Often. Solo, in a group..."

"Ah."

"But I'm not taking this personally, go on..."

"In any case I'm sure you never do what a certain performer did to me last year. It was in a town, in Bengal. The invocation person went on and on for... guess how long?"

"Half an hour? Forty five minutes?"

"A full hour and a half. Can you imagine? There I was, waiting in the wings, ready with my sitar tuned. But the lady just wouldn't stop. First she did the Saraswati Vandana, then she moved on to Bhajans, then Ghazals, then, can you imagine, to Sufi Qawalis! The audience was hooting and jeering, but she was unfazed. She had her eyes closed," he did a comical mimicry "and just refused to budge! The organizers sent in chit after chit, requesting her to stop, but she never did. She ploughed on, like the tractor in the fields outside the hall."

He was a fantastic mimic, realized Nomita, though she should have known. Mimicry, the ability to imitate others, at least in voice, but also body language, was a known component of the whole talent that a person had for music. Great! She thought. If we can laugh like this sometimes, the marriage will be quite a success.

"Anyway, finally – some more coffee for you? No? Sure? – Anyway, finally, it was Kamalda who saved the evening, such as was worth saving. After all I was supposed to return to Kolkata after the performance, I had a flight to catch early next morning. It was he who persuaded the organizers to draw the stage curtains, pull them close, you know."

"Ah..."

"Yes. Undignified and insulting, but it had to be done. In any case, the lady herself wasn't aware of the fact that the curtains were drawn. She was still singing with a great deal of sincerity..." he quickly sketched out her posture, his body language mimicking hers exactly, his eyes closed, a soulful expression on his face, his right hand placed affectedly on his heart to indicate the depth of his feelings... "and she continued. But then her accompanists stopped accompanying her, and the organizers rushed in and practically forced her to get up."

"You're exaggerating, of course," she said, still laughing.

"No no, not in the least, you can ask Kamalda. He made enquiries later, it turned out the lady hadn't managed to land a programme for months. She was pretty desperate, so she naturally couldn't bring herself to stop when she did land one. These days, he makes sure that no "Desperate Type", he calls it, is given a programme to perform an invocation song before mine comes on."

"How does he do that?"

"He has his ways. I don't enquire too deeply." He smiled and added, "If you're done, shall we go?"

He hailed a cab for her outside the café as they emerged, blinking, into the din and the heat and the dust of the Kolkata street. Once more, there was no mention of an offer to drop her back or anything like that. In the café, his presence had been unremarked, but now she couldn't help noticing that several passersby looked at Kaushik Kashyap with recognition as he stood on the pavement. Nobody actually came forward to ask for an autograph, not yet, but it was probably only a matter of time before that young girl, egged on by her mother standing nearby, came up with a paper and pen and asked for his signature. She could understand why he seemed to be in a sudden hurry to get back to his apartment again.

She noticed, once again, how careful he was about his arms, his hands and especially his fingers. A rather large man with a fat briefcase came close enough to jostle him. In what was probably a very well practiced gesture, Kaushik Kashyap moved his hand out of the briefcase's way. It would hardly have hurt if the briefcase had grazed his arm, but the gesture was telling. Just as she, and other serious singers, spoke in a comfortable pitch that did not strain their vocal chords, just as they were careful about such things as the weather, their sleep, their rest, and their food, in fact anything that could affect the quality of their voices. For Kaushik Kashyap and musicians like him, the arms needed to be kept away from even the slightest scratch. Was this another reason why not too many women were to be found playing the sitar or sarod or even the violin at the topmost rungs of classical music? Chopping vegetables, washing clothes...domestic chores were demanding, resulting in little nicks and scratches that, negligible otherwise, were huge impediments when one had to have the freest use of one's arms and hands in order to coax out music from the instruments they played

A yellow Ambassador came to a halt before them. He opened the door for her. "Make sure he doesn't go too fast..." he said in a lowered voice as he leaned forward to close the door. "Traffic accidents happen all the time here. The place where Amir Khan Saheb met with his end is just down the road, you know."

She looked enquiringly up at him from her seat inside the car.

"And lock the door," he added. "Amir Khan Saheb was flung out from his car while it was negotiating the roundabout there at breakneck speed. They were coming back from a concert, it was late, the roads were empty. If the door had been locked, he would be alive today..."

But as the taxi crawled slowly along to its destination, she couldn't help feeling a vague sense of dissatisfaction. She couldn't figure out why this should be so. After all the man had done more than she had any right to expect. He was a busy man, here for a very brief visit. He had shown her his sitar collection, obviously a place to which not many were admitted. He had even revealed a little humour. What more could she ask for? A little romance? Well, this was an arranged marriage, and after all this was only their second, no third meeting. He was a decent man, that was for sure, and he probably didn't want to upset this small town girl before him by doing things that...that he would with Lucia?

Maybe she should have asked him a bit about his past, about the girls who no doubt had peopled it. She remembered Guruma's and

Deepak's and Rati's faces, the way the voices changed, ever so slightly, and their glances slid away when they spoke of this man. If he really had had a bit of a fling that all of Kolkata knew about, it would have been good if she knew about it before settling down with him. If for nothing else, just to parry the pointed remarks that came her way.

Back again at what she was beginning to consider "home," Rati was almost ready to leave. Most of the staff were lined up on the verandah, waiting for her to come out.

"There you are, Nomita, I was just going to call you. Didn't want to miss you before leaving." She reached out a hand affectionately from her seat in the wheelchair as Nomita went up to her, and said, "My goodness, you look hot and dusty. Not at all like somebody who's just come back from a visit to her fiancé." She turned to the woman hovering behind her chair, and said, as courteously as always, "Tell them in the kitchen to bring something cold for this poor girl..."

"I'm so sorry to have to leave you, like this, but then..." she shrugged. "Anyway Deepak will be here."

"It's just a day, anyway, we'll be leaving tomorrow too in any case." Impulsively, she reached forward and gave the older woman a hug. "It's been so wonderful here, these last few days in your home... and the music and everything... what can I say..."

"Don't say anything..." smiled Rati Mittal. "So. Invite me to your wedding, I'll try and make it, I promise. In any case you'll be staying here afterwards, won't that be nice? We can meet all the time."

Deepak Rathod had come into the room while they were talking. "We really must be going, Rati... you know the traffic at this time..."

"There's no need to drop me at the airport, I've told you so many times..." protested Rati. But Nomita, attuned by now to many of her hostess's expressions, noticed her eyes. They looked, no, not happy, but a little less like the pools of despair that they had been that evening at the jalsa.

Guruma, too, came in. The contrast between the two women as they hugged each other was so striking that Nomita found she had to look away. Her eyes rested on Deepak. He, too, was looking somewhere else, away in the middle distance.

"Thank you, Rati, it has been such a wonderful visit..."Guruma was murmuring.

"Come on Sandhya, you know this is your home when you are here. In Kolkata. And now its home for Nomita too. Her parental place in this city after her marriage..."

"I'll be going straight to the office after I drop her off, so don't wait for me for lunch," said Deepak as he wheeled his wife out to the waiting car.

They went back to their rooms, a little spent now that the music for which they had come was over. A thought suddenly came to Nomita. How would it have been if Deepak and Guruma had been alone in this house? She was Sandhya Senapati's student, of course but was she also here as a chaperone? Was this why she had been brought to Kolkata, then? Nomita shook her head in confusion, but Kaushik Kashyap's words the other day about being careful as an accompanist seemed to have planted some poisonous weed in her mind.

Of course it was nonsense. What a thought to have about one's own Guruma. In any case... in any case, why did they need her? But it was impossible to forget the expression in Deepak's eyes that evening. Those had not been the eyes of a man listening to the singing of a very good friend surely. And yet he seemed to be a caring husband.

Now that the mistress of the house had left, Nomita felt freer to wonder about her marriage. It wasn't just the fact of the two peripatetic lives that occupied this marriage. What about Rati Mittal's disability? Would it hinder, well, would it hinder them from having sex? Had they shared the same room at all? Certainly they had been on the same floor, but had they been in adjoining rooms? She wished she had paid more attention to such things. It seemed to her that Deepak had a different room. Well, maybe the rich liked to live like that. Maybe the rich needed space in a way that the merely middle class, like she herself, did not.

Why on earth was she thinking like this? It was quite possible for Deepak and Sandhya Senapati to spend the night together in a bedroom now, and she would be none the wiser for it. Nor, probably would anyone else.

Did Rati know this? Had she known this all along, but decided to keep her peace?

Everything was so complicated. She washed her face, and decided to have a pre-lunch nap to clear her head. They were to go for some last minute shopping to the sari places in Gariahat, to supplement the ones they had bought at New Market and Park Street earlier, during one of Guruma's relatively free mornings.

Later, that evening, Deepak suggested that all of them go out for a meal on their last day here.

"Nomita must be bored with this ghar ka khana all the time... Where shall we go? Shonar Bangla? Grand? Taj?"

Nomita looked at Guruma. She herself would much rather stay at home. It had been an exhilarating but exhausting ten days here, and now she felt drained, in spite of being happy.

"It's up to you, Nomita, decide..."

There was something in her eyes, too, a kind of tiredness, unusual in her tranquil face. She had been busy, these last few days, even after her own concert was over, with interviews, meeting up with her old co-students, those tabaliyas and harmonium and sarengi players who always accompanied her when she came here, or went with her to the other tours. It was etiquette, and expected of her, to keep in touch with them all while she had been here.

And perhaps – the thought came to Nomita's mind – there was also the strain of staying in her "special friend's" house while his wife was with him.

Quickly, she said, "Well if it's all the same to you, I'd much rather stay at home. A quiet evening, you know..."

They sat on the rooftop terrace that last evening before returning to Tamulbari, listening to the muted sounds of the city around them, feeling the soft monsoon breeze on their faces as they talked of this and that.

25

There were calls between their parents all the time now. Calls about dates, venues, and much else besides. Shikha Sharma was always reporting at the dining table over a meal, "Spoke to Tirna today."

"Not *again* Ma!"

"Well a wedding doesn't happen just like that, there's lots of planning to be done, lots of things to be discussed, what would you know about it? You're just the bride, one of the two least important people in this entire thing."

"Who's the other unimportant person?"

"The bridegroom, of course. Kaushik Kashyap."

"Ah I see. Of course. We are just the excuse for the rest of you to get busy…"

"Get busy? Hmm, nice sarcasm there…"

Whenever she was with her co-students these days, or with Guruma when they were all singing a Managalacharan or a Guru Vandana together, Nomita felt a twinge of worry. Like today, for instance.

Over a period of time, Jhankaar's Mangalacharan had gained a great deal of local fame. The Sanskrit Slokas that Guruma had put to music, and taught her students, indeed brought in an atmosphere of sobriety, of calmness.

Today, too, they were here in one of the smaller halls in the town. The usual group of Mangalacharan singers had assembled. Last minute rehearsals were on, getting the pitch and rhythm right.

These days, along with Geeti, Sujata, Shrabana, Indrani and the others, Panchali and Rupa, too, had become almost permanent members of the Mangalacharan group. True, their role was still confined to only singing the most basic portions of the songs. Their function was to allow the other singers to get back their breath before they embarked on the complex portions that Guruma kept adding to the songs. But neither Rupa nor Panchali thought their role was in any way inferior to that of the others in the group. Indeed, going by their airs, it was possible to mistake them for the lead or solo singers, in any performance.

Now, listening to the group critically in the greenroom before they were called on stage, Nomita felt that same worry surface. No doubt about it, they were sounding good. Much practice, and numerous performances, had honed their ability to perform as a group. They sounded almost like a single instrument, with tablas and violins and harmoniums blending in with the human voices in almost perfect homogeneity. Almost. Not unusually for her, Panchali had missed the cue leading in to the second stanza. And Rupa, who had a tendency to go off-key in the higher notes beyond the middle octave, was singing a part not meant for her.

How could these two, who were so obviously mediocre in their musical ability, fail to recognize that fact? Nomita was faced once more with the conundrum that was bothering her.

It was never possible to gauge one's performance if one went only by the comments of the audience. Nobody in Tamulbari spoke badly of an artiste to his or her face anyway, though they more than made up for this when they spoke of the performance behind the artiste's back. Of course Guruma would give the student her own feedback, but this was always done in private. No comment except a quiet "wah" ever left Guruma's lips during these jalsas, though the students who had performed that evening were required to stay back after the concert. One by one, in the seclusion of the otherwise empty music room, Guruma would speak to the students, giving them words of encouragement as well as correction, the one as gentle as the other.

Musicians were routinely taught to evaluate themselves. These days, technical aids such as live recordings while performing at a concert, helped the musician to listen to how he or she had sounded to the audience. A slip in reaching a particular note, a missed beat in the rhythmic cycle, these were all unforgivingly recorded in the small cassette players that most middle rung musicians carried around with them. Feedback was extremely important. One needed the recording to critique one's own performance.

If only etiquette allowed Gurus to tell their less-talented students the truth. Of course there were the usual critiques that took place during the lessons themselves, but nothing, as final as telling them to stop wasting their time.

No Guru, no teacher ever said these words even though they knew on the very first note that a student sang, exactly how much talent he possessed. She remembered, how, over the years, she had seen a procession of students of both Tridib Barua and Sandhya Senapati troop into the music room.

She remembered Binod, a thin boy with a scraggly beard who had attended Tridib Barua's classes for a long time. He was always dressed in a khadi kurta and pyjama. His sandals were always down at heel. It was obvious, from his speech that he came from a rural background. His voice was good, but that, she felt was about it. No doubt in his little village, he was a good singer, of folk melodies, perhaps, or Bihu songs. But perhaps somebody had told him that with his voice, he should train to be a classical singer. It would put him on a higher plane altogether.

Nomita remembered Binod's struggles during the classes. His voice was perfectly pleasant for the enjoyable river songs and Bihu melodies that he had grown up with, and no doubt music would have given him a great deal of pleasure but now, as he struggled to master the lessons that Tridib Barua tried so patiently to impart, he cut a pitiable figure. Neither his voice nor his temperament was suited to the classical. But Tridib Barua never lost his patience, no matter how many times he corrected the boy before him. Was it just a question of more riyaz, more practice?And what about her? How was she to know where she herself stood? Of course she had judgement enough to know that she would never be the kind of musician that Guruma, or Guruji, or Kaushik Kashyap was. Yes, she had some spark, but was it enough to continue? Could she make a career of it? And if she was not good enough to make a career in singing classical music in a highly competitive world, where did that leave her? True, her voice was good, it was getting better. But was that enough?

When a star of the stature of Kaushik Kashyap fixed a date for his marriage, the importance of the traditional almanac, the book that laid out the auspicious days and hours, paled in importance. What was of more consequence was his programme schedule. Tirna Ghosh and Shikha Sharma spent hours on the phone, working out the common denominators between the requirements of the planets in the skies for the auspicious moment, and the demands of the organizers of the music functions at the beginning of the busy season.

"Yes, of course fifteenth of November is probably the best from the point of view of the conjunction of planets. Rahu, Ketu, everything is auspicious, that's what the Pandit said. But you said Kaushik has a programme on the sixteenth?" Nomita, finishing her breakfast, looked at her mother on her cellphone. Shikha, oblivious to all else, was concentrating on the words pouring out from the other end, looking frowningly at a large notebook that she was tapping absentmindedly with a pen. The notebook was, Nomita knew, the Wedding Planner. Guest lists, lists of assorted menus to choose from, lists of things that needed to be done, things that needed to be bought – this book was going to contain it all.

"Okay then, December. But there are no auspicious dates after the fifteenth, right up till mid-January, remember. So... all right then eighth of December? Or tenth? That's a Saturday, ah, not very auspicious to welcome a bahu into the house. That's right. So, eighth of December? Final? Okay good ... we can think of printing the cards and booking the pandit and the decorators and the cook ..."

"You're getting married on the eighth of December," Shikha said, shutting off her cell. "Gives us enough time to prepare."

"Enough time? That's not even a full four months away... !"

But Shikha was already leafing through the pages of the planner, looking for some other list. She looked up abstractedly at her husband at the other end of the table once, and asked, "Eighth of December. Okay by you?"

"Anything you say..." he assured her, finishing off his coffee. "There's enough time, we can make the arrangements quite comfortably. Weather should be good at that time, hopefully it won't rain."

It was true that a wedding in a family like theirs was always an elaborate affair in Tamulbari. It was a celebration, an occasion for family and friends to get together, to sing, to feast, to enjoy themselves. The bride and the groom merely provided the excuse. It was the time for the siblings of the parents to gather, to fly in from distant places and spend at least four or five days partying.

"Now that the date's settled, we'll have to inform your uncles and aunts and cousins. Thank goodness there's the phone these days. When I got married, everybody had to be informed through handwritten letters because many people didn't have phones, not in the remote village where my grandmother lived anyway." She rifled through a few pages and pushed back her chair. "No point waiting. May as well start. I'll begin with Radha."

Among Nomita's friends too, Rahul was the first recipient of the news that the date had been fixed.

"Eighth December," she repeated, "make sure you apply for your leave and stuff right now. There's enough time..."

"Actually there's hardly any time," said Rahul unexpectedly.

"What do you mean? Well, I suppose..." Suddenly she was conscious of a fluttering in her stomach, a dizziness in her head. But she took a deep breath, closed her eyes, and waited for the feeling to go. Stage performers knew how to deal with these symptoms of nervousness, of stage panic. Sure enough, she felt calmer in moments. He was the first person to whom she was saying, "I'm getting married on the eight of December, do come." No wonder she was fluttery. It sounded so definite, so *fixed* when it was said like that. Written in stone.

Bride-to-be nerves, she supposed.

"It's all relative anyway, time I mean..." Rahul was saying when she felt composed enough to pay attention to him again.

"What? Why are you talking as though you're Einstein? Listen Rahul, don't you dare... *don't you dare*... tell me you're being sent to the US or Canada at that time. I just won't have it..." The thought of her wedding happening without Rahul around was beyond the pale of possibility.

"No no of course not," he soothed. "I'll put in my application right away."

Uncharacteristically for a conversation between them, there was a pause. "Well... I'm off then..." said Nomita finally.

"Yes. I'm at work too... Bye, I'll call you tomorrow."

Somehow, it soon became common knowledge that the Tamulbari girl who was going to marry Kaushik Kashyap was none other than Nomita Sharma, the singer. How did the town know? Nomita hadn't a clue, for she hadn't told anybody about it. Besides Guruma and Guruji, and of course Rahul and his family, nobody else had known to begin with, and it was unthinkable that any of them could have spread the word. Perhaps the news had been given out by Kaushik's entourage, then. Or maybe Kaushik Kashyap had told his accompanists the real purpose of the visit to this remote, unremarkable town?

No matter what the source, it was soon impossible for Nomita to move out of the house without people coming up smilingly and congratulating her. Her colleagues in school, even the children whom she taught, now knew that she was getting married to a maestro.

"How wonderful, Nomita, our very own music teacher getting married to none other than Kaushik Kashyap himself!" The teachers' common room at school was all a-twitter at the news. Their pleasure in her engagement was simple, unalloyed by other emotions such as envy or surprise. They assumed that marriage to a maestro would be every music teacher's dream-come-true. "When is the wedding, Nomita? Don't forget to introduce us to him when he comes next time! We'll be sorry to lose you though."

A senior teacher who had taught Nomita and Rahul in school, added, "I spoke to Shikha when I met her this morning. I must say I was surprised! But I'm so happy for you. Congratulations! We'll miss you, and I know the children will, too!"

Nomita, deluged by such genuine and warm good wishes, found herself unable to ask, "But how did you know?"

The whole of Tamulbari seemed to be excited about the marriage, more excited, she sometimes thought, than she herself. The kind of people who came up to her, or her parents, to congratulate them on her upcoming marriage never failed to surprise her. Total strangers seemed to know about her marriage. It gave her a weird feeling. Sometimes it seemed that they knew more than she herself did.

The mother of one of her students came up after class and introduced herself. "Hi, I'm Nayantara's mother. I just wanted you to know how happy we are about your engagement. Really, we are so proud of you. And how is Kaushikji? When can we meet him? Not right now, I suppose. He's in Frankfurt, isn't he? I read that his concerts in Europe are attracting huge crowds..."

Trying not to look blank, Nomita smiled as non-committally as possible, leaving the questions unanswered.

At the radio station, though, when Nomita went for a recording, the reception was quite gratifying. The Programme Executive normally patronized her during recording sessions, barely deigning to acknowledge her presence even as she sang. Today, however, he greeted her with a warm smile that had been quite well-hidden from her all these years.

"Nomita, I've been wanting to congratulate you...what great news! I'm so happy!" The insincerity was quite apparent in his voice, but Nomita decided to ignore it. She was becoming quite adept at smiling insincerely herself, she thought, as she directed a falsely warm look at him. And if just being engaged to Kaushik Kashyap was going to bring her such good behaviour from otherwise snooty people, she was quite looking forward to being married to him.

Nomita came out of the studios feeling quite pleased not just with her performance, but also with the attention she was getting from the officials in the radio station. She spoke to Rahul about her feelings in the evening.

"It feels really good, you know, this kind of behaviour from yobs like that PEx. He was so patronizing before. Stuck-up, nose- in-the-air fellow," she said, with relish.

"Ha, star mannerisms already!" said Rahul. "Soon our Nomi will be a local Naomi, hurling objects around if things are not just right..."

"Naomi ?"

"Campbell. Naomi Campbell, even you must have heard of her..."

"Don't be ridiculous Rahul. But you know...umm...I was thinking...one could get used to this. I mean - all this adulation is not even for anything I have achieved. After all, getting engaged to Kaushik Kashyap can hardly be termed an achievement. But the way people are saying I have brought some kind of glory to Tamulbari, you'd think I'd done something great. Like winning Indian Idol or becoming a Voice of the Nation or bagging a playback contract in Mumbai or something. I mean very few classical singers are even recognized, leave alone adulated..."

"Hm. But he's a Star, don't forget. And on TV all the time, advertising this and that..."

"Yes, but I'm not. Certainly not a Star, just a middle rung singer, aspiring to be a little better... And Guruma is so unstarry, I've never really been exposed to this kind of thing before..."

"I hope you never become a Star. You'll lose that special gift you have, the gift of teaching music to children."

Rahul's voice had been uncharacteristically sober. Surprised, all Nomita could say was "Oh? But that's different. I love teaching the children, I love the way they respond... ah, did I tell you about Debojit's music lessons with Guruji?"

It was now impossible to live in Tamulbari and not know that Nomita Sharma was the Chosen One. The papers and journals were full of speculation about how Our Nomita had floored the maestro when he had come to Tamulbari for his concert. Her good looks and polite and respectful demeanour had won him over so much that he had immediately conveyed his intentions to her parents, who, of course were happy to agree to the match. Such an honour for Tamulbari.

"Long, black hair falling like a curtain almost to her waist". Hm. That made her often unmanageable mane sound quite romantic. "A beautiful wheatish complexion, and what eyes! Liquid, like a doe's. Not overly tall, beautifully proportioned. No wonder Kaushik Kashyap, so well travelled, was bowled over by her beauty."

This was embarrassing, besides being bad journalism. However, the target audience was probably lapping it up. In any case, it was not every day that one found oneself described in such glowing terms. She wished the absent fiancé could see this. She would rise several notches in his esteem, she was sure, enough, maybe to dislodge the Lucia- shaped resident there. She could barely tear her eyes away from the page, though opposite her, Shikha Sharma was tittering helplessly. "Liquid, like a doe's!" she repeated several times, explaining to her husband as he sat finishing his coffee, "Nomita's eyes, believe me. That's what's written there..."

But there was more.

"Of course Nomita Sharma is beautiful, and a good singer, too. But what really attracted this star to a girl from our town was her simplicity. Have you noticed," the columnist had chattered on in a gossipy vein. Her air was insufferably know-it-all, but Nomita couldn't help reading on, "have you noticed how men who are sophisticated and well travelled prefer to have women from smaller towns as their wives? It's not a coincidence, girls. There's a reason for it. Weary after their travels, tired after their work in the wide world, they want to return home to simplicity and warmth. Not to those sleek metro-maidens whose sophistication stops outside the kitchen. Yes, a man wants a home-cooked meal when he returns from his work, and it is we smaller town girls who can see that it is provided to him..."

She seemed to have become some kind of symbol, a triumph of small town ideals over the perceived harridan-like qualities, the slumping moral values and poor housekeeping skills of wicked metro-maidens. Too amused to feel disturbed, she continued reading.

"Nomita Sharma is a familiar figure on the Tamulbari stage, and one hopes that she will continue to grace it even after she is whisked away by her fiancé after the wedding, to the larger stage of Kolkata.

But more than her music, it is her small town grace that has appealed to this well travelled man…"

Was that her they were talking about so earnestly? If this was what being affianced to a famous person meant, then being married to one would be infinitely worse. And what, she wondered fleetingly, was the star himself subjected to at all times?

"We have something that metro girls don't, and let's not forget it…"

A national daily ran a rather learned article about the "Rise of the Small Town" in its regional page. Most of it was about cricketers, notably Dhoni of Ranchi. But one section of the article was devoted to how people who had been born and brought up in the metros now looked for spouses in the smaller towns. This, it seemed, had not been very common some years ago, with boys and girls from Delhi, for instance, hardly looking at a place like Jhumri Tilaiyya for their spouses. Famous personalities whose spouses came from small towns while they themselves were from metros were listed. Nomita was interested to see that sarod maestro Amjad Ali Khan's name was there, with his wife, Subhalaxmi from Sibsagar, which was not too far from Tamulbari. Reading on, she was astonished to find written: "Kaushik Kashyap, the jetsetting sitarist who has done so much to promote classical music around the world, is getting married soon. Not to a Beijing beauty as you might have supposed, or a Madrid maiden, or even a Seattle sylph. No, the girl comes from a small town in the periphery of the country, in faraway Assam, a place called Tamuli Bar." Of course they had got the spelling of the town wrong, rather spoiling the effect of the piece itself. Still…

True, because the piece was located on the regional page, only small townees like herself would actually get to read it. The metros had their own supplements, so all this self-congratulatory flood of opinions would not even be seen by the opposite party. Thank goodness for that, thought Nomita as she folded away the papers and stashed them where they would not be easily found again.

Nomita decided not to read any more about herself and the marriage at least till the wedding actually took place. In any case, none of them seemed to care enough to find out what she herself was like. It didn't seem to matter. She was just a five-day wonder, like that baby with two heads born to a poor couple in a village in South India. The TV channels and the print media had been full of it a week or so ago. Now, after being pushed into the more obscure pages, the baby was not newsworthy any more.

It was Guruma who advised her to just stop reading about it if she wanted to remain herself.

"It's amazing what they are writing about me these days in those journals," Nomita had said as they chatted for a few moments after her regular class was over. "Nothing really bad, true, at least not yet... But you know, the patronizing tone, or the breathlessly adulatory one... I mean both are so irrelevant. I'm either annoyed or embarrassed when I read anything about the wedding these days. I wonder how Kaushik manages... though he's out so often, I suppose he hardly gets to see them. Lucky him."

"I suppose his Secretary clips and files the reviews and the write-ups about him or he probably subscribes to one of those clipping services. But let me give you some advice. Just stop reading any of it. It's not very easy to read something and then ignore it. I know I am always a little influenced, for a while, by things that are written about me. Or my music. If some critic writes that my Bistaar was good, I find I concentrate on that in my next concert. And if they say the opposite, that it was not upto the mark, I tend to move to the next phase more quickly than I would otherwise, glossing over the Bistaar portion."

Nomita nodded. 'That's very understandable..."

"It's not good either way. Music, and behaviour, and thinking, must be part of your individuality. We must guard who we are, our individuality, as much as possible. I've stopped reading reviews about myself these days, unless they are by reviewers like Nilaksha Gupta, for instance, critics who are impartial, and knowledgeable, and not easily swayed by frills such as glamour or goodwill. He calls a spade a spade, and I respect that. But nowadays almost every rag carries a Friday arts page, featuring "reviews," so called, by people who know very little about music. It's better to ignore the stuff, I find. Plus I think it will be better for your peace of mind, now and later, if you just stop reading about your wedding, na? "

The Kolkata trip had brought the two of them closer together, but even then, this was a long speech by Guruma's standards. She probably felt deeply about the Press as indeed, which famous person did not, reflected Nomita.

They began to walk away from the music room. They had just finished preparing for an upcoming show, though not with the monsoon Raags any more, for the clouds of Sawan had long gone. Instead, they performed melodies that evoked Hemant, and looked forward to the time, a few months later, when they would be able to sing the songs of spring. Basant, Bahar, and similar Raags that evoked the Holi festival. At this point, though, the evening shadows now came in quicker as daylight began to fade faster, in anticipation of autumn. The music room was already in a twilight haze, the light curtains fluttering like ghosts in the gloom. But outside, there was still enough light to see by.

"Actually, I really feel that students, especially senior students, should be given media management classes nowadays. You know, how to deal with interviews, the Press ... it's necessary, really."

"Well, why not?" Nomita looked at Guruma's face. It was still tranquil, but her eyes sparked with a kind of exasperation for which "anger" would be too strong a word.

"Yes. It can save a lot of heartburn. How to hold Press Conferences after a show. How to send invitations to the most influential journalists and critics. What to put in your Press Kits, the kind of selective information that should appear in the biodata ..."

Nomita was surprised. She had never heard Guruma speak in this way before. She looked again at her, and was reassured to find that Sandhya Senapati was smiling now. There was no bitterness in her face, none at all, only a kind of detached amusement.

"It's amazing," reflected Nomita, "how much there is of things that have nothing to do with one's music in order to become what is known as a 'successful' artiste ..."

"Well, yes and no. There are so many definitions of 'successful.' For one artiste, it may be the ability to hold a crowd, riveted, with one's music. For another, a programme is a success only if that crowd is located in some foreign country, preferably in Europe or America. At some other levels, 'success' is defined by the number of shows one gives, the number of foreign trips one has made. Quantity, not quality. But I know that for many traditional Ustaads and Pandits, it was never about the venue or the number of concerts, but the quality of the audience, the knowledge level of the rasikas, the patrons of the music. Of course those days have long gone. And one has to find ways of earning one's living even if one is a musician. After all there are no temples, no Kings or zamindars who can look after the material needs of a musician while he just sits and makes the most exquisite music. One must have marketing savvy, and the Press plays a huge role in building an image."

Guruma was talking, thought Nomita, like a corporate executive herself, and not like any traditional classical musician.

"But not everybody goes on that path," she pointed out, refraining from adding, "After all, neither you nor Tridib Barua manipulate the media in any way." But it was true.

"Well, no. Actually, in the long run it doesn't pay. You have to be good to survive for years, decades. But on a level playing field, when two performers are more or less equal in their talent and their ability to give good performances, it is the person who is media savvy who gets the initial push. Sometimes this is all that's required to put one ahead in the race, for success builds confidence, and that brings on more success..."

"Media management classes," smiled Nomita. "Now that would be nice."

"Well, a hundred years ago, there was no such thing as educating students in the use of the microphone, for instance. Or even sixty years ago. How to modulate one's voice, how to turn one's face away, or bring it nearer the mike, for effects. How to hold the sitar or the sarod or the rudra veena, how to bring in effects such as diffusing the sound by moving one's body away from the mike. How to get the correct pitch and timbre by adjusting the base and treble, how to listen to the feedback monitor and adjust one's performance accordingly, simultaneously, even as you perform. I mean all this is almost basic knowledge now. Every beginner knows how to use the microphone to best advantage. They are taught that, alongside the traditional riyaz methods. "

"Well, maybe I could deal with media comments on my music, even if they are unfair. But it's this ... all this, you know, irrelevant and embarrassing stuff about marrying Kaushik Kashyap. That's what I'm finding so difficult to deal with ..."

"There'll be more of that after your marriage. As I said, just ignore it, if you can't laugh at it. It will be difficult to laugh at many things, so just stop reading those magazines or columns that carry those stories."

They parted at the entrance, and Nomita, lucky for once in getting an auto right at the gate, phutphutted back home. She wondered if Guruma knew about the innuendoes about herself and Deepak Rathod that had appeared in various journals, insinuations and gossip that Rahul had told her about. Probably she was speaking from experience then.

But did it bother her that Rati Mittal, too, had probably read these, or heard about them? Did the seeming easiness of their relationship seek to cover some horrific chasm? Or did Rati Mittal, knowing everything, just choose to look the other way?

The musicians that she knew in the town were ambivalent in their reactions to the news of her marriage. Several came up to her and congratulated her. But there seemed to be something – a shiftiness in their eyes, or indeed their inability to look her in the eye at all as they wished her, that made her think that they were less than sincere. Several others were too enthusiastic, especially considering the fact that Nomita barely knew them.

At Jhankaar, they were, for the most part happy for her. Mixed with this was the glow that was reflected on them, as being "close" to her, and thereby able to tell the rest of the town what kind of person she was, what kind of preparations were going on, what she told them.

Considering that Nomita was careful not to speak about Kaushik and the marriage to the other students of Jhankaar, they had to draw freely on their creative abilities to fabricate these tales.

But it was Panchali and Rupa whose sudden change of attitude towards her amused Nomita the most. From being condescending and aloof towards her, they were now almost fawningly friendly. It wasn't always possible to avoid them. Nomita had to grit her teeth and endure their talk.

"Nomita, you're looking *soso* pretty today, you're positively *glowing*," they would say, archly, their bulky bodies standing in her way so that she couldn't move forward. "What is it? Tell us! Did Kaushikji telephone? Yes, that's it, for sure. How long did he speak? What did he say? Sweet things, come on, you can tell us..."

They were even more unendurable now than they had been earlier.

It saddened her, though, that some of the people she would miss the most seemed to have little or no idea that she would soon be leaving them. Or even if, like Silsila, they knew that Nomita Ma'am was getting married and going away, it didn't seem to affect them in the way she had expected. Perhaps it was difficult for them to grasp more than the immediate future. Perhaps, thought Nomita, this was a good thing, a protective device, to help them get through their difficult lives. The less one saw of the future, the better it was perhaps. Seers were never happy people.

26

It was amazing how fast time flew. The four months, which had seemed quite sufficient to prepare for the wedding, now seemed barely adequate. Lists were made, torn up, remade; arrangements were finalized, re-finalized, then modified again.

People dropped in at all hours, giving the house a festive air weeks before the actual ceremony. The women sat around drinking tea and discussing trousseaus and rituals, while the men sat in another section of the drawing room, happily partaking of the spirits that Pradeep Sharma plied them with, and solemnly discussing finances and inflation.

"Expensive business, a wedding," was the general consensus.

"But so much fun," said the women from across the room, where saris and mekhela sadors had been spread out for their inspection, and the jewellery brought out for evaluation.

"Give her lots of Assamese jewellery, she'll really stand out in Kolkata when she wears our Loka Paro earrings with the enamelled pigeons dangling from her ears."

"Also a Sayn set…you know, the necklace with the pendant shaped like an eagle, set with Burmese rubies. And a ring and earrings to match."

"I'm giving her my own Sayn set, I hardly wear it these days…" said the mother of the bride.

"Have they, you know…?" asked a heavyset matron, Maya, a cousin of Pradeep Sharma's. She was known to be a difficult person who thrived on creating rifts and ill-will between people.

"What? Have they what?" asked Shikha Sharma apprehensively. She was anxious, as were all mothers of brides everywhere, that the whole thing should go off smoothly, with happiness and joy all around. The ultimate aim of the whole series of ceremonies was to see Nomita blissfully settled in matrimony. If women like Maya told her that it was necessary to propitiate all manner of planets and deities in order to ensure that bliss, then she would personally see to it that it was all done.

But Maya was not thinking of flawed planetary positions. She pushed up a thoughtful finger to her thinning hair out of habit, and asked, "Have they asked for dowry? You know, money, cash, or maybe cars and flats, things like that?"

All around, the women abruptly stopped fingering the mekhela sadors and saris before them, and quickly withdrew their hands from the gleaming gem-encrusted gold on the tables. The enjoyment so far evident in their faces vanished. Dowry. That was a taboo word, something they prided themselves on not having in their society. But it occurred to each one of them, with a pang of sympathy for Nomita and her parents, that of course it was true that the giving and taking of dowries was common practice in the land she was going to. Kaushik Kashyap was a prize, no doubt about it, and if he had married in his own land there was every likelihood that his bride would have come richly dowered.

This was a possibility that had not occurred to anybody before. But now that the dreaded D word had reared its ugly head, there was no ignoring it.

"What do you think, should I come straight out and ask Tirna ..." Shikha asked her husband later. "We don't want to seem like cheapies after all. If they expect a pouch of cash or a flat or something, maybe ..." She was too flustered by this new eventuality to think coherently.

"Don't be silly, just because that hag Maya brought it up, it doesn't mean that we should run around like headless chickens ..." replied Pradeep Sharma in his usual composed manner. "They would have mentioned it, given us a hint of some kind long ago if they had wanted something ..."

Nomita had been trying to get in a word for a while. When her mother took a breath, it was finally possible to do so. "Ma, listen to me. This is final. If there is any mention of any money or something like a car or a fridge or a flat that is wanted, that's it. No wedding. I couldn't bear the shame of it."

"Shame?" Shikha asked.

"Of course. As though I was a commodity, a flawed one, needing speed money to get me off my father's hands..."

Her voice was beginning to rise dramatically, but Pradeep Sharma cut her off with a laugh. "Calm down Nomi, there's no need to take on like this. Trust that Maya to sow discord wherever she goes. Dowry! Here, give me my cell. I'll settle the matter once and for all."

"Pradeep, you're not going to ask them just like that?" Shikha couldn't make up her mind if the agony of not knowing was greater than the embarrassment of asking them something so delicate in such a blunt way.

It was finally decided that they would sleep on the problem, and take a decision the next day. Sure enough, at breakfast, all three of them were amazed that they had taken the whole thing so seriously last evening.

"That Maya, there's something in the way she speaks. Dowry! Why are we insulting Tirna and Rana by even thinking that they would want money or material goods? Really, I must have lost my mind..." Shikha buttered her toast, quite happy to forget completely her reactions of the previous night.

"Amazing what one poison tongue can do," agreed Nomita. It was impossible to think of shy Rana Ghosh or motherly Tirna demanding material goods.

"Though I think you would have liked making that statement, Nomi," said Pradeep Sharma, the solemnity of his voice belied by the twinkle in his eye. "Do you regret it?"

"What? Regret what?"

"Well, it would have made headlines. 'Fiancée spurns renowned musician, refuses to succumb to dowry demand.' You would have become terribly famous."

"Really, Deuta," Nomita said, exasperated. She looked up and saw the gleam in his eye, and laughed. "The things you say..."

Repeating the incident to Rahul that night on the phone, Nomita wasn't surprised to hear him say, "Hmm, well yes, that's a lost opportunity. Never mind..."

"Really, you too, Rahul..." she felt obliged to say, but she was smiling.

"Well it's true. Already you are famous, for being about to marry - not yet married mind you, but about to marry only - a famous man. You'll be even more famous if you decide, at this last moment, not to do so..."

"Famous? How can that be called fame?"

"Why not? It won't be notoriety, there's nothing really *bad*, I mean, like, morally, in dumping a fiancé, is there? At most it is a bad error of judgement, but rectified before the actual wedding. Causing a lot of bad blood and inconvenience and anguish, true. But better a jilted fiancé than a divorce, later. And you'll be talked about with even more gusto than you are now. So that's fame, isn't it?"

He sounded quite flippant, but something about what he was saying caught Nomita's mind. "Well yes, there's still time, isn't there?"

"What, for him to dump you? Yes there is, you better be careful..." The familiar teasing voice was comforting, but that was not what her mind had caught hold of. She realized with a start of surprise that her mind had become fleetingly happy, for a second, that in spite of all the preparations around her, all the money that had already been spent, and would soon be spent, in spite of the invitation cards that had been sent out and the accommodations that had been booked for guests, in spite of the seeming finality of it all, she still could, if she wanted to, change her mind. Not that she wanted to, of course, but if – just in case –

"...where is he now, by the way?" She came back to Rahul's voice at her ear.

"Ummm...in Tokyo I think. Osaka? Some place in Japan anyway. Do you know, I'm becoming so good at geography these days..."

"You always were," he responded instantly. "Remember how you insisted once that Alaska was in Australia? Class five I think it was.

Quite the little genius. You even had Das Ma'am the teacher confused for a while."

"Rahul, I wish you were here..." she began, "I would get you for that..."

But suddenly it was more than just that. A wave of some emotion swept over her. She couldn't identify the feeling exactly...but of course it was longing. He was her best friend, and the telephone just wasn't enough. She wanted to be able to see him face-to-face, watch the expressions in his eyes, the mobility of his mouth as they spoke of the many things that they always did. He was her best friend, from as far back as she could remember, and he was the one who understood her more than any other person on the planet. Just as she understood him best.

She would make this last, she thought as she said her final "bye, take care," She would make sure that the friendship continued, even though she would be married in a few weeks to another man. Once again she thought of Guruma, and paused. For the longest time, she had thought that Guruma and Deepak Rathod shared that sweetest of relationships, a friendship. But she could no longer think that. She did not know, did not want to know whether they had a physical relationship. If they did not, it was not for lack of opportunity. It was obvious that they sought out opportunities, and cared very little for what people said. Perhaps if one was as rich as Deepak Rathod, or as beautiful and as noted a performer as Sandhya Senapati, it did not really matter what other people thought. But both of them cared deeply about what their spouses thought. Of that, Nomita was sure. If they had not actually slept together, it would be because of consideration for their spouses...

There were so many new equations between the sexes to be seen these days: look at Abanti, whose marriage had been full of fractious discord. After an acrimonious divorce, though, calmness had descended on her, and she was now best friends with her ex-husband. "We are meant to be friends, not spouses," she had told her surprised relatives only the other day. They went out to restaurants and shows together, leaving the children in the care of one or the other of the ex-mothers-in-law. It was almost as though the bitter years in between, when they had been man and wife, had not existed. To friends and relatives who asked if they were about to get married again, they replied, surprised, "Why?"

And then there was Sheelu, who had married wheelchair-bound Paban. Sheelu never looked anything less than happy as she wheeled in her husband to attend the shows that the children put up at intervals. Sheelu was a well known poet, and also held a job as a college lecturer. She had married Paban knowing fully well, it was said, that he would never be able to father children. It was obvious though that they were very good friends. Perhaps Sheelu had only got married in order to stop wagging tongues. After marrying Paban, she would be viewed as something of a Devi, out of reach of gossip. Yet it was only by marrying Paban that she could, with society's full sanction, do what she wished to do most. Look after her friend, take care of his every need, and enjoy his companionship. Sex did not come into the picture, not yet.

But as the preparations around her continued, and reached a crescendo, she found she had less time to analyse and think things through. She was caught up in the excitement about her, an excitement that centered on her but seemed to have a life of its own. It seemed the whole town was infected with the same enthusiasm. So what if they could not attend the actual ceremony?

A couple of evenings later, coming out of the room where the music lessons were held, she saw Debojit sitting on one of the cane chairs on the verandah. He was humming something in a low voice, his gaze in the middle distance, oblivious of his surroundings. He only became aware of her when she walked up to him and spoke.

"Sorry Ma'am, I didn't notice you..." he said, coming to a sense of his immediate surroundings with a start, and standing up. Nomita was not unfamiliar with that feeling, of being in the zone, when the only reality was the melody that one was developing in one's head, or the rhythmic cycle it was set to, while the immediate physical surroundings receded as though they were the unreal objects, and melody and rhythm the only solid, substantial things left in the world.

But for her, that usually happened when she was in her music room, or on stage. To lose oneself totally in this way, oblivious to surroundings that were not familiar, that too at such a young age, was unusual, indeed. A sign of genius? "How are you, Debojit? Classes going on all right?" She meant school. But he obviously thought she was referring to his lessons with Tridib Barua, for he replied, "Yes, I'm waiting for Guruji. He told me he was returning from his Allahabad concert today, but the train is late, it seems. No problem, I'll wait for him."

Sandhya Senapati too was on the verandah now. She reached out an affectionate hand and ruffled the boy's head. "Why don't you sit inside, you will be more comfortable ... ? Your Guruji has reached the station, anyway, he will be here soon, but I don't think he'll be able to take classes right away..."

"No no, that's all right," Debojit assured her. His voice, Nomita noticed, was no longer as husky and unpredictable as it had been all those weeks ago, just before the concert. Tridib Barua's gentle vocal exercises had helped considerably. "I want to sit here, so that I can see him immediately when he comes in through the gate ..."

The hero worship in his voice and eyes was moving. Leaving him where he was, the two women walked slowly away.

"He's like a son to your Guruji, you know," said Sandhya Senapati when they were out of earshot of Debojit. "He has so many students, and of course they are all his protégés, he's a father figure to them all. But in Debojit he's found something, some need that fits like a piece in a jigsaw puzzle to his own need. It's not just about music either, though of course music is the bond that binds them. It's a bond that's growing stronger every day. Debojit is the son he's never had, the child who should have inherited his talent."

Nomita was quiet. This was the first time that the conversation between them had touched on something that was this personal in nature.

They paused beneath the large tree at the edge of the driveway. The leaves were thinner now than they had been at the height of the monsoons, and the breeze that came in through them was almost cold. There was a nip in the evening air, a chill that was not uncomfortable yet, but made one want to draw one's dupatta or anchal closer around one's shoulders.

Sandhya Senapati's voice was as soft as always, but her eyes as she looked steadily at her friend now glistened in the reflected light from the porch. "He's the one, I have always thought, who has needed a child. Flesh of his flesh, his own blood and bones. Strange, the maternal instinct gets so much importance, but we forget that men have this nurturing instinct, too, some stronger than others. My husband has a … what shall I say… a strong feminine …"

The pause was so fragile a cough could have shattered it. Nomita held her breath till Sandhya continued, hesitantly, "What I mean is, he has a very strong fostering instinct. That may be one reason he is such a very good, such a brilliant teacher. Of course a good Guru is supposed to be a parental figure but with him, it's something more. It's as though he is, what shall I say, it's as though he is sublimating his childlessness in the relationships he has with his students."

She looked away, and they began to walk slowly up to the gate.

"But with Debojit," she continued, "it's something else, I've noticed. Maybe because the boy is so much younger than his other students, maybe because he has a vulnerability, like he himself…"

Once more, the pause. The sound of traffic on the road was loud, and Nomita had to strain to hear to catch Sandhya Senapati's words.

"A different kind of vulnerability, of course, but even then …"

A gust of wind rustled the leaves of the tree beside them. Nomita couldn't hear Guruma's next words. Only when the sound of the truck that roared past died away could she hear her voice again …

"… it's what he wants to do. If it makes him happy, I'll be happy, too. For his sake …"

"What?"

Guruma looked at her, startled.

"No, I mean I didn't catch what you just said. The traffic …"

"About your Guruji wanting to adopt Debojit? Well yes, he does."

"But Debojit already has a parent. His mother. His father passed away some time ago, I believe. I mean it won't be possible, will it? Will she give him up, just like that?"

"No, not like that, I mean not in the modern sense, with signed papers and everything. Of course he knows that won't be possible, obviously Debojit's mother will hardly allow it, even though she's a single parent struggling to make ends meet. But he's been thinking about it. You know in the old days, the students would stay with the Guru, in the Gurukul, like his own children. Well that's what he wants to do, with Debojit."

"Raise him like the old days, as though this house..." Nomita waved to the large old building behind them "was a Gurukul?"

"Not exactly as in the old days, no," said Guruma slowly. "Debojit will need a modern education too. He will continue going to your school, but he will stay here during the week, so that morning and evening he will sit with his Guru for lessons. He can visit his mother on weekends. Actually, why not, if she wishes, she can stay here, with us. The house is so large and empty. Yes, that's an idea. I'll talk about it to your Guruji, to Debojit's mother. I would like having another woman in the house. She can have that set of rooms at the back to herself." She paused, then went on, "Debojit has talent, we all know that, and Debojit's Guru feels if he can get him to himself like this, he will have repaid his own debt to *his* Guru. By passing on the knowledge to the next generation."

"...I see...Certainly that should be possible. Have you talked to his mother yet? I can arrange it, if you like..."

"Would you? Thanks, that would be nice," said Guruma, patting Nomita's arm gratefully. "It means so much to him."

"And you? How do you feel about it?" she was emboldened to ask.

"It's good of course. If this is what he wants, of course it's wonderful. Having a child around the house, a child of Debojit's age, musically inclined, is perhaps going to be good for me, as well. But it's his idea, Debojit will be his student, not mine. I owe it to him to make him happy. After everything..."

Nomita wanted to ask what that "After everything..." meant, but it wasn't possible, not yet. In any case, not everything had to be spelled out. Some things were better understood for remaining unsaid.

27

The Raags that resonated at Jhankaar throughout the evening classes changed colour. Malhars, Desh and Jaijaiwanti were set aside for other Raags, those of another season. The students began to rehearse Raags that would embody the coming mood of Spring, which, was still some months away. Nomita, brushing up on a Basant-Bahar for an upcoming concert, was glad. The Raags of spring were always happy, lively ones. The melodies pepped her up. She loved the lyrics too, the ones that described the flowers of the season, the buds of spring, the butterflies that evoked a garden bursting with blooms. They were quite unlike the traditional lyrics of the monsoon Raags, where bejewelled and adorned women waited futilely for absent lovers to return from distant places. The women in those lyrics pleaded with the black, rain bearing clouds to take a message to the absent lover, entreating him to come back before she pined away to a shadow.

Maybe it was those Raags she had practised for so many months that had got to her. Often, she found herself feeling sad, unaccountably so. She was glad that till she got married and went away, she would be singing and learning the happy Spring songs. Maybe they would cheer her up.

Relatives began arriving for the wedding several days before the first ceremonies were slated to begin. This was after all the wedding of Pradeep and Shikha Sharma's only daughter, it wasn't as though there would be a similar celebration again in the house. The guest rooms filled up, cramped with close relatives, while the more distant ones were accommodated in a couple of houses nearby, rented temporarily for the purpose. The rooms began to echo with laughter, talk and music.

Nomita, sitting with them, found she had little to say. There was a tiredness in her limbs and mind that made even responding to them difficult. Luckily, it seemed that as the bride to be, all that was required of her was simply to be present. An occasional smile was all that was needed.

"Wedding songs, how come we are not singing any wedding songs?" demanded two of Nomita's aunts, her mother's sisters, who had come a week ahead of time.

"That's right," chorused the other women happily, looking up from the chores they were busy at.

"This is the wedding of a world famous musician to another great musician, our own Nomi. And no music?"

"Classical?" asked Nomita's cousin doubtfully. "Now?"

"Don't be silly, no classical-wassical. Those are for concert halls," replied Diksha Jethai, Shikha Sharma's elder sister, her grin as broad as her person. "These are our songs. Biya Naams. Wedding songs. Come on, I'm starting, who'll join me?"

She tucked the end of her sador into the waist of her mekhela, cleared her throat, and began in a strong voice,

Janakor Jiyori, Sita Patesweri,
Aei Ram, Aasey Sintakul Hoi, Hei,
Ketiya Ahibo, Xadori Xahu Ai
Aei Ram, Hatot Tel Sindur Loi Hei,
Janak's daughter, most beauteous Sita,
Sits there, steeped in worry,
When will she come, my mother-in-law,
With unguents and sindoor,
To claim me for her son?
The other women joined lustily in the chorus,
Ayodhyare Nari Logot Loi Ahisay
Aei Ram, Aasey Kolor Gurit Bohi Hei…
Bringing with her the women of Ayodhya
She sits there, under the welcoming fronds
Of the auspicious banana plant…

Diksha broke off abruptly, and turning to her sister who was singing as happily as the others, said, "Shikha, that reminds me, they're from a different community, obviously they don't have the Joron like we do. But it's sad that our Nomi won't have the happiness of being welcomed into her husband's house by her mother-in-law..."

"No, Tirna will not be putting sindoor on Nomita's head like we do here. The bridegroom will do that, the way they do in the rest of the country. But I like our custom best. All the women come a day before, and claim the girl for their family, giving her gifts and clothes and jewellery, putting sindoor in her hair. But what to do, I didn't feel like suggesting it to them."

"In any case they would have been shocked, I suppose," opined Disksha wisely. "People from other parts of India just can't understand how in our weddings, the mother-in-law, and not the bridegroom, puts the vermilion on the bride's head."

Nomita, listening, agreed with her mother. It would probably have been more appropriate in the present case if Tirna Ghosh were to claim Nomita with a thick streak of vermilion on the parting of her hair. After all, it was on her initiative that the marriage was taking place at all. The bridegroom had come into the picture much later, and even now, was a peripheral presence. As women, both of them had bonded so well, in spite of the age difference. The mother-in-law/daughter-in-law relationship, she was well aware, was weighted with difficult histories. Even now, before the relationship between the two of them became official, there was supposed to be a tension between them. It was taken for granted that there would be acrimony between them in the years, decades that stretched into the future. But it was not necessary to go down that route, and Nomita herself was quite confident that their relationship would not be like that.

She and Tirna now conversed on a daily basis. Often Rana, too, joined in. Diffidently, but the affection in his voice was very real. True, Kaushik phoned too, but at much rarer intervals, and at odd hours, depending on where he was at that moment. Their conversations even now were stilted, and one sided, with Kaushik doing most of the talking during the brief calls.

Impossible to tell Kaushik about the things that were closest to her heart. Perhaps understanding each others' passions would come to them later, gradually. Her involvement with children like Silsila and Pallavi, his love of fusion music.

Rahul's parents were in and out of the house, but Rahul himself arrived only a few days before the actual ceremony. He came to Nomita's house straight from the airport, without stopping by at his own house to freshen up. Nomita, waiting at the gate for him, was shocked at his appearance.

"Rahul...you've lost so much weight!" There were circles under his eyes, and his face looked drawn. His body too was thinner, much thinner.

"I haven't slept for over twenty-four hours, what you expect?" he asked, touching her cheek briefly. His eyes seemed strange, no, it was his expression, which had an intensity she hadn't noticed before. Surely it wasn't just lack of sleep? "This comes of working in an IT firm. I had to wrap up a lot of things before coming. But don't mind me, I'll be quite ok in a couple of days."

A searing worry flared in Nomita's mind. Twenty-four hours without sleep could not be the reason for this loss of weight. He was used to going without sleep, just as she was. He could catch up on a few hours of sleep after a couple of days without a wink and still be as good as new. An engineer working in today's IT industry was supposed to have become immune to changes in sleep cycles. No of course it wasn't that. Was he ill? Why hadn't he told her he was sick? Rahul was bad with illness, he needed to be mollycoddled even when he had a cold. She had spent chunks of time over the years pampering him with Vicks headrubs and neck massages when he had had even a slight fever. Strange he hadn't mentioned any illness during all those telephone conversations. Strange and most unlike him. He liked to dramatize his ailments, even if it was a thorn on his thumb or a blister on his foot.

"Rahul, are you all right?" she began, but he said at the same time, "You look a bit tired, Nomi? Not like the glowing bride I expected ... ?" He looked at her, and then away at the shamiana behind them.

"Wow, that's impressive! Beautiful!" He began to walk towards the marquee, and Nomita had no option but to follow, murmuring, "I've ordered some fresh momos for you, just wash up and we'll sit and have a plate..." But she did not know if he heard her. Probably not. She trailed into the shamiana, feeling, after Rahul's words, that the structure before her was better looking than she, the bride, was.

Her parents were pulling out all the stops to make this marriage an affair to remember. They were happy, very happy for her, in that quintessentially Indian way, of being able to give their daughter away to a "boy" of "good family" who could "support" her comfortably. They were delighted that their daughter's interest in music would be supported and carried forward by the family she was marrying into.

Nomita, trailing after Rahul, found that he was immediately surrounded by the men under the shamiana. Her father came bounding out from the corner where he had been supervising the placing of the chairs, his face a combination of worry and joy. The latter emotion grew predominant as he enveloped Rahul in a hug.

"Rahul, I really missed you. So much to do, and no able-bodied young man around..." Both Pradeep and Shikha Sharma had always looked on Rahul as their son.

"Sorry, I just couldn't come earlier..." Rahul's voice was pitched at an uncharacteristic mumble. Then, in a brighter tone more like his usual voice he added, "But now I'm here, just let me know what's to be done. We'll sit down and make a list..."

They walked off towards the house, Pradeep Sharma's arm wrapped affectionately around Rahul's waist, since the younger man's shoulder was too high to do so with comfort.

Nomita, left behind, looked around. It was certainly true, she thought, that one could be surrounded by crowds of people, and yet be lonely. There were so many people here, under this newly erected marquee in shades of magenta and peach, standing or sitting around, talking, laughing, listening. They were all here, ostensibly because of her, Nomita. Many of them had come at great inconvenience to themselves, spending precious days of leave and money on tickets, only because they wished to join their family at this celebratory time. A wedding was the time for families to gather, after all.

And yet Nomita felt alone. She had thought she would feel better if Rahul was here, but now that he was, she only felt worse. There would clearly be no time to talk to him alone in this house bustling with people and activity. And later… after she became Mrs Kaushik Ghosh, who knew? Would she be expected to move around in the footsteps of her maestro-husband, making sure that everything was just so, so that he could focus undisturbed on his work? A kind of glorified Kamal Basu, was that to be her role, then? Booking tickets, looking after dates and payments…

A group of younger women were sitting cross-legged on the floor in a corner of the drawing room. Before them was a heap of mango leaves that they were sorting and then threading into strings. A dot of vermilion would be put on each leaf before the strings were put up above the doors, and at the entrance to the compound, to signify the auspiciousness of the occasion.

"Do you know," her cousin Maitreyee from Delhi was saying, "It's really sad the way I've lost touch with so many of my friends. After all I grew up here, in Tamulbari, and I've only been in Delhi since I got married. That's eleven years now. Of course I have lots of friends there, from work, and through Varun, but there's nothing like old friends to really brighten up one's life, is there?"

The others murmured their assent. "Actually, it's easier to keep in touch with the girls," added Sanjana, who had come in with her husband and toddler from Mumbai. "No matter how busy they are. And aren't we all busy these days, with children and home and unreliable help and jobs?" She was a graphic artist, working hectic days, and commuting long distances. "With the internet and sites like Facebook, we can all be in touch if we want to. I find that it's the girls who come forward, wanting to re-establish contact. The boys in our group in college were such nice guys, such great friends to have. They seem to have vanished from the face of the earth, now. I've tried so hard to find out where they are, but it's like they've been elevated up to some other planet or something. No news of them, nothing…"

"But men make great friends, don't they, even though they don't seem to be too good at keeping in touch over the long term," said Ranjana, who had come in several days ago from the tea garden where her husband worked. "There are such few people in the neighbouring tea gardens with whom one can have a reasonably stimulating conversation. Mostly, I find that when we go to a new place, it's easier to make friends with the men. The women are a different group altogether, they take much longer to become your friends. They are so much more complicated..."

Savitri Mahi, coming over briskly with a large tray of tea for the mango-leaf-stringers, heard the later part of what Ranjana was saying. She set the tray down on the floor, waiting for the younger women to take a steaming mugful each before helping herself to the last one. "Do you know," she observed, "women of my generation would not be having the kind of conversation you are having here, at all. Keeping up with men friends – that's something that we could never do when we were your age, or younger. It was difficult enough keeping up with one's women friends, because relatives-in-law and relatives seemed to take up all one's time, whether one liked it or not. But men friends, they were just not allowed!"

"Men make better friends than women," said Tara.

"Well, my generation doesn't even know how to make that comparison," said Savitri Mahi, sitting on a chair and curling her palms around the warmth of the mug. Arthritis had stiffened her limbs, and she could no longer sit on the floor. "Any contact that was more than a superficial one, between a grown woman and a man who was not related, was suspect. Husbands were suspicious as well, they used to feel quite threatened if the wife had a very good friend who happened to be a man. Things are so much easier now. You can have men friends, and your husbands will be quite ok about it."

The younger women laughed. "True," agreed Ranjana. "Good friends are precious, no matter whether they are men or women..."

"But tell me," asked Savitri Mahi, "really, looking at the boys and girls now, I often wonder... how do you know the difference? The closeness that my nieces for example have with their boyfriends doesn't seem to me to be all that different from the closeness they have with their friends who are boys. So what's the difference?"

Nomita, sitting at the edge of the conversation, leaned forward a little to hear better.

There was a chorus of voices as each one of the young women replied.

"Actually, friendship is the base, I would think. Unless you are friends, you cannot move on to becoming lovers," said Sanjana. "Husbands have to be friends, though not all friends can be husbands."

"You can't have a successful marriage without the spouses being friends," added Ranjana.

"But in our days it was all arranged marriages," said Savitri Mahi, the sindoor in her white hair glowing in the light. "We hardly met the boy before marriage. Where was the question of being friends before marriage? My grandmother for example only saw her husband's face when they were both seated in front of the sacred fire, being married by a priest reciting mantras that they did not understand at all. She was thirteen, he was seventeen. Yet I would say ours were – are – successful marriages."

"But you're friends now, aren't you, Mahi?" pointed out Maitreyee. "Of course you are. And lovers, too."

"What!" Savitri Mahi sounded shocked at the word on her young niece's lips.

"Don't blush Mahi, we've seen the way you look at each other when you think nobody's watching."

"You're shameless, you lot," said Savitri laughing. "When I was your age I wouldn't have dreamed of saying these things to a woman twice my age."

"We say things, pronounce words that have been kept hidden for a long time," said Maitreyee.

"Like 'lover'. And 'sex'," agreed Sanjana, stringing the final mango leaf. She looked up and smiling cheekily, added, "And 'vagina.' And 'pe...'"

"Stop stop, I can't listen any more," said Savitri Mahi, but she was laughing. "Here, if you've finished, I'll take the mugs... just hand them to me... oh my here's the bride, what are you doing there in the shadows, so quiet, Nomita? I know, I know you have nothing to do. Well then..." she peered closely at Nomita, "just go to your room and lie down with a face pack or something. You look tired, poor child. It's stressful, being in a marriage house. Being the bride means you just have to hang around, getting more and more tense. Just rest a bit..." she bustled away.

At this time, the bride was expected to be surrounded by cousins and friends, laughing, giggling, having fun. True, her cousins were here, but they were all in their own groups. Nomita, over the years, immersed in her pursuit of music, her long hours of riyaz and her shows, her work in the Tamulbari Public School and the Shishu Kalyan institution, had not kept up with them, or their lives. It was nice, really nice of them to gather here for her wedding, in spite of their busy schedules. But after the first fifteen minutes of laughter and teasing, Nomita found that there was not much she could talk to them about. The Tamulbari friends she had grown up with had either gone away or were now so busy with their own lives that they had lost touch. True, Sheila, Jimli and Ranjita had come over one day, sipped the tea and snacks that Rina had provided, and left, promising to come early on the wedding day so that they could be part of every single ceremony. They had talked mostly of the absent Rahul at that time, how well he was doing in his job, the name he was making for himself. Did she know that he had bypassed several seniors on the way to this latest promotion of his? She hadn't, though of course she knew about the promotion.

There was no other person in her life that she could call her "very good friend" in the same way as she did Rahul. Rahul. Where was he, then? Instead of going to bed to rest as advised by Savitri Mahi, she wandered out again, looking for him, threading her way unnoticed through the groups deep in talk and laughter. He was supposed to be here for her, why was he talking with... ah there he was, listening intently to her uncle from Sivsagar.

"...all the young people are leaving, tell me is it a good thing? My own children...the house is empty now, such a huge house, built by my father's father. Why would anyone want to live in those tiny rooms in the poky flats that are coming up all around? Come back to your own place, young man..."

Nomita expected Rahul to say, "Come back, to what, Jetha?" as he usually did when elderly people spoke in this way. It was quite common. But instead he just nodded and kept quiet.

"There's the bride," added her uncle. "What, Nomita, have you been working too hard? Too many functions and programmes stretching to the early mornings, is that it? We expect to see you on the national platform now, you know. This is going to be a huge boost for your career, isn't it?"

"That's not why I'm marrying him, Jetha," said Nomita, careful to keep her tone mild.

"No no, of course not, I'm not implying that for a minute. But the fact remains...it will be excellent exposure, you should make the most of this chance..." he smiled, and wandered away, called by a group of similarly elderly people across the lawn.

"Do you think I'm marrying Kaushik Kashyap because I have an eye on the main chance? Do you, Rahul?" she demanded.

He looked down at her, his face as tired as hers, the laughter missing from his eyes.

"No," he said, slowly.

"Why are you saying it like that? You don't sound convinced."

"No no, it's nothing like that. Of course you're not marrying him to further your own career. Of course not. That never works, does it? You have to make it on your own steam, whatever your line of work. Just being married to somebody, or being born to a parent who is a master in a particular field, is hardly a guarantee of success. No...you're too intelligent to think that. In any case, teaching music, especially to children like those in Shishu Kalyan is more your interest, rather than stage shows, isn't it? "

She knew him too well to think that this was all he had to say.

"But...?" she prompted.

"But. Actually..." he trailed off.

"No, tell me. This is important," she insisted.

"What is there for me to say? Surely you know the reasons why you are getting into this marriage, you're a grown girl."

Suddenly she remembered the surprise she had for him. "Come with me," she said, feeling happier and brighter than she had in a long while.

"Where? I need to go home and wash..."

"Come on, you can do that later..." She took his hand and walked with him across the lawn, to the garage where their cars were parked. "Get in," she said. The keys, she saw, were dangling from the ignition as they usually were in the daytime.

She watched, smiling, as Rahul automatically began to move towards the driver's side of the Alto.

"No no, not there, the passenger's..."

He turned around, his eyes laughing at last. "Nomi! You never told me! Keeping such a secret...but have you got a license? Or are you still a learner? I don't want to get killed!" He was sounding like himself now. "I..." she said grandly, sliding into the driver's side, "am now licenced, fees all paid up, examination taken and passed, with flying colours if you please. You don't have to look nervous, come on, relax. I'll be driving you better than those so-called chauffeurs that you see wrecking cars all around town."

She backed out smoothly from the garage, and going past the lane, moved to the main road. The streets were full of early evening vehicles, but Nomita wove her way through them quite confidently.

"I'm impressed," said Rahul. "See, I'm not even holding on to the door latch any more. My palms have stopped sweating." He waved them around their faces. "But seriously, why didn't you tell me? This is majorly majorly good. You won't have to hang around waiting for rickshaws or autos in front of Jhankaar any more."

Briefly, she took her eyes off the road, and looked at him.

"Ah, I forgot," he said, not missing a beat. "Stupid me." His voice was soft again, the excitement gone from it. "Well anyway. You'll be your own mistress in Kolkata, not depending on anyone for a lift...

though I suppose they have a chauffeur-driven car, several in fact. You may perhaps not even need your driving skills there..."

His words were running into each other, a monotone with no pause in between. Her own excitement had evaporated, too.

There was silence in the car as she drove on. Soon, they had left the heavy traffic behind, and were moving on towards the open road. House lights twinkled here by the side of the road at intervals, interspersed with patches of darkness. Looking carefully at the rearview mirror, as she had been taught to do, she pulled over in front of one of the dark areas.

They waited, without speaking, for what seemed a long while.

"Rahul," she said finally.

She could sense him turning to look at her. His breathing came to her, shallow and faster than it usually was.

She had been with him, sitting side by side any number of times in her life, but she had never felt like this before. Her own breathing was shallow, too.

There was so much to say. So much to discover. And yet it wasn't possible. She was aware, though they weren't even touching, of the beating of his heart, just as he was, no doubt, aware of the thudding of hers.

A truck came down the road, its headlamps lighting up the interior of their car. His eyes were bloodshot, she realized. And. Oh God, no, they were wet.

It was too much.

"Rahul, Rahul," she wept, groping for his hands, his face. "What have I done?!"

They clung to each other, not saying anything, not needing to. His hands smoothed back the hair from her face, hers rested on his shoulder. Tears mingled.

How many times had their bodies touched in the past, but it had never led to this. She had known, of course, what his hands, his arms, his body felt like when it came into contact with hers fleetingly, as they were moving on the back of his bike, or as they sat side by side in his home, or hers. All through their growing up years, she had known. Just as, no doubt, he had. When his body had suddenly grown lanky, and his voice had changed from a sweet soprano to an unpredictable tenor, she had known the feel of the down on his cheeks. He had proudly taken her hand and rubbed the back of it on his cheeks himself. Over the years, the way they had touched had changed. His hand never brushed her breasts, even by accident. She had been careful, unconsciously, about getting too close to him, physically. Even when riding pillion, there was always a certain distance between their bodies. No matter how tired she was, she had never even felt the urge to rest her face against his back, though it was just a few inches away.

But this sudden awareness of his body now, this was something that she had never had in all the years that they had known each other. There had always been that physical distance between them, a distance that was created in their minds rather than in the space between them. Now, when it was too late, the wall between them had suddenly crumbled.

"It's not... we shouldn't," he said finally. The throb in his voice echoed the emptiness in her mind.

"It's too late," he said after a while. He pulled himself away.

"Why did we not realize this before?" she thought, but her thought was a whisper.

"I did," he said. "I always knew..."

"You never said..."

"I never thought I needed to. And then suddenly it was too late."

28

The bridegroom, with his entourage, was coming that day. It was not going to be a big group, but after all, the entire bridegroom's side had to be kept happy and satisfied. The mere mention of a "borjatri" always sent shivers of nervousness and apprehension up the spines of the bride's side. What if they took umbrage? What if some small unintentional slip snowballed into a huge fiasco?

Pradeep Sharma, as usual, was depending on Rahul for support and help. He had deputed Rahul to be in charge of receiving the bridegroom and his people at the airport, and bringing them safely and ceremoniously to the Guest House that had been booked for them. It would be unseemly for him to go there, he would meet them at the Guest House. Now that he was coming as a bridegroom and not a maestro, Kaushik Kashyap was flying direct to the small Tamulbari airport. Thank goodness for that, said the bride's side to each other. Imagine if he had come to Guwahati airport, that would have meant a journey time of a few hours.

Nomita listened to the discussions and excitement that enveloped the rest of the house from behind the closed doors of her room. She did not feel like facing the phalanx of relatives, though a few cousins had knocked at her door and come in, wondering why she was still inside.

"I'm not too well... I have this headache, it's awful..." she had said. And it was true. Unable to sleep for even a few minutes the previous night, she had spent much of it pacing up and down her room.

They had nodded and looked worried and left her alone. "Yes, you're looking quite..." Tact had prevented them from saying the word "horrible," or "haggard," but Nomita had known that the words had been at the tips of their tongues.

Last evening, she had come straight up to her room after returning from the drive. Her newly acquired skill had deserted her, and after a few moments of shaky driving during which the car had swerved madly from one side of the road to the other, Rahul had taken the wheel. They had returned in silence. There was, after all, nothing to say now. Her thoughts had a single focus. How could she have done this! How could she have mistaken her closeness with Rahul for "only" a friendship? Her mind had known that it was much more than that. Probably it had been trying to tell her for a while. But she had been so overwhelmed by the music that she had not been able to think straight. And now... it was too late.

She didn't hear Rahul respond to her father's directions, but she knew that meant nothing. He would meet Kaushik Kashyap and his parents and the others at the airport. This time, of course, there would not be any Committee waiting with garlands for the sitarist, but only a few people from the bride's place to escort him to the Guest House.

She could barely think straight. She wished she could talk to somebody. But as always, the "somebody" came down to one person. Rahul. Of course she couldn't speak to him about this now. No. Just as he couldn't speak about it to anyone else. Now or ever.

On the other side of the door, she could hear her father and his brothers discussing the arrangements. She knew Rahul was there, the remarks were addressed to him, though she didn't hear a word he said. He must be tired too, she doubted he had slept very much, even after so many hours without sleep.

"I don't really trust these hired chauffeurs on that stretch from the airport to the edge of town. They come at such speed. That bit is really a danger zone. You come in the lead car Rahul; sit with the chauffeur, the others can follow. There should be six cars, with four people each plus the driver... I think you should sit with the bridegroom, in the same car, make him feel welcome, you know. Let me know as soon as... be in touch on the cell..."

The voices droned in and out. Her mind ran in a mad circle of thoughts that chased themselves round and round. She barely registered that they were talking about the bridegroom's arrival with his family to her town, to get married to her. She felt drugged, as though she had taken too much of that cough medicine that she sometimes sipped before a performance when her throat was acting up.

She should go out, she knew. She should mingle. All these people, well-wishers, were here because of her. It was the height of bad manners to stay confined to her room like this. She should talk to them, smile, laugh, allow herself to be fussed over, to be teased, to be made much of. She should look demure and shy, she should glow, so that all the visitors and guests could say later, with satisfaction, "What a wonderful match! Just to look at our Nomita was enough to know how *happy* she was. Who said arranged marriages don't work in this day and age? Look at Nomi and Kaushik ..."

A knock, and Sanjana put her head in cautiously through the door.

"How are you feeling, Nomi?" she asked softly. "There's somebody come to see you ..."

The last thing she wanted now, with this turmoil within her mind, was to make small talk with somebody she barely knew.

"...your Guruma. Sandhya Senapatiji ..." she continued. There was awe in her voice.

She realized, suddenly, that subconsciously, this was exactly what she had been wanting, hoping for, that Sandhya Senapati would come, drop in for a visit. She no longer thought of her as Guruma. After Kolkata, especially, Sandhya had become, in a way, her closest female friend. She would know what her student was talking about. She would know her feelings.

She hurriedly straightened her hair, her clothes, began to walk out of the door, came back again, and put on a dab of kajal and some lipstick. She peered into the mirror in the darkened room. She looked worse if anything, like death painted over. Death. It was inauspicious for a bride to even think the word. She decided against rubbing off the colours, and walked out of the door.

At four in the morning, as the early eastern dawn had lightened the horizon, she had sat down with sheets of paper, and scribbled furiously on them. They were still there on her writing desk, pages of them, topped with a glass paperweight. She hadn't finished with her writing when she had been called out for her breakfast. She looked at them as she went out, only half remembering what she had written.

Guruma, tranquil and golden-skinned as always, was sitting in the drawing room with her mother and aunts, already being plied with tea and snacks. "Thank you, no more laru please, I've just had a late breakfast... ah, there she is..."

Nomita, feeling an upsurge of gladness at just seeing Sandhya Senapati, went up to her and bent to touch her feet. It was more out of habit now. Of course her respect for her teacher was, if anything, greater than before. But their relationship now had a new dimension, something that did not need to be put into words.

A sudden spark appeared in Sandhya Senapati's eyes, quickly veiled. It was surprise at her appearance, Nomita knew. She made an effort to smile, but it was a wan effort. She felt the coolness of her teacher's hands on her head and arms as she raised her gently, and said softly, "May you have a long and happy life, Nomita, now and always."

Shikha Sharma murmured something about having to attend to the lunch, and left, followed by the others. Rina arrived to clear away the teacups and snacks and plates. And then they were silent, sitting together in a sudden pool of quiet in the middle of the wedding-house bustle.

Without preamble, Sandhya Senapati leaned forward and put a cool hand on Nomita's fevered arm. "Tell me, Nomita, what is it?" she asked, her voice softer than the breeze, meant only for her student's ears. She looked around, and added, "If you like, we can go somewhere else. Your room, perhaps?"

Nomita remembered that her bedroom was a mess, the bed still unmade, but she got up immediately and led the way. Once they were inside, she bolted the door, and tried to neaten up the bed. She hadn't spoken a single word to Guruma since her arrival. She didn't trust herself to speak, not to this woman who knew every nuance of her voice even better, perhaps, than she herself did. Instead, she gestured to the chair, and sat down on the dressing table stool.

"Tell me…" said Sandhya Senapati again. She sounded caring and concerned, but also as though she knew what the matter was likely to be. "You'll feel better, maybe," she added after a pause.

"But it's too late, isn't it?" asked Nomita, careful to keep her voice neutral. It sounded different even to her own ears. Dead, flat and husky, without the cadence or resonance that it normally had.

There was no need to tell Guruma what the matter was. It was apparent from the compassion in her voice and her eyes that she knew. But something struck Nomita as she looked at that calm face.

"How long have you known?" she asked.

"Well – not known, exactly," Sandhya Senapati replied slowly. "But I have wondered right from the beginning, when this marriage was arranged. After all, in all the years that you have come to me for your lessons, I have been watching you with Rahul. Of course you thought he was just a friend - but it's been apparent, at least to me, that he's more, much more. Especially when we were in Kolkata… there was something in your voice when you were speaking to him on the phone. It wasn't there even when you went to meet your husband-to-be in person."

"And now it's too late…" repeated Nomita.

Sandhya Senapati looked at Nomita as she sat a little below her, on the stool, as befitted a student, who could never sit at a level higher than that of her Guru. She got up and went towards the hastily made bed. Straightening the folds of the coverlet, Sandhya Senapati sat down on it.

"Come and sit here, Nomita," she said, smoothing a place beside her. "I want to tell you something…"

They sat there, side by side, watching the garden with its shamiana outside the window for a while. Then softly, in a voice that Nomita had to strain to hear, she said,

"You know, when I was in Kolkata, training under Guruji, Deepak was one of the few people my age that I knew in that city. Well, of course

I knew the other students, girls and boys, the tabla accompanists who came and went, even Guruji's sons, but it was not... how can I put it... those were very casual friendships. Acquaintances. But with Deepak, it was very different."

She paused, her hand moving slowly over the coverlet, continuing its movements, even though the fabric now lay quite smooth on the bed.

"His world and mine were – are – so different. But that hardly mattered. Our temperaments were different, too. He was always more of an extrovert. I was always focused on my music. That was, you know, my entire world. Riyaz, practice, sadhana. I was walled in by the constant need to go deeper and deeper into melody, into the intricacies of Raag and Sur and Taal. It was a well whose depths you could never plumb, because it was bottomless. It was, for me during those years, a kind of addiction, you know?"

"Addiction?" Nomita would not have used the word, but she knew what Sandhya Senapati meant. Her teacher's voice, taking her back to her own past, distracted her momentarily from her own despair, which now thudded heavily within the depths of her being as though a large Nagara, a kettle drum was being thumped aimlessly in her mind. Yes, it could be like an addiction. No wonder so many classical musicians, especially of the older school, were an unworldly lot, hopelessly out of place in the demands and needs of the modern world. Absent-minded when out of their musical surroundings, brilliant when within it, they were sustained and energized by this addiction, this maddening need to delve ever deeper into the wellsprings of melody and rhythm. They were like Sufi dervishes, whirling round and round, trying to find the source. The source of all music, the Naad Brahma, the Ultimate Divine Sound, which resonated throughout the Universe and all Creation, the root of all music.

"But Deepak... his world was different." Nomita's wandering mind came back to the reality of Sandhya Senapati's voice. "Somehow, in spite of all the differences in our temperaments and professions and backgrounds, in spite of all odds, we became friends. Such good friends. And it was through him that I learned of the existence of another world. True, I lived in Kolkata, but the Manicktola house that Guruji lived in, and his in Ballygunge, were practically in different places. Guruji's was a traditional household, Guruma ran a traditional kitchen. True, Deepak's was a traditional family too, but he was very much a part of that life, in Kolkata, in those days. Being a boy, he was given much more leeway by his family than the girls were. Deepak was the one who took me to Eden Gardens to watch cricket, making me forgo for those days of Test matches, my afternoon riyaz. He was the one with whom I saw the stars of the Universe... well in the Planetarium, but it was, I remember, almost like the real thing. He was the one who took me to eat puchkas on the Maidan, ice cream at Kwality's... But more important, talking to him, I got to know about different kinds of music. Classical musicians here tend to be" – she smiled a little disparagingly – "you know, a little insular. As though ours is the only valid kind of music, the rest is trash or something. That's not true, of course, that's probably just a sign of insecurity... Or maybe it's because we place a lot of importance on the spiritual aspect of our music..." She took a deep breath and added, "But you know all that. I think I'm boring you. You're under a lot of stress... I just want you to hear me out, and then make your decision. I'm trying to get to the point, just... bear with me..."

"Of course I'm not bored, how can I be?" Nomita protested. It was true. She looked at Sandhya Senapati. Her cheeks now were slightly flushed. Nomita realized that this was probably the first time she had spoken about this to anyone. It was as difficult to talk about it now as it must have been when she too had been called upon to make a decision, all those years ago.

"Marriage to Deepak did of course enter my mind, many times. Ours was a friendship that flourished, remember, more than twenty years ago. It was only in the anonymity of the big city, a place where hardly anybody else from Tamulbari lived, that I could be such good friends with Deepak. He, too, came from a very conservative North Indian family, a joint family at that time. True, he was sent to the best schools and colleges, but from a very early age it was known that he would be expected to marry into a business family similar to theirs. But Kolkata – Kolkata at that time - was big enough for our friendship to flourish undisturbed. Even then, with our kinds of backgrounds, it was inevitable that the question of marriage, of having something other than just friendship between us, would enter our minds. Deepak tells me that he thought of it often at that time too, though we never actually spoke of it. In any case, both of us knew that his family, and mine as well, had something different in mind for us when it came to marriage. In fact his people would probably have been much more difficult to convince if we had decided to get married. My parents would have come round in the end, I suppose. But our friendship was in itself a wonderful thing, unusual also, and we really enjoyed it. Cherished it, even then."

There was a feeling of déjà vu in the air. But of course it hadn't been the same between them as it was now between her and Rahul, thought Nomita. Two decades separated their stories, decades during which so much had changed in people's minds and attitudes.

"Anyway..." Guruma looked apologetically at her student... "I'm trying to put things in perspective, I'm sorry I'm becoming so lengthy. It's the first time I've spoken about it to anybody. I didn't have many women friends in whom to confide. The pursuit of classical music is demanding. You move around, you spend your time in riyaz and meditation, in listening to the music of others, attending Conferences... it leaves you very little time to nurture friendships. Which was why my friendship with Deepak was like a miracle. That too, in a city where besides my Guruji and his family and my co-students I hardly knew anybody. Nobody with whom I could really strike a deep friendship..."

"In any case..." ventured Nomita, knowing exactly what she was saying, "in any case, a friendship like that is extremely rare and therefore valuable."

"Yes." Guruma did not look at her. Her gaze was focused unwaveringly at the window, and the people moving around under the shamiana outside.

"And then... so many things happened. My parents wanted to get me married. Understandable, of course. In our society it is the duty of every father, every householder, to see his children settled in life. And for women, even women with hugely promising careers, 'settled' meant marriage."

"It still does…"

"But not to that extent, I think. Anyway, my parents did their best. And Tridib was – is – an absolute gem. The best husband material that one could find, given my career. Only…"

Sandhya Senapati hesitated, and swallowed. Nomita looked enquiringly at her, but she was silent. Something trembled in the air, a thought, a fact, on the edge of being spoken out loud.

The moment passed. Reaching across to the jug of water on the bedstand, Nomita poured out a glass and handed it silently to her Guru.

"Thank you, I've been talking so much…" said Sandhya Senapati, finishing the water. "Anyway. And at the same time, Deepak was sent off to do a course in Management in the US. It was a given, of course, after all that was what sons in their kind of families always did. Go off to America, that is, get a degree in Management or Engineering, and come back to add value and newer inputs into the family business. And that… that's where he met Rati."

"Ah. Was she already…?" Nomita did not know how to frame the question further. Indeed, it was a crass question that had formed in her mind. But Guruma knew exactly what her student wanted to ask.

"Well, hers is – was – a progressive disease. Muscles wasting away, but only, thank God for small mercies, in the lower limbs, I think. No, she wasn't wheelchair bound then as she is now. But there was something, something not quite normal, in the way she walked. A little lopsided, but not always. Sometimes she would need some help to get up from a low chair, like an older person. Though we were all quite young at that time. She had a kind of limp the first time I met her, after they married and came to Kolkata. Quite a while after they got married, actually. She looked – interesting. She is from a business family, too, her people stay all over the world. Nairobi, Durban, Singapore, London, whatnot. And of course in India too, in Rajasthan, and in Kolkata. Very cosmopolitan. Yes, she had some problems with moving around when she met Deepak, but it was nothing like this. And of course she has always had a really really brilliant mind, you could see that for yourself, na?"

"Of course. And so nice, too…" She wondered, too late, if Guruma would mind if she praised Rati. But Sandhya Senapati added, quite sincerely, "Yes, isn't she? So unassuming, though she's worth who knows how many millions." She paused again, and said in a different voice, "But she told Deepak that her disease was likely to put her in a wheelchair. That in twelve, fifteen years, she would be unable to walk."

"It didn't matter to him…?" asked Nomita curiously. Had he been so much in love with her, in faraway America then? Had he not thought even once of the golden skinned, golden voiced girl who had been his companion…?

"I…" Guruma spoke slowly, her gaze fixed on something outside the window. "I'm trying to explain this. Objectively. Of course he was attracted to her. She had – has – such a quick mind, and then their interests jelled, he says, from Day One. Deepak, going from the controlled economy of our country, at that time, breathed the freedom of the marketplace. That heady fragrance, he tells me, was always mingled with the personality of Rati in his mind. They talked and debated and argued and laughed…yes, they became the greatest of friends, very soon. He would call me in Kolkata or Tamulbari. No cellphones in those days, everybody listened to what I said to him in Guruji's house. I had to shout to make myself heard. He wrote, too – no email, remember? – and Rati said this, Rati feels that, was always part of it."

"Who got married first?'

Guruma turned to look at Nomita, her eyes focusing on her student with some surprise. "Actually, me. But only because it was logistically easier, I think. I mean Tridib and I lived in the same place, the same region anyway. Whereas a lot of people spread across a lot of countries, continents even, were involved in their marriage. But still, I would say that we both knew, after he left for America and my parents began to look for a boy for me, we both knew that we would be married soon to other people."

She turned around to look out once more through the window. Nomita followed her gaze. Through the glass, under the shamiana, as though in a silent film, or something that was happening underwater, she saw her relatives moving around. Hardly any sound from the rest of the house entered her room. A car came up to the gate of the shamiana, and a person she did not know got down. People, her relatives, were walking up to him, speaking, gesticulating. There was such urgency in their gestures, the way they spoke. Yes, a wedding ceremony was imminent in this house, that was obvious.

In the same voice, Guruma continued, "He told me once that when he knew that Rati's condition was likely to become worse, that she was quite likely to become immobile, he felt duty-bound, in a way, to marry her. If she had not told him about it, with the most honest of intentions, of course, he would perhaps not have married her, but remained good friends. I understood what he meant. He was always very idealistic, you know. It would be unimaginable for him to leave if he knew something of that kind."

"So, from friends, they became husband and wife," said Nomita slowly.

"And on the other hand, we, from deepest friendship, moved to, what shall I say, a circumspect one. A kind of wary friendship. Guarded. For a while at least. Oh of course we kept meeting, off and on. He has business interests here, his tea gardens and broking house. And I have to keep going to Kolkata, all the time, for my music. Or we sometimes met up in other cities, Mumbai, Delhi, once even in Singapore when they had a Traditional Music Festival of Asia there. There was, in the beginning, something... no, not strain, but a kind of cautiousness between us. We were married to other people, after all, we, who could easily have been..."

Have been husband and wife. Sandhya Senapati did not say the words, but they were there, anyway, hanging between them, as though they were heavy, tangible things, carved in stone.

Still looking at the past but gazing out of the window, Nomita saw that her father was speaking into his cell. There was a kind of strain in his body language. Yes, he was the father of the bride, a huge responsibility was on him. His brother, her uncle, was speaking with the person who had got down from the car. Everybody was so busy, so engrossed in their work. The ceremony was almost upon them, so what if the bride had had a change of heart? Whoever heard of things coming to a halt now, at this late hour, for a frivolous reason like this? The show must go on…

She brought her confused thoughts back to the room. "And Guruji?" she asked. It was a deeply personal question to ask of her teacher, she knew, but after the events of the past few months, it came easily to her.

Sandhya Senapati did not reply immediately. When she finally spoke again, her voice was different. She looked her student directly in the eye, and said, "Do you know, my parents were right. They made a very good choice for me, isn't it obvious? He gives me so much freedom, so much, what's the word, *space.* I've grown as an artiste greatly. He's a good man, a fine artiste. Without him around, I doubt if I could have reached quite this point as a singer, you know." She brightened up suddenly, and added, "You know, Debojit coming into his life has made so much of a difference. It's so good to see them together, the way they are bonding… I am so happy for them."

"And you? How do you feel about this?"

"Well…not maternal, that's for sure. I am more like the outsider. But in a way I always was…"

Nomita, feeling rather than understanding that enormous burden, getting a sense of just the tip of it, looked at her, speechlessly.

"He never wanted to get married, you know," Guruma continued, helplessly. "But Tridib's people – there came a time when he could no longer say no. He tried to tell me about the way he was, when we met at functions while the talks were going on. But I – I just didn't understand. I mean this was two decades ago…when such things were not discussed, not even understood. I don't blame his mother, or his people. They had no knowledge of what was…"

She paused and took another sip of water. Through the window, she saw that her mother and aunts had joined the men on the lawn. Their backs were to the room, but they all seemed to be talking together. Her mother walked to a chair, and sat down, while her father kept talking into his cell. This was unusual. He was not the kind of person who spoke a lot, that too on the phone. It was her mother who did that. But her mother did not seem to be speaking at all at the moment. She was looking at her husband as she sat there. That too was unusual. But then the wedding of an only daughter was not a routine thing that happened in households, all responses were unusual for the people involved.

"He has suffered, much more than me. It's not that he has had relationships out of wedlock. I know he hasn't. He is lonely, very lonely, in spite of his status as one of the best musicians in the country. But he... I mean... we are extremely good friends, colleagues even. But not husband and wife." She lifted her eyes, and looked at her student. Nomita was startled to see the anguish in them.

She put a hand out to clasp Guruma's, and still their uncharacteristic restlessness. "I understand. It's sad... more than sad... a waste, really... Yes, I understand." She didn't want Sandhya Senapati to go through the additional torture of trying to explain.

Another car had come to the gate. More people had gathered there. Quite a crowd, in fact. Nomita recognized her neighbours, but also several others who seemed to be strangers. They all seemed to be talking at the same time, though from here, they could not be heard.

"Does Deepak know this?" she asked.

"I haven't told him, but I think he does. You're the first person..." she swallowed, and continued, "For a long time, my friendship with Deepak was blameless. But gradually, I don't know how or when, it became something more. Something deeper, something that is now, for us both, one of the most important things in our lives. Yes, we are both passionate about our professions, our careers. His children, Tridib, Rati, they are all so important, true. But also what we have with each other is too precious to ignore. You know, Nomita, when we were young, we were very good friends, but we did not recognize that what we had could grow into something much more. And now that it has, it has come at a time when things are not so simple any more. Anyway, I just wanted to tell you ... though maybe I should have told you before this. In any case, I wanted you to know how it was, how it has been, in my life, in the lives of the four of us ..." She sounded incoherent, but her student understood exactly what she meant.

"What will you do?" asked Nomita after a pause. "Can it go on like this?"

"I don't know. Anyway, there's nothing to be done. Neither of us wants to do anything. He can't hurt Rati, though I feel she knows, but is too intelligent to say anything ... And I can't bring myself to say anything to Tridib. He is too good a person, and nothing is his fault, anyway. And he has been loyal to me, he has never ... it has been terribly hard for him. It's not his fault that he was born at the wrong time, wrong social environment. For him, his work, his music is everything. He has immersed himself in it, been kind to me always. If I do tell him, he will understand I am sure. But no, I can't ... it will be as though I am blaming him for something that is not his fault. And I'm not. I can never put any blame on him ..."

For some reason, all the people outside on the lawn had turned, and were looking at the house now. They were not laughing or smiling. That was strange. In fact, they were all looking at the window of her room. Nomita knew that they could not see inside, it was too dark compared to the bright light outside. But it seemed as if they could see her as she sat there. And they had closed, troubled expressions on their faces.

She watched her mother get up from the chair. Her aunt was holding her hand. Her father, too, was coming this way, his arm around his wife's shoulder.

Slowly, the dull ache in her mind began to deepen into a sharp pointed pain. Her heart began to thud loudly. Guruma, too, had noticed what the people outside were doing.

"Something's the matter ..." she began, her voice edged with concern and worry. She stood up.

"Yes," murmured Nomita, her eyes riveted on the people walking towards the house.

In a moment, they would be inside. In a moment, she would know… She took a deep breath, and looked at the door. She was aware that Guruma, beside her, was doing the same, composing herself for whatever news the people were bringing to them.

The knock came, soft and hesitant. It was her aunt Savitri who came in first.

"Nomita, you must be strong, something's happened that you should know about…" She hesitated, then looked over her shoulder. Obviously her role was to prepare her for the news, whatever it was.

Savitri Mahi looked at her again, reaching out and placing a hand on her shoulder. "Sit down, child…" she said kindly.

"What is it," said Guruma quietly. It was a statement, not a question. Her arm was around Nomita.

Pradeep and Shikha Sharma entered the room. Savitri Mahi made way for them, and left the room after giving Nomita a quick hug.

Sandhya Senapati moved towards the door. "I'll be outside," she began, but Shikha Sharma interrupted her, "No, please, Sandhyaji, please stay…it's good that you are with her, she is like your own sister…"

They were all looking at her, not knowing, probably, how to begin. "Tell me," she said quietly, not allowing herself to think of all the many things that could have happened.

"Sit down," said her father, swallowing, but his voice was steady. And kind.

"We just got the news…" he paused.

"What? What news? Tell me…"

"There's been an accident."

"Who…I mean to whom…who was involved…?" There was a huge lump in her throat that refused to go away no matter how hard she swallowed. Her breath came shallowly.

"It was the first car, the limousine we hired. A truck coming from the opposite side smashed into it…" Her father licked his dry lips, and continued, "The bridegroom was sitting at the back, behind the driver. His right side is injured. His humerus, maybe his clavicle, they're probably broken. Maybe. His arm is bleeding. His wrist, something is wrong there. It may be multiple fractures. And perhaps his ribs, I wouldn't be surprised. We'll only know the full extent after a proper examination. No, not life threatening, but they are all being taken to the hospital. I'm on my way there…"

Nomita barely heard the last couple of sentences. She heard her father's voice saying, just a little while earlier, "I think you should sit with him, in the same car, make him feel welcome, you know."

"They? Who else?"

"The driver is injured, certainly. No head injuries, probably, but broken bones in the arm. And Rahul. He was sitting in front, beside the driver. He was thrown to the front, he's got gashes… but nothing can be said till they are examined, X-rayed, scanned…"

29

Rahul. Injured. Gashes, her father had said, but she knew very well that it could be something more, something deeper. She was not a doctor's daughter for nothing. She knew perfectly well that an innocent-looking gash could very well be the tip of the iceberg, hiding something much more serious. She got up quickly, and said, "I'm going too, I must be there. Beside Rahul..."

Her parents looked at her, their eyes reflecting her own feelings.

"There's no need. No, its best if you stay here just now, they will be in Casualty anyway, you won't be able to see them..."

"But Rahul... he'll need me..." she said, preparing to leave.

"Wait," said her mother, her voice gentle. She looked at Sandhya Senapati, and then back at her daughter. "We'll go across a little later, let your father see them first..."

Nomita didn't pay any attention to her. She was looking around the room, searching for something. "I'll give him a call, his mobile..."

Taking up her cellphone, she speed dialled Rahul's number. But the voice she heard at the other end droned in measured tones, "The number you have dialled is not reachable..."

She imagined him lying there, unconscious, in a pool of blood, his cellphone smashed so unrecognizably that it was impossible to get through. Smashed, like his body, his head...

Her own was almost bursting. "No, I'll go with you," she said. "I can't sit still here, anyway..."

She moved towards the door, and waited for her father to come. He looked at her and said, quietly, "All right then. Wait for me; I'll be ready in a minute."

She stood, at the door of her room, impatiently, waiting for her

her father to come out. The rooms beyond this were full of people, waiting now with sombre faces. They had come for a wedding: these were not the expressions and looks they had thought would be required of them.

They went straight to the hospital to which the injured had been taken. They walked into Casualty, the sisters on duty there allowing Nomita in because after all her father was a senior consultant, and her fiancé was lying there, injured.

But it was not Kaushik Kashyap's bed that Nomita raced to. Taking off her shoes, she entered the room and looked around for Rahul. It was clean and airy, the tiled floors sparkling from a recent phenyl mopping. Machines blipped and clicked and hummed in low tones all around her, accentuating the quietness of the room. Monitors were attached to the forms lying supine on the beds. Nurses in white and doctors with stethoscopes slung around their necks moved with silent and urgent steps from one form to the other.

Her father, entering, paused to speak in low tones to the sister on duty. Nomita didn't stop. Looking around, she recognized Rahul's long legs in his jeans on one of the beds. She walked quickly up to it.

His eyes were closed in his pale face. She saw the large plaster stuck to his forehead, making him look strange. Vulnerable. She was careful about not letting any of her distress escape with an "Ah" from her mouth. She consciously quietened her breath that was coming out in short gasps now.

But Rahul seemed to sense her presence. Or perhaps it was the intensity of her look that caused his own eyes to flutter open.

"Ah Nomi ..." His voice was strange.

She reached out a hand to his, and tried to calm the tumult in her mind. "How are you feeling?"

"It's nothing, just a scratch."

"Does it hurt?"

"A bit ..." he admitted. Now that his injuries were so much more serious than any he had had previously, he had become a better patient. Or perhaps it was because she was now about to be married to another man, and it would be unseemly for him to burden her with a litany of aches and pains. She shook her head, trying to dislodge these thoughts. “The truck just came round the bend, hogging all the space on the road.” He was quiet for a moment, then asked, “The driver. How is he? And the other passengers? Kaushikji and I were in the same ambulance, his hand was ... omygod, his *hand* ...”

The full implication of what a hand injury meant for a professional instrumentalist struck Rahul only then, at the same moment that Nomita realized that her father was beckoning her towards another bed.

She left with reluctance, telling Rahul, “Don’t talk, just lie there, I’ll be back ...”

She tried not to look at Kaushik Kashyap’s face when she went up to him. But there was no way she could avoid that. His eyes were closed, his face looked greyish. Much of his hair had escaped from his ponytail, and was now spread in disarray over the pillow under his shoulders. Her eyes went to his right hand. It was tied up from wrist to elbow in white gauze that was already blotched with red patches. His kurta, too, was splashed with a brownish red across the front.

Nomita tried to fight back the sudden nausea. She had no idea where that came from. Certainly, she had not felt this when she had been looking down at Rahul. She noticed a tube attached to Kaushik’s elbow, its other end snaking into a bottle of reddish fluid. He was being given blood.

She realized that her father had come and was standing next to her. “He’s been sedated. Tests are still going on, the preliminary ones don’t show any head injury, but we’ll need scans and things to be sure ...”

“His hand though ...” she said, hesitatingly.

“Yes. Very unfortunate that he was sitting on the right. He took the brunt of the smash along with the driver.”

She was glad that he had his eyes closed, and was seemingly oblivious to their presence. She wouldn’t have known what to say to him, what to do in this situation.

She realized her father was saying something. “... we’re hoping that at least his fingers are all right ... looks bad though ... a plastic surgeon is coming..." His voice, she noticed, was calm, professional. He was a doctor now, not the prospective father-in-law of the sitarist who lay there, bloodied, with a shattered hand.

She realized that there was another person she would have to see now. Torn between reluctance and concern, she went slowly to Tirna Ghosh. Kaushik's mother smiled weakly at her as she lay there.

Nomita reached out her hand and stroked back Tirna's hair, which had escaped in uncharacteristically untidy strands around her face. "Does it hurt?" she asked, the words sounding lame even as she said them. She wondered if Kaushik's parents knew about the condition of their son.

"I'm ok, just a little bruised..." she said, her voice little more than a whisper. "The driver though... he's probably the worst hurt of us all, how is he?"

"Broken hand and leg, hopefully nothing more. Of course the tests are still going on..." Nomita's father had come to stand beside her again.

"What happened?" blurted out Nomita.

"No, it's okay, don't talk, tell us later," said her father immediately. But Tirna Ghosh, her eyes on Nomita, said as though she hadn't heard, "I don't know, it was so sudden. One moment we were going down the road, and then the next there was this truck that seemed to be right on top of us. The driver of our car swerved, in any case he was well on his side, he is a good driver..." she looked directly at Pradeep Sharma, as though aware of the lakes of guilt that were pooling in his mind like blood gushing from a severed artery. "He did swerve, I think, but then there was this tree... It was the trucker's fault, he was coming at quite a lick. I hope they nabbed him?"

"The police have caught him, of course, he's in custody," said Pradeep Sharma.

Tirna reached out a hand and held Nomita's gently. She noticed that Tirna's face was already forming dark bruises on her cheeks. Her arms, too, looked livid.

"The others, how are they?" she asked. "There was a lot of blood..."

Her eyes were closing. Probably she had been sedated too, and was fighting to keep them open. "Kaushik, he's..."

"All the tests are being done," said Nomita's father. "He's... he should be all right, nothing that can't be mended..." his voice tapered off.

"His hand though... so much blood..." mumbled Tirna, her eyes closed. She didn't seem to expect a reply this time.

Rana Ghosh was lying with his eyes closed in the next bed, unaware, like his son, of their presence. "Nothing serious here, still, the tests will confirm..."

Nomita wanted to go back to Rahul again, but she forced herself instead to return to Kaushik Kashyap's bedside. He lay there supine, just as she had left him. She could not bring herself to touch him, even to smooth back his hair, as she had done his mother's. Guilt and a sense of dread prevented her from making any such move.

She looked over at Rahul's bed. His eyes, too, were closed now, but the colour seemed to have returned, somewhat, to his face. She went across and looked down at him again. Several other doctors were moving around, coming towards them. Gesturing to her father that she was going, she slipped out, and took an auto home.

Cousins and aunts crowded around her as she went in through the gate. "How is he? How are they?" they asked, but in soft tones, considerate.

She murmured something that was unintelligible even to herself, but the cousins and aunts looked at each other with understanding. This was a terrible thing to happen.

The question was: what would they do now? Could the wedding take place according to schedule? It was just five days away, but still, if the scans and x-rays showed no internal injuries, it might be possible to have the wedding formalities.

As the day progressed, the guests, sitting around the house now without the sense of purpose that they had had a few hours ago, murmured "I can't stay too long, I mean if it is not going to happen..."

"But maybe it will... I mean we can ask the priest to keep it short, just the very essential rituals..."

Nomita, moving aimlessly from room to room, heard the murmurs, hastily suppressed when the cousins saw her. She pretended not to have heard, and said nothing to them. She needed to talk to her parents, but her father had not yet come in from the hospital, though he had called periodically to say that there was no really serious injury to any of the people who had been in the car, either the driver or the passengers. Still, there were a few more tests that needed to be done.

What was a serious injury, in any case? A broken arm was a routine part of childhood for many people. But the same broken arm, on one of the country's best – the world's best – sitarists was a totally different matter. There would be the weeks when it would be in the plaster cast, the months of physiotherapy, the years when twinges and aches would prevent the sitarist from playing at the same speed and standard as he had previously...

Yes, he would certainly need all the support he could get now. From his friends, his students, and certainly from his fiancée.

30

They were all out of the hospital within forty-eight hours. The bridegroom and the driver of the car were the last to be discharged. The others – Tirna and Rana Ghosh and Rahul, with hardly any injuries except trauma and concussion, were on their feet in less than a day.

Kaushik Kashyap, his right hand in a sling, was taken straight to the guest house where the rest of the bridegroom's party were already being looked after. Technically, it was still possible to hold the wedding ceremony at the scheduled 'auspicious' time. True, the preliminary celebrations would have to be curtailed or cut out totally, but the essential ceremony, the seven circumambulations around the sacred fire, and the exchanging of garlands which was still three days away? Would the bridegroom be up to it though? He had just been discharged from hospital after all…

At the bride's house, the atmosphere was very different from what it had been like just two days ago. There was none of the hustle and bustle, though most of the relatives who had come in for the wedding were still around. There was no song and laughter. People spoke in subdued tones, even after they came to know that nobody had suffered serious injuries. What was particularly difficult to bear, especially for Nomita's family, was the fact that this terrible accident had happened in their own town and that the foremost sitarist of his generation had broken his right arm.

It was actually Kaushik's wristbones that were smashed. And the right side of his body, his torso and thigh, had several large bruises. The pain in his side was temporary, nothing that a few weeks of rest would not cure. It was an inescapable fact that had it been a broken foot or leg, the consequences would have been negligible. True, a few concerts would need to be cancelled, and travelling restricted for a while but his music would have remained untouched. However, as things stood now, it was apparent that the attending orthopaedic and plastic surgeons and the other doctors had done what they could. They made it clear to the family that this was only an emergency, stop gap arrangement and more extensive treatment than what their small town could provide was urgently required. Probably an operation, or even several, would be needed over months, in order to set the bones thoroughly. Tendons had been badly torn, muscles slashed. The doctors had done what they could, and felt that actually the man should be in hospital for a while more, but given his otherwise fit condition and the circumstances, they were ready to release him, provided of course that he understood that the treatment they had administered would need to be followed up as soon as possible. In any case, they felt that it would need months, possibly more than a year of intense physiotherapy for Kaushik Kashyap to be able to even heft the sitar into the playing position, leave alone play it. It would be physically impossible for a long time to come. Of course the doctors said that he would be able to do it eventually, and come back to the stage as an even better performer perhaps. It was certainly possible for even they, who knew very little about artistes, had heard of cases such as Sonal Man Singh's, the Odissi dancer who had been in a bad road accident. Her backbone had been injured, they had heard, when the case had been discussed in medical conferences. Yet through sheer grit and determination, she had come back as a dancer again, lighting up the stage with her performances. And there was Sudha Chandran, the Bharatanatyam dancer who performed on a Jaipur foot after she lost her right leg in an accident. Her movements on stage, even with the artificial foot, were as nimble and artistic as before.

What they left unsaid was that there were many other cases where such miracles did not happen. Healing was an art, like music or dance, and there were so many other factors that needed to be taken into account for a successful convalescence leading to a complete cure. Mental strength, and of course the loving support of family and friends counted for at least as much as did access to the best doctors, medicines and physiotherapists. The doctors at the bride's father's hospital had paused at this point, and said, "Of course he will have a new bride by his side. We can count on Nomita to do everything that is required. He won't be bedridden of course, he will be ambulatory, so in all other respects he can have a normal life. Now if he had been a vocalist, it would not have mattered in the least. As it is though... The important thing is to keep his morale up. Mental strength is everything. If he begins to think negative thoughts, there will be huge repercussions..."

The anxiously waiting wedding guests at home would want to know exactly what was happening at the hospital, what was the prognosis for the patient. Dr Sharma repeated everything to them all faithfully, in a reassuring professional manner. Nomita, listening to the frequent health bulletins, said nothing.

After that first time, she had gone once more to the hospital. Tirna and Rana Ghosh as well as Rahul and the driver had been released by then, and only Kaushik among the passengers of the car was in hospital. She followed her father to the best private room in the building.

Two middle-aged people were sitting by the bedside of the patient, speaking in low tones with each other. The woman's face was so much like Tirna Ghosh's that she had to be related. Her sister? Introductions were made. She was indeed Tirna's younger sister, come with the wedding party of her nephew.

"Nomita," said Kaushik Kashyap's aunt. She looked kindly at her, and reached out a hand to pat her shoulder. "Are you taking care of yourself...? This is terribly traumatic for you..." She didn't add "You look terrible," but Nomita heard it in her voice. Of course it was expected of her to lose the radiance that a bride was supposed to have after this kind of an incident. The aunt was not to know that this bride had never looked radiant.

The bridegroom was dozing, unaware of the people around him. "He's under light sedation," said Nomita's father. "But the doctors told me he's doing fine. They are satisfied that they have done a good job. An interim one, of course, but good nevertheless."

Nomita was thankful for the presence of these others in the room. And also for the fact that the patient was asleep. The relief made her turn to the aunt and say in a low voice, "I hope you are being looked after well at the guest house? Is everything suitable? The food, the beds?"

Of course several people from their home had been deputed to look after the comfort of the bridegroom's party, and she was in no doubt that they were being looked after well. But it was polite to ask.

"No no, don't worry, we are just fine, as far as the guest house goes. But you just take care of yourself..."

Nomita made herself turn to the bed to look at the patient. He was pale, his hair spread in a circle around his head. Sleep made him look younger. More in need of caring, of understanding. She looked quickly away, trying to ignore the sudden upswell of guilt in her mind.

The aunt and uncle were trying to move tactfully out of the door, in order to leave Nomita alone with her fiancé for a few minutes. She stopped them, saying, "No, please stay, I'm going. There's no point in waking him up, is there?"

Resolutely she had stayed away from Rahul. He was back home, she knew that, and all right, more or less. Nothing that a couple of days more in bed couldn't cure. She hadn't spoken to him since that day in the hospital. He had made no attempt to call her, either.

But now a decision needed to be made.

Would the wedding be held according to schedule, or would it be postponed? The doctors had said the bridegroom would be able to carry out his part in the rituals, provided the ceremonies were kept to the bare minimum. Pradeep Ghosh went to talk to Tirna and Rana Ghosh, and came back with the news that they were in favour of having at least the Civil Marriage ceremony, if possible even the traditional one. The Magistrate who was due to conduct the Civil Marriage had been notified, in any case everything was arranged for the evening after the traditional ceremony. That would take only a few minutes, surely they could go ahead with that?

The relatives at home, listening, nodded with relief. True, a civil ceremony was not nearly as much fun as a traditional one, but at least the job would be done. The marriage would take place, doubtless in a truncated manner, but then in these circumstances it hardly mattered. The bride would leave for her in-laws' place, and they could all go back home again, with no major disruptions to their schedules.

The relatives were beginning to move away. At last, it was permissible to smile. This accident was most unfortunate, of course, but at least the marriage would take place. How terrible if...

But they were halted in mid-smile, mid-sentence by a loud voice that made no effort to disguise its scorn.

"But do you think this marriage should take place at all, at least at this point of time?" Maya looked around the roomful of relatives, her basilisk gaze swivelling this way and that as she fixed now this aunt, now that uncle, with her baleful eye. "Do you? Well *I* don't. It's terribly inauspicious, this accident. The bridegroom himself has been injured. Under the circumstances, this wedding can't happen now. I am sure the priest will corroborate. The stars and the gods need to be propitiated, a fresh auspicious date will need to be fixed. This is a sign. To go ahead with the wedding now will be to go against a clearly given signal..."

"Ah...I don't think..." Pradeep Sharma began, but he was cut short by Maya's loud voice again.

"I would speak to the priest if I were you. After all, a warning is a warning, who knows what kind of disaster you'll be inviting on your daughter's head by going ahead as planned?"

"Umm..." This was a new perspective. Which father would condemn his daughter to sure doom, after the warning had been given? The relatives, who had been silenced by the sheer force of Maya's voice, began to whisper among themselves. Shikha Sharma looked dazed, but Pradeep Sharma said bravely, "Well, let's see. We'll have to talk to the bridegroom's side, of course. Again. We'll see what they say. But it seems they want to go ahead..."

Maya shrugged and moved away. Her gait said, more clearly than the bluntest words, "Don't blame me when something bad happens to your daughter. When, not if. *When* something bad happens to your daughter."

Nomita, listening, felt the huge bubble of relief that had first fizzed through her mind shrink. No, it was no use. Tirna and Rana Ghosh were not superstitious. They would hardly view this as a sign, an inauspicious omen. They would take the accident for what it was: a piece of pure bad luck, made worse by the location of the injuries that the bridegroom had suffered. They would want to finish what they had come for, and go back as soon as possible, their daughter-in-law by their side, so that the work of rehabilitation of Kaushik's wrist could begin as soon as possible.

Of course she could take matters in her own hands, and declare that she agreed with Maya. She was shattered, she could say, at this turn of events, the accident being such an inauspicious thing to happen. She needed time. She would do the rounds of temples, a new date would be fixed, and in the meantime the bridegroom could concentrate on healing his wrist. Then, later…

Later was another day. She would figure out something by then. The bubble grew large again.

People began to move out of the room, whispering among themselves, looking resentfully at Maya. Trust her to put difficulties in the way of a smooth resolution. Only the bride was looking gratefully at her aunt. This was probably the way out, then. She grasped the straw she had been handed with gratitude, her mind racing ahead, as she went back to her room, to the many benefits that following this course would take.

She lay down on the bed, and stared up at the ceiling. There was the Press, for instance. Already the Tamulbari print media was full of news of the accident, complete with pictures. Several days after the accident, it was still making front page headlines. The electronic media, the TV channels, too, were full of young and earnest anchors spinning out their stories in front of the hospital to which the accident victims had been taken. One of them had even asked the question, "Now, will this marriage take place?" though most of them had concentrated on that other question, the more important one, surely, of "Now, will Kaushik Kashyap, the foremost sitar exponent of his generation, ever play the sitar again?"

The national media, too, were full of the news. Besides, people from all over the world were calling the family, through Kamal Basu and on Kaushik's cell, full of anxiety. Was he all right? Was his hand going to heal? Was he up and about, was he still in hospital? His students from Europe and America, his Guru living there, all urged Tirna and Rana to bring their son immediately, as soon as possible to some good hospital. Where was this godforsaken place they were in now? What did the doctors at that mofussil hospital know about healing shattered wrists? Particularly, they emphasized, *this* shattered wrist, belonging to Kaushik Kashyap? Yes, immediately, they were to come immediately. A hospital in America would be best. It wouldn't be a problem, they would arrange everything. But time was of the essence. And yes, the marriage could wait. Why not? This was urgent, an emergency.

What would have happened, Nomita thought suddenly, if something like this had happened to Guruji after his wedding had been finalised? And Sandhya Senapati? What would they have done? A broken hand wouldn't have mattered, of course, but what if, abruptly, it was discovered that he had some disease that made a career as a vocalist impossible, at least temporarily? What then? Tuberculosis, or something like that? If, every time he attempted a note in the upper octaves, he had an uncontrollable bout of coughing, because of nodules that were growing in his larynx?

In spite of all that was going on around her, and her own quandaries, Nomita found herself thinking often of Guruma. Why had she felt the need to deny the fact, the indubitable fact, that Guruma and Deepak Rathod had a relationship that was intimate? Infidelity was common enough. It was hardly worth commenting on. Yet, because of their position in society, because they were so well known, and of course because both were married, people talked. Besides, there was the fact that Guruma looked conventional, and sang songs that had a deeply spiritual tradition. The moral dichotomy between her career in music of a spiritual kind and her betrayal of her legally wedded husband was too delicious not to talk about. Who was bothered about the state of her marriage, anyway? From the outside, if one discounted her "friendship" with Deepak Rathod, her marriage looked perfect. Indeed, she herself had thought theirs to be an ideal marriage.

Why had she been in denial then, even though all around her, gossip about Guruma's relationship was rife? The answer came to her as she walked around the lawn. It was her own need to see Sandhya Senapati, her Guruma, as a "moral" person. It was her own need that had blinded her to what was so glaringly obvious to everyone else. It had needed Guruma's own words to show her what the truth was. People like Panchali and Rupa had stumbled on the truth, while she had been blind to the evidence before her.

She had placed Sandhya Senapati on a pedestal.

But even though Nomita now knew different, she realized that her feelings, even her reverence for her teacher, who had become so much more than a Guru to her, had not changed. If anything, her feelings had deepened. It was complex. She felt a kind of empathy with her, a fellow feeling. They had shared many things, been together on many occasions. She did not feel the need to idolize her any more. She herself had gone through too much recently to need that kind of umbilical cord. Sandhya Senapati's humanity, flawed though it was, still appealed to her, as strongly as ever. Indeed, perhaps, more strongly than ever before.

Nomita met Kamal Basu when he came over to their house to talk with Dr Sharma. He looked more distracted than ever. There was only worry on his face now. No laughter. Understandable, thought Nomita. After all, "Brand Kaushik Kashyap" was what put the food on his table. If this fell apart, there would be all kinds of problems for him, personally.

"Ah, Nomita," he said when she came out to the lawns to meet him. The shamiana was still standing, after all the wedding had not yet been officially postponed. The chairs were still placed around the lawn, and there were festive decorations up around the marquee even now. Yet the place looked forlorn. A look of surprise, then a kind of understanding, came on his face. It said, as clearly as though he had spoken aloud, "God, she looks terrible. But then of course that's quite understandable. Poor thing. She must be under terrific stress. Not as much as me, of course, but still ... poor thing. Terrible thing to have happened to us all, terrible ... Trust these small town drivers to botch up a straight drive from the airport to town."

He came forward to speak to Nomita. "He's better, thank God. He can move his hand around a bit, but ..." Kamal Basu bit his lip and looked away. Then, controlling his emotions, he turned back to her, and told Nomita, "Actually, I wanted to speak to your father. What are his plans, will the ceremony go ahead as scheduled ..."

Dr Pradeep Sharma was already coming forward, his walk betraying his anxiety.

"Ah, yes, Lucia called," remembered Kamal Basu. "Actually she's been calling very frequently, practically every hour. Anyway, she was enquiring about you when she called from Delhi airport."

Nomita looked questioningly at him. Her mind was fuzzy. Of course. She had thought Lucia was in Italy, not India.

"Oh, I thought you knew. She took the first flight out as soon as she heard of the accident. She's in Delhi already, she'll be here tomorrow. Morning flight to Guwahati, then the taxi ride here. Practically direct from Italy to Tamulbari."

"Ah. Of course."

"Yes. She's very concerned. Kaushikji had asked her many times to come for the wedding but she had declined. Now of course she feels ... after all they spent a lot of time together this last summer, during his Europe tour. She's a perfect student. More than a student actually, in so many ways. Anyway, she was enquiring about you, how you were, what you were doing. I told her that you were as well as could be expected under the circumstances ..."

"Tell me, Kamalji, what is it ... ?" her father asked, his direct question and abrupt manner betraying his anxiety. Hosts were supposed to utter welcoming words to people as important as Kamal Basu, offer a seat, and ply them with tea, before coming to the point.

Leaving them together, Nomita wandered aimlessly off again. Her head felt heavy, the thoughts moving around fuzzily, as though they were people on Jupiter, crushed by an invisible weight that pressed down relentlessly on their Earth-reared bodies.

So that was another thing. Lucia.

So many absolutely valid reasons for her to go up to Kaushik Kashyap, and, tell him and his waiting bridegroom's party, "No, sorry, the wedding can't happen. Not now, anyway. How can we? Ask any priest, any person who can read omens and signs, ask any shaman or diviner. An accident while coming to get married is one of the most inauspicious things that can happen. It's worse than a black cat crossing your path, much worse. Ah, you didn't know your bride-to-be was superstitious? I didn't either. But it's all a blackness in my mind now, it must have been latent all this while... in the face of this, I can't go forward with this at all, please forgive me for the trouble I've caused you, and I'm sorry about your hand, but..."

She gulped, trying to brush away the picture that had sprung up in her mind. Kaushik, his arm in a sling, hair in a ponytail, looking at her, uncomprehending. This small town, aspiring classical singer, not even a B High grade, was rejecting his offer of marriage! His eyes would mirror his disbelief, and then, quickly, anger. But she would have to keep looking at him, because if she looked around, she would meet the eyes of Tirna and Rana Ghosh, as they sat, bandaged and bruised, at the side of the room.

No, perhaps that was too harsh. But there were so many options. She could make it seem that she was postponing the marriage for his own sake, for his own good, given the omens and signs. Only a postponement, of course. What was marriage, anyway, a mere formality. She would be at his side, metaphorically of course, because after all she couldn't accompany him to the US where he would have to spend months in excruciating physiotherapy. But everything needed to be done, urgently. If they were to wait till they got married, it would be a delay of two, three, four days. Four crucial days, during which tendons would set in wrong ways, bones would turn misshapen. Now that he was on his feet again, he should take the first flight out to Kolkata, then after a brief rest, just jet off to Europe or

America. Whatever the medical experts said. She would understand. He was not to worry about her.

Yes, that would probably be the best line. Mask it with layers of overt concern. That was in any case the role she was expected to play, wasn't it?

And yes, she thought, standing at the edge of the lawn, staring without seeing, that would be best from the media point of view, too. Kinder, for all concerned. "The wedding is postponed indefinitely as Kaushik Kashyap is rushed out of the country for emergency medical treatment." Yes indeed. So much better than "Small town girl jilts sitar maestro at the eleventh hour. That, too, after he was injured in a road accident." And the subtext, "These small town girls ... they promise to marry a man when it's all smooth sailing, but opt out the minute things turn difficult."

So many options were open to her. "How to tell your Betrothed You are Opting Out in 7 Easy Steps" she thought humourlessly. Her mind played with ideas as they came to her, examining them from each angle, seriously, as though it didn't yet know exactly the course of action she had to take. As though it was feasible, even, to think of these things, with a houseful of guests waiting patiently for the ceremony to happen so that they could all sigh with relief and get on with their lives again. True, there would be trouble ahead for the married couple, but then that was life. Fate. They would shrug mentally, offer what help they could, and point out that every life had its problems. Every marriage had its dark side.

And her parents? She looked back at her father, now listening, head bowed, to something Kamal Basu was saying. They were totally out of their depth now. What would it be like, later? She felt a brief flare of anger. What was it that Basu was telling her father? Whatever it was, how dare he make this man feel so, so *guilty* for something that wasn't his fault at all?

She remembered, suddenly, the sheets of paper that still lay on her desk in her room. She went in, and glanced through them. Written before this accident, they now seemed empty of meaning to her, a mockery of what had happened to the person they were addressed to.

She hadn't yet finished, of course. She had not yet got around to the main point. She had been leading upto it, slowly. Or had she merely been beating around the bush?

"Dear Kaushik," the letter had begun. Written before the accident, the letter was now irrelevant. It had served to clear her mind, though.

Events had overtaken them all. In any case, much of what she had written didn't apply to him any more. Was he, would he still be, in six months time, the musician he had been a week ago?

A sitarist with a broken right wrist. Though - right, left, did it matter? Both the arms, both hands were needed, all eight fingers and two thumbs had to work synchronously if sounds had to be converted to music. The tendons were severed through, the nerves, too, were squashed and cut. Kaushik Kashyap's mind would conceive tunes and melodies and rhythmic patterns as before, but his hands would be incapable, for a very long time yet, of executing those concepts. If at all they ever did.

Nomita's mind, even now, kept looking for a way out, a reprieve for the artiste, and through that a reprieve for her, too. Technology and medical science had made enormous progress, it was making great strides all the time. Limbs could be replaced, and made to function as though no accident had ever occurred. Bharatanatyam had taken a new dimension, and gained a magical new facet, when Sudha Chandran had got on stage after months of painful but gritty determination, her Jaipur foot as much a part of her technique as the flick of her wrist and the arch of her eyebrows as she executed mudras with consummate ease.

Yes, it was possible. Kaushik Kashyap's career would not have to be curtailed by this accident. In any case, he would definitely be playing the instrument again. The question was – when? And with what degree of excellence? Would his body and mind compensate, like that drummer she had heard in Rahul's room, and make the music flawless again? Or would he give up the fight, and turn listless and unenthusiastic, too shattered to work his way up again? Nomita doubted that this would be the case.

And yet she knew, even as she was rationalizing in her mind, that all this was only a veil, a way of covering up the terrible thing that she would now have to do. Something that would haunt her for the rest of her life. But if she did not do it, that too, would haunt her. If Kaushik's hands recovered from this accident, and he began to play again, in the same way as before, things would be easier for her. But even if he didn't recover, and had to spend the rest of his life unable to play a note on the sitar, even then, it would not alter the course of what she was about to do.

31

So many options. So many ways to get out of the situation, smoothly, without arousing comment.

Nomita went out of the back door of the house to the garage. All the guests were congregated around the front. None of the wedding guests, or her parents, noticed her. Refusing the chauffeur's offer of help, she took out the Alto, and went smoothly out of the gate. Soon she was on the main road, driving herself to the guest house where Kaushik Kashyap's wedding party was housed.

So many options. She toyed briefly with each as she dodged rickshaws and autos in her path.

She suddenly remembered that Lucia would quite likely have arrived by now. So that was another option, if she cared to use it. "I'm sorry, but it's obvious there's something going on here. How can I marry a person who is tailed by some Italian-shitalian person like a devoted wife?" Yes, take the offensive, take the ball to the opponent's court. That was the way to do it. "People have been hinting about that relationship to me, only I was too dumb to catch on. Well, let her be with you, I have no problems, you'll need her during the treatment. It will be in the USA, she'll know what to do. I will just be a liablility, anyway. Just let me opt out of the whole thing now..." Yes, he would probably be relieved to be let off the marriage promise.

The guest house came up ahead. At this early morning hour, there were very few people around. Thank goodness for that. Having to listen to commiserations and sympathies on her fiancé's shattered wrist was the last thing she wanted now.

She found an empty slot inside the compound, and parked in one fluid motion, nicely parallel to the other cars in the row. Locking the doors, she twirled the keys thoughtfully as she walked up to Reception.

For the last time, she went over all her options. Superstition. Concern. The need for specialized medical attention, speedily. Suspicion and affront about the beautiful foreigner who tailed her fiancé around. Her own shock, leading to a state of mental imbalance, almost.

As she entered the hotel, she threw them out of her mind, one by one. She owed Kaushik Kashyap an honest explanation at the very least, no matter what the consequences for him and for her.

This accident had happened just after she had finally made up her mind to call off the wedding. It meant that it was even more difficult for her to go through with her decision. The accident had come out of the blue. To test her resolve. To see if she really knew what she wanted? Would she be able to stick to her decision despite what had transpired?

If she did not succumb to the awfulness of what had happened to Kaushik Kashyap, if she did not feel obliged, after this, to become his wife, immediately, and his nurse and support later, well then, it would be her punishment. She would have stood up a man at the altar. That was bad enough. But she would have abandoned a fiancé who had suffered an accident, whose musical career now hung in the balance and that was far worse. What kind of a woman would do that? This accident was her punishment, and it was something she would have to live with for the rest of her life. It was a punishment for not realizing, much earlier, that Kaushik Kashyap, the greatest sitarist of his generation though he might be, was not for her.

Everything, they said, happened for a reason. Better to make the final break, however painful, however horrible, now. Sandhya Senapati and Deepak Rathod had tried, so many years ago, to move down the path she was on. They had taken the step, they had not stopped at the point she was willing herself to stop at now. But, in spite of their best intentions, it hadn't worked for them. It wasn't working.

Better now, than later. No matter what the consequences.

But the accident had happened, and her change of mind would

be looked at with deep suspicion. Even opportunistic. Now that Kaushik Kashyap's career no longer shone with the same rosy glow Nomita Sharma had decided to toss him, and go for an IT guy who was moving off to America soon. Yes, that was how it would be construed. For a long time, maybe even for life, people would whisper to each other when she entered a room, and point to her and say, "See that white haired woman? Long ago, she was in all the papers. She jilted her fiancé on the eve of her wedding day, can you imagine? But wait, there's more. She threw him over after he had an accident that shattered his wrist. He was one of the finest sitar players of his generation ... How could she do it? No conscience, no sense of duty ... and look at her now, shameless, partying without a care in the world ..."

Yes, that would be her punishment. The brutality of what she was about to do now would be her sentence, her punishment. But, it would also be, in an oblique way, a relief.

Kaushik Kashyap would not realize it now, but maybe he would, later. Looking at Guruma and Deepak Rathod, and knowing their story there was no way she could go ahead with the wedding now.

She would talk to him. He would be the first one to know of her decision to pull out of the wedding, in spite of this accident that had shattered so much more than his wristbones. She would tell him, too, that she had taken her decision before the accident. She could not change her mind back again, in spite of his smashed wrist and splintered career. He deserved that. And then, afterwards, she would tell her parents, and his. And then, only then, Rahul.

She would go to Rahul after all this was over, and tell him that she would go with him to America. A small ceremony would have to take place before that, but the ceremony itself was incidental, just a way of getting the sanction of all the people around her who would have been scandalized otherwise. If possible, she would try to get some training in music as therapy, especially for children. And when they returned to Bangalore again, a couple of years down the line maybe, she would find some organization that had children like Pallavi and Silsila, and she would teach them music. Her own music would continue in her life, but it would take a back seat. Her focus would be on teaching the children.

That was the way she wanted it. Her mind was now as clear as the winter sunshine that lit up the garden at the entrance to the guest house.

She took a deep breath and asked the sleepy-looking boy who manned Reception, "I want to meet Kaushik Kashap. What room is he in? Ok, ring his room. Tell him Nomita Sharma has come to meet him, please..."